Caffeine

C000227185

~STEAM, SMOKE & MIRRORS~

Colin Edmonds

with insights and extracts from the secret
journals of

Professor Artemus More PhD (Cantab) FRS

Fiction aimed at the heart
and the head.

Published by Caffeine Nights Publishing 2015

Published in Great Britain by

Caffeine Nights Publishing
4 Eton Close
Walderslade
Chatham
Kent
ME5 9AT

www.caffeine-nights.com

British Library Cataloguing in Publication Data.
A CIP catalogue record for this book is available from the British Library
ISBN: 978-1-907565-94-6

Cover design by
Mark (Wills) Williams
Everything else by
Default, Luck and Accident

Dedicated to the memories of four of the most inspiring people
I have ever known.

Harry Edmonds 1908-1993
Bob Monkhouse 1928-2003
Tom Press 1996-2007
Peter Prichard 1932-2014

Acknowledgements

My sincere thanks must go to David Tyler and Geoff Posner for their 'Pozzitive' support and encouragement at the beginning and to Darren Laws at Caffeine Nights for his unwavering enthusiasm right up to the end.

Garry Bushell, the widely published author, pointed me in the right direction and Sarah Abel, my keen eyed editor, kept me straight along the way.

Among the hundreds of books I referred to, two were outstandingly useful, *'M – MI5's First Spymaster'* by Andrew Cook and *'Lillie Langtry – Manners, Masks and Morals'* by Laura Beatty.

Lucy Edmonds with her BA (Hons) in Publishing was my invaluable adviser, Mark Edmonds with his technical acumen was frequently my saviour and Kathryn Edmonds with her serenity and wisdom was always there.

And to Steampunk enthusiasts everywhere, I do hope I have done some justice to the genre we all love.

www.steamsmokeandmirrors.com

~STEAM, SMOKE & MIRRORS~

~IN THE BEGINNING~
"Conjuring is the only absolutely honest profession.
A conjuror promises to deceive and does!" – Karl Germain

1

Well, it was no secret the evening started off badly and went quickly downhill from there.

And not just for my dearest associates, the Music Hall magicians "Michael Magister, the Industrial Age Illusionist, and Phoebe, the Queen of Steam and Goddess of the Aethyr". Yes, I know the billing doesn't trip off the tongue with any great deft, but I like to think it pretty much does its job in telling the crowd what to expect, then shocking them when it delivers much more. So, anyway, Michael and Phoebe were gracing the stage of The Metropolitan Theatre of Steam, Smoke and Mirrors in London's Edgware Road, performing the first of their twice nightly shows and building to their baffling spectacular finale.

The stage was stygian black, save for menacing swirls of soft-lit smoke, blue and green. The only noise was that excited thrum you get from an expectant audience. Then, with a vicious electrical fizz, a narrow column of brilliant white light sliced down through the blackness to illuminate him. The figure standing left of centre stage, intense, commanding: Michael Magister, the Industrial Age Illusionist.

In his late twenties, lean, clean shaven with thick, neat brown hair and, you know, it must be said far more handsome than was really necessary. Not that he needed telling. Michael wore a black frock coat, frothy white shirt and metallic gold cravat. The gold silk lining of his coat kicked back the light as he gestured and smoothly addressed this eighteen hundred-strong sea of totally engrossed faces in a manner which made each of them believe they were the only person in the theatre. In the front stalls, the rear pit, the fauteuils, the balcony, the gallery and the boxes, they oozed, all of them, they oozed that unmistakeable smell of an audience, that pungent cocktail of armpits, mothballs, beer, cologne, cigar smoke and halitosis; the sweet scent of box office takings. Oh, yes, with their cloth caps, bowlers, top hats, bonnets, all West London human life was here. From all walks, all classes.

This was our first capacity house since we opened the show three months ago. An indignant local clergyman, quoted in yesterday's *Paddington Mercury*, had described the Magister show as 'the most rabid concoction of blasphemy, lust and sin ever seen on stage in our Victorian era'. So, one must only assume the evening's capacity crowd felt the need to venture along and judge the precise level of such shameful un-holiness for themselves.

"Ladies and gentlemen, as you have witnessed this evening, the very presence of my beautiful muse, Phoebe, the Queen of Steam, the Great Goddess of the Aethyr, has enabled me to defy death a dozen times!" Michael's accent had been American, but a decade in Great Britain had softened that nasal hardness so associated with the Bronx. It might also explain, to this crowd, his uncommon use of the English language. "But a Goddess with such wondrous ability cannot remain in our world. So the time is now come for me to cast her back to the dimension from whence she came. But to make such an event happen, it demands power, it demands passion – and *this* machine!"

With an elaborate wave of his arm and a furious hiss of steam the front centre stage suddenly burst into dazzling yellow light to reveal a metallic gold coloured sheet, covering an object which, from its vague shape could be an ordinary armchair rather than some fabulous machine.

Michael strode towards the mysterious object. "Yes, ladies and gentlemen, I – Magister the Magician – can now reveal the inter-dimensional mechanical masterpiece that is… The Throne of Disintegration!"

Michael grabbed the back edge of the metallic sheet and with a flamboyant sweep, heaved it forward to reveal The Throne itself. And, oh, what a Throne it was! An imposing, brooding beast, broad and tall, the frame, legs and arms were of burnished oak and polished metal, swathed in snaking brightly coppered piping. The seat cushion and back were firm ox-blood leather, dimpled with brass rivets. All at once The Throne jolted, jets of steam hissed and wheezed from various pipes and joints, as if its very revelation had imbued the machine with life. The crowd ooh'd and aah'd their amazement, awed by the barely suppressed throbbing power of this fearsome industrial asthmatic.

"And to grace The Throne," continued the magician, "I summon once again, from the mysterious Aethyr, the great Goddess herself, the magnificent – Phoebe!"

In a burst of acrid blue steam she was suddenly there, stage right; summoned, as promised, from the Aethyr!

In fact, she'd simply been lofted up from the void beneath the stage, aboard the hydraulic platform which served the stage right trap door.

Phoebe, the Queen of Steam, the Goddess herself, was every bit as magnificent as Michael had claimed. No doubt about it, you know, she was a stunner; a slender, well-bred, titian-haired twenty-two-year-old stunner. Clad in a red corset, boned with silver metal, wearing long black fingerless silk gloves, black lace cuffed ankle boots and black taffeta costume skirt, slashed at the front to reveal more than the occasional tantalising glimpse of lissom thigh and skimpy French knickers. I know...

Now, in case you're sitting there wondering how we were permitted to display this, shall we say 'liberating female look' right under the noses of the representatives of the Lord Chamberlain's office, those Government censors in all matters theatrical, the explanation is quite simple. We realised very early, that many of these guardians of public decency, these official upholders of morality, quite happily signed us off as approved when liberally plied with French wine and a generous cash incentive. I just thought you should know – now back to the show.

For those discerning connoisseurs of physical perfection, let me tell you, Phoebe was far more alluring than any of those stark naked but stock-still Living Statue lady poseurs, which usually pitched up in the English Music Hall. Once again, the less prudish among the packed audience, which, frankly, amounted to most of them, cheered their approval at the sight of Phoebe in yet another stunning outfit. For many of the gawping menfolk, they had witnessed more naked thigh in one hour than they'd seen in a dozen years of marriage.

Towards the centre of the auditorium, in what are called the Pit Seats, the dog collared Father Connor O'Connor, a son of somewhat unimaginative parents and the author of yesterday's damning newspaper review, suddenly rose to his feet in fury. This final sensuous appearance of Phoebe, Goddess of the Aethyr, had clearly been too exotic for his catholic juices.

Shaking his gnarled fist, Father O'Connor hollered: "Be damned the godless shaman and this wanton temptress! Be damned with their steaming engines of Satan!" Unfortunately, his pious indignation was immediately met with a veritable torrent of foul mouthed abuse and a murderous battering about the head from everyone within stick wielding distance.

"Thank you, sir, but please, ladies and gentlemen!" protested Michael Magister, looking to quell the commotion. "Please, do not strike the holy man's head! Please! You'll only knock some sense into him! Thank you. Please return to your seats. In fact, I had no idea our friend was with us this evening! I just assumed it was the breeze from the brewery!"

The priest slumped, still defending his bald head as the audience hooted their joy at the barrage of put-downs from the stage. In fact, encouraged by their enthusiastic response, the magician milked the situation still further.

"Yes, ladies and gentlemen, how good is this, that a man of the cloth should donate his brain to St. Mary's Hospital for the furtherance of medical science. But at least he might have waited until he died first!" More shrieks of laughter. "I'd like to get on your good side, Father, but it looks to me like you're now sitting on it!"

The crowd roared and clapped, as the humiliated holy man slid ever lower into his seat. "Swait Jasus," thought Father Connor O'Connor, "Is there no one pure and righteous left in the world?" He then gestured the most lurid hand signals at the stage, while shouting the vilest invective – all in the good Lord's name, you understand.

2

While The Metropolitan Theatre of Steam, Smoke and Mirrors was in unholy uproar, eleven miles to the west, at The London County Lunatic Asylum in Hanwell, the mysterious events which were to dominate our next two days, were beginning to unfold. Senior Warder Winfield Trout, a small, jaundiced looking fellow with a face like a rabid shrew, held a large ring of iron keys, close to his blue, coarse cloth double breasted uniform tunic. He found himself ushering none other than The Right Honourable Mister William Ewart Gladstone along the dimly lit corridor, to the rhythmic sharp clack of their footsteps. All the patients were in their beds snoring or shuffling, and all the night staff were tucking into a hearty supper over in the refectory.

Gladstone strode with calm authority, resplendent in his black, long-coated suit. A black cravat was tied in a bow beneath that broad, rumpled face which had been locked in a look of permanent disapproval for what seemed like decades. The half-light of the corridor caused the few thin wisps of grey hair, which sprouted defiantly from the back of the old fellow's head and from his cheeks, to effect the illusion of a saintly halo.

As for Winfield Trout, he scurried and bowed in a most obsequious manner, much like a spatchcock chicken might when trying to ingratiate himself with a vegetarian as Christmas approached.

"My sincerest apologies that you became lost within the confines of our humble establishment, Mister Gladstone," he fawned. "Pray, I cannot conceive of how it might have happened, but, I do submit, it is somewhat easily done."

"This place can hardly be described as humble, Mister Trout," proclaimed the former Prime Minister. His normal tone of voice was proclamation. "It is the largest establishment of its kind in the country and whilst the pioneering policy of Moral Therapy and education are much preferred to the shackle and the lash, the treatment of the high security patients down in the basement requires further attention. As for yourself, Mister Trout, you are nothing less than a malevolent disgrace."

"You are most kind, sir," said Trout.

"Pray now, let me take my leave of your godforsaken company."

With a firm clunk, Winfield Trout unlocked the door at the entrance to the Female Wing of the asylum and swung it open to the outside world. Gladstone felt the rush of cool evening air upon his face. He paused and closed his eyes. Trout escorted the great Parliamentarian across the crunching gravel, past a splattering fountain, towards the looming brick built arch of the great gatehouse, barred with gates of black, vertical iron.

"Mister Gladstone is leaving us now, Mister Gint. Allow me the honour of opening the gate for him," oozed Trout.

Bevis Gint, the tall, thickset uniformed Gatehouse Warder, stroked his tobacco-stained walrus moustache, peered down, met the gaze of what appeared to be the grey, slight figure standing beside Trout, and blinked. He then unhooked a large key from his thick leather belt and laid it upon the waiting, sweaty palm of Senior Warder Trout. Another well-oiled click and the small pedestrian access, the Judas Gate, swung silently open.

"Do not wait up for me, Mister Trout," said Gladstone with a dismissive wave as he stepped through the gate, before turning right and sauntering off down the busy Uxbridge Road towards Ealing. Winfield Trout then returned the key to Gatehouse Warder Gint and set off to the refectory for his dinner – it was cauliflower cheese tonight. Bevis Gint, a former Metropolitan Police Constable who had been forced to take early retirement and then somehow landed the cushiest security post in West London, relocked the gate and returned to the gatehouse room and his newspaper. And, do you know, at no point did either man question why, after evening lock-up, the former Liberal Prime Minister, William Gladstone , would be found wandering the corridors of The London County

Lunatic Asylum. Nor, better yet, how it was even possible? Considering he'd been buried in Westminster Abbey for the best part of a year.

**

Of course, thirty minutes later, Trout, having just recovered from an unusual headache, had been summoned from the dinner table and was still wiping cheese from his moustache with a napkin, as he clattered down the cast iron spiral staircase to the basement below the Female Wing. Ward Attendant Miss Damaris Gunthorpe, I think her fine name was, the tough, corpulent one with a belly like an unpricked sausage, had apparently been making the first of her evening rounds, ensuring the continued welfare of the sleeping patients, when down in the basement Secluded Area she made a discovery of a most alarming nature. As the Asylum regulations demanded, she sent for the man responsible for securing the establishment, Senior Warder Winfield Trout.

"What do you mean she's gone?" demanded Trout, arriving outside the Secure Room. "No one *goes*!" It was either rising panic or the cauliflower cheese which was starting to gnaw at his stomach lining. "That door was definitely locked fast! I turned the very key myself, so she must be here." But she wasn't. And a look inside the small room revealed the white padded walls, the birch wood bed, the horsehair mattress, the goose down pillow, the tall ceiling, the dim lamp above. In fact, all appeared present and correct – except for the all-important patient. He looked around again, but there was no doubt about it. For the first time in the history of Trout's tenure at Hanwell, someone had escaped. Miss Gunthorpe slipped away to make a discreet telephone call, leaving the Senior Warder standing in the centre of the room feeling as if the white walls were closing in on him.

"Damn the woman, damn her to hell!" he gasped.

Then he saw it. Written on the wall behind the door. One word. In blood.

"MAGiSTER".

3

Richard Norman Shaw's iconic design for the purpose built Metropolitan Police headquarters, called New Scotland Yard, down there by the Thames on the newly completed Victoria Embankment, you know, was splendidly gothic. So much so, one night passers-by were convinced they witnessed Mary Shelley's monstrous creation lurching from the building, but it turned out to be the Prince of Wales, following a session on the absinthe with the Police Commissioner. The red brick, white Portland stone and grey granite building, topped with turrets and high chimneys, had been finely described, as 'a constabulary kind of castle'. I can't recall by whom, so I'll claim it as mine.

In his second floor oak panelled office, Superintendent William Melville, a round-faced Irish fellow, all but fifty years of age, with a thick, black moustache and a not quite so thick head of receding hair, sat at his desk, reading the report of one of his best informers, a louche Russian émigré called Sigmund Rosenblum, and wondered if it wasn't time to change the fellow's name.

Melville was a career law enforcer, having signed on as a young constable in 1872, working out of Bow Street. A man of calm courage and integrity, Melville, with an impressive record of arrests, had been promoted from P.C., working the tough Covent Garden beat, to Detective Sergeant within the CID, before being seconded to the Special Irish Branch. Melville was one of a dozen detectives working in the SIB, a department dedicated to thwarting the Fenians who had sought to terrorise British cities with a bombing campaign known as 'The Dynamite War'.

In 1893, Melville was given command of the Special Branch, at a time when anarchists were successfully plying their trade across Europe with the assassinations of the French President, the Prime Minister of Spain, the former Prime Minister of Bulgaria, the Empress of Austria and Tsar Alexander II, all adding to their tally thus far. Many heads of state visiting Great Britain had cause to be grateful for Melville's skilful protection, including those two real political beauties, the Shah of Persia and Kaiser Wilhelm II. And only three years ago, in 1896, while guarding Tsar Nicholas II up at Balmoral, it required Melville's herculean diplomacy to persuade the Tsar's jittery Imperial Secret Police to suspend their security policy of shooting on sight anyone they didn't like and tossing the bodies into the nearest river. Thanks to Melville during their stay the Dee remained corpse free.

As a consequence of his skill and success, William Melville was entrusted by Queen Victoria with the little matter of ensuring, not only the safety and security of her Royal self, but also that of the entire nation. At least this prized cup, or poisoned chalice, whichever way you wish to view it, paid the rent on Melville's small family house in Clapham. But it also meant that whenever the candlestick telephone on his desk rang, day or night, *especially* at night, it was hardly ever going to be good news. And now that telephone was ringing. He lifted the earpiece and in a soft melodious voice, graced with a trace of County Kerry, simply said, "Melville."

The Superintendent listened carefully. The steel-nibbed pen by the blotter on his desk remained untouched. He rarely scribbled notes, preferring to commit details to memory. One of those little espionage fads they pick up, I suppose.

"Magister? Confirm the spelling for me please. And this was the only word written? Kindly ensure a second thorough search of the premises is conducted. We will notify all points of local transportation. And, if you please, may I be very clear, *nothing* is to be touched within the room. Thank you."

Melville cleared the line, then dialled zero. He was in the middle of asking the Scotland Yard telephonic plug-board operator to connect him with the Archivist three floors down, just as Detective Inspector Walter Pym tapped upon the open door of the Superintendent's office. Melville beckoned him with a nod. Pym was one of those splendid, working class, well-made Bethnal Greeners. His full ruddy face was topped with a mop of untameable red hair and complimented with a thick ginger moustache. Following a stint in the Royal

17

Artillery and an eight-year career in police uniform he now wore a three-piece suit in black, much like Melville's, only tighter about the corporation. Keen and loyal, here was a man you'd always want at your side. If Melville was the long arm of the law, his Detective Inspector was the strong arm. Pym remained standing and listened carefully as Melville listed his requirements to the Archivist.

Five minutes later, Pym was peering over Melville's shoulder as they both skim-read the three newly delivered document files. One, a thin wallet, contained material concerning an unimportant American immigrant Music Hall turn, a conjuror cum illusionist, apparently. But the other two files, ah, they were vastly thicker. One was packed with in-depth information detailing the life of the conjuror's young English female stage assistant. The other file contained a comprehensive appraisal of a middle-aged female incarcerated for the last decade in several mental institutions. Both these bulky files also bore the same stark words, stamped diagonally across the front pages: 'Top Secret'.

"And *he* definitely won't get involved without *her*?" asked Pym, pointing between the file of the conjuror and that of his on-stage assistant.

"Of that you may be certain," said Melville.

"Bloody hell, if you'll pardon my French, sir," said Pym, the multi-linguist, as he once again sifted through the pages of the file on the young English woman, "This has all the makings of a proper effin' balls up."

"Indeed," said Melville calmly. He reached for his telephone and asked the Scotland Yard plug-board operator to connect him with the office of the Prime Minister.

***

Little more than an hour later, Detective Inspector Walter Pym was making elaborate highly classified arrangements and speaking with some big shot called Lieutenant Colonel Sir Arthur Bigge. On the Edgware Road, another Special Branch man, Detective Inspector Gersham Skindrick, was stationed beneath the broad glass canopy which ran along the front of The Metropolitan Theatre of Steam, Smoke and Mirrors, trying not to look overly conspicuous. He stiffened when he saw the black Clarence carriage pulled by two sleek black military horses approach and draw to a clattering halt in front of him. Skindrick was a slender, sharp featured fellow. Indeed he was so pointed of chin, if he had not followed the police service path he would have carved himself a successful freak show career as a human ice pick. The Detective Inspector wore his thin hair slicked back over his ears, his mouth was frozen in a permanent sneer and he exuded the cheery disposition of a consumptive undertaker. And those were his finer points. Skindrick had been seconded to Melville's Special Branch upon the personal, out of the blue, recommendation of an Assistant Commissioner. His police record was blemish free, his arrest rate high and his attitude tenacious. So he was certainly not to be trusted.

In contrast to Skindrick's narrow pallid face, Sergeant Bilsten Coxhead, a long-serving police driver, possessed a bulbous red face attached to which was a bulbous red nose which dripped like a split tomato - a disorder, I'm told, which is not uncommon among the carriage driving fraternity. While Coxhead held his horses steady Skindrick unfolded the passenger steps of the carriage. Superintendent William Melville was the first to alight.

"All clear, Inspector?" he said quietly.

"Aye, sir, all clear it is," replied Skindrick, who was of Glaswegian lineage, judging by his accent.

Having satisfied himself with a deft glance in either direction along the pavement, Melville looked up into the darkness within the carriage. "If you'd be so kind, sir,"

Skindrick swallowed hard as the imposing figure dressed in a smart black mourning suit stepped down from the carriage. The Prime Minister, Robert Gascoyne-Cecil, 3rd Marquis of Salisbury, looked all of his sixty-nine years and whatever hair that was missing from the top of the old boy's head, was more than made up for by a dense, impenetrable beard which hung down way below his wing collar and tie, like a woollen muffler. Salisbury was followed from the Clarence by a delicate, baggy-eyed cove sporting a brown moustache. It was Arthur Balfour, the Leader of the House of Commons, or 'Bloody Balfour' as he'd been dubbed by the Irish and 'Pretty Fanny' by his small circle of friends for reasons probably best not asked about. Balfour wore much the same cut of frock coat as his uncle. Yes, Robert Gascoyne-Cecil was also Balfour's uncle, hence the expression 'Bob's Your Uncle'. To suggest nepotism was rife in Government would not be unreasonable.

"Damnably short notice, Melville," protested Arthur Balfour, making little attempt to disguise his irritation at this diversion. "The Prime Minister was forced to leave the Commons in the midst of a debate on Local Government fundamentals in Ireland for this ridiculous diversion!"

"For which I am inordinately grateful, Superintendent," said Lord Salisbury merrily, who, but for the thick beard, may well have been seen to be smiling.

"You understand I require the highest official approval, sir," said Melville.

"Quite so, old man," said Salisbury. His voice which was set in a high register, sat quite at odds with his austere image. "And you were quite correct to assume I might wish to view the persons in question for myself."

Last to step down was Sir Cumberland Sinclair; a late middle-aged, thoroughly agreeable and totally ineffectual Assistant Commissioner of Police in the Metropolis. The stooped Sir Cumberland sported a headful of grey hair along with a pair of mutton-chop whiskers which fought a constantly losing battle to prevent his jowls from wobbling. "This is all very mysterious, our Melville!" he grinned, rubbing his hands together and gazing at the blaze of electric lighting outside the theatre.

"Ye're in time tae see the finale, sir," said Skindrick. "This is their second performance o' the night and despite an audience greater than expected, this entrance will lead us directly to a box within the auditorium in a suitably clandestine manner."

"Shall we?" said Melville, not wishing to have the group

exposed in the open for longer than was necessary. He scanned the Edgware Road back and forth once again. No one could have possibly known the Prime Minister was visiting the theatre at such short notice, and in this part of London few would give a huddle of well-dressed toffs a second glance. But constant vigilance was Melville's stock-in-trade

"Sergeant Coxhead, this will take no longer than twenty minutes," Melville told the driver as he held the single frosted glass door open for the party to enter. Melville then pulled Skindrick close to him and whispered: "Detective Inspector, you may stand watch outside the box."

Skindrick nodded, while Sir Cumberland rubbed his hands together excitedly. "Quite splendid. I understand this chap Magister is quite the conjuror."

Quite the conjuror, indeed.

4

Symmetrically either side of the stage of The Metropolitan Theatre of Steam, Smoke and Mirrors you would find two large audience boxes, almost within touching distance of the stage. The Prime Minister's party slipped quietly and unnoticed into their seats in the stage left box. It was what we grandly called The Royal Box, lest the Queen ever felt the need to come to see our show. But thus far, for some reason, she had not.

As in his earlier performance that fateful evening, a spotlit Michael Magister told the crowd that the gorgeous Phoebe, the Queen of Steam and Goddess of the Aethyr, would be returned to that mysterious dimension from whence she came. He revealed the very machine with which he would perform this feat; the magnificent Throne of Disintegration. The new audience gasped and then cheered when Phoebe re-appeared in a puff of blue smoke.

"My–my," whispered Sir Cumberland Sinclair, as he settled into his seat next to Salisbury.

"So now, ladies and gentlemen," Michael told the audience, "For the continued safety of the world, I must dispatch the Goddess back to the Aethyr!"

The audience murmured as Phoebe began to slink seductively, ominously towards Michael.

"You may issue such a decree, Magister," she breathed, "but I have decided tonight, because of this enthusiastic audience, I shall be returning nowhere!"

The crowd cheered, thoroughly pleased with themselves, having brought about this change of heart.

"But, Goddess Phoebe, you forget! I am armed with the ultimate talisman... The Hypnotic Timepiece of Hyperion!"

Then, as if from nowhere, *actually from up his sleeve,* Michael suddenly produced a fob watch; clear glass on both sides, enabling anyone with decent enough eyesight, to clearly see the glinting cogs and crisp movements within. The Hypnotic Timepiece of Hyperion dangled from a golden chain, as Michael swung the mystic pocket watch back and forth, back and forth. But with a haughty turn of the head Phoebe smiled and scoffed, "Ha! Magister, no man-made trinket can enchant a Goddess!" Her voice was clear, defiant, all but on the way to being, dare I say, posh.

"Yea, well I reckon this'll enchant her!" hollered some rough-type from the stalls, as he stood and pointed down at the front of his dark moleskin trousers.

"Thank you, sir, but for that size of trinket the Goddess would need a magnifying lens the size of a window just to see it!" Michael's put-down was like a stiletto in the rough-type's heart, and after the great roar of mockery and laughter subsided, Michael knew he needed to rebuild the tension.

"But The Hypnotic Timepiece of Hyperion has been handed down through the ages from Queen Elizabeth's Astrologer Royal, Doctor John Dee himself, via Sir Isaac Newton, and now to me. I control its great hypnotic power!"

With a graceful flourish he again swung the watch back and forth, and then suddenly it was gone! Vanished! *He simply dropped it down into a pouch sewn within the pleats of Phoebe's skirt, on the blind side of the audience*. With a dramatic second wave of his hand the crowd "Oooh'd" as they witnessed Phoebe's entire body suddenly stiffen and her head slump to one side, totally hypnotised.

"While it's true, no ordinary man *can* enchant the beautiful Goddess, never forget, I am The Magister! And in The Trance of the Living Dead, Phoebe, the Queen of Steam, yields to the blackest depths of her unconscious mind!" intoned Michael firmly, as he led his now compliant, vacant-looking assistant by the hand towards the hissing, snorting Throne of Disintegration.

"Pheebs, check the Royal Box. Four men just came in," whispered Michael.

"Really? The Professor must have sold the tickets," whispered Phoebe, despite the depth of her supposed trance. She even managed a surreptitious glance across at the usually empty Royal Box to her left. "Oh, my days. Michael. It's Salisbury."

"What, *Lord* Salisbury? Prime Minister of England Lord Salisbury?"

"And perhaps even Balfour's with him," whispered Phoebe. "But I don't recognise the other two. I'll take a closer look when I get up there."

Michael seated Phoebe upon the leathern cushion of the heaving Throne of Disintegration and quickly buckled the heavy, ox-blood leather straps about her wrists and ankles.

"Witness how the Goddess Phoebe is unable to resist the awesome power of The Throne!" Michael told the audience. "Even I, Magister the Magician, am rendered humble!" Michael then confirmed his new found humility by whispering, "Do they offer Americans knighthoods? Is that maybe why he's here?"

Phoebe's pithy response was lost as Michael gripped the metallic sheet and raised it to hide the apparently unconscious Phoebe from the crowd.

Once hidden, she quickly unstrapped her wrists and ankles from their phoney leather restraints, all within fleeting, well-drilled moments.

Michael lowered the sheet, affording the audience another look at the head and shoulders of the still seemingly 'fluenced Goddess. The Throne discharged a burst of steam and Phoebe's eyes suddenly widened as if in shock.

"Feel the sensual power of the Throne of Disintegration!" incanted Michael, as the chair began to rhythmically chug and throb. Michael dramatically raised the sheet once more.

Under cover of which, Phoebe released the trap door set in the seat and slipped her legs down into the void beneath the chair. She opened a red tapped valve which released another surge of steam.

The pipes embracing The Throne strained and complained as the pressure and throbbing increased. Again, Michael lowered the sheet allowing the audience another good look at Phoebe, while she opened her mouth and let out a pleasured gasp, just before she was hidden again.

Then, out of view and with the throbbing quickening, Phoebe shimmied down into the seat void, twisted the valve for

24

another burst of steam, and with a hiss, a metal arm, supporting the outline of a false head, swung forward, falling to rest where Phoebe's head would have been.

The aroused audience stared with wide-eyed wonder as the steam pulsed and the Throne itself began to undulate, faster and louder.

Phoebe then struggled, legs first, out through the back of The Throne, re-set the false seat door and slipped back, away and free into the upstage blackness.

Michael heaved the entire metallised sheet back and over the false head piece and let it rest there. As far as the audience could tell, the helpless Phoebe was still strapped to the now furiously rattling, steam-snorting monster.

"No more shall the Goddess Phoebe – exist – as we return her to her own – dimension!" Michael shouted above the climactic crescendo. A great scream of white steam ejected upwards, as he now whipped the sheet back and over…

Taking with it the arm of the false head!

… to reveal, in the immediate silence of a dissipating cloud of white steam – the completely empty Throne!

The silence continued as the audience stared open-mouthed until their bewilderment gave way to a great thunderous wave of applause and cheering. Michael gestured, bowed, and tried his very best to look modest. But, of course, rather than disappearing, Phoebe had already slipped out of her stage dress and scampered past Wicko the Dwarf, our manservant, who from the prompt side wing of the stage, controlled the show's unique lighting using a great panel of gauges, pipes, wheels and circuit breaker levers, much akin to a Great Western Railway signal box. Wicko spun a few wheels and prepared himself to throw a couple of hefty circuit breakers. Unseen above the audience, spot lamps swivelled and tilted in readiness for Wicko's command.

Phoebe threw open the stage left Pass Door and sprinted up a small flight of stairs, two at a time, and into the passageway ahead. On stage, Michael firmly gestured for the crowd to settle.

"Has the Throne of Disintegration banished her spirit to the darkest recess of her own dimension?" shouted Michael, as if he understood any of what he was talking about.

Phoebe sprinted along the corridor towards the sneering, slick haired, pointy-chinned oaf in the brown suit who was standing outside the Royal Box. As for Detective Inspector Skindrick, he barely had a moment to take in what he saw. A slender vision of breathtaking loveliness, dressed, if that was the word, in a red corset and black knee-length boots. The vision then pointed and called, "Look out behind you! It's John Wilkes Booth!" Even as Skindrick turned to look, he knew he'd been duped – but it was too late. Phoebe had yanked open the door and slipped through the black curtain at the rear of the Royal Box. She sashayed smoothly past the four seated dignitaries with a quick "Excuse me please, gentlemen, Goddess coming through," and leapt up to stand on the lip of the balcony, all in one fluid movement. Skindrick entered the box, pistol drawn, but Melville calmly held up an arm to bar his way.

"Is her fleshly body banished to the recess of her own heavenly world?" declaimed Michael, from down on the stage.

"Not just yet, Magister!" The clear female voice rang out through the theatre. All heads turned up towards the box. Wicko pulled his levers and a handful of pinpoint shafts of white light fired downwards upon her. Suddenly, she was there for all to see. Arms aloft, imperious, standing like some deity of the exotic, there to be worshipped.

"Ladies and gentlemen – the Queen of Steam and Goddess of the Aethyr - Phoebe!" yelled Michael. The astonished crowd rose as one to roar their approval. Even those plagued with rickets or haemorrhoids felt the need to stand, braving the inevitable consequences. You know, even the Prime Minister, whom Melville had quickly pulled back into the shadows and out of the light felt compelled to applaud. Phoebe then pointed dramatically at the magician on stage.

"For tonight, Magister, I do return to the Aethyr, but I take you with me!"

Then Phoebe leapt from the box safely into Michael's waiting arms. He spun around a complete revolution, shouted, "Farewell!" and then the crowd saw them both vanish in a vicious burst of steam. Right before their very eyes.

Below the stage, gears turned and a piston pumped as the trap door dropped them down into the void in less than a moment. The audience cheered and applauded at length as clouds of steam billowed about the centre of the stage. For half a minute the crowd yelled, then cheers became a collective gasp, as Michael's swirling face appeared, as if conjured out of the haze, huge, nine feet high, green and uncanny.

The moving image was back-projected using a tinkered-with version of the Theatroscope, invented by my old friend Robert Paul. I used the dense steam as a wall or screen onto which I could project the images of Michael's animated face. The effect was eerie and convincing. I much preferred Robert's projection equipment to that of those two Lumière Brothers. They were Frenchmen, you know. I need elaborate no further.

At his control panel, Wicko pulled the wooden handle of another circuit breaker and a voice filled every corner of the theatre. Upon the console at Wicko's elbow sat what looked to be a black dinner plate, clamped firm and still. Beneath the plate a circular bed revolved quick and steady, and it was from this arrangement the spoken words emanated, captured by a brass horn and then fed along the network of tubes which embraced the auditorium.

"Ladies and gentlemen, this is Michael Magister. I have been transported to that unworldly dimension known only to Phoebe, the Queen of Steam and Goddess of the Aethyr. Nevertheless, I shall be back tomorrow for two shows, so please share the news with your friends. In the meantime, stay safe and keep an ever watchful eye over your shoulder. Does the Goddess walk amongst us at will? Or is it just Steam, Smoke and Mirrors?"

The photographic soliloquy concluded with a sharp fizz and Michael's image shattered into a hundred pieces, which all floated gently like snowflakes, dissolving in the steam. The audience gasped and applauded once again as Wicko sharply plunged the theatre into total blackout, before fading the house lights slowly up, transporting the crowd back to their ordinary world of stark Victorian reality.

"Thank you, Wicko," I said. "Could you ring down the Iron for me?"

"Who? Me?" demanded Wicko the Dwarf. Admittedly I usually rang down the Safety Curtain, myself, but tonight I was expecting a visit from an old friend. Wicko's reaction was the expected loud, irritated tut. But then he had always been the most lazy, recalcitrant employee, not just in the theatre, but the entire world.

"So, Pheebs, did you get a look? Who was it really sitting up there in the box?" asked Michael, as they both took the platform riser, an invention I called the 'Lift-and-Shift', back up to stage level. "Was it the real Lord Salisbury or someone with a fairground novelty Prime Minister beard?"

"No," said Phoebe. "It was most certainly Salisbury. And Balfour was with him. But I couldn't place the other two."

"Pheebs, if the Prime Minister of England and this Balfour, whoever *he* is, suddenly pitch up to see us, word of mouth must be really getting around. That can only be a good thing."

But Phoebe's reaction was a more thoughtful, "Do you know, Michael, I'm not entirely sure it is…"

5

Thurlow Weed, the hunchback Station Master of Hanwell and Elthorne railway station saw Dan Leno, the most famous comedian in the land, performing at the Theatre Royal, Drury Lane only last year. It was in a pantomime, a lively diversion, entitled 'The Forty Thieves', as he recalled, and rather amusing Mister Leno had been too, all done up to look like a woman. But, stone me, if that very same Dan Leno wasn't now sitting in the station waiting room and at all of eleven o'clock at night. Weed would later report he had been studying the railway timetable at his Station Master's desk, by which we may safely assume he was, in fact, slumped forward, dozing and dribbling, when Mister Leno tapped him on the shoulder, enquiring about the next train to London.

"Who'd have thought?" said Weed to no one but himself. Fortunately he recognised Dan Leno's off-stage appearance, because the performer's caricature was clearly featured on the front page of the *Penny Illustrated Paper* which lay open on his desk. Thurlow Weed, cruelly afflicted with rheumatics of the feet, the price paid for a lifetime's loyal service to the Great Western Railway, now carried a chipped enamel mug of scalding tea from his office to the waiting room. As he shuffled along, the steaming gloop slopped over the rim of the mug, splatting onto the platform.

"That's a bloomin' waste, Thurlow", he said to the breeze. It was by far the freshest, strongest brew of the evening, containing enough tannin to stain a regimental saddle.

Weed stopped to peer in through the waiting room window. At first he saw his own reflection in the glass, the familiar bearded, pustulant chops. Then he focussed on a fearsome sight which fair took his breath away, so it did. Standing in the light of his pristine waiting room, warming her hands by the glowing fire, was a pale, slender, middle-aged woman! Her head was swathed in a headscarf and she wore a grey dress with an off-white pinafore covering – which happened to be the very fatigues as worn by them up at the Hanwell nut house, by God! He'd been telegraphed that a women had escaped a bit lively, like, been advised to be on the lookout – and blow me down if that weren't her right there! Caught like a rat in one of his traps.

Station Master Weed threw open the door of the waiting room, shouting, "Here! What's all this?"

"Just keeping the chill at bay, m' fellow" said Dan Leno, dressed in dark overcoat and silk red scarf, warming his hands at the fire, as the red glowing logs popped and spat.

"What? But, where is she, sir? Where'd she go? The mad woman! From out the asylum!" Weed's perplexed bewilderment, caused his red face to flush deeper and resemble a bearded beetroot. "I just saw her, not this second ago, standing right where you are now, sir. A wretch of a thing, she were, and no mistake. Where'd she go?"

"Appears it's only me here, m'fellow. Perchance you witnessed a ghost?" said Leno, looking around and then taking the now half empty mug of brown liquid. "I felt no other worldly presence and I do possess some experience of the supernatural, for we can boast many a spectre at Drury Lane. The lost spirits of the Man in Grey and Charles Macklin rattle around the dressing rooms. And Grimaldi the Clown haunts the very stage! Upon my word, sir, I believe we have more walking dead at Drury Lane than they do in the House of Lords!"

Weed chuckled, mostly out of respect for the famous funster, but deep down he was disturbed by the situation. Greatly disturbed. In fact, you know, he later reported that such was his state of flabbergast he had to take off his smart peaked cap and scratch his head.

"So now, Mister Station Master, the next train to London shall be when?" said Leno.

"Well, see now, sir, the next Paddington bound service due through here is a milk train in two hours' time," said the Station Master. "But it dun't stop here, sir."

"Upon my word, m' fellow – I believe the train *will* stop for me." And with that, Thurlow Weed watched as Dan Leno savoured a welcome sip of his thickly stewed brew.

***

With the safety curtain, the fire-proof barrier between the
stage and the auditorium now lowered in place, Michael
Magister stood stage left, shuffling a deck of cards and very
politely taking no notice whatsoever of Doctor Arthur Conan
Doyle's effusive ramblings. You see, ACD was a dear old
friend of us all, and a frequent backstage visitor, but Michael
was hoping to have found the Prime Minister backstage full of
congratulation and wide eyed puzzlement. Especially as,
having lived in this country for these past ten years he'd grown
to love everything about Victoria's Britain. And he'd paid his
taxes. Well, some. So what else did you have to do to qualify
for a face to face chat with the Prime Minister? In fact, surely
being a brilliant stage magician was enough! Evidently not and
instead Michael was lumbered with dear old Arthur Conan
Doyle. Again.

"I am totally baffled," said the creator of the world's greatest
consulting detective. In fact, ACD even waved his arms to
underscore the sheer extent of his bafflement. "Three times
I've witnessed your Throne of Disintegration illusion and I
still cannot for the life of me fathom the method employed. So,
come now! Be damned with all that deductive logic. Please.
Just tell me how does Phoebe do it?"

"Doctor, how could you even ask such a thing," called
Phoebe, clattering across the stage from the dressing rooms.
"Once you know the secret you will be applying for my job.
And I do believe the costume rather might suit you."

Doyle felt his face flush as Phoebe flung her arms as far as
she could about his chubby frame and planted a red smacker
upon his fleshy cheek. "Lovely to see you, Art."

Believe you me, much had changed since the fourteen year
old Phoebe spent holiday time with Doctor Doyle, her
guardian's former student. Phoebe stayed with Arthur and his
wife in Montague Place, about the time Arthur set up his
disastrous ophthalmic practice in that first floor front room of
number two Upper Wimpole Street. It was there, while waiting
in vain for any patients, myopic or otherwise, that ACD,

dressed in a Harris Tweed three-piece suit, passed the time scribbling more stories for the *Strand Magazine*, and soberly attired Phoebe whiled away the hours poring over Arthur's student medical books. Well, that's what he told me. Now, eight years on, ACD was still wearing the same style of Harris Tweed three-piece suit, but Phoebe's look was now thoroughly more vibrant. A long black taffeta skirt, black leather boots tipped at the points with silver metal. A front-laced purple corset wrapped her top half, her tiny waist accentuated by a thick black leather belt decorated with an array of silver key rings. Her arms were covered with long black lace gloves. The entire ensemble was set off with a black and purple lace choker.

"My, if dearest Phoebe had worn that outfit whilst working for me," thought Arthur Conan Doyle, "I might have attracted a few customers through the door! She'd have certainly driven a few blind!"

Phoebe's drive, and it was a drive, to push the boundaries of Victorian acceptability was never more apparent with her radical approach to fashion. But how anyone could change quite so many clothes, quite so often and so quickly was a mystery known only to Phoebe. Why, since the show finished Michael had barely had time to unknot his gold cravat.

"Oh, and Professor, I rather think I *would* like to enlarge the opening down to the void beneath the Throne," Phoebe said to me as she looped in a silver hooped earring into her left lobe to complete the pair. "It will enable me to make a much smoother escape." ACD was now smiling, having heard this vital clue to the trickery, so Phoebe tapped his chest adding "And don't you tell a soul, Doctor Doyle!"

In case you're wondering, I should explain my involvement in all this gallivanting; I am Michael and Phoebe's '*ingenieur*'. It's one of those old words the French use to aggrandise one's position. It simply means 'engineer', one who fiddles with or makes or uses engines. I use my engineering and scientific knowledge and my modest mathematical skills to conceive and build the various magical illusions which we use in the show. An old dog with new tricks, you might say. I was born in Boston and studied in the Rogers Building at what we called 'Boston Tech', and what is also known as The Massachusetts Institute of Technology. I could bore you with details of my life, my Cambridge Professorship of Abstruse Mathematics, but that was another life I led, and now is probably not the time.

"I was just showing Arthur these 'Goggle-Eyes'," I told Phoebe, as ACD pulled the pair of newly constructed goggles-with-a-difference down over his eyes. The Goggle-Eyes were our latest joint venture. Much like ordinary eye protectors which were buckled about the back of the head with leather straps, these lovelies had not the usual clear glass lenses in front of the eyes, but a pair of adjustable miniature telescopes. Bolted to the Goggle-Eyes and sitting above the wearer's ears on either side sat a pair of brass cylinders the size of cigar tubes. These contained the science which controlled the 'scopes. In fact with the 'scopes fully extended the wearer tended to look not unlike a constipated toad.

"Mmm. Mmm," nodded Arthur Doyle. I'd never known anyone with such unbridled gusto for, quite frankly, everything. "D'you see, by brilliantly utilising Röntgen's discovery, Artemus here is well along the way to creating a visual device which enables the user to actually see clear through a solid door and view whatever lies beyond. By Jove, it's a remarkable breakthrough in ophthalmic science, is it not, Michael?"

Michael agreed, but his thoughts were elsewhere.

"Michael, I rather think if Salisbury had really planned to come backstage he would have done so by now," said Phoebe, with pragmatic certainty.

"Oh, you're wondering about the old PM?" said ACD. "I bumped into him only just now as he was making his way to the exit. I had no idea he shared our fascination with magic. His Lordship interrupted his party's animated discussion about security to commend me on my latest novel *The Tragedy of the Korosko*..."

For Michael that was the clincher. If the Prime Minister still had the time to hand out artistic praise, then Michael wasn't about to miss out. "Thanks, Doc. Come, Pheebs. We can still catch Salisbury."

"Why ever not," agreed Phoebe. "I am rather keen to learn why the old goat was here. Shall we take The Drain?" said Phoebe.

"It's the only way," said Michael.

"Best hurry," said ACD, still wearing the Goggle-Eyes. "Oh, I say," he then gasped as he found himself gazing straight through Phoebe's dress and underwear. "Don't these work splendidly…?"

Michael and Phoebe quickly crossed the stage to the dimly lit prompt side wing and a black metal door, much like a safe, set in a black painted brick wall. Unless you were looking for it, you'd pass straight by, which was the idea. Michael turned the small, well-oiled metal wheel bolted to the wall beside the door. Behind the brickwork, cogs were heard to engage and the door swung open with a hiss. Michael took Phoebe's hand, and, ever the gentleman, let her slip through the doorway first. A platform lift then dropped them both ten feet down into 'The Drain', a name we coined, you know, long before the Waterloo–Bank underground railway line was opened. Suddenly, lamps fizzed into brightness to reveal a brick built tunnel, much akin to one of Joe Bazalgette's sewers, but instead of a flow of brown ooze flowing along the bottom, there ran a mono-railway line.

Phoebe sat in the plush leather seat and swung her legs within the streamline brown oak nosecone, braided with hoops of riveted brass. Michael stood upon the platform behind the cockpit, yanked a lever which changed the points on the monorail, flipped the brake and clung on for dear life. With a great gasp of compressed air and a whine, the capsule lurched, then hurtled at alarming speed along the seventy yards of tunnel, as it curved to the right then decelerated to a fearsome halt, mercifully, before the solid brick wall at the other end. It was a pneumatic electro-magnetic monorail system which I had commissioned utilising the old service tunnel originally constructed for the Edgware Road District Railway Line underground station across the street. It was put together originally for Phoebe to be transported at breakneck speed to make an impossibly rapid re-appearance in another part of the theatre. Only tonight she had opted for the P.M.'s box.

An equivalent lift mechanism at the other end of the tunnel then pushed Michael and Phoebe up to ground level and to a door which opened directly onto the pavement of the Edgware Road. The entire journey, from stage to street, took less than a dozen seconds, perhaps enough time to intercept the Prime Minister before his departure.

"I just don't get why he'd come to see the show, then not want to meet us afterwards?" puzzled Michael.

"Michael, you must remember, Salisbury is a typical politician," said Phoebe. "He's all talk, all show and precious little substance."

"Shame on the man," sniffed Michael. "That's my job."

Michael and Phoebe had stepped out beneath the awning of the theatre, not fifteen yards from the official looking black Clarence carriage and pair parked at the kerbside, which stood in stark contrast to the cabs lined up and waiting for big tipping fares. Clearly, Salisbury and his party had still to battle their way out of the theatre, caught up in the great audience surge for the exits, the usual ugly morass of pushing, shoving and elbows, with everyone keen to get to their drinking dens before closing time. Within the foyer, Arthur Balfour was most put out by his close proximity to the awful electorate and their womenfolk, and was indeed about to express himself loudly as such. But that was before Melville calmly instructed him to keep quiet, keep his head down and keep moving. In this kind of crowd, no one would recognise the Prime Minister, so long as Balfour could be dissuaded in no uncertain terms from making another damned fuss. In fact, thought Melville, if Balfour hadn't stood to complain so bitterly about that Royal Box security lapse, they may all have been well on their way to Arlington Street by now! It was only with great fortune it seemed that anyone in the audience beady eyed enough to have spotted Lord Salisbury had dismissed his presence as a mistake, rightly wondering why the great national leader would waste his time visiting a magic show, when there were far more pressing matters of state to consider.

The hold-up, Michael and Phoebe heard, was caused by a bizarre accident not five minutes earlier, down there to the right, by the corner of Chapel Street, near Edgware Road Station. Apparently, a flatbed wagon, carrying a dozen barrels of rancid pork fat, bound for who knows where had, for some reason, careened across the street and collided with the red hot brazier of a hot chestnut vendor. The wooden barrels brim full with white sloppy gloop had reacted badly with the shower of sparks thrown up by the toppled brazier and went up like a rocket. Apparently, the red flames at one point roared aloft by as much as twenty feet. The driver leaped clear and scampered off, while the horse broke loose and was last seen galloping toward Maida Vale. Blazing barrels rolled across the street scattering pedestrians and carriages like some hellish game of skittles and the nauseous whiff of burnt pork crackling permeated the entire area. Although, by now, the inferno had lost much of its spectacle, Michael and Phoebe could still clearly see the reflection of the glow upon the grimy windows of the buildings opposite. The burning debris of strewn and flaring porcine spillage coupled with the crowd of onlookers served to congest more than usual the southern end of the Edgware Road

It meant, of course, that Driver Sergeant Coxhead, having fed and watered his black military horses was now figuring out his detour route. But if the gathering crowd about the Clarence carriage was becoming a problem, his concern was very short lived because every man and woman of them backed up a brisk step or two when both horses suddenly decided to snort, nod their heads and empty first their bladders, then their capacious bowels in perfect, steaming unison.

"Mindful of Salisbury's proximity, one might have expected a greater police presence," said Phoebe. "Of course their attention may be drawn to managing the fire."

"That fire is a classic distraction, Pheebs. Maskelyne knows we've got Lord Salisbury in the audience and he's created that mayhem so no one sees us with the Prime Minister."

"It seems rather a lot of trouble to go to," said Phoebe, wondering why a rival magician should have prior knowledge of the Prime Minister's visit.

"But it's working. I mean, see across the street. The only person not interested in the accident is that old Nanny pushing that pram."

Phoebe, looked over at the coarse-faced woman, dressed in a black full length dress and black bonnet as she shoved her ancient baby carriage across the cobbles of Linton Street with such juddering force as to shake the poor infant senseless.

"And to me that's not right, Pheebs," shrugged Michael. "At this time of night, a little child should be at home and in bed asleep. Or maybe up a chimney. Ow! It was a social comment, not a joke."

It was at that moment a group of well-heeled gentlemen forced their way out of the theatre and headed for the Clarence. A path had been forged for the Prime Minister.

"Pheebs. Here he is. It's the Prime Minister!" Beaming with star struck enthusiasm Michael waved, calling out, "Sir! Sir! Michael Magister, sir! And Phoebe!"

But Phoebe was ignoring the excitement at the front of the theatre, and her focus was trained intently upon the Nanny.

"That is a rather good point, Michael," said Phoebe to herself before tugging on Michael's jacket sleeve firmly enough to draw his attention away from Lord Salisbury. "Why *is* that woman out with a baby at this time of night?"

Michael turned to look at the old girl and saw it; a glinted reflection in the amber glow of the street lamps. Fished from the folds of her voluminous dress, the Nanny was holding an ornate pistol.

"She's got a gun!" gasped Michael, "Pheebs, she's gonna shoot the baby!"

"Oh, my days," said Phoebe, now seeing the weapon for herself. "Not the baby. She's going to shoot the Prime Minister!"

6

Even in the brief moment it took Michael to make sense of the situation, Phoebe was already halfway across the Edgware Road, smartly weaving between the melee of carriages, omnibuses and cabs.

"Wh...? Wait. Okay – why does she always do this?" Michael sighed. He glanced at the Prime Minister in two minds what to do, ignored his natural instinct to flee in the opposite direction and found himself chasing his fearless assistant and *towards* someone toting what looked to be a gun! As he slipped through the traffic, Michael began to hope Phoebe had some kind of plan figured, because *he* sure as hell didn't.

"Good evening!" said Phoebe, sweetly smiling as she approached the coarse looking Nanny, whose face upon closer examination proved to be not so much coarse as, frankly, repulsive. The flustered child-minder quickly shoved the pistol back into the pocket within her skirt folds as Phoebe continued: "Please forgive this intrusion. But I wondered if everything was well with you? I only ask because it's a rather drear evening and your well-being, in addition, of course, to that of your infant, was of particular concern to myself – and, indeed, to my equally cavalier associate."

Her equally cavalier associate now stood at her shoulder. having just narrowly avoided being hit by an omnibus. "Good evening, ma'am. And straight off can I say, I do love the bonnet. Not many can carry off that Jane Austen funereal look, but you certainly can. By the way, I am Magister the Magician, may I present Phoebe the Queen of Steam, and no doubt you'll recognise us from our starring roles at the Met just across the way there! See the poster? That's us, but so much better looking in real life." Michael gestured grandly across to the brightly lit theatre, but the Nanny remained sourly unimpressed. In turning, Michael saw the Prime Minister's driver crack his whip and shape the horses around, to catch a break in the traffic.

"Magister, perhaps you might enthral this lady's lovely infant with a little playing card prestidigitation?" suggested Phoebe.

"Indeed I certainly could, oh Queen of Steam," said Michael, still trying to figure out a plan. With one hand he produced, as if from magic's proverbial thin air, a deck of playing cards, *from a hidden pouch inside his waistcoat* and then with one finger swirled them into a fan. "But not before I gaze upon her precious little bundle of joy." Michael looked into the pram, but immediately recoiled, gasping: "Ergh! The kid's hideous!"

The Prime Ministerial coach was now exploiting a gap in the traffic flow and Driver Sergeant Coxhead rattled the reins and coaxed the horses into movement with that "C'muh!" order that all coachmen, fluent in Equine, tend to use. Now the coach was starting its U-turn in the street, an arc which Michael calculated would swing it directly in front of them. If this old crone truly was an assassin, the coach and everyone aboard were turning straight into an ambush.

"Be gone, the pair of yous!" growled the Nanny in an accent that was less English than Michael's, and from the dry rasp, Phoebe figured the grotesque woman was either afflicted by that phlegmy chest contagion which was doing the rounds, or that 'she' was, in fact, a 'he'. And, yes, the latter proved indeed to be the case when the Nanny's calloused hand once again drew the pistol, the like of which Michael and Phoebe recognised. It was a decorated weapon of remarkable beauty, capable of firing not bullets, but pulses of energised Aethyr to powerfully destructive effect. It was called a 'Pulsatronic pistol' and only two such similar weapons were known to exist in this country. Both belonged to Michael and Phoebe, and both were built by me!

Instantly, and, I suspect, more in panic than plan, Michael sprayed the entire deck of sharp-edged playing cards straight into the eyes of the gun-toting Nanny-man. The corners of each red card were edged with sharpened copper, inflicting a vicious pattern of paper cuts around the man's eyes. The blinded would-be assassin triggered off a desperate shot. The ball of vicious purple energy missed everything and everyone, before exploding into the front wall of the theatre and showering the pavement in shards of terracotta brickwork. Suddenly, everywhere was a blur of mass panic. Carriages skidded, horses reared up, women, and men, theatrical types mostly, either fainted, screamed or scarpered.

"Drive on! Drive on!!" hollered Sergeant Coxhead, cracking his whip. The Clarence lurched forward, its rear end fishtailing wildly and its wheels throwing up a shower of sparks. Next, the odious baby sat bolt upright in the pram revealing himself to be another stubble-faced assassin brandishing another Pulsa pistol. Phoebe raised her booted foot and with a mighty shove, toppled the straining pram over onto its side, spilling the squat, loathsome man-baby out onto the pavement.

"Hello! Police! Over here!" waved Michael, bravely. "We have assassins! Over here! See! The ugly ones!"

Police whistles mingled with the shrieks of the panicking crowd, distracting Phoebe enough to not notice the prostrate man-baby in a now skewed nursery bonnet aiming his Pulsa directly up at her pert chest. But Michael saw it and only just managed to shove her to one side, as the weapon discharged a volley of energised shots which soared and smashed into the chimney of the corner house on Linton Street. Thoroughly miffed by such audacity, Phoebe retaliated by aiming a firm kick with the point of her boot straight across the gunman's snarling mouth and yelling, "How dare you!" as she did it.

As the Pulsa fell from his grasp, the man-baby screamed, as best anyone could with a freshly fractured jaw, and rolled backwards. One assassin down and one to go. Unfortunately, the one to go had other ideas. Michael found himself staring straight down the metalled barrel of the Nanny-man's Pulsa. While he heard himself squeal, "Anywhere but the face!" from his pocket he was producing a small black metal tube, which with a squeeze, suddenly extended itself top and bottom to form a walking cane which struck the Nanny-man a blow to the chin. *It is spring loaded and when released simply spirals out to full length.* The Nanny-man's head jolted backwards before Phoebe took great delight in bringing her knee up between the folds of the assassin's skirt, connecting with his free-dangling scrotum and causing him to now snap forwards. In spite of his confusion and pain the assassin managed to trigger off another pulse of super-charged Aethyr before his weapon fell to the pavement. The purple tracer streaked hot and fast by Michael's ear, straight across the street and shattered one of the decorative electric lamps suspended below the theatre canopy, fusing out the circuit, plunging the entire theatre front into darkness. Screams and further chaos ensued as the crowd fought to flee in any available direction. Within the wildly skidding Clarence, Melville covered Salisbury with his own human barrier, while Balfour and Sir Cumberland both simply whimpered and cringed and watched in astonishment as Inspector Skindrick flung open the carriage door and jumped out into the street.

"Yous lot! Wi' me!" he shouted in full Scots brogue, and led a posse of boys in blue, with black moustaches and matching truncheons who were, at last, converging on the battlefield from all directions. The two failed assassins (the first was later described in witness reports as: small, thick-set and brutish wearing a baby's bonnet and trying to hold his face together; the second as: tall, bloody of face, apparently female and nursing her testicles) scrambled to make good their painful escape in an easterly direction down Bell Street.

"Arrest those men!" ordered Michael, pointing in the direction of the fleeing miscreants, only to be bundled aside by the stern-faced constables.

Then Skindrick arrived. "You! Th' weapons! Did they still carry th' weapons?"

"He took them! The man dressed as a baby!" said Michael.

Skindrick cursed, before bravely continuing the pursuit, unaware that Michael had, with a deft boot, managed to hide one of the discarded pistols out of sight beneath the upturned pram.

Out on the road, urgent whip cracks, coupled with the clatter of horses' hooves, signalled the speedy departure of a now safe and most certainly un-assassinated British Prime Minister. Michael and Phoebe watched as the black carriage rattled past them, so near they could almost reach out and touch it. From within the passenger compartment the impassive Lord Salisbury looked out and returned their gaze before drawing up the window blind.

"You're welcome," murmured Phoebe, as the Prime Minister's coach sped away, then quickly screeched a right turn into Earl Street and charged eastward towards Lisson Grove. In fact, had the assassins been savvy, they might have intercepted the Clarence on Lisson Grove itself, but the fight had been well and truly slashed, beaten and kneed right out of them.

Melville assured himself of the well-being of the Prime Minister, the Leader of the House and the Assistant Commissioner of Police of the Metropolis. He was acutely aware that had the assassins been successful, it would have amounted to one of the greatest outrages ever committed upon the streets of London. Balfour sat ashen and shaking, while Sir Cumberland was pale, clammy and gently whimpering. Salisbury, by contrast, you know, appeared entirely untroubled by the incident.

"I assume, Sir Cumberland, you have never before experienced an assassination attempt," he said. "Allow me to assure you, they only become dangerous if they are successful. By which time it is probably too late to worry."

"No, sir, this is something I am not in any way used to," replied the Assistant Commissioner, failing to appreciate the humour, his hands still shaking. "But I wager, our Skindrick and his uniformed confederates are apprehending the foul perpetrators, even as we jolly well speak! Wouldn't you say, old chum?"

William Melville ignored the Assistant Commissioner. Instead he slid aside the metal panel which connected the interior of the bullet-proof carriage with the driver up-front and called: "You may reduce your speed now, thank you, Sergeant Coxhead! It is clear we are not being pursued!"

"In which case, Inspector Melville," said Sir Cumberland, dabbing his sweated forehead with a 'kerchief, "It might be prudent to briefly stop to allow me to alight the carriage. I fear my churning stomach may cause the Prime Minister further distress and myself much embarrassment."

Melville couldn't have agreed more. An up-chuck in the PM's carriage was thoroughly undesirable. In fact, the Assistant Commissioner's behaviour throughout the entire incident had been nothing like one might expect from a high ranking officer of the law. In the great pecking order of national importance, Assistant Commissioners were two a penny, and if Sir Cumberland Sinclair wanted to be let out, that was entirely his own decision. Melville's immediate concern was the safe return of the Prime Minister to Arlington Street.

"Sergeant Coxhead, please be kind enough to draw to a halt!" ordered Melville. The last he saw of Sir Cumberland Sinclair that evening was the Assistant Commissioner leaning back against a set of tall railings in Portman Square, retching and mopping his brow.

"Was that altogether wise, William? Are we certain he is capable of making his own way home to South Kensington?" wondered Salisbury. Melville cared not a jot, but felt it an opinion which served little purpose in being expressed.

Leadership roles in the Metropolitan Police had always been a cause of concern for rank and file Bobbies. Since the creation of the post of Commissioner, thus far six had been drawn from the ranks of the military, and all six had fruitlessly tried to run the Force upon military lines. Of the other two past Commissioners, Richard Mayne and James Monro, neither was a serving copper, instead coming from the civilian world. Both were lawyers, which was just as hopeless, and while Mayne became aloof in the role and badly mishandled The Clerkenwell Bombing outrage, Monro had made a better fist of raising standards and morale following the Ripper debacle, under that idiot Charles Warren. But, you know, even Monro had worked as a civil servant in India and rumour was it was he who brought his civil service matey, Sir Cumberland Sinclair, into the fold.

"Prime Minister, tonight's two security incidents at the theatre present two different concerns," said Melville, quietly.

"First, for Detective Inspector Skindrick to allow any unauthorised entry to your box was dereliction of duty in the extreme."

"It did, however, enable me to witness the subject of our disquiet at very close quarters. And admire her tenacity," said Salisbury. "Your second concern?"

"Understanding how tonight's assassins gained knowledge of your presence in the Edgware Road. It was a short notice arrangement known to only but a few."

"Does that suggest we have a traitor in our midst?" piped up Balfour, his pompous, lofty air now seemingly restored. "And if so, Melville, I wager the traitor must dwell in your policing circles, sir!"

"Mister Balfour, whatever his position in the world, be assured it is a conundrum you may safely leave with me," said Melville pointedly.

The rest of the journey Salisbury spent deep in thought. The only sounds to be heard were the rhythmic clopping of the horses' hooves occasionally disturbed by the dreadful digestive protests emanating from Arthur Balfour's stomach. Balfour, of course, looked splendidly furious, realising confidential decisions of national importance were being made from which he was being manifestly excluded. So he passed the time gazing at the drawn window blind and by twiddling his thumbs, as opposed to thumbing his twiddle, as dear Miss Marie Lloyd might have quipped.

Despite the unplanned passenger drop off, Sergeant Coxhead still had his three important charges safely delivered to number twenty Arlington Street, Lord Salisbury's residence in less than twenty minutes. In the Prime Minister's private office Melville declined the offer of a large measure of ten-year-old Macallan.

"After tonight's excitement, your little Hanwell Asylum problem appears insignificant, by comparison," said Salisbury.

"Be assured, sir, it remains neither little or insignificant," Melville assured the Prime Minister, firmly.

"Based upon your briefing, and upon what I have now seen for myself, I concur, it is unlikely the American will agree if the girl is not involved," said Salisbury, before knocking back a decent measure of Scotland's peaty finest. "Mother is at home and apprised?"

"Indeed," replied Melville.

"William, this must not become any more untidy than it already is."

"It will not, sir."

Lord Salisbury drained his glass, and then nodded. "So be it. Proceed."

Melville thanked the Prime Minister and sought permission to use the telephone in the outer office. He requested a Whitehall number and when connected simply but firmly said, "Take them."

7

The Metropolitan Theatre of Steam, Smoke and Mirrors was one of the most modern playhouses in the land. The designs of dear old Frank Matcham, the architect of The Met, had drawn much interest, especially as Frank had managed to shoehorn this spanking new building onto the cramped, triangular site of the old Metropolitan Music Hall, here at the confluence of the busy Harrow Road and the even busier Edgware Road. The result was a beautiful playhouse, containing the strangest shape for a stage anywhere in the world: it was thirty feet wide at the proscenium opening, nineteen feet in depth, but narrowing all the way to less than three feet at the down stage back. Of course, from the perspective of the crowd looking through the proscenium arch, the stage appeared perfectly regular, but that was just another illusion. As you might imagine, during the planned stages I prevailed upon Frank to adjust and augment various aspects of his blueprints for the convenience of magic performance and a few, shall we say, hidden and behind the scenes adjustments and refits, which were even now on-going.

In fact, following opening night, one critic opined thus: *"Every part of the theatre has been enlarged and the entrances and exits multiplied. Occupying as it does the same ground space as the old hall, the great increase in the size of the present theatre was a veritable triumph of artistic vision, and quite practised skill. After all, Mister Frank Matcham, the architect, already had fifty-three theatres and Music Halls to his credit. The audience capacity is two thousand six hundred crimson seats in the fauteuils, stalls and pit seats, four private boxes, plus the balcony, along with standing room for two hundred."*

A quite splendid review, don't you think? And those of you with an abacus to hand, will not need me to inform you that a nightly full house with a minimum ticket of four shillings and six pence amounted to quite a box office take by the end of the week. Our plan, and by 'our plan' I mean to include myself,

Michael and Phoebe (and Wicko if we must), was to create a venue to rival John Nevil Maskelyne's long-established, wildly successful magic emporium at The Egyptian Hall in London's Piccadilly. True, it was a tall order given Maskelyne's right and proper status as the godfather of British magic, the top dog. But, you know, I felt we possessed the capability. Certainly since Phoebe had joined the act.

Now the auditorium was empty, the bars closed, but the walls, the ceiling, the very guts of the place still seemed to tingle. Almost as if it had absorbed all that laughter and applause like a sponge of stone and plaster. Far more important, of course, for me was the vast void beneath the stage, the under stage, what we called The Dungeon. Set within the excavated foundations of the old Music Hall the large space was illuminated by half a dozen suspended electric lamps, the designs of which I'd borrowed from Joseph Swan, an old friend of mine, you know. It was Joe's fine work which lit the first theatre in Britain, The Savoy, all of two decades ago, can you believe that? Few realise dear Joe, with that fine Geordie accent and his fulsome beard, was years ahead of Tommy Edison when it came to the incandescent light bulb. But back to The Dungeon. Down here, amidst a handful of cast iron red oxide pillars supporting the wooden stage above, stood the performance paraphernalia of the working magician: cabinets, cages and gothic contraptions of more than a dozen terrifying stage illusions, some so vicious even Tomas Torquemada the Grand Inquisitor himself might have shaken his head and tutted in disapproval. All were cast, carved, fashioned or wrought in all manner of metals, woods and materials, some supposedly not yet invented and hefted up onto the stage through a trap door, aboard our Lift'n'Shift, the steam powered rising platform based upon the notion of a scissors jack. These conjuring contrivances, the cabinets and such like, all had a solid industrial muscularity about them. Vivid colours, fringed with gold, all swathed in shining cogs, brass and copper pipework, brown leather or gothic green ironwork, superbly reflected the substance, beauty and technical innovation of this forthcoming new Millennium. Well, I thought so.

Over there, to one side was my workshop where we conceived, designed and constructed most of everything we used in the show. A bazaar of pneumatic and steam powered cutting and riveting machinery, wall-mounted wrenches, screwdrivers, drills and hammers of all sizes from sledge to toffee. In fact, it was so nicely equipped it was not unlike a small scale Menlo Park. Menlo Park, you probably know is the research establishment Tommy Edison set up with John Pierpont Morgan's money in West Orange, New Jersey. What you won't know is that I flounced out of there in high dudgeon at the same time as my great chum and workmate Nik Tesla. You see , Edison wouldn't give Nik due credit for generating electrical power far more effectively than his Direct Current malarkey could ever manage. So together, we quit, right there and then. Nik still writes, but Tommy doesn't.

Anyway, my mini Menlo, right here under the stage at the Met, was designed for the development and experimentation of matters chemical, technological, and industrial, and how they could be applied to magical illusions. You see, in this day and age, you must strive to stay ahead of any new developments.

Michael, you know, was the first magician to use electro magnets rigged beneath the stage for a weight lifting illusion. Oh, yes! For the trick, he'd pull the biggest strapping great fellow he could find among the audience and invite him to lift a stone and a half metal weight which, of course, the fellow could manage with ease. Then Michael would pronounce that the mere presence of Phoebe, the Queen of Steam and Goddess of the Aethyr, would sap all of the man's brute strength, rendering him weak and wan. I would then throw the switch on the electro magnet bolted beneath the stage and when the poor fellow tried to lift the weight this time, he would be completely unable. No matter how much strain and sweat he expended, the weight would not budge. Not, you understand because of Phoebe's exotic powers, but because of the pull of the magnet.

In addition to Joe Swan's lighting, The Dungeon was also driven by a network of overhead pipes of burnished copper and brass. Against one wall stood a console of dials, meters and gauges, each mounted in a solid brass housing. A phalanx, don't you love that word, a phalanx of hefty circuit breakers and wheel valves controlled the pipework which spewed from various orifices in the console. Let me see, what else? Oh, yes, I can also boast a wooden frame in the corner into which are built towers of metal cogs which, one day, when I finally get around to completing it, should perform any mathematical function. My good friend, poor Charlie Babbage, who had known such personal tragedy in his life, was well into his dotage when we both sat, not a stone's throw from this theatre, and discussed his Analytical Engine. His lovely Ada, the Enchantress of Numbers, would be ashamed of my idleness and rightly so. Did you know that like Charlie, dear sweet Ada Lovelace also passed away not too far from here? But look, here I am side-tracked again…

Michael and I had just strolled down the street to examine the scene of the accident. Nosh Clutterbuck, the roast chestnut purveyor who had been working that roadside pitch for years, was all but inconsolable, having lost his livelihood. His brazier had been so flattened by the impact of the pork fat wagon it resembled a black rusty pancake. The old curmudgeon's charcoaled face was streaked with tears, and where once he boasted a thick head of wiry hair and a fine beard, both had now vanished, thanks to the shower of sparks which had set his entire head alight. I'm told Nosh looked much like a flaring safety match as he ran screaming to quench the blaze in the nearby horse trough.

However his spirits took a lift when Michael slipped him enough large pound notes to purchase a new brazier and a fresh supply of nuts. The sum involved also proved more than enough to encourage him to recount the finer details of the entire incident. Not in half a dozen years, he said, had any traffic come even close to skidding into his brazier – until tonight.

"Look around, Prof," said Michael. "No wheel marks for a skid, the ridiculously flammable cargo, the driver running off. All points to something deliberate. This was perpetrated by someone with a true and lasting hatred of Nosh Clutterbuck's roasted chestnuts."

Again, Michael's observations were uncanny and accurate, but his logical assessment of those observations, as ever, was completely and utterly wrong.

"Or perhaps by someone intent upon distracting the police contingent, and steering the Prime Minister's coach into the path of the assassins?" I suggested.

"Yes! I didn't think of that..." said Michael. "But that is why, Professor, you are a genius!" His praise was somewhat *more* effusive, of course, but modesty forbids...

Upon our return to the workshop area of the Dungeon, we were welcomed by an intense blue crackling light of an acetylene torch flame, slicing easily through the metal seating framework. With the escape flap on The Throne of Disintegration now suitably enlarged, the deft metal worker in the brass rimmed safety visor and full length leather apron and a backpack of twin gas bottles, removed a slender hand from a gauntlet and twisted the red wheel control valve half a turn to kill the vicious flame.

"Your opinion, please, Professor?" breathed Phoebe, as she lifted the visor.

I peered down at the newly widened aperture, its orange-glow edges now darkening and clicking as they cooled. As I would have expected, it was a nifty piece of work from an extraordinary person. She'd make someone a wonderful wife one day. As if. I nodded in genuine appreciation, "Splendid! Although I do believe that was Wicko's task to perform."

Wicko sat relaxing on a leather travelling trunk bounded with brass strips, his feet up, reading *The Paddington Mercury*. "My diphtheria's playing up a bit shocking," he said tapping his chest, "but I offered."

"He very kindly did," nodded Phoebe, as she pulled off the helmet and visor and let her titian hair tumble free. "You know, Professor, it rather occurs to me those assassins must have had precise knowledge of Salisbury's whereabouts. That elaborate Nanny charade certainly suggests planning with intent."

"And, you know, the fire along the street looks to be part of the plot," I nodded.

Michael was frowning as he distractedly poked a finger at the circular blade of a work in progress illusion called 'The Steam Saw Of Gore'. Unfortunately the blade was unbolted and dropped to the stage with a clang.

"And all those constables chasing down the shooters like some comedy troupe, but none of them come back to take statements from Pheebs and I. And where's the press? Prime Minister under gunfire, saved by magicians, bizarre weapons used, shooters dressed as women and babies – that's got to be unusual, even in West London."

"They will play down the entire incident. Behave as if nothing of the like ever happened. Sweep it straight under the Establishment's thick pile Axminster," said Phoebe, with some authority. "And, technically, it's 'take statements from Pheebs and me'."

"Really? Okay. And as for those Pulsa pistols, Prof, where did the gunmen get those beauties? Not from any gun shop around here. No wonder that detective was asking after them," said Michael.

"I reckon them German buggers have stolen a march on us, Artie," said Wicko. Much as I resented his calling me Artie, I could hardly disagree. In my left hand I now held the Pulsa recovered from tonight's battlefield. In my right hand, was the Pulsa I had constructed. The ornate design and exquisite skilled metal working of both pistols was quite similar. But, the assassins' weapon was heavier and more bulbous. And Wicko was quite right. It might well have been the work of Theodor Wulf and Walther Nernst over at Walther's Institute of Chemistry and Electrochemistry in Germany. The town of Gottingen to be precise. Walther Nernst, as you may have guessed, is a good friend of mine. When Wicko and I paid him a visit some years ago I copied his prototype plans for an energised Aethyr weapon. It was possible that Walther and his young God-fearing pupil Theodor had made significant advancements with their Pulsa pistols since then. Not that it explained how they came into the possession of our assassins.

"This will require an examination of some detail," I told Michael and Phoebe. "Wicko and I will work into the night."

"I won't," said Wicko, somewhat alarmed.

"So you two take yourselves home," I told Michael and Phoebe. "And sleep content in having performed two shows and saved a Prime Minister."

"Just so long as you're careful when you jemmy the Pulsa open, Prof," advised Michael.

'Jemmy it open.' I did enjoy Michael's wondrous grasp of scientific vernacular. Michael and Phoebe bade me goodnight with instructions not to labour too long and both rode the Lift'n'Shift up to the stage and the Stage Door lobby.

"I'd help if I could, Artie," said Wicko, folding up his paper and slipping off the trunk, down onto the floor. "But I'm fair bushed."

"Yes, yes. But if you could bolt that blade back in place before you do, I'd be grateful," I told him, pointing at the silver sharp-toothed circular saw which still lay where it had fallen.

"Who? Me?" I could not help but smile at Wicko's face, a picture of irritated malcontent.

***

"Beautiful waxing crescent moon tonight," observed Phoebe, peering up at the night sky through the toughened glass window, set within the fortified Stage Door. She waited for Michael to tap out a six letter word on the "qwerty" keyboard of the Remington typewriter which rested on the Stage Door desk. It was the code to unlock the Door. Following a quick sequence of clicks and clunks as the bolts were released, the door then swung outwards with a hiss and they both stepped out into the cool night air of the yard outside. Lights flickered on to illuminate the steps down to White Lion Passage and behind them the Stage Door hissed and closed.

"Two full houses. The life of the Prime Minister saved," said Phoebe, happily slipping her arm through Michael's, "I still rather enjoy this job..."

"Just another night's work for..." Michael then stopped. "Pheebs. I think we should maybe go back inside..."

"Michael? What is..."

Suddenly they were engulfed in darkness! Sack cloth hoods? The click and burn of the wrist-shackles? The faint, soporific whiff of chloroform? The muffled words: "Into the carriage with them..."

8

"Pater dimitte peccata, indigni!'" incanted the two men as they knelt, basically begging forgiveness for their unworthiness By and large, this was a remarkable feat, considering one of them could barely spout the Latin thanks to his shattered jaw, and the other could barely kneel as a consequence of his battered scrotum which, by now, had swollen to such alarming proportions it looked much as if he was smuggling a melon in his trousers. By Hansom cab and then on foot, they had hauled their bloody, broken bodies, wincing at every bump and step of the way, to this, their pre-arranged refuge – a place of worship in Soho.

But instead of offering thanks for their success before an altar adorned with a tall solid silver crucifix and the solid silver goblet and salver of Holy Communion, the failed assassins were bowing in sorrowful penitence. The flames atop two black candles danced and spluttered in scornful defiance of the many cold draughts which pervaded the small church.

"You are indeed unworthy, for you have failed us," growled the firm and menacing voice which echoed about the small chapel. "The heathen Salisbury still breathes our Holy Lord's air and walks his earth, but in losing one of our weapons you heap danger upon our Blessed Society. And upon me!"

From the shadows and into the flickering light stepped a tall, upright, imposing figure dressed in a full length black habit, its face hidden, enveloped within the dark recess of the hood. The figure stood before the altar, bowed to the crucifix and then turned to look down upon the two cowering wretches. Their dishevelled disguises made them appear all the more pathetic.

"Holy Farver, find it in your 'art to forgive us," rasped the one who had most control over his jaw. They stared up at the face of the holy man in black. A face of horror, half hidden now, but pale skinned with long strands of hair which hung down past his ears. Little wonder he was known to those who followed and feared him as 'The Black Bishop' and 'The Hairy Monk'. His dark cruel eyes blazed with a religious fervour that might have even put the wind up St. Peter himself. Then suddenly the holy man's attitude softened. His bearing remained powerful, but his tone became distinctly more benevolent. One might even say sympathetic.

"But it is clear that misfortune blighted your course of action, my sons. The blame should not rest entirely upon your shoulders. This is as much a failure of mine, as yours. And I am proud to see you bear your physical pain and mental torment with such fortitude and grace. Our Gracious Father knows of your commitment and he forgives your sins. And so, before we partake of the Blessed Sacrament, let us give thanks for your safe deliverance."

As the priest in black turned and knelt before the altar, the newly absolved pair glanced at one another, both visibly relieved. Truly, men less valuable to the Society, less experienced in arts of murder and mayhem would most certainly have been struck dead by now. The scent of smoky incense wafted around the altar as the bishop in black stood bowed and prepared the sacrament.

"The body and the blood," said the Holy man, administering the wafer and wine to each of the grateful supplicants. He then blessed their poor souls… to eternal damnation!

His face contorted with rage and the veins in his neck throbbed as through gritted teeth he hissed. *"Stipendium mors est propter defectum haeredis!"* Death is the reward for failure!"

Both men barely had time to catch a breath before the all-consuming pain ripped through them. They clutched their throats. They tried to stand. It felt as if their insides were ablaze, consumed by the fires of hell as the bitter, white foam bubbled in their mouths. Gasping, they looked up to The Black Bishop for some sign of mercy – but none came forth, and they both slumped forward and lay twitching either side of where the holy man stood. Until they twitched no more.

"Pones in infernum, haeretici!" intoned The Black Bishop. Burn in hell, heretics.

"Amen," added a second man, who, having observed the entire shocking ritual, now emerged from the shadows. Detective Inspector Gersham Skindrick bowed to the altar, blessed himself with the sign of the cross, and then looked down at the corpses with contempt. "I'll ha'this filth weighted with stones and thrown in the Thames within th' hour, Excellency."

"You attend me well, disciple," nodded the Holy man.

"A crowd o' West London filth all bore witness tae the explosive power of th' weapons at work, but I kin ha' the occurrence dismissed as the work of the conjuror. But, Excellency, might I share an additional concern," asked Skindrick, narrowing his already narrow eyes still further, until they looked much like two knife slits.

"Share that concern with your spiritual guide," said the Bishop.

Skindrick looked down upon the two bodies lying at his feet, their faces twisted in a rictus of agony. "If this Godless scum spoke truth and the magician told me lies, our lost weapon may reside in th' keeping o' Michael Magister and his wanton slattern."

"You must investigate and recover the weapon!" hissed the Bishop. "And if circumstance requires, you have my blessing to guide these magicians down the pathway of certain truth, as we have done lo these many centuries."

"The power of prayer, Excellency?"

"The power of torture!"

"Ha! That, Excellency," grinned Skindrick, "that shall bring me much joy…"

"Bless you, my son," said the faceless Bishop.

Skindrick then knelt and kissed the holy man's black signet ring of office, the ring upon the third finger of his left hand, the ring stamped with the symbol IXXI.

9

I believe the chloroform, or whatever it was, must have been of a much diluted tincture, more soporific than somnambulant. I cannot believe I've said that, because Michael and Phoebe quickly felt themselves restored with clear heads, as clear as possible when shrouded in a debilitating gentle haze of brown sack mustiness. They had felt themselves borne with great efficiency aboard a waiting carriage, then driven off at a whip-cracking lick, the reins of the carriage clearly in the hands of a lunatic who had learned his horse driving skills from reading Lew Wallace's new novel *Ben-Hur*.

The quilted leather bench seats were firm but comfortable; the only debilitation came from their shackled hands, which now rested quietly in their laps. Some twenty minutes into their frantic ride and slumped together on a quilted leather carriage seat, Michael inclined his hooded head toward the warm body leaning against his.

"Pheebs?" he murmured.

"Michael? Who are these people?" she whispered back.

"Someone we've really upset."

"Which rather narrows it down to the hundreds."

"I've counted the corners, the straight line runs, we're going in circles."

"Yea, no talking, please, sir!" barked the voice opposite.

A Londoner, thought Michael. Respectful, too. Very nice. Military? Quite possibly.

The carriage then swung sharply left, and the wheels, rather than rattling, made a crunching noise, as if they were rolling across gravel. Now the sound of the horses' hooves began to echo, suggesting an enclosure, a courtyard maybe? Their short journey had barely skidded to a halt before the carriage door was whipped open and Michael and Phoebe were manhandled down, into the cool open air, across gravel, onto a cobbled walkway. The entire abduction occurred with a kind of slick speed, which meant Michael and Phoebe were most certainly in the hands of professionals. People who were well-versed in the dark art of kidnapping. And most kidnappings did not end well.

***

"You cunning pair of Gottingen rascals!" I heard myself say with a chuckle.

You see, only seconds before, beneath the stage of the Metropolitan Theatre of Steam, Smoke and Mirrors, I had been puzzling over the Pulsatronic pistol Phoebe and Michael had secured from the scene of the farcical shooting. The design of the weapon, the workmanship involved, was exquisite. It was perverse that such instruments of awesome destruction could also possess such beauty, both aesthetic and artistic. My attention was drawn first to the deep brown cherry wood grip-stock, which was riveted to a block of forged copper coloured metal, an amalgam of which I had yet to identify. The revolving cylinder was much the same as a common usage revolver like the Browning, but possessed no flute holes for housing bullets. It was outwardly solid, set to the fore of the barrel, and contained its critical power generating mechanicals within. The trigger and its trigger guard were similar to a regular weapon. This new Pulsa weighed a full six ounces heavier, oh, but the firing mechanism was ingenious. The release of the safety catch and the first squeeze of the trigger, allowed the cylinder to loudly whirr and spin, suck in the air and energise the Aethyr. A second squeeze of the trigger discharged a purple pulse of destructive energy from the barrel at tremendous velocity. It zinged across the Dungeon and with a loud thud embedded itself into the side of a pile of sacks filled with damp sawdust, where it briefly glowed before dying. But here's the difference. Because the cylinder revolved continuously, so did the charging mechanism, enabling the trigger to be pulled again almost immediately, in seemingly limitless rapid-fire succession. My Pulsatronic pistol was whiskery, almost medieval by comparison requiring first the hammer spur to be thumbed back, causing the barrel to spin before a shot could be discharged. While mine could only generate a single pulse every ten seconds, the Gottingen Pulsa could fire off six.

In gazing upon this new extraordinary version, you know, I felt a sense not of envy, but growing dread. My Pulsa was built purely with technological novelty in mind, to look for a spectacular twist on the Catch-The-Bullet-In-The-Mouth illusion you understand. Although in practice catching a ball of scalding energised Aethyr in the mouth was proving somewhat difficult to try out. Michael's unwillingness was understandable to say the least. But this Gottingen Pulsa? It was a doomsday weapon. One which criminals, armies and even governments would kill for.

I do consider myself a renegade, a rebel scientist steadfastly refuting the accepted tenets of academia, the old boy's network. But I could never, in all conscience, unleash such destructive ordnance upon the outside world. Nor, I firmly believed, could Walther. We scientific genii must adhere to a strict moral and ethical code. I remember thinking that very thing as I rummaged through his designs while he was over-trustingly elsewhere.

With fascination, but also a growing chill of dread, I swung the angle-poise arm of the large illuminated magnifier round and trained the thick lens upon the weapon. The secrets to rapid fire lay within the spinning chamber. And Michael's warning... in addition to his looks, skill and charisma, Michael could be an infuriating whelp; but only a fool would ignore his instinct. A scientific and technological plagiariser I may be, but a fool, no. Oh sure, the retaining screws which held the two halves of the heinous weapon together were so easy to spot, Blind Pugh could have seen them. But the array of additional grub screws which loomed large through my magnifier, also appeared very easily accessible. Perhaps seductively so.

Had the German fellows taken some precaution and installed a safeguard within the body of the beast? I know I would have done! Pulling Arthur Doyle's Goggle-Eyes over my head, I clicked the power-slider to 'ON' and was immediately grateful I had. The heavy frame whirred, as it does, the lenses extended and retracted, pulling the blurred image into focus, as those remarkable Röntgen rays penetrated the outer metal casing.

And that's when I chuckled: "You cunning pair of Gottingen rascals!"

The cylinder housed the kind of array of cogs, copper coils and magnets, everything I would have expected to energise the Aethyr. But just there, tucked behind the spindle was the added element, the ingenious mounting of super-charging booster cogs which effected the continuous charging. However, this bit was a puzzler, a tinkering, which caused me some concern. Set within the stock of the Pulsa, lay a circular container, no bigger than a penny piece, thrice as thick, but lead lined and determined to shield its contents. The container was connected to the Aethyr generator by a single one-eighth diameter copper tube, and was protected by a pressure spring. A bloody booby trap. Prise the pistol apart, the spring would be released, forcing a massive charge of Aethyr down the tube to ignite whatever explosive lurked within the lead box. The reward for opening up this little treasure box was to be your head being blown from your body in three different directions. Then I heard the noise, removed the Goggle-Eyes and saw Wicko, wearing a blue and white sleeping cap and yellowing linen nightshirt, looking distinctly unimpressed.

"I hope you're not looking to be firing that thing all night. Some of us need our kip after a hard day, y'know!"

10

"This is an outrage! A contravention of human decency!" yelled Phoebe, albeit somewhat muffled from within her hood, while she and Michael were firmly escorted into what must have been a building, because a door banged behind them. Suddenly there was warmth, and their walking pace became urgent.

"My advice, sir? It's never good to mess with a lady who can use those kinds of long words." Michael's homily was met with surly silence. At least he took it to be surly.

Now he tried appealing to their better natures. "Listen, if this is just about us stepping in the way of your assassination stuff with the Prime Minister, let me tell you we've learned our lesson, and we will never be doing that again anytime soon. So listen. You seem like reasonable, easy-going fanatics, so why not just let us go and we'll call it quits, how about that? You'd have to be crazy to turn down an offer like that?" Silence. Just more walking.

"Sorry, Pheebs," he whispered. "Looks like they're crazy. Much like these Derby Pattern handcuffs."

It was just as he was finally beginning to admit that this situation was not looking much in the way of encouraging, Michael suddenly tripped and fell against Phoebe. Both felt the flagstone floor on their hands and knees before they were hauled back onto their feet, marched up a flight of stairs and along a thickly carpeted corridor. Next they heard a knock on a wooden door, the rattle of a handle, and following a few more paces were forced to an abrupt halt.

"Any ideas where we are?" breathed Phoebe.

"Estimating the time, the speed and counting the turns, I put us somewhere near Green Park," whispered Michael confidently.

"Welcome to Scotland Yard," said the gently modulated voice, as Michael and Phoebe felt their hoods whipped away and the wall of yellow light bleared and seared their eyes.

"Close," shrugged Michael.

"Really?" whispered Phoebe.

As their eyes grew accustomed to the brightness, they found themselves staring up at Queen Victoria. Not the real thing, of course, that would be ridiculous, but that three-quarter length painting. The watercolour portrait of the monarch knocked out in 1885 by Lady Julia Abercrombie, copying Heinrich von Angeli's picture. It's the one where it looks like she's holding a pair of white bloomers. The portrait hung upon the wall behind a large, tidy oak desk.

The man sitting behind the desk then said, "Good evening. I am Superintendent William Melville of the Special Branch."

Despite the hour, and the trauma of the evening thus far, Melville was impeccably calm. "May I introduce your escort, Detective Inspector Pym. I am sure he has been firm but gracious."

"Apologies if the necessary hoods dishevelled your hair," this Pym said to Phoebe.

"Accepted," said Michael.

Phoebe sighed, "Special Branch…"

"Indeed," said Melville.

"And that would be the Special Branch of what?" asked Michael.

"The police, can you believe?" said Phoebe exasperated, which given their treatment thus far, was not unwarranted.

"The police?" A flicker of concern crossed Michael's face, but only briefly. "You found my mahogany walking cane? It's the one where blue smoke can pump out of one end and you can pull two dozen handkerchiefs from the other. I thought I lost it, or Nevil Maskelyne picked it up, to see how it worked."

"It does not concern your walking cane," said Melville.

"Okay. If it's about our stage act with all its exotic… we think of it as art…"

"The content of your stage performances will not breach national security," said Melville. Certainly the man had Jobian patience, which with Michael was always a necessity.

"National security?" Michael flashed an alarmed glance at Phoebe.

"Mister Magister, we are not unlike your Secret Service, as created by President Lincoln," said Melville. "We are the unseen guardians of Her Majesty's realm, if you will, toiling in a quest to thwart anarchy and treachery both at home and overseas. Be it the Fenians, the Balkanites, the Boers, the Bolsheviks. "

Michael nodded, seemingly impressed. "And that's just the Bs!"

"Apart from the Fenians," whispered Phoebe, who frequently displayed a scholarly edge when it came to matters of the alphabet. "Now behave."

"Well, Mister M – if I can call you that, now we're acquainted – I have to say this is a very smart office you've got yourselves here," said Michael, looking about, weighing up the large room with its high ceiling, air of opulence, dark wooden furniture, the smell of polish, the heavy, rich curtains drawn together, thick pile carpet, which alone had taken the wool of the backs of a dozen flocks of sheep. Oh, and the outline of a secret door set within one green, floral papered wall, he certainly didn't miss that titbit. "Special Branch must be doing pretty well for itself."

"So, Superintendent William Melville of the Special Branch, I sincerely trust you are about to explain why we are under arrest?" said Phoebe, holding out her handcuffed wrists. "Because depriving of us of our liberty can surely be the only explanation for these."

"Miss Lan..." Melville had only uttered those two syllables before she cut him off sharply.

"Le Breton!" said Phoebe sharply. "My name is Phoebe Le Breton!"

Melville nodded, "Indeed. Miss Le Breton. My apologies too for the handcuffs, they were purely for ease of transportation. Detective Inspector Pym, we may now dispense with their services, if you would be so kind."

"No, that's okay, Mister Melville," said Michael, rattling his cuffs. "We've got this."

Before Walter Pym could even reach into his waistcoat pocket to bring out the handcuff keys, both Michael and

Phoebe had, with a glorious flourish released their hands and were laying their open nickel-plated shackles down upon Melville's desk. It is worth pointing out here that history will record that Mister Harry Houdini effected the very same stunt for Melville at Scotland Yard, and perhaps he did, but do be assured my magicians performed it first.

So how did they extricate themselves from Scotland Yard's finest handcuffs with such ease? The big mistake the police made was to handcuff the two magicians with their hands at the front. You will recall when being marched along the flagstone corridor, Michael and Phoebe feigned to trip and fall? Well, both had cracked their handcuffs at a precise angle against the hard surface of the stone floor, causing the internal locking mechanism to unspring itself. It was a design fault common to this model of handcuff and common knowledge among most magicians, escapologists, and now the police...

Pym stared down at the open cuffs in wide-eyed wonder, but if Melville shared Pym's reaction, he masked it with aplomb, simply saying, "Ah. Most helpful!"

Pym took both pairs and examined them minutely for anything which might indicate the magicians' method. Saw cuts, drill holes, even teeth marks, there must be something, but as hard as he looked, the way they cracked the locks refused to reveal itself. He looked at Michael. "Here, hold on. These are cuffs we only use for the most hardened criminals..."

"How enlightening to learn that that is how you perceive us, Detective Inspector," said Phoebe.

Pym flushed and glanced at Melville before adding a flustered, "No, well, what I meant was, if these things are so easy to escape out of, I reckon we should know how it's done."

"A magician never divulges his secrets, Inspector," said Michael.

"And no manner of beatings with a rubber gas hose will ever make us talk," said Phoebe.

"That's not strictly true," added Michael, quickly. "But if, gentlemen, this whole getting arrested misunderstanding is about Pheebs gate-crashing the Prime Minister's box tonight, let me tell you straight off I take full responsibility. I put her up to it. Pheebs was only doing what I insisted, no, what I forced her to do, forced on pain of death, for added magical and dramatic effect."

"Mister Magister," said Melville.

"Yes, sir?" said Michael.

"Please be silent," said Melville.

"With pleasure," said Michael.

"Oh my days," said Phoebe, looking at Melville as a realisation dawned. "You! You were up in the box with Salisbury and Balfour. You and another man with grey hair, genial but ineffectual."

"That would be the Assistant Commissioner, Sir Cumberland Sinclair," said Melville.

"Well, I have to say, Superintendent Melville," continued Phoebe, her blue eyes flashing in fury, "if we *are* being arrested for breaching the Prime Minister's security, I believe the blame rests squarely on the shoulders of yourselves, most especially that thin faced bruiser supposedly standing guard outside the box. If he had been in any way up to the task, I should never have slipped past with such ease."

"Skindrick?" hissed Detective Inspector Pym, bitterly, looking at Melville. "Useless…"

"Miss Le Breton, Mister Magister, that matter is in hand and please be assured your presence here has nothing to do with Lord Salisbury's security. Additionally you are both free to leave at any time."

Phoebe perked up. "In which case, thank you, gentlemen, we bid you a very goodnight. I'd like to say it's been a pleasure but frankly it's been far from it!"

Michael then pitched in with another theory. "Pheebs, wait up. I'm thinking this has nothing to do with you getting into the box. This is more about those two assassins. Those guys were carrying some pretty fancy ordnance and I'm guessing we're here to be rewarded with cash certainly, medals probably, after foiling that attempt on the lives of the Superintendent here, the Prime Minister – and what's the other guy's name, Baleful?"

"Balfour," corrected Phoebe. "But it is close enough…"

"Begging your pardon, Mister Magister," Detective Inspector Pym piped up, "I've met a good few Americans, but I've got to say your accent and how you say things is all a bit odd."

"New York you see, Detective Inspector," shrugged Michael, gesturing apologetically before returning to Melville. "Anyway, after we noticed the assassin's gun Pheebs led the charge across the street, so I vote Pheebs deserves a medal for bravery. At least."

"I regret the bestowment of accolades falls outside the remit of my authority," said Melville.

"But any publicity you can rustle up for tomorrow's newspaper front pages, that kind of thing will never hurt ticket sales. Although 'Magicians Save Premier' as a headline will never top last week's 'This Show Is Godless Filth'." Michael was now smiling that confident smile.

"I regret a veil of secrecy has already been drawn over the events of the entire evening and any attempt to lift that veil will be discredited with ease. You will understand, of course, Miss Le Breton," Melville said firmly looking at Phoebe.

"So, if we are not being arrested or rewarded, it rather begs the question, why *are* we here?" Again, Phoebe's eyes flashed with fury.

"Quite simply we require Mister Magister's assistance," said Melville.

"I can understand that…" nodded Michael.

"Assistance?" said Phoebe, taking not the slightest notice of her flattered associate. "Superintendent, you have had Michael kidnapped, sedated, hooded, handcuffed, and dragged into the night halfway across London in great discomfort and totally against his will in this entirely illegal clandestine farrago, just because you require Michael's assistance!? Did it not for one moment occur to you to knock on his door and politely ask for help? No! Simply because Michael is just a stage performer, and worse yet an American, you believe that gives you the right to mete out this kind of underhanded, no, heavy handed treatment. But please not to concern yourself with my opinion, after all in your eyes I'm just a nuisance woman."

"How can anyone not love her?" said Michael. "But it's all true. If you want my help, why put Pheebs through all this cloak and dagger hokum?"

"And what would have been your reaction had I requested your assistance in a matter of extreme national importance, but had no need of Miss Breton's?"

"Then, sir, I'd have said, thank you, but no thank you. We come as a team. I don't care how extreme the national importance – Pheebs is all part of the set up. No Pheebs, no me." Michael was sincere and determined.

"Precisely my appraisal of the situation," said Melville. He then turned to Phoebe, adding: "And, you will understand why I am required to seek approval of your involvement at the highest levels. Hence the Prime Minister making time to visit your theatre to satisfy himself."

"Wait," said Michael, shaking his head in confusion. "You need Lord Salisbury's official okay for me to bring in Pheebs?"

"And it does not stop there, Mister Magister!" A woman's voice suddenly filled the room. It was deep, resonant, commanding and it came from somewhere behind Michael and Phoebe.

Phoebe's eyes closed and her heart sank. "We're not in Scotland Yard, are we?" she whispered.

Melville suddenly stood. Phoebe knew, but Michael didn't, which is why he glanced back over this shoulder to see who was talking, and was rewarded with the most heart-stopping shock of his life. There, in a wheeled bath chair sat a small, thickset woman. She wore a black velvet dress and a veil of black silk swept back, which tumbled down over her shoulders. The air was filled with the scent of lavender. The wrinkled jowly face, that pronounced nose, those deep china blue eyes; Michael was now looking at the most famous face in the known world – the woman in the painting on the wall.

So, while the usually silver-tongued Michael Magister, master of the glib put-down was rendered instantly mute and paralysed with shock, Phoebe turned, bobbed a curtsey and said, "Your Majesty."

11

Beside Queen Victoria stood an imperious, bearded, turbaned Indian. His tunic, buttoned to the neck, was sharp, smart and of the finest blue silk. Unmistakeably it was Abdul Karim, the Munshi.

"Mister Magister," said the matronly monarch. "We are content to receive your presence." Michael bowed deeply. He tried to speak and despite his mouth opening and closing in the manner of a spawning sea trout, no sound came forth.

"And you, Miss Le Breton," the Queen was now looking directly at Phoebe. "We observe you have lost none of your spirit. So like your mother. And quite unlike your… We are pleased but unsurprised to hear of your courage and fortitude this evening."

"Without fortitude and courage is not any woman lost, ma'am. As you have always shown."

"And it is for those reasons we find no objection to your involvement in the matter which so exercises Superintendent Melville. The decision is, of course, for you alone. As for you Mister Magister, you may be pleased to now stop bowing, lest we begin to fear for your back," said Queen Victoria. Michael eased himself upwards, returning to a vertical position, but still remained bereft of speech.

"You may approach, child," said the monarch, holding out a hand. Phoebe took a few steps toward the Queen, close enough to hear her whisper, "We remain gratified by your continued discretion and integrity. Be assured Doctor Bell often speaks of your well-being. It is much the Superintendent asks of you now. Especially as you and your Mister Magister may find yourselves led to waters most treacherous."

"Ma'am, I am rather used to swimming against the current," said Phoebe. Victoria gave a gentle nod, glimmered a smile.

Once Phoebe had curtseyed and returned to her place beside Michael, the Queen addressed them all. "God's speed in your continued endeavours Superintendent Melville and Inspector Pym. And we thank you most sincerely, Mister Magister and pray you restore your powers of speech before your next theatrical performance."

Michael bowed again. "Thank you, Your Majesty. Oh. How about that? And can I just say, I am such a fan!" His recovery now caused Phoebe, Melville, Pym and even the impassive Munshi to simultaneously raise their eyebrows.

"Quite so. And, child," the Queen said to Phoebe. "Be assured of our contentment."

Then Queen Victoria waved a regal hand. Melville and Pym bowed, Phoebe curtseyed and gestured for Michael to bow. The Munshi released the oak handled brake, and drew Her Majesty back through the secret entrance, into the darkness beyond and closed the door.

"Whatever drug you put in that hood, Inspector Pym, it must have come from China Town," said Michael, "because I really thought for one minute there I was talking to the Queen."

"You were," said Phoebe.

"Wow, Pheebs. How about that? Because I've seen her face on a thousand postage stamps and I thought she'd be taller. And, I'm betting we're nowhere near Scotland Yard."

"You were not too far from the mark with Green Park, Michael, "said Phoebe. "We seem to be in Buckingham Palace."

"The office of Her Majesty's private secretary, Lieutenant Colonel Sir Arthur Bigge," said Pym nodding, "my former commanding officer in the Royal Artillery, as it happens."

"Buckingham Palace? Queen Victoria? Pheebs, can you believe this ?" said Michael, still red cheeked with joy while Phoebe was looking daggers at Melville, as if he had committed a most heinous crime.

"Whatever it is that exercises your concern, Superintendent I trust it is worth this. For what reason do you require Michael's assistance?"

"A locked room mystery," said Melville.

"Any magician can get his head around a locked room mystery," said Michael. "And while we're flattered… why the rigmarole? And why pick us?"

"Because this is in The London County Lunatic Asylum, Hanwell."

"Yes, that pretty much explains why," said Michael, nodding, convinced.

"Here are the standard terms regarding recompense for your consultancy work in this matter. All highly confidential." Melville pushed a sheet of paper across the desk to Michael, who took one look at the offer, raised an eyebrow and showed it to Phoebe, who raised an eyebrow.

"Wow, you are really keen to secure our services," said Phoebe.

"At seven a.m. a police carriage will collect you from your homes and take you to Hanwell to look around the room," said Pym. "Once you've worked it all out we'll bring you home again."

"No disrespect, Inspector but we've just experienced your transport," said Michael. "We'd prefer to spend the journey fully conscious, so Pheebs and I will take our own transportation. We'll meet you outside Hanwell by eight. But sharp. Don't be late."

"Thank you, Superintendent Melville. Detective Inspector Pym. Very much." Phoebe's thanks implied not a jot of genuine gratitude. For the past year she had found stability and happiness, and now she could feel the rug being pulled from under her feet.

"Needs must, Miss Le Breton," said Melville. "Needs must."

12

Detective Inspector Gersham Skindrick gritted his teeth as he heaved on the oars, hauling his small row boat through the low mist and whatever was floating and festering on the surface of the River Thames. At least he could content himself in the knowledge that his battered, flake paint vessel would be less heavy on the return trip. The current looked to be pulling everything east out towards the Pool of London and at a fair old lick tonight, which was perfect. In the moon shadow, tucked between a pair of the huge imposing columns which supported the wonderful Joseph Cubitt's Blackfriars Railway Bridge, Skindrick stowed his oars and with the boat wobbling wildly, he threw back the tarp which hid his grisly cargo. He awkwardly lifted first one corpse and pitched it over the side, then the second. Both bodies plopped into the thick water, then quickly sank. Their arms and legs bound with sisal and their pockets heavy with rubble, a trail of tiny bubbles rising to the surface was their only memorial. In two days' time they would be bloated and blackened beyond recognition.

"An' while y're there, y' can quaff on a drink o' this, too, y' bawbags," sneered Skindrick, before unbuttoning his flies and relieving his bladder into the river which, frankly, I believe to be a thoroughly unnecessary gesture, but, nevertheless, you know, quite summed up the vile nature of the man.

Directly above, a Chatham-bound train thundered across the wrought iron bridge, sending down a deluge of grit and rust flakes causing Skindrick to squint to protect his eyes. Suddenly, Skindrick was dazzled by a bright yellow light pointing directly at his face. A voice from somewhere in the darkness shouted "Ho, there! River Police!" Skindrick raised a hand to shield his eyes. It was the focussed beam of a bull's eye lamp aboard a police rowing galley. That quite snuck up on him, he thought. One of the river boys' new Supervision steam launches Skindrick would have easily heard, but not this old time man-powered patrol vessel with its crew of three peak capped blue serge officers, probably sailing out of the

Waterloo Pier Police Station. Skindrick cursed under his breath. Because of their wretched stealth, he had no idea how long they had been observing him, but whatever the circumstances he knew he had a serious problem. The River Police were a tenacious, professional outfit, proud of their history as the world's first organised police force.

"What's the game here, lad? Hold fast while we come alongside!" ordered the voice, as the prow of the galley hove into view.

Skindrick certainly couldn't out-pull these boys on the oars, or give them the slip in the darkness. So he figured there was but one solution. As the galley drew alongside and the faces of the three bearded crewmen became clear, Skindrick pulled the Pulsa from his jacket pocket, the cylinder span and whirred, before he fired off a bolt of purple energy which winged one constable and sent him cartwheeling clean overboard into the filth. Another shot caught a second constable, the one holding the bulls-eye lamp, in much the same fashion, and both he and his lamp went over the side. The third river man hollered in fury and launched himself into Skindrick's craft. He forced Skindrick to topple back, into the bottom of his boat. The river officer raised his billy club, keen to beat his assailant senseless, but not before Skindrick fired his Pulsa pistol at short range. The purple ball of energised Aethyr struck the policeman in the midriff and forced him upright. His belly now sported a hole you could put your arm clean through. His tunic then erupted in bright purple fire, but only until he toppled back and hit the water with a dense splash.

Skindrick gasped, staggered to his feet and looked at the Pulsa with renewed respect. He was about to slip the weapon into his waist band when a hand from the depths rose, grabbed the side of the boat and yanked Skindrick off balance. The Pulsa fell from his grasp and splashed into the Thames. Now Skindrick roared with fury, scrambling to the side to see in desperate hope if the weapon was buoyant. Then he felt the grip on his shoulder. It was the river policeman with a gaping but cauterised wound to the side of his head, who loomed out of the murk like some vengeful emissary of Neptune.

Skindrick wrenched the hand from his shoulder, pulled on the slimy head and cracked it hard against the side of the boat. The policeman slipped gently beneath the surface, presumably this time, for good.

Gasping for breath and trying to regain his composure Skindrick looked about for further witnesses. No, all was quiet. The Pulsa was gone, but that he'd survived was God's will. Skindrick knelt, placed his hands together in prayer, looked up to the Heavens and whispered, "Blessed Lord, thank you for your support and guidance in ridding your world of this Godless vermin!"

Gersham Skindrick made the sign of the cross, just as another train passed overhead sending down a further cloud of debris.

***

Ironically, it was Assistant Commissioner Sir Cumberland Sinclair, who seemed to be enjoying the least eventful evening. Having made his roundabout way from Grosvenor Square, he had enjoyed a milky coffee laced with cognac, served up by his manservant, Pockney, and now slept soundly in his warm cosy bed in his magisterial villa in South Kensington. Dreaming, no doubt, of assassination attempts, magic and that very splendid Phoebe woman.

***

"You know, even by our standards of lunacy, that was quite a night, Pheebs," said Michael. He and Phoebe once again found themselves sitting side by side in the police carriage, this time in considerably more comfort, unshackled and unhooded. "Two full house shows, two street fights, saved a Prime Minister, got hauled off to Buckingham Palace and then hired to help The Special Branch. Didn't I say working in the British Music Hall was going to be fun? Did I miss out anything important?"

"I don't think so," said Phoebe, shaking her head and turning her mouth down. "Oh, there was that moment, I suppose, when it appeared as if the Queen and I had met one another before."

"No, I don't think that was it," said Michael, unboxing his deck of cards. "You would have mentioned it before now."

"Except that you never asked."

"That's fair," nodded Michael, riffling and cutting the cards. "So, let me now slip that nugget into the conversation right now with something like, 'Oh, Pheebs, I know this is a long shot, but do you happen to know the Queen of England and if that's a yes, how, might that be?'"

"Through my parents."

"Parents? I thought you were like me, an orphan. Cast into the world to fend for herself."

"I am most definitely an orphan. It's just that I happen know who my parents are."

"Do you want to tell me?"

"No," said Phoebe.

"Okay…" said Michael. But it wasn't.

Phoebe then leant across and whispered, "At least… not here." before casting a nod in the direction of the driver.

The rest of the journey continued in silence with Phoebe resting her head on Michael's shoulder, still reflecting upon how this development would affect them both. Michael clearly remembered Arthur Doyle bringing Phoebe to the attention of both Michael and myself, enthusing about her determination to make a life for herself on the wicked stage, how quickly she picked up the illusions, her natural showmanship, and her spirited attitude to life. And, you know, Michael had said to me at the time, "Prof, this girl has just got something, I don't know what it is, but she's got something."

The carriage driver, a retired constable with the splendid name of Canker, pulled up his team, as instructed at the corner of Westbourne Terrace and Bishops Road, just along the way from the Paddington Railway terminus. Michael thanked the driver profusely and tried to tip him handsomely, only to be told firmly that that would not be appropriate.

As Michael and Phoebe walked arm in arm along Westbourne Terrace, huddled against the dark night chill and with the clatter of the carriage disappearing safely into the distance behind them, Phoebe took a deep breath and broke the silence. "My parentage... actually, Michael, unless you wish to spend the rest of your life in the shadow of mortal peril, it's really best you don't know."

"Peril?" winced Michael.

"Mortal," nodded Phoebe.

"Really? That bad? You know, you're right, I shouldn't ought to pry." Then after walking a score of steps it was Michael's turn to break the silence. In fact he stopped, looked her straight in the eye and said "No, this is killing me. Pheebs, I really want to know. And face it, if it is a state secret, then Melville and his gang of police spies are going to think I know anyway. Mortal peril I can cope with. Death is a worry, but mortal peril that's okay. Let me put it this way, I'm keen to know, not simply because I love and respect you, but because I am a very nosy person. So, if you want to tell me, you have my permission."

It was then that Phoebe took a deep breath and for the first time in her life revealed her state secret: "My father is the Prince of Wales and my mother is Lillie Langtry."

You know, Michael tried very hard not to look shocked, but just couldn't make a terribly good fist of it. After a few moments of open mouthed contemplation, he finally cleared his throat and whispered, "Okay, just so we're clear and not confusing this with some other couple who might just happen to have the same names, your parents are *the* Lillie Langtry, who's the beautiful, gorgeous, world famous actress and race horse owner Lillie Langtry, and *the* Prince of Wales who's the future king Prince of Wales."

Phoebe nodded, sadly.

"Pheebs, that is incredible! The Prince of... and Lillie... Oh, yes. You know what that makes, you?"

"Michael, I've known exactly what I am since I was eighteen. A scandalous embarrassment. An establishment cover-up. A threat to the succession. A dangerous secret. A troublesome bastard. Take your pick."

Michael held both Phoebe's hands and looked at her. "It doesn't stop you being Pheebs. Or a real life Princess."

"Michael, you must understand why I couldn't confide in you. And would never have done, if this whatever it is nonsense with Special Branch had not sprung up. I could not willingly place your life in jeopardy, especially when you consider the Whitechapel murder spree a decade ago, following the Prince Eddy scandal. But now I fear my lack of candour will affect our relationship."

"Pheebs, are you kidding me? Remember that day, eighteen months ago, when the Prof and I told you magic is all about discretion, distraction and deception and a whole long list of other words that probably mean the same thing as deception but don't begin with D? Well back then, I really thought I was the master of deception. The Magister. The great deceiver. But, when it comes to holding cards close to your chest, you are by far the best there is. If I was proud of you before, Pheebs, believe me, I'm a whole lot prouderer now."

"Thank you, Michael," said Phoebe, squeezing her arm around his waist. "By the way, it's not 'prouderer', the expression is 'more proud'."

They crossed the Westbourne Terrace Bridge flanked on either side with its iron arches, brutal and grey and spanning the dozen rail tracks which splayed out of Paddington Station and Paddington Goods Depot below.

"Pheebs, this locked room mystery up at Hanwell," said Michael. Phoebe knew that alarm bell in his head was jangling. "It's not the whole story."

"What are you thinking?"

"To figure out a locked room puzzle he can use any London conjuror with a top hat and a wand. So why me? Why us? He already knew I would never make a move without you, so went ahead to get a whole bunch of high rankers to give their okay. Why risk opening a can of worms and exposing your secret? Remember this Mister Melville is just like us, he deals under the table. Whatever's happened over at Hanwell, it has to be big. "

They turned right into Harrow Road and walked alongside the vast Paddington Goods Depot which, despite the hour, was still bustling with shunting engines pushing and pulling wagons from one line across to another like a complex steam driven chess game. The magicians stopped beside an inconspicuous metal barred gate set within the railings between the railway sidings and the pavement. Michael hinged open the metal lid of a panel set into the fence to reveal a block of enamelled keys like a typewriter. He tapped in a sequence of numbers. With a hiss of steam and a firm click the metal door juddered and swung open.

"I'll come by about six forty-five. Then we can find out what Melville's game really is. Sleep well," said Michael, as Phoebe slipped through the gate and closed it behind her.

"Oh, and Pheebs. This thing with you, about being Royalty... do I have to start bowing and say 'Your Highness'?"

Phoebe pecked a kiss upon Michael on the cheek, through the bars, all before smiling and saying: "If you do, I'll kill you myself."

~IN THE MIDDLE~

"The world which wishes to be deceived..." – Sebastian Brant

1

"Isambard Kingdom Brunel was a wonderful fellow, you know, a Great Briton, taken from you at the far too tender age of, what, fifty-three? Disgraceful. To call him a genius is to do the fellow a great injustice, I mean, those of us called 'genii' are commonplace, two a penny. No. I contend that The Great Man of The Great Western should be revered as a deity, to be praised and worshipped. I frequently slope across to Kensal Green Cemetery to give thanks and bow before his grave. I never knew him, of course, which was a huge loss to both of us, but his smartly perceptive son Henry Marc is a good friend of mine. I am minded to mention the Brunels because that particular morning the purple haze of dawn's early light was growing brighter by the minute before beginning its daily battle to penetrate Isambard's three magnificent glass canopies spanning the platforms of Paddington's railway station. I prefer to use the expression 'railway station' rather than 'train station', don't you, it's so much more British, and, as the British pioneered the railway per se, I am, always at pains, you know, to heap much requisite praise, as much as is possible, in their direction. I also like to ensure the comma is never underused in prose.

But anyway, a delayed milk train belched and hissed and squealed itself to a halt alongside Platform One. The handful of smartly uniformed porters, leaning on their sack barrows, rubbed rheumy eyes in disbelief for so many reasons, not least when they watched the toff alight from the brake van at the rear of the train and stride along the platform bidding them 'good morning'. A toff who bore a marked semblance to a not long buried Liberal statesman. The deceased politician then strode calmly down the concourse to where the Hansoms were ranked, woke the stubble-chinned driver of the first cab and politely asked to be conveyed directly to the market at Covent Garden.

Half an hour later, and much to the cabbie's shock, the gentleman he picked up at Paddington was certainly not the figure he was now dropping off in Long Acre. As the driver later explained to his tea-slurping, disbelieving colleagues, "I had that William Gladstone in the front of the cab, this morning. Well, not him on accounts as he's brown bread an' that, but a ringer for The Grand Old Man he was nevertheless and that's a fact. But then – right – then, stone me, when he's got out he was a woman! A 'nemmo'! Plain as y'like! All done up in a grey blue dress and white pinny, with this blue wrap around her 'ead, slippers on her feet, the lot of it. So then she's stumped up her two bob fare, right enough, but it's all in ha'pennies and farthings. Well, don't get me wrong, money's money to any man or beast and the change is 'andy an' no mistake. But now I can't find a single brass farthing of any of them coins the bint give me. Not a one of 'em. I'm telling you what, lads, the whole world's turning into a proper mystery to me. A proper mystery and no mistake."

Despite the derision of his sewer-mouthed associates, the cabbie's inconceivable report could not have been more accurate! A woman, pale and slender as described, did indeed step down from the front of the Hansom cab, before setting off towards the early morning noise and bustle of Covent Garden Market.

2

Home, for the time being at least, for Miss Phoebe Le Breton
was a railway carriage; but not just any old out of service
beaten down car, no, far, far from it. This was a dwelling of
elegance and luxury, furnished with care and decorated with
style. It was divided into four separate rooms. The sleeping
area enjoyed soft furnishings and a décor of powder blue and
white, much, you know, in the palette of Wedgwood china.
Cherry wood graced a chaise longue, a dressing table and
wardrobes a-plenty fashioned by the hand of Thomas
Chippendale. One end of the room was dominated by the bed,
a dramatic Queen-sized statement with gently carved cherry
wood pillars rising from each of the four corners, making it
impressive for aesthetes and one might surmise, practical for
entertaining purposes.

***

Phoebe was now awake, up, and completely naked as she
completed her morning routine, dodging punches thrown from
my steam-driven boxing contraption 'The Jabber-Blocky'. I do
enjoy giving my inventions witless sobriquets. The Jabber-
Blocky was exactly what it says it was. Built within a tall, dark
wood polished upright cabinet, which masqueraded as one of
Phoebe's wardrobes, a dozen fist-sized holes were cut into the
front at various heights, then hidden behind hinged doors. Six
pairs of boxing gloves filled with sand and bolted to pistons
upon retractable arms lurked within each hole, calibrated with
various sizes of brass cam to punch out the gloves in a
haphazard order. The notion was for the athlete to duck or
block this barrage of fast action blows and the Jabber-Blocky
either sharpened the defender's reactions or bruised their flesh,
it was as simple as that. Each jab was accompanied by the hiss
of the piston and the speed could be adjusted by a twist of a
control valve.

Throughout this morning's ten minute bout, Phoebe had
defended herself without injury against a sustained volley of

jabs ranged at her from various angles. Suitably exercised, she twisted the red wheel valve to the closed position, and the mechanical pugilist fell silent with a grateful sigh.

Beaded with sweat, Phoebe slunk from her bedroom through the spacious parlour with its sofa and chairs stuffed with sheep's wool, atop a thick pile powder blue carpet. A Chippendale dining table and four chairs graced the area by one of the windows. The wall panels below the blue, silk curtained windows were lined with row upon row of books. And not just for ornamental decoration. This was a reference library, a repository of knowledge covering all manner of subjects, you know, which would have even impressed old Ptolomy the Saviour. I didn't know him, by the way, he lived two thousand years ago. Maybe one day...

The door beyond opened into the kitchen where a glass of green gloop, some lumpy cordial confected from cress, celery and other rotting, though invigorating vegetable matter was waiting upon the Chippendale dresser. She took the glass, drank it down and then slunk through into the bathroom area. The large, white roll-topped enamel bath sat in the centre of the space and Phoebe stepped over the edge and slid down into the warm, foamed water and began soaping her body.

Her mind drifted to my recounting the rumour about two of President Ulysses S. Grant's finest Secret Service agents who resided and travelled around the U.S. aboard their own railway train, while pursuing their national security adventures. However, and quite between you and I, on the subject of railway accommodation, I always felt it best not to broach the subject of Phoebe's mother, the beautiful 'Jersey Lily', who ten years ago, as a successful actress, was transported around and about the U.S. in her own private railcar, a ten-roomed seventy-five foot palace of the tracks, built, I was told, to Mrs Langtry's s own specifications by a former American Civil War veteran, one Colonel William D'Alton Mann. He claimed to be a friend of mine, but I never much cared for him. The American carriage was called 'The Lalee', not that that matters much.

Despite trying to focus on railway trivia, Phoebe could not prevent her thoughts, how could she, from drifting back to yesterday's extraordinary events. Now Michael knew of her well-hidden past, would that, despite his assurances, affect their association? Today would tell.

Steam from the warm bath had condensed against her bathroom mirror. She closed her eyes, then opened them again with a start, sat bolt upright amidst the bubbles and stared up at the mirror. Finger-written upon the steamy glass were the words: "Morning, Pheebs – I'm waiting outside!"

Phoebe, now in a purple silken robe and with her wet, dark red hair quickly tied up in a towel, flung open the front door of the railway carriage. A blast of cool air hit her, along with the great wave of noise from shunting wagons and chuffing engines . Standing upon her raised purpose-built platform she found Michael Magister, shuffling a deck of playing cards and leaning nonchalantly back against the carriage. Despite the cock's crow hour, he looked annoyingly handsome, wearing a brown frockcoat, black trousers, gold waistcoat and brown top hat worn at a rakish angle, goggles strapped around the headband.

"How's the bath?"

"You couldn't just have knocked like any normal person?"

"Pheebs, how bored would you be if I was any normal person?" said Michael, screwing up his nose. "Besides, you were beating up the furniture at the time, didn't seem right to disturb you in mid fight."

"I'll be ten minutes."

"I know. I'll be in the Steamo," said Michael.

Phoebe stepped back inside the carriage to dry and dress. Michael always admired the external beauty of this particular railway carriage. The polished maroon lower half, with the windows bordered in white and trimmed with mahogany. The carriage was set in a siding by the Goods Depot of Paddington Station. It was untroubled by railway traffic in and out of Paddington Station, or by Depot drivers and track workers, tappers and shunters, who merely assumed the carriage formed part of the Royal train and was standing by for coupling-up as and when required. The faux Royal coat of arms stencilled on the flanks helped perpetuate the myth. I had previously effected the appropriation, or rather misappropriation of this Great Western carriage, well, they had so many I figured they wouldn't miss just the one, dressed it up in new livery and installed the spruce new internal living space which we insulated against the sounds of a working railway outside. Employing those infallible instruments of my style of negotiation, namely cold hard cash and the provision of exotic entertainment, those usually stuffy railway bureaucrats allowed me to set the carriage here, in its own siding with a dedicated platform. Phoebe skipped down the stone stairs, through the gate and onto the street where the Steamo was now parked, waiting.

The Steamo, you ask? Ah. This was an abbreviation of 'Steamotivator', the name we imposed upon our four wheel horseless carriage, which, I suppose, looked almost like any other carriage but with a distinct absence of any horses.

Instead of the equine pulling power at the front, motivating propulsion came from the rear via a steam powered piston engine, much like a locomotive but with a good deal less of that brutal, ear bending chuffing. And that was all part of the Steamo's stylish elegance, you know, it didn't chuff, it gently chugged. She was wrought in sheets of dark green, supported by four thick wheels. Adorning the front of the vehicle were four large lamps, useful by night and beautiful by day. The enclosed passenger compartment was accessed by a sliding door on either side, mechanically operated with a lever. The interior upholstery was of the most exquisite crimson leather, the panelling of magnificent polished oak. The driving compartment was also accessed with its own pair of sliding doors and topped by a retractable roof. Two driving seats faced an assemblage of levers which regulated the steam and speed of forward motion, while a four-spoked leather sleeved wheel took care of the steering.

If you're in any way interested, needles on the various brass rimmed gauges danced and waved to indicate varying levels of pressure and output, all of which Michael and Phoebe could operate but none of which Michael remotely understood.

At the rear, two small brass chimneys rose unobtrusively aloft for the release of spent steam, both stacks served by an elegant array of burnished copper piping. The entire vehicle, you know, was sturdy but sleek and tried not to be too showy. Nothing too conspicuous, apart, of course, from the hoarding lashed between the two smoke stacks which read: "Magister the Magician – now appearing at The Metropolitan Theatre of Steam, Smoke and Mirrors, Edgware Road, W." It pays to advertise. Pedestrians and road users within the metropolis were in no way impressed or alarmed by the sight of this purring beast steaming through their streets. They were already quite familiar, you know, with horseless electric motor cabs like the Bersey. But while those vehicles were simply sparking, fizzing pretenders which could only manage 30 snail-paced miles before requiring re-charging, the Steamo could clock up at least a hundred cushioned comfy miles at a fair old lick, on little more than a tank of water and half a scuttle of nutty slack.

Michael was waiting behind the wheel. A pull of a lever caused the door on the passenger side to slide back and Phoebe climbed aboard next to him.

"Good morning, Mister Garrideb," said Phoebe turning around to the anonymous figure sitting behind in the passenger compartment. Mister Garrideb, in his back frock coat, his face obscured by a gas mask, sullenly made no effort to respond.

"And so our mysterious gallivant begins!" said Phoebe. "To the asylum, please, driver!"

3

Sir Cumberland Sinclair sat at the oaken dining table in the capacious dining room of his palatial home in The Boltons, South Kensington, breakfasting upon coddled eggs and buttered toast when his liveried retainer, Pockney, knocked and entered. He was a stubby, well-nourished fellow of a certain age and who not so much walked as waddled. Folds of flabby skin hung from his face, long and creased, not unlike a bloodhound in mourning.

"Detective Inspector Skindrick awaits without and requests an audience, Sir Cumberland," he droned. "Do you wish to receive him, sir? He has wiped his feet."

"Skindrick? Why of course! Thank you so much, our Pockney, do be awfully kind and show the chap in! Show him in!" The Assistant Commissioner, dabbed his eggy lips with a crisp white linen napkin. "Come along in, Detective Inspector, come along in. Now look, I fancy you'd care for a little of the coddled egg? What do you think, our Skindrick? Fresh from the hens of Guildford."

"Nae, thank y' sir, I've a'ready partaken o' ma breakfast," said Skindrick, looking around at the elegant, inherited opulence with jealousy and resentment. Gersham Skindrick had been brought up the youngest of a family of eight sharing two squalid tenement rooms off the Gallowgate where they would have never seen an egg at all, coddled or otherwise, had it not been for the beneficence of the church.

"Now then, our Skindrick, about your gallantry last evening. It was highly conspicuous. *Highly* conspicuous. Why, leaping from the carriage like that in order to save the Prime Minister was most impressive. So, what do you think? A word from me in the Commissioner's good ear to secure you a nice little commendation, I think so, old chum, don't you?" Sir Cumberland then tapped the side of his beaky nose, in a knowing manner.

"I'd be much obliged, sir. It would sit well in ma record book, but whatever you see fit. And pardon ma asking, sir, but did Superintendent Melville ever offer any explanation as to why he summoned the great and good of the land, like yourself, and force you all to view this attention seeking conjuror Magister, and his bumptious floozy?"

"Do you know, our Skindrick, there came not the slightest whisper. Something's afoot, but the old Superintendent is devilish adroit at keeping his own counsel," said Sir Cumberland. "Now I trust you bring me news of the apprehension of those two diabolical assassins?"

"Despite extensive searches by half the divisions of London, sir, neither hide nor hair has yet t' be found. Word about has the pair already slippin' the net by nefarious means. N'er the less, the men will continue about their endeavours."

"Well, I believe their efforts should be redoubled, old chum, redoubled. So inform your colleagues that these types of anarchistic scoundrels must at all costs be found and damn them if they aren't brought to book. Why it is just their very sort who give our decent criminals a thoroughly bad name," said Sir Cumberland earnestly.

"I'll be sure tae tell them, sir," said Skindrick. "Doubtless the men'll be much inspired by your leadership."

4

At the stroke of eight o'clock, Phoebe and Michael drew the Steamo to a hissing halt directly outside a vast, imposing grey Gault brick archway: the entrance to The London County Lunatic Asylum. Melville and Pym, were already speaking with Winfield Trout. You'll remember him, that obsequious little Senior Warder charged with maintaining the asylum's security. While Melville simply raised a quizzical eyebrow at the magicians' mode of transport, Pym could not conceal his marvel and fascination and Winfield Trout's thin-lipped grin barely masked his scornful indignation at the exhibitionism of these two theatrical peacocks.

"Look at that hussy! It's a disgrace!" thought Trout.

Phoebe's titian hair hung down beneath the small, black bowler fascinator set at a fetching angle. She wore a black blouse with a black cravat beneath a wasp-waisted black leather bodice which was adorned with a wide leather belt with silver buckle, and a large silver cased fob watch. Covering her legs and knee-high black leather kitten-heeled boots, was a black full length taffeta dress. Her arms were covered with tight-fitting fingerless gloves. As ever, she was a breathtaking vision. Oh, and she also carried her trusty silver parasol. You know, she rarely went anywhere without it.

Trout couldn't make out much of the anonymous person sitting in the back of the vehicle, only that he was wearing a top hat and for no apparent reason a gas mask. Superintendent Melville and Detective Inspector Pym doffed their bowlers to the female baggage, but he, Winfield Trout, for one, had no intention of extending any such courtesy. Never. Truth be told, he bitterly resented this entire insult, this questioning of his version of what happened last night at his asylum. And what on earth had it to do with Special Branch anyway?

"Good morning, gentlemen," said Phoebe, as Michael helped her down from the driver's compartment. The man in the gas mask attempted no form of greeting and simply remained seated.

"Mister M, Detective Inspector Pym. I'm guessing a locked room mystery in an asylum is another way of saying someone's upped and escaped," said Michael.

"A euphemism," added Phoebe.

"Indeed," said Melville. "First, note the arch, secured by a locked gate to which only the Gatekeeper and Senior Warder Trout here possess the keys. You will also witness through the gate, the clear, open area and circular driveway between the gate and the locked main entrance in that panoptic tower. A hundred yards at least. The escapee is of slight disposition and in no condition to breach the boundary foliage, or scale the outer wall."

"We contend she cunningly picked all the locks between the cell and the gate when effecting the escape. It is keenly the obvious solution," simpered Trout.

"She?" said Michael, picking up Trout's careless slip of the tongue.

At first sight Phoebe found the Senior Warder to be a slimy lickspittle, a simpering jackanapes. Michael just plain didn't like him. But there was nothing intuitive or deductive about that. Anyone who ever met Winfield Trout thought the same thing.

"So at least we've established the person who escaped was a woman," said Phoebe.

"Yes, the patient in question was of the female variety," fawned Trout, cursing his stupidity.

"Mister M, can Pheebs take a look at the lock on the Judas Gate?" asked Michael. His question was answered with a nod, and Phoebe handed Michael her parasol.

The Judas Gate was a smaller pedestrian entrance set within the larger double gates. Trout looked Phoebe up and down. What would she know? Who was this slip of a thing with her fancy posh tones?. He tut-tutted under his breath at such a brazen display, and then tut-tutted a darn sight more when Phoebe lifted her left leg to reveal a fair expanse of knee and, God forbid it, thigh. Was that even legal? Not that it stopped him gawping, of course. Melville barely noticed, he'd seen as much on stage the night before, but dear old Pym's eyes nearly popped out of their sockets.

From a slim leather pocket stitched to the side of her left boot, Phoebe produced a small brass container, much like a box of matches, from which, at the press of a button, two metal prongs sprang. It was a little contrivance I designed and dubbed 'The Picker-Nicker', for practice of escapology, or just this kind of lock-smithery. Phoebe twisted the winder on the side of the casing before offering it up to the large keyhole. The two shiny prongs buzzed and oscillated, conforming to the shapes within the lock.

"What you got, Pheebs?" asked Michael, keen that she continue to impress her audience.

"There are no scratch marks evident. Also a lock of this size and strength requires rather significant leverage when unlatching with traditional skeleton keys. Gentlemen, contrary to what you might read in the Penny Dreadfuls, lock picking is far from simple. A century ago a gentlemen named Joseph Bramah designed and built a lock and then offered a two hundred guinea purse for anyone who could open it without a key. Following hundreds of attempts, it was seventy years before someone finally came along and managed to pick the Bramah lock – and it still took him sixteen days."

"She reads far too much," said Michael.

"So, I'm afraid I have to disagree, Mister Trout," continued Phoebe, "Despite your earlier assertion, this gate lock was certainly not picked." With a firm click the gate swung open. "At least, not without a device like this."

"Thing is you see, Mister Trout, Pheebs is one of the country's leading experts when it comes to locks and bolts," said Michael. "And that is only because she learned her craft from the best teacher there is."

"And whom might that have been?" oozed Trout with ill-disguised ire.

"Me," replied Michael, in a tone which underlined the stupidity of the question. You see, Trout's disrespectful attitude to Phoebe had rankled Michael right from the moment they stepped down from the Steamo, so now he was naturally predisposed to try and belittle the greasy snake at every opportunity.

"May we go in?" smiled Phoebe.

The site of The London County Asylum was more vast green open space than complex of functional hospital buildings. William Alderson designed the original Middlesex Paupers Lunatic Asylum and construction was completed in 1831, making this the first purpose built asylum in England. Covering the best part of sixty acres, and more like a self-governing village with all attendant trades and services including a chapel, burial ground and, would you believe, until ten years ago, a brewery! The property was bounded at the front by the busy road to Uxbridge and at the rear by the Grand Junction Canal. Over the years the hospital had become a recognised institution of mental health excellence. Fresh air and activity was the key to this establishment, and shackles and restraints consigned to the histories of a misguided past.

The gatehouse opened onto a quadrangle skirted on three sides by a double story building, stretching forward on both sides like long welcoming arms. A long gravel drive bordered with flower beds split left and right around a central fountain and met again to form a carriage-drive circle. Beyond the fountain stood a three-storey, eight-sided panoptical tower which served as the main entrance. It was the centrepiece of two stretches of double storey buildings, both displaying arched, glazed windows. The entire building was one of those masterpieces of simple, easy on the eye symmetry.

"Within the block to the left are the wards for male patients and to the right the facilities for the females. Now, if you'd care to follow my good self," simpered Trout. Once inside the tower, he ushered Melville, Michael and Phoebe to the right.

Pym remained behind at the solid arched gatehouse to continue questioning Gatehouse Warder Bevis Gint, whom he knew to be a former police constable, who had left the force quietly under murky circumstances, and had done very well from it.

"This escape tomfoolery must be a bit of a pain in the rump, Mister Gint. Especially with you enjoying the quiet life these days," said Pym, offering him an Ogden's Guinea Gold cigarette.

Gint shook his head. "Pipe man, me, sir. But your Special Branch file on me will have told you that a'ready. Yes, Constance Dill is the first patient we've lost since I been here, sir, but if you're pumping me for clues, there's nothing I can tell you, and you know I would. The whole thing is as peculiar to me as it is to you, and that's the God's honest truth of it."

Pym nodded, shook Gint's hand and told him he was a good man. But there was something former P.C. Gint dare not divulge, not to Mister Trout, the Special Branch nor anyone. This morning he had discovered that his old service pistol, the Webley Break Top revolver, always kept in the locked drawer in his gatehouse, had vanished. From a locked drawer, just disappeared! And Gint was convinced Constance Dill had taken it.

***

"And we're certain your patient's vanished?" asked Michael, as he, Phoebe and Melville followed Trout along the corridor of the Female Patients' Wing. "She's not laying low in the eaves, lurking in an outbuilding? Just because you can't see something, doesn't mean it's not there. "

"Be assured a complete close-down followed by a top to bottom, nook and cranny search has yielded nothing," said Melville confidently.

"And our beautiful grounds were searched exhaustively by a full complement of my trained staff at first light. That also drew a blank, gentlemen," said Trout proudly.

Patients peered at the strange group as they strode along the corridor. Despite the early hour all the hospital's female patients were up and about; some bright, some vacant, some spry, some shuffling, but all dressed in smart regulation grey dresses with white pinafores, and setting about their occupational therapies.

"Three new faces for the ol' place, eh, Mister Trout?" shouted a thick set woman with several chins, a broad smile. "Proper fine. Look like you'll fit in well here, luvvies!"

"Thank you most kindly, ma'am," said Michael, bowing to the woman with a flourish. He turned to Phoebe and added with a smile, "How well she knows us."

An elegant woman with long grey hair and a lofty air stopped mopping the perfectly clean floor to tell them all she was Her Majesty the Queen's cousin and it was all a terrible mistake. Michael almost quipped that Pheebs could mention her plight at the next family get-together at Osborne House, but somehow resisted the temptation.

Miss Damaris Gunthorpe imperceptibly nodded at Melville, who returned the compliment in an equally unnoticed way. Well, not entirely unnoticed, because Michael spotted it. He later surmised that Melville was an on-the-quiet roué; and he and the magnificent nurse might be enjoying a clandestine relationship. Phoebe more accurately figured Melville's only interest in Miss Gunthorpe would be her eyes and ears.

Michael counted four doors, from the roadside archway gate to this corridor alone, four doors, each of which had been locked at the time of the disappearance and each requiring a different key to open them. This was looking not so much a mystery of a locked room, but of a locked building. At the end of the corridor, Senior Warder Trout led them in single file clanking down a metal staircase which spiralled into the basement. A few steps along the well-lit, though musty subterranean hallway brought them to a series of three doors.

"Might I present The Seclusion Area, gentlemen. We consider these dwellings to be a safe refuge of peace and tranquillity to enable the aggrieved patient to help restore their calmer disposition," smoothed Trout. "Do now be pleased to step inside, for this is the very place from whence the female vanished as if into thin air. It is a mystery which presents itself as so utterly baffling as to be the very stuff of Grub Street, I'm sure you'll agree."

At first glance, Michael and Phoebe noted the white painted door was of stout wood, with an open peephole bored through at eye level. Trout pushed the door inwards with the toe of his boot. The room was lit by a bulb of such poor wattage Michael was convinced if you switched it off the place would suddenly become brighter. The ceiling was high and the white walls were a patchwork of painted leather pouches stuffed with horse hair. The straw filled mattress rested upon the floor. The Padded Cell had been pioneered by a Doctor Connolly, in this very asylum some sixty years earlier.

Michael looked around, up, down, stamped a heel on the floor which seemed solid and secure, then tapped his knuckle on one of the padded walls which seemed soft and secure. Then he swung the door back and forth to examine the hinges and suddenly raised an eyebrow. "Pheebs. Now I know why we're here."

"Why?"

Michael swung the door completely closed enabling Phoebe to see the eight letter word written in red on the wall.

"Oh, my days," said Phoebe.

"Indeed," said Melville quietly, from outside in the corridor. "A woman disappears from a locked asylum cell and the only clue she leaves behind is your name: Magister. Now. How might you explain that?"

5

Out on the Uxbridge Road, Pym had left Gint in his gatehouse and was taking a good hard look at the vehicle in which Mister Magister and Miss Le Breton had arrived. The machine was a work of artistic contrasts. A beautiful monstrosity. Sleek, but solid. However, what intrigued Pym most was the enigmatic fellow who remained within, a kind of watchman, he supposed. A watchman wearing a black overcoat, bowler hat and full-faced gas mask.

"Hallo!" said Pym.

Nothing. The fellow remained still, staring straight ahead.

"Here, I said hello there! Who are you? I said who are you?" After half a dozen tries, Pym was quickly tiring of this ill-mannered refusal to communicate. "Oi. What's up with you? I am an officer of the law. Are you deaf of hearing, or what?"

One must only imagine the Detective Inspector's surprise when our Mister Garrideb suddenly shrugged his shoulders and turned his head to look down at Pym. Behind the lenses of the gas mask, Mister Garrideb's eyes glowed bright green, as if illuminated. Then Garrideb's voice, sounding much like a Catalonian with catarrh told the high ranking policeman in no uncertain terms to: "Bugger off and move away!"

In fact, so unnerving was the encounter that Pym felt compelled to draw his revolver. Then with a whirr and a click Mister Garrideb shrugged his shoulders and faced forward again. Pym waved his pistol and demanded the gas masked man learn some respect, ordering him to step out and identify himself to an officer of the law, or bloody well face the consequences. Again, Mister Garrideb shrugged, turned and told Pym to bugger off and move away. The late night and the early morning had done nothing to ease Pym's mood and in losing all patience decided to haul this insolent geezer down and out of the carriage and learn him a bit of respect.

Unfortunately, as soon as Pym touched the door handle on the Steamo, there was a vicious sharp buzz, and a dull ache fizzed up through Pym's arm, propelling him back from the

Steamo. Pym's own studies and bomb disposal skills were more than enough to make him realise he'd just been shocked by a zap of electricity. Shit and derision. Magister's vehicle was booby trapped! And it was only when the stand-off continued, with Mister Garrideb sternly repeating his charmless green-eyed 'Bugger off and move away!' routine that it finally dawned on Pym... He was trying to conduct an increasingly acrimonious conversation with quite the most extraordinary thing. A mechanical man.

***

"I can't explain why my name is written on the wall, but patience, Mister M. Given a few moments we shall," Michael appeared smoothly confident, but gave Phoebe the raised eyebrow look.

"Michael, this is written in blood," noted Phoebe, looking closely at each red letter which made up the word 'MAGiSTER'.

Michael screwed his nose up. "I've had better fan letters."

"In the absence of pen and ink, slicing a finger on the edge of the hinge and using the blood makes for an effective writing implement. Examine the hinge." Melville seemed keen to let the magicians know that he was himself not without deductive observational skills.

Even Trout then felt the need to chip in with his own revelation. "The word 'Magister', gentlemen, is the self-same word the patient was calling all day long, the day before she disappeared. Repeating the word 'Magister' seemed only to make her increasingly more anxious as the day wore on, causing such disquiet the doctors felt she be best served by a night within the Secure Accommodation. This was for safety's sake, as I know you'll all understand. Naturally, we had no knowledge this peculiar *word* was in fact a person's *name*."

Michael, Phoebe and even Melville; each would have taken great delight in clipping the little ratbag about his large ears, but instead, Michael asked, "Okay. So the door was locked?"

"Of course, sir, locked fast by my own hand," Trout nodded earnestly.

"And there's no indication of tampering," confirmed Phoebe, after a fiddle and check with the Picker-Nicker.

"Walls and floor secure. Door secure. Nope," said Michael, turning to Superintendent Melville. "In my expert opinion Mister M, Mister Tripe here is quite right."

"Trout, sir, the name is Trout," corrected Trout.

"Mister Trout is quite right. As a professional magician I can confirm that the woman who occupied this cell officially vanished into thin air. So, now that Pheebs and I are done here, if you could send our fee on to the theatre we can be on our way. After you, Pheebs. A pleasure doing business with you, gentlemen."

"Wait," said Melville, with just a hint of exasperation. "Mister Magister, we both know that is not the case."

"There's no conjuring involved here, Mister M. No illusion, no sleight of hand. But there's certainly deception. Because other than just plain vanishing, there is only one possible logical answer," said Michael. "Pheebs?"

"Whomever you locked in the room, Mister Trout, was a person with a full set of keys, who opened all the doors and simply let herself out," said Phoebe.

"Outrageous suggestion!" snorted Trout. "Absurd!"

"I rather think so too. So the answer must be – someone *else* with a full set of keys opened all the doors and let her out," said Phoebe.

"Superintendent, I crave authority to put an end to this nonsense immediately," Trout had become puce with embarrassment or rage, or quite possibly a bit of both. "The only persons in possession of full sets of keys are myself and a few highly trusted, professional staff. What this person asserts is impossible!"

"Impossible is what we do best," said Michael. "We are also very good at absurd incidentally, but there's no mystery here. The doors were unlocked and she walked straight out. Once again, case solved."

"None of which explains why Michael's name is scrawled on the wall," said Phoebe, suspiciously. "How is Michael involved?"

"Aha! Him and you aided her escape! That's his signature, to mark his cunning work!" shouted Trout triumphantly, as the idea fell into place. "The conjuror, Superintendent, he picked all the locks! Seems to me as if you've been caught red-handed by your own petard, as it were, Mister fancy-magician!"

"Please be quiet, Mister Trout," said Melville patiently, "Thank you, Mister Magister. You have confirmed my suspicion."

"Always a pleasure, Mister M," smiled Michael. "And before we leave to spend our fee on wild living and in Phoebe's case clothes, just how did I confirm your fear and suspicion?"

Melville looked Michael directly in the eye. "The woman who escaped is Constance Dill."

Michael reeled. It felt as if he'd just been struck square in the chest with a sledge hammer. For several moments he struggled to find the breath to stammer anything.

"Michael...?" said Phoebe, alarmed by his reaction, which was even more marked than coming face to face last night with Queen Victoria!

"Connie Dill? *The* Connie Dill whose stage name was Connie Lamal was right here? In this cell? Well, that's exactly how she escaped, Pheebs. The doors *were* unlocked for her. And these people have no idea they helped her do it."

6

Young Nebuchadnezzar Dunnalump, (understandably called Neb for short) in his cloth cap and brown apron tried to coax a whistle from his parched lips as he struggled to barrow half a dozen wooden crates of sweet smelling fresh picked pears along the alley to Covent Garden. For generations the unfortunately monikered Dunnalump family had worked the fruit and veg market. The P at the end of the family surname was supposed to be silent they had always insisted, but naturally for the purposes of ribald humour none of the earthy porters and costers who pushed, pulled and packed in the market took the slightest notice. Young Neb, developed for his age, why he was all of twelve, stopped to strike a match to relight his cherry wood pipe, dream of breakfast and his first foaming tankard of the day when he heard, "Where's you taking those pears, lovely boy?"

Neb Dunnalump, remember, the P is silent, stopped and looked around. From a doorway stepped a pale, slender, rather tired looking woman. Not much taller than himself, she wore a blue scarf, a grey dress and off-white smock, the likes of which young Ned had never seen in the market before.

"Me pears? What's it to you, you pox-riddled ol' crone?" snickered the young coster. By tradition, males of the Dunnalump clan were ill-disposed to any form of chivalry or charm, which they keenly displayed on a daily basis, but not often this early.

"Just that those pears of yours are all rotten," said the woman.

"Ha! Give over, you filthy stinking cow! Them's all fresh pears them! Now sling yer bleedin' 'ook out of it!" suggested the silver-tongued rapscallion. He then blinked, looked at his crates of firm, sweet smelling Bartletts and staggered back in shock and revulsion. His pears were a seething mass of writhing maggots, feasting voraciously on a tower of brown, decaying fruit flesh.

"That's the thing, lovely boy. You see precisely what I want you to see," said the woman, smiling benignly, before taking a bite out of a perfectly formed freshly picked pear. "Now then. There's a little something I want you to do for me."

***

"Michael? Who is Constance Dill?" asked Phoebe, as they stood in The Seclusion Cell.

"When I first landed in England, I toured in vaudeville, a Music Hall show which headlined Alfred 'The Great' Vance with Vesta Tilley, and Connie Dill was third top. Her stage name was 'Connie Lamal'. I was way down with the wines and spirits at the bottom of the bill, almost below the name of the poster printer. Connie was a mesmerist, a hypnotist and I'm talking about the best there was, Pheebs, ever. She was truly fantastic. Connie could 'fluence anybody to do anything, and the crowd loved the act and loved her."

Michael stared at the empty cell recalling the show stopping brilliance of Constance Dill, now a fugitive from an insane asylum. "How she did what she did we could never figure out. A quirk of nature? Whatever it was, Connie only had to glance at someone in a certain way and snap, they were under."

Michael recalled the fateful night, December 26, 1889, while playing the Christmas week at The Sun Music Hall, that little theatre over on the High Street, Knightsbridge.

At the start of Connie Dill's spot, a boorish loudmouth infused with several bottles of the Christmas spirit yelled from the stalls, "If you're a mesmerist I'll eat my hat!" And Connie proved she was a mesmerist when she 'fluenced the fellow to eat his hat. He was on stage, sitting on a chair hungrily chomping bites out of his own bowler. The crowd lapped it up. It was a sensational stunt, quite hilarious. It was a week later, when the police came by to arrest her, we found out the loudmouth had died from some digestive malady like inflamed gastritis. All from eating a hat.

"Modern medicinal science would have identified mercury poisoning," explained Melville. "Hatters apply mercury to cure the felt they use to make the hats. Often, over a period of time, they became mentally afflicted by the fumes. Consuming much of a filthy hat would have the same effect." It seemed Melville had read the dusty trial report which was tucked away in Constance Dill's Special Branch file.

Michael continued the story. "So, Connie was arrested for manslaughter, and was so horrified at causing the death of a punter, she didn't bother to defend herself. Just copped to the charge and none of us knew what happened to her next. Until now. But who'd have figured she'd wind up in a place like this."

"A complete miscarriage of justice?" said Phoebe.

"It is unfortunate she admitted the charge so readily," said Melville.

"Gentlemen, I do pride myself in stating that the unfortunate Dill woman was under our kindly supervision, lo, all of this ten-year," simpered Trout. "And model patient she was too!"

"Mister Magister. You confirm with confidence that Constance Dill used her mesmeric ability to convince the guards to let her out?"

"Oh, that's exactly how she did it, Mister M. In the blink of an eye Connie could have convinced anyone here she was another person, a visitor, a nurse, or even Mister Trout here," said Michael. Trout squirmed. He was far from happy at the way all this looked to be heading in his direction.

"But to return to the question of why, after a decade residing here in quiet anonymity, did Connie suddenly feel the need to call for Michael, daub his name on the wall and then make her escape?" said Phoebe.

It was no surprise that Michael had become preoccupied with his name, written in such desperate, vivid red on the wall behind the door. And, you know, something in particular, a minor detail caught his attention. "She's written the 'i' in Magister without a dot over the top of it. See? The 'i'? That's not like Connie. She was always very tidy, very precise," he heard himself say aloud. "But, I guess surviving in a place like this for ten years it's going to send anybody crazy…"

"As I humbly explained previously, this Seclusion Room was but a temporary measure until she regained her usual equanimity," simpered Trout. "Her more permanent abode is located above."

Trout led them back upstairs to Connie's aforesaid more permanent abode off the main Female Wing corridor. It was a fifty-patient ward, the beds set out much like those found in general hospitals the length of the land, two rows of twenty-five beds facing one another. Connie's comfortable bed was bounded by wooden bedside tables and backed by an arch shaped window which overlooked a laid to lawn exercise area. Melville reported a search of Connie's cabinets revealed little in the way of clues or personal possessions. But then, you know, why would she when everything she could have possibly needed was supplied by the institution?

"Cosy," said Michael, looking about, but he really didn't mean it. With patients out and about attending to whatever therapeutic duties comprised their morning routines, the ward was entirely empty.

"No, there's nothing here to explain anything, but hey, at least we found that missing dot over the 'i'." Michael pointed to a small blob of red daubed on the whitewashed wall behind Connie's bedside cabinet. "At least she's not forgetful..."

"That really is rather peculiar..." said Phoebe, intrigued and approaching the red dot which until then only Michael had spotted. "Why would she daub the dot there? Unless it was to draw Michael's attention..."

"What you doing, young woman?" snapped Trout, as Phoebe removed a lace glove and dabbed her index finger at the dot. Trout looked at Melville for support, but got none.

"Superintendent, would you mind very much taking a look at this please? The dot appears to highlight a hole bored into the pointing of the brickwork. May I?"

"Indeed," said Melville, as Phoebe unclipped a pin from her skirt and used it to ease a small roll of paper out of the hole. She passed the roll-up to Melville, who carefully unfurled two long and narrow pieces of newsprint. One slip had been snipped from a theatrical weekly called *The Era*, the other from *The Performer*. Both were critiques concerning the show at The Metropolitan Theatre of Steam, Smoke and Mirrors headlined by Magician Michael Magister, the Illusionist of the Industrial Age and Phoebe, the Queen of Steam and Goddess of the Aethyr!

"These clippings are most recent," Melville told Michael and Phoebe. "Neither has browned with age. They both concern critical notices regarding your performance at The Metropolitan." Melville turned to Trout. "Did Constance Dill read newspapers?"

"Not a-one, sir," oozed Trout. "She never once expressed the slightest interest in the outside world and all its doings."

"So, how might she have come by these?" asked Phoebe, as Melville passed both cuttings to Michael who was instantly absorbed with his own reviews.

"Mister Trout, was Constance Dill ever allowed visitors?" asked Phoebe.

"Allowed, most certainly, she was, but received never a single one, sir," replied Trout turning to Melville. "Nor did she ever once express the desire to receive any. Positively eschewed them, one might say. With the exception, of course, of the Reverend Brother Morten."

"And the Reverend Brother Morten is…?" asked Phoebe.

Again, Trout turned to Melville. "A fine, upright man of the cloth and a friar to boot, sir, despatched from St. Bernard's Convent along the way and sent in lieu of our recently indisposed regular priest. We have always believed in the benefit of the teaching of the scriptures, the receiving of confessions and the ministering of communion, to be most enriching for the patients, sir."

"Mister Trout, as I posed the question I would very much appreciate your also directing the answer to me," said Phoebe firmly.

Michael was re-reading his favourable notices when, without looking up, he chipped in with. "Take my advice, Mister Trout. It's best not to mess with Miss Le Breton."

"So, when did this Reverend Brother Morten first begin making his visits to Constance?" asked Phoebe.

"Came offering his Godly services about the end of March-tide," Trout told her, with barely concealed bitterness.

"Less than a fortnight ago," said Melville, quietly taking it all in.

"I suggest you question the friar himself. He is due to make a visitation this very morning," said Trout, looking at Phoebe sideways, with narrowing eyes, before adding under his breath, "Bitch."

The next thing Trout felt was the gut-wrenching agony of a vice crushing his scrotum, while being slammed back against the wall. He tried to scream but no sound emerged as his throat was locked shut by Phoebe's parasol pressing firmly across his scrawny neck. Trout looked in terror at Phoebe's eyes. Blue, fixed and determined.

"Never, I repeat, *never* speak to me, or any other woman, in those derogatory terms *ever* again. Do I make myself clear, Mister Trout?" The steel in Phoebe's voice was matched only by the tightening grip on his dry testicles. "I said do I make myself clear?"

"Told you not to mess with her, Trouty," said Michael, still not looking up.

Melville raised an impressed eyebrow at the encounter, then took the news cuttings from Michael and held them to the light in search of further clues. With watering eyes and purple cheeks Trout nodded as best he could. Phoebe released her hold and Trout doubled up in pain, and sat heavily upon Connie Dill's bed. The hand now between his legs was his own.

"Assault! I warrant this is common assault!" whimpered Trout. "I shall summon my staff... I shall complain to the highest authority!"

"I *am* the highest authority, Mister Trout and I have neither time nor the inclination to listen," said Melville, just as Detective Inspector Pym sprinted breathlessly into the ward calling, 'Superintendent Melville!'

Pym could not help but notice the sight of Winfield Trout slumped on the bed with a face as red as a beetroot and holding himself in a manner most undignified. What with that, the mechanical man and now the news he brought the Superintendent, it had been a bit of a morning so far. And it was only eight-thirty. "Word's just arrived. Constance Dill has been found in Covent Garden. And she's asking for Mister Magister."

7

Meantime within The Dungeon beneath the stage of The Metropolitan Theatre of Steam, Smoke and Mirrors, I once again poured over the assassin's Pulsa pistol which lay there before me upon my work bench. Last night, you may recall, while wearing my Goggle-Eyes peer-through device, I determined the nature of the deadly booby trap which protected the secrets of the weapon's enhanced fire power. But I was not about to let something trivial like danger to life and limb stand in the way. So I asked Wicko my dwarfish associate to crack the Pulsa open.

"If you think I'm getting anywhere near that thing you're off your head," was his unhelpful and somewhat selfish reply.

So, with Wicko and his favoured precision instrument of the true artisan, the ten-pound club hammer, suddenly unavailable, how might I neutralise the explosive? The solution came as the kettle in the corner boiled for my morning brew. The Aethyr can only be energised in a dry environment, so I would steep the Pulsa in the finest Industrial Elixir of the Age – steam! Thus, with tongs I dangled and danced the pistol in the cloud of grey magical vapour which gushed from the kettle spout, then carried it back to my bench, twisted open the retaining screws, opened the pistol housing and freed the section of booby trap, the tubing and explosive, with such surgical precision as could teach Sir Robert Liston a thing or two. With all threat of danger thus removed I could now set about filching the improved ideas from this weapon and imposing them upon our own version of the Pulsatronic pistol.

Not that you're beginning to wonder about me, but I'll explain a little anyway. I had worked as a theoretical scientist and abstruse mathematician, heading a faculty at one of the smaller Oxford colleges. But frankly, I tired of working for a living and began applying my intellect to the entirely more agreeable business of industrial espionage, namely filching the discarded, or half-formed, discoveries of eminent contemporaries and then improving upon their originals. A minor disagreement with an aggrieved party forced me to flee at speed to New York where I became fascinated with the craft and science of magic and where I discovered Michael. A major disagreement with an aggrieved party then forced us both to flee at speed back to London. Truth be told, in addition to my genius I can also point with pride to being an enigmatic, lying, cheating, plagiariser. Perfect qualifications for a new career in show business, I think you will agree.

"I'll take a mug a' tea if that kettle's boiled," said Wicko, as he began reading the second chapter of Arthur Doyle's *The Tragedy of the Korosko*.

***

Benevolent suburban traffic coupled with a certain knuckle-gnawing urgency meant it was less than an hour before Michael was steering the Steamotivator smoothly up London's Long Acre. Past the Odhams Press building on the left, the site of the old Queen Theatre and a stone's throw from The Eden Palace of Varieties on Great Queen Street, where Michael and I first saw Charles Morritt 'The Yorkshire Conjuror' perform. As well as baffling trickery with the balls, the cards and the cut flowers, Morritt performed an impressive mind reading act with his wife.

Charlie Morritt was not a real mind reader, of course. His act was a variation on Robert Houdin's spoken code word routine: Houdin's assistant would ask him, "What is it here that I am holding?" a specific phrase which tallied with one item on the list of objects Houdin had memorised. Another agreed phrase would be associated with another object and so forth. Morritt's nifty spin on that idea was to have his wife use the same words every time, "Here. what is this... pray tell?", but Morritt's clue to the code was in the lengths of the silences between the words. For example, gaps of three seconds and four seconds meant item thirty-four on the pre-memorised list! Michael spotted the silences and I figured out the significance. But that was then and this is now and back to the plot...

Superintendent Melville sat up front with Michael, while Detective Inspector Pym felt he'd struck more than lucky by sharing the passenger compartment with the gorgeous Phoebe. Of course, he also had to tolerate the imposing mechanical man in black. Pym took exception to being told to "Bugger off and move away!" but only because Miss Edie Clutterbuck had said those very same words to him last week round the back of the Commercial Road stables, on their second and, as it turned out, final date.

Michael had convinced Melville and Pym to share their ride to Covent Garden, and while the Superintendent would normally eschew anything which drew unnecessary attention to himself, like a chugging metallic horseless carriage steaming down the street, the promised expedience was an overriding factor. Nevertheless, Melville had insisted upon the removal of the advertising banner at the rear of the vehicle, claiming it was akin to chalking a target on their backs.

"Constance Dill, Mister Magister," said Melville, loudly above the noise of the London traffic. "Her hypnotic powers remain undiminished over the years. Having worked closely with the woman, you must have some notion of the chicanery involved. How does she make this mesmerism work?"

"That's the thing, Mister M. Spiritualists, fortune tellers, mind readers, there's always a method, a trick, a deception," explained Michael. "And it's the same with stage hypnotists. Many of them use stooges. Plants in the crowd who are part of the act, pretending to be hypnotised. Other hypnotists can convince genuine punters to pretend they're being 'fluenced."

"How so?"

"They just tell the crowd that it's impossible to hypnotise a dumb-ass. So straight off whoever they get up on stage is not going to want to look like a dumb-ass. The performer only calls up punters who look like they'll play along. Compliant is the word they use. Otherwise they look for loudmouths who'll want to get laughs. Those kinds of punters up on stage are putty in your hands. But Connie Dill was no fake, Mister M. She really could make you believe anything with just a look. If you met her gaze and she wanted you to believe she was The Ghost of Christmas Past, then you would be looking at the very Yuletide Phantom Charles Dickens described. Don't ask me how she managed it, because I truly don't know. How does a sheepdog control a flock with a look? It may even be God-given. If you believe in that kind of stuff."

Behind, within the passenger cabin, Pym's questioning of Phoebe was markedly less cerebral. "So about your lifelike talking dummy...?" said Pym.

"Michael?" said Phoebe. Pym chuckled and gestured a thumb at the Garrideb. "No, this... mechanical man, or whatever you want to call him."

"Ah, Mister Garrideb," said Phoebe. "He's our 'Mechannaquin'. A Motorised Mannequin. He has a terse manner and is a rather effective deterrent to thieves and the overly curious. The Steamo also had additional methods of discouragement worth avoiding."

"So I discovered," said Pym rubbing his still aching arm. "I've never heard the name, what is it, Garri...?"

"Garrideb. It's a rather tortuous acronym. It stands for 'Guardian Individual Defence Embodiment'. And you're quite right it makes very little sense. The only person I know who actively likes the name is Arthur Conan Doyle."

As Michael steered the steaming beast through the bustle of Long Acre, a voice from a brass horn by his shoulder was heard to say: "At the next junction turn right. Turn right. Then turn left. Destination lies after seventy feet on the right!" The voice was Phoebe's, feeding him directions by way of the mouthpiece of a black candlestick telephone while reading her copy of Stanford's London street map which rested, unfolded on her lap.

Covent Garden Market was the capital's vast principal fruit, vegetable and flower trading area. Originally part of the orchard owned by Westminster Abbey, known as 'The Garden of the Abbey and the Convent', the name was eventually shortened to 'Covent Garden'. Yes, very well, even I will admit it was a more apposite abbreviation than 'Garrideb'.

As the Steamo was teased round into King Street a great wave of noise and smells readied the senses, steeled the sinews, in preparation for the enormous onslaught of colourful hustle and bustle which lay before them as they turned into the

110

market square. Porters shoved and hauled barrows and trollies while yelling great eloquent volleys of abuse, profanity and uncommon oaths at anyone who stood in their way, and, indeed, anyone else, who didn't. Their speed, strength and the sheer tonnage they shifted was astonishing to behold. But even these gritty no nonsense toilers were struck dumb as the Steamo forced a path through the hordes, avoiding the sacks, baskets and wagons piled high with produce, many slung over with canvas tarpaulin. Michael brought the vehicle to a gasping rest in the square directly in front of the columned and white stone faced Palladian portico of St. Paul's Church, renovated and altered over the decades but still owing much to its 1631 Inigo Jones design.

A decent turnout of Bow Street's uniformed finest were already in attendance, along with, rather oddly, a single London County Council Fire Brigade horse drawn steam fire engine, manned by half a dozen former sea dogs all in their woollen tunics and shiny brass helmets. But it fell to a grizzled, grey haired bearded Police Sergeant with a bottom jaw the shape of a dustpan to update Melville on Constance Dill. Several wolf whistles met Michael as he stepped down from the Steamo which he acknowledged with great grace and with a cheery wave. The manly fellows of the Veg Market weren't predisposed to admiring the ornate fashions of a stage magician. But that, of course, all changed when the Steamo's passenger compartment door slid back with a gentle hiss and Michael proffered his hand to assist one of his passengers. The ribald crowd firstly cast their eyes upon a long black, pointy tipped shiny leather boot, followed by a longer, slim bare - thigh, followed by a gorgeous, titian-haired young woman. It was then that a great lusty cheer of lewd appreciation swelled up from market porters, costers, firemen and it must be said policemen as well.

"Constance Dill is to be found at the rear of the church, facing the graveyard," Melville told Michael and Phoebe as he led them briskly through the stone archway at the right of the church and along the gravel path towards the yard at the rear.

"She says she will talk with no one other than Mister Magister."

"I can understand that," said Michael nodding, although his self-appreciation was quickly rewarded with a sharp dig in the back from Phoebe.

"Otherwise she claims she will jump," continued Melville.

"Jump?" Immediately Michael's bright look of bravado became a dark face of concern. "What do you mean 'jump'?"

"And doubtless to her death from that height."

Michael swallowed hard. "From that height? Where exactly is Connie?"

Melville gestured with his head to the roof and pointed his thumb over his shoulder, "Up there."

Michael's dread-filled eyes followed the angle of Melville's twitching thumb and, oh my, sure enough, there, high up, extremely high up, at the end of the church's pitched roof, with one foot either side of the apex stood the figure of Constance Dill.

8

She was dressed in what certainly looked to be the fatigues of a patient at Hanwell Asylum, and her head was swathed in a blue cloth scarf. She was staring out toward the distant west, her arms wide and outstretched in a manner much akin to that of the Messiah, or that agreeable inebriate on Paddington Green who lets the pigeons perch on him while he sings a chorus of 'When The Old Dun Cow Caught Fire'.

"The height. Does that present a problem, Mister Magister?" asked Melville, now quite fully realising that it did.

"No," lied the magician, shaking his head and again swallowing hard while still looking up at Connie Dill. She certainly looked precarious balanced up there unsupported. Some head-spinning distance below her lay the churchyard with its many graves. The irony was too disturbing to contemplate.

Either side of the main building, two single storey brick built extensions had been constructed, to broaden the entrance vestibule within the church. Their flat roofs stood the best part of twenty feet from the ground so quite why Connie couldn't have chosen to pose on one of those instead of scrambling up a further forty feet onto the church's pitched roof Michael couldn't fathom. Well, yes, admittedly the greater the height the greater the theatrical impact. Although 'impact' was not really the best word for Michael to find drifting into his mind at that moment.

"You know, Mister M, keen as I to scramble up there, , I'm wondering if this ought to be a job for one of your specialised constables. One of those highly qualified in the art of talking women down from high church roof types of policemen."

"In that division we find ourselves currently deficient," said Melville. "Additionally Constance Dill insists she will converse with you and you alone. I remain confident that to resolve this scenario with minimal disruption you will suppress your irrational acrophobia and acquiesce."

Michael glanced at Phoebe with one of those, 'and, in plain English, that means?' kind of looks.

"You have to go up," said Phoebe, with a sympathetic look. "Unless you'd rather I…"

"Pheebs. Please. Do I look like a man even remotely concerned? Admittedly I'm better with depths than heights having plumbed a few in my time." Michael squinted up at Connie, the sweet and gifted mentor he so dearly remembered from his early days on the English stage. And, truth be told, there were a dozen questions which only Connie could answer. How had she wound up in that asylum? Why, after so long, did she decide to escape? Why was she so desperate to see him? "I owe Connie too much to let her down now, Mister M. I'm going up." He removed his jacket and handed it to Melville. "And don't try to stop me."

Nobody did. The route to the roof was a slow, rung by rung climb up three wobbly wooden ladders hastily lashed together by the Fire Brigade. The first ladder was propped against the right hand side extension. The next up leant against the high pitched roof and took Michael as high as the metal guttering. The third long ladder was laid up on the slope of the tiles, to the ridge, much of which Michael climbed with eyes tight shut. The terror of opening his eyes to clamber the last foot or so onto the apex all but fair took Michael's breath away.

"Gorn, son!" came the yell from somebody below. I believe it was a tattooed, hefty woman who smoked a clay pipe and sold buttercups in the churchyard; at least it was positive. She had earlier been rebuked by police for imploring Connie to "Jump, y' bitch!"

You know, it wasn't so much the encouragement that suddenly steeled Michael. It was the realisation that he suddenly had himself an audience. A gathering crowd all looking up at him, pointing and taking bets. It was show time!

Michael let go of the ladder, found his footing on the tiles and stood at the apex of the roof, one foot either side of the ridge. It must be said, you know, the views over London from the roof of St. Paul's Church, Covent Garden were quite marvellous. Over to the left there, slender, brown and vicious, stabbing upward was the sharp gothic tower of Big Ben. Back over here was the arched canopy of Charing Cross Railway terminus and way over on the south bank of the river when the distant mist parted you could just make out the Lambeth tower of Messrs Walker, Parker and Company, manufacturers of gunpowder and shot. None of which was of the slightest interest to Michael Magister. Instead his eyes remained focussed dead ahead as he shuffled, slowly step by slow step, arms adjusting his balance. Connie, by contrast, remained stock still, quite at ease, with her back to him and her arms outstretched. The air was cool as it always seemed to be, but the breeze welcome, drying the film of moisture on his brow and across his top lip. A murmur of approval buzzed around the crowd below. Michael stepped closer, buoyed by their admiration.

"I've got to say, Connie Dill, there are easier ways to grab my attention. A postcard maybe." There was no reaction. "Connie? It's me. Young Magister. Here I am. Came as soon as I heard you wanted me."

Again, not the merest flicker from Connie Dill. Not a turn of the head over her shoulder to look back at him, not even a shrug, nothing. Michael recalled that Connie could somehow do this, 'fluence herself into some kind of trance. She found it relaxing. Soporific he thought she'd called it.

"Connie, isn't this all a little, what's the word I'm looking for? Oh, yes – dangerous! And high. And you know how I love 'high'. So what do you say we both come down? I don't know how you got up here, but look, I brought ladders. And I don't like you being right on the edge there."

Michael was now just two yards behind her, and as he shuffled closer, so Connie for the first time began to move. Michael took another step. Then she began to sway. Back and forth, back and forth. It was as if the effort of standing there for such a time was beginning to take its toll. More and more she swayed, and now to such a perilous degree she was on the verge of toppling forward.

"Connie! Oh... hell!" shouted Michael as he found himself lurching to grab her by the shoulders. Got-her! But to his horror Connie's foot slipped, dislodging a chunk of concrete parapet. Michael tried to keep a grip but Connie's bodyweight began pulling away. She was going! Beyond the tipping point! She slipped through his fingers and she plummeted away from him. The horror was so overwhelming he felt no sensation as he was yanked backwards; just the voice which shouted, "I've got you!"

A lace gloved hand steadied Michael's shoulder and found his centre of gravity. A great cheer rose up from below and a lusty round of applause. But to Michael, his mind racing, his heart pounding, never had the approval of an audience sounded so hollow, so sour.

"Pheebs? Pheebs! Connie's gone. I couldn't hold her. She slipped away. I couldn't hold her!"

"Michael, calm. Deep breaths. Melville has that in hand. Come forward with me. Can you bear to peep down? I promise it will gladden your heart."

Phoebe helped Michael edge forward and to look down. Beside the rear entrance to the church he saw Connie's body, not broken and bloody, but caught in a great sheet of brown sack tarpaulin. The great Jules Léotard himself would have been impressed. Michael felt a great wave of relief engulf him.

"A makeshift safety net hastily stripped from the vegetable wagons, on Melville's instruction."

"Pheebs, what are you doing up here?" demanded Michael.

"Hooking you back with this," Phoebe showed the handle of her parasol. "And did you seriously expect me to miss the opportunity of getting involved in something as exciting as this?"

It transpired that the murmur of approval that Michael heard had been no reflection on his climbing to the top of the roof, no, it was more to do with Phoebe starting up the ladder behind him and the view her dress afforded to the assembled heroes below, who all just happened to be looking up at the time.

The return to solid ground was enormously welcome, as were the enthused pats on the back as Michael and Phoebe ran to where Connie sat, propped up against the back wall of the church, a constable fanning her face with a handful of cauliflower leaves.

"How is she?" called Michael.

"Impossible to determine," said Melville. "Best you see for yourself."

"Oh, my days..." said Phoebe, bending over Connie.

Michael's heart sank, "Pheebs, is she...?"

"Heavens no, Michael, quite alive," said Phoebe, turning to look up at him. "But... since when was Constance Dill... a boy?

Michael peered over Phoebe's shoulder. Most definitely, below the headscarf were the unmistakeable features of a teenage boy , dressed in the fatigues of a female Hanwell inmate . One, who they later learned, went by the name of Ned Dunnalump. Melville shook the lad firmly by the shoulder. "Where's Constance Dill, young man? Where is Constance Dill?"

"She said t'give this t'Magister," said Ned Dunnalump finally, in a weak, disinterested monotone. The lad repeated the sentence again and again as he felt inside the pocket of his pinafore and offered up a rolled sheet of paper. Melville prised the paper from the boy's fingers and unwound it like a miniature treasure map. It seemed like a list of names. No. An advertisement of some sort. Melville handed Michael the page saying, "You're mentioned again."

"Michael?" said Phoebe.

"It's a playbill," said Michael, sharing the quarto sheet with Phoebe. "For a Music Hall show. My first show. I appeared with all these people. There's me down there. There's Connie's name. She kept this playbill all this time?"

Despite being a decade old, the paper had weathered remarkably well, with the print clear and showing little sign of fading or browning. One could easily make out the billing:

117

SUN MUSIC HALL
KNIGHTSBRIDGE.

Director ... ... Mister C. DE CHASTELAINE

The "SUN'S" Brilliance known to all
ALFRED 'THE GREAT' VANCE
Lion Comique – as given before Nobility!
MISS VESTA TILLEY - Male Impersonator!
CONNIE LAMAL   - Mesmerising Hypnotist!

'STRONG-ARM' ARMSTRONG
Great 'Feets' – and Hands – of amazing strength!
ANNIE SAUNDERS - The Game Gal with the Golden
Gullet!
LEZ WARZO - Avian Antics A-Plenty!
FEK YU TU - Official Juggler to the Emperor of China!
MAGISTER,   THE   AMERICONJUROR   -
Prestidigitator from the Americas!

POPULAR PRICES.
Boxes, 10/6 and £1-1s Fauteuils, 2/- Stalls, 1/-
Balcony, 6d

Acting Manager . . . . Mister CHARLES MERRION
A. Carter, Printer, 226 Southwark Bridge Road, S.E.

"The Americonjuror?" said Phoebe with a quizzical smile.
"At the time I thought it was a word," countered Michael.
"This is more important," said Melville. "The writing upon the reverse."

Michael turned the page. There was a familiarity to the neat hand-script on the back of the playbill, happily this time not in blood, but lead pencil. There were twelve words, twelve words which would cast a grim shadow over the lives of the two magicians for the next two days.

"Do not try and stop me. They all brought Death on themselves!" said Michael quoting them aloud.

"Written in Connie Dill's hand?" said Phoebe.

"Without doubt," nodded Michael. "Okay*, 'Do not try and stop me. They all brought Death on themselves'.* Whatever it means it's not going to be good."

"I believe it to be a credible threat," said Melville, nodding.

"Oh my days, Michael," said Phoebe. "I rather think you're on a death list…"

9

Detective Inspector Gersham Skindrick skulked along the Edgware Road trying to look innocent, well, as innocent as any disagreeably pick axe-featured fellow could. He rattled each of the six pairs of double doors that fronted the Metropolitan Theatre of Steam, Smoke and Mirrors, but all remained stubbornly locked tight, even unyielding to the weight of his shoulder, but that was not unexpected. The abominable policeman pulled a scornful face as he ran his fingers over the scorched pits which had been blasted into the brickwork the previous night. He could not believe the stupidity of those two idiot gunmen. All they needed to do was saunter up to the Clarence and discharge their merciless weapons at The Prime Minister and the Leader of the House. They could have even blown great holes in the accursed Melville and the fool Sinclair. And those ridiculous disguises served no purpose, thought Skindrick. No honest to goodness assassin would dress himself up as a woman, or for that matter a baby? Not even a Frenchie.

Skindrick recalled with contempt how those two buffoons had somehow managed to lose an Aethyr generating pistol as they made their getaways. Somehow he conveniently ignored the fact that he himself was responsible for allowing the second pistol to wind up at the bottom of the Thames. The magicians must have nabbed the first pistol, he was convinced of it.

With his rage building, Skindrick cast a bitter eye over one of the beautiful colourful posters pasted on the wall, advertising the wonders of Magister the Industrial Age Magician and Phoebe the Queen of Steam and Goddess of the Aethyr. He ripped the blasphemy from the brickwork, tore the poster in half and cast it onto the pavement before quickly passing along the street and turning into White Lion Passage, the long narrow cut through leading to the Harrow Road, passing the yard and the theatre Stage Door, along the way. The Stage Door, Skindrick figured, might pay a dividend. It was less conspicuous back here and he could certainly take his time trying to force his way in.

Skindrick ran a finger up, around and down the edges of the door and its jamb. A very tight fit and oddly there was no outside handle to force, or any lock to pick. A shove, followed by a heavy shoulder barge served only to jar his neck. Inset within the door, about eye level, was a window of clear glass about nine inches square. Skindrick peered inside, but saw nothing, it was too dark. Suddenly a leering face appeared on the inside; hideous, deformed, monstrous and satanic. Skindrick recoiled with a start and all but fell backwards down the five stone steps to the yard.

"Police! Open your cursed door, y'hackit huddy!" Skindrick stormed, hammering his fist on the door, but his demands were met with insolent silence. He chanced another look in the window, then rapped it with his knuckles but the face from hell made no reappearance. "Police, I say, open up! I saw ye! Open in the Queen's name, damn you, you obnoxious creature!" screamed Skindrick, unused to such flagrant impertinence.

He pulled his truncheon from his jacket and took a mighty swing at the glass. The hardwood club struck it beautifully but instead of hearing the expected sound of shattering, Skindrick saw the truncheon bounce clean off the surface of the glass and spin out of his hand before feeling a numbing agony as the truncheon smacked him squarely on the nose.

With blood now dripping down onto his top lip like a scarlet moustache, Skindrick screamed, "I shall be back! Mark this well, I shall be back!" before turning and retracing his steps along White Lion Passage while holding a grubby handkerchief to his nose. Mercifully he did not hear Wicko's hearty laughter filling the Stage Door lobby, the click of his heels as he danced a jig, nor his shout of "I'll give you obnoxious creature!" while making gestures through the Stage Door window which suggested a lack of respect most unbecoming. Wicko pulled himself up to sit on the huge stage trunk which stood by the desk and then said aloud, "What's a hackit huddy?" I never had the heart to tell him.

"Oi, you coppers! Woss all dis? Lemme frew!" bellowed one Nicodemus Dunnalump, as he pushed aside the crowd of Covent Garden costers. "Dey reckons it's my boy as fell darn offa da roof. Dey reckons it's my Neb!"

"Stop right where you are," ordered Pym, fearlessly stopping the bullish progress of what turned out to be Dunnalump the Elder. Nicodemus was a bushy bearded, overbearing porter, the size of a cart horse, with one of those lovable Cockney punch-first-ask-questions-later dispositions. But Pym stood firm and stared him down before gesturing at Dunnalump the Younger and saying, "You know this lad?"

"Dass my Neb. Is 'e orlright? An', 'ere, why's 'e all dressed up like a slag?" demanded Pere Dunnalump. You could tell where the boy got his eloquent charm from.

Pym gave way and allowed the father to accompany his son to the waiting Ambulance before reporting to Melville, Michael and Phoebe. "Seems the scally up on the roof works here, guv'nor, goes by the name of Nebuchadnezzar Dunnalump. Aged twelve and a resident of Poplar. Worked on the market these last two years. He's restored to his senses well enough to claim he has never heard of anyone called Constance Dill, though he has a vague memory of talking with a strange looking woman, before enduring a blinding headache."

"Being of similar height and size, Dill no doubt happened upon the boy with a view to exchanging clothing and then set him up on the roof to deliver this threat." Melville quickly hatched a plan. "Mister Magister, you can provide a list of addresses for all these performers under threat?" He tapped the playbill as if to emphasise the precise performers to whom he was referring.

". Okay. Alfie Vance is dead. I know Tilley's in France, but all the others live within half a dozen miles of here."

"Then you will kindly furnish Detective Inspector Pym with that information. If they are to be the intended victims of

Constance Dill, they also offer our greatest opportunity to affect her recapture."

"But why warn us? And better yet who'd want us dead? That show was ten years ago. And it was never *that* bad," said Michael. "In the light of her escape, we discount anything Constance Dill now does or says at our peril. That is to say, your peril," said Melville, coldly.

As soon as Michael had dictated the addresses and while Pym had dispatched officers with instruction to post police guards outside the properties, Melville told the magicians that their assistance thus far had proved remarkably invaluable, but now their task was complete.

"And that's it?" protested Phoebe.

"Your obligations have been entirely fulfilled," said the head of Special Branch firmly. "And now, Mister Magister, with this threat to your life you will return to wherever you feel most secure. Detective Inspector Pym will arrange a police escort."

"But...!" was all Phoebe could say before Michael cut in.

"No. That's fine. I get it. I'm in danger, we're going home. And, Mister M, you can stand down any of your highly trained, fully armed men who might guard me. I've got Phoebe."

"We shall nevertheless position surveillance officers at your theatre. Expedience is imperative. Until later I bid you good day." And with that, Melville tipped his bowler and walked briskly away with Pym in his wake.

"Michael. ?" from Phoebe's tone he knew that she knew he was plotting something.

"I'll tell you on the way." Michael wrapped his arm around Phoebe's shoulder as they made their way back to the Steamo, where Mister Garrideb, the mechanical man, was impassively braving an onslaught of ill-tempered abuse from porters who, having brushed against the vehicle, had received painful electric shocks for their trouble.

"I take it we're not returning to the theatre?" said Phoebe.

Michael shook his head. "Connie warned me we were all going to die. It's up to me to warn everyone else."

10

From his office on the third floor in the Scotland Yard building, Detective Inspector Skindrick held the earpiece of the candlestick telephone close to his ear and waited, as the external connection he requested was still being plugged through. Having somehow failed to retrieve the missing weapon from the Metropolitan Theatre, with nothing but sore knuckles, a bruised shoulder and a bloody nose to show for his efforts, Skindrick finally felt his fortunes had taken a turn for the better. He had just received a telephone call from an old colleague, one from his Sergeant's days back in V division at Wandsworth, a bobby by the name of Bevis Gint. Former Police Constable Gint had been required to hand in his notice under something of a cloud following the un-godly midnight incident in the camel house of London Zoo, witnessed by a now dead reporter from the *Daily Sketch*, involving senior law enforcement colleagues. To ensure Gint's continued loyalty and indeed silence, Skindrick had arranged for his man to secure a new, cushy sinecure as a Gatehouse Warder up at Hanwell's London County Asylum.

Not five minutes ago the same Bevis Gint had told Skindrick of Superintendent Melville's peculiar interest in the escape of an asylum inmate."

"A proper puzzlement it is this Constance Dill escape, causing a fair load of angst in certain quarters, boss, and no mistake. Melville, Pym and a pair of conjurors off the stage, a dandy man named Magister and a fair good looking piece of a girl," Gint had said.

Skindrick's ears pricked up at the news and, now, three minutes after thanking his old colleague, Skindrick was engaged in another clandestine telephonic conversation.

"Speak," said the voice at the other end.

"Forgive the intrusion, Excellency," whispered Skindrick. "While I can report nae progress on the recovery of the weapon lost by those two incompetents, I do bring news of the detested Melville."

"Continue," rasped the voice of The Black Bishop.

Skindrick repeated everything Bevis Gint had reported concerning the recent drama over at the Hanwell Asylum and how Special Branch had conscripted the help of those two blasphemous illusionists.

"Ma informant tells me this Dill woman had been incarcerated for the best part of a decade, she has," Skindrick continued. "Then last night she suddenly just upped and escaped, leaving not a single clue as to how or why. Strange under normal circumstances, you'll agree, Blessed Excellency, but having consulted the files, the lunatic Constance Dill is said to possess great hypnotic power, the like of which has never been known before."

"Great these powers must be to warrant Melville's attention." The Black Bishop paused to analyse this intriguing new development, a pause during which Skindrick glanced anxiously about him like a robin on a lawn, watching for any lurking predator. Then, The Black Bishop deigned to speak once again: "The time and attention Melville is devoting to this woman suggests only one thing. Dill's satanic ability is of such significance he fears her freedom shall result in her falling in with those who will be at odds with his precious National Security. Falling in with people like us. Skindrick, you shall place all schemes to recover the weapon to one side. Focus your attention on the appropriation of this hypnotist. We will test her deviltry. If not found wanting she will prove to be a more powerful weapon than a Pulsatronic pistol ever could be. You will confound Melville, I care not how, find Constance Dill – and bring her to me."

"As you command, Excellency."

***

"I figure we've got at least a ten minute start on Melville's men," said Michael as he fired up the Steamotivator, engaged the gearing and yanked on various levers to get the vehicle underway. "So now, let's think this through. The Sun Music Hall headliner was Alfred Vance and he's dead. Vesta Tilley's out of the country. Of everyone that's left, how about we start with Sid? He's closest to where we are now."

"'Sid'?" puzzled Phoebe.

"The juggler."

"Sid? But he is billed as 'The Official Juggler to the Emperor of China himself, a Mister Fek Yu Tu," said Phoebe, from memory.

"The closest Fek Yu Tu got to China was the tea service Tilley bought him. He's originally from Watford and his real name is Sid Picket!"

Michael steered the Steamo past the offices of the George Newnes' *Strand Magazine*, then swung her left into the Strand itself, while wrestling to avoid all manner of horse-drawn traffic, none of which seemed to have any predisposition toward courtesy, much less a sense of direction.

"Michael, this is a cast you haven't worked with in a decade, but you still know where they all live?" said Phoebe, holding on to the edge of her seat as Michael suddenly veered left to avoid the chock full horse drawn omnibus advertising Nestlé's Milk and Bovril.

"These performers were my first family, Pheebs. Years later as they retired, the Professor fixed them all up with lodgings. As a thank you. And he still pays their rent."

Without wishing to sound too conceited, but what the hell, it was quite true. I have a philanthropic side which I try to keep secret, but often fail so to do. You see all these so called stars of the Music Hall live such peripatetic lives, always moving from one town to the next, from one theatre to another, year upon year and never setting down roots. Music Hall performers truly are of no fixed abode. So when the time comes, as it inevitably must, and they retire from the stage, or as more often happens the stage retires them, many find themselves penniless and very quickly out on the streets. Michael and I cannot help them all, but we do what we can for those with whom we have worked in the past, especially those who had been so welcoming when Michael first came to England. Whoever thought I would be associated with philanthropy...

The Steamo chugged past the arched façade of Somerset House over there on the right, then just before St. Mary Le Strand, the second of those two churches built so ridiculously in the centre of such a busy thoroughfare , Michael swung her left into Drury Court, drawing the vehicle to a steaming halt in the wider end up by Drury Lane. From there the magicians walked quickly back on themselves down to Wych Street. This was a dark, narrow turning little wider than a lane, flanked on either side by buildings four and five storeys tall. Some of the wooden properties survived the Great Fire, and it was they which stooped forward as if to scowl upon any newcomers passing below, while being supported by the more modern buildings either side. Residential premises in Wych Street were more than outnumbered by degenerate public houses and disreputable bookshops, but despite its rough reputation, the pedestrian paving and street cobbles appeared remarkably spruce and clean.

"Pardon me," said a fellow stepping out of their path and onto the street, his cap turned down over his eyes, having no doubt just purchased a copy of the lewd 'Nunnery Tales: Cruising Under False Colours, A Tale of Love and Lust' by T.N.R., and trying to conceal it beneath his overcoat. Not that I knew anything about that kind of lascivious literature, you understand.

"If they moved quickly, the Special Branch may already have men posted at Sidney's home," said Phoebe.

"But Sid won't be at home. Every morning he comes here..." said Michael, pointing at a three storey flat-roofed building.

The cream bricked Olympic Theatre, at the corner of Wych Street and Newcastle Street stood out as the only bright modern landmark in the area. The words 'The Royal Olympic Theatre' were beautifully carved in capitals upon the stonework above the front entrance, although, like The Met, quite when, or indeed if, the Queen, the Prince of Wales or any minor regal ever patronised the theatre was given to some ambiguity. Certainly playhouses had occupied this site for more than a century, but this, the third incarnation, designed by Billy Sprague and Bertie Crewe a decade ago, had quickly spiralled into terminal decline.

"Sid appeared here when the place was The Olympic Theatre of Varieties," explained Michael as they approached the Stage Door. "Said it was the finest theatre he ever played."

"I know this theatre. The final season here was a series of Shakespearean tragedies," said Phoebe.

"No wonder the place folded."

"Yes, I'm rather certain it was here I saw Henry Irving's *Coriolanus*."

"That's Roman togas for you."

But Michael's glib quip was rewarded with a blow to the shoulder from Phoebe's parasol. The Stage Door of the Olympic was to be found around the corner in Newcastle Street. Unlocked, it was an easy open to anyone who gave it a forceful shove. Immediately the daylight streamed in revealing a damp brick walled lobby and the broken window of the Stage Door Keeper's booth. Michael eased the door back into the jamb and led Phoebe along the dark corridor, then down a flight of half a dozen stairs. You know, it was tragic this three-thousand seater was dark, because the Olympic had greater potential than The Met, with many more dressing rooms and huge spacious wings. Who was it said a theatre devoid of an audience has no purpose? Probably me.

"At this time of the morning you'll always find Sid here, on the stage all by himself, practicing his juggling," said Michael. "He believes Fek Yu Tu still has a place in show business. And he's right, it was a terrific act. Set in a Chinese laundry, Sid would juggle wicker washing baskets, then for no reason anyone could figure in a Chinese laundry he then juggled plates, chairs and his big finish was cranking down the lights and juggling half a dozen flaming torches. All while dressed as a Chinaman in long silk gown, eye make-up and long, thin moustache."

Michael shoved open the Pass Door to the prompt side wing, a massive space, dark, yes, but not dusty, or littered with the discarded detritus one might expect in a dying theatre. No lengths of wood, coils of frayed rope, torn canvas scenery or the odd discarded Yorick skull.

"Sid keeps the place tidy," Michael nodded in appreciation. The old-timers all shared this kind of spiritual respect for the theatre. The building itself was their church and the stage its altar.

"Michael, what's that?" Phoebe, wrinkled her nose at the distinct whiff in the air. Not of a wood fire or a burn-up of rubbish, more a hog roast.

"Sid. He dips the tips of his juggling torches in a bucket of whale oil before setting them on fire."

"Michael, I'm not terribly sure that is whale oil…"

"Sid? Sidney? It's Michael Magister! Permission to step onto your stage, sir!"

The vast half lit stage was fully enclosed by the 'fourth wall' iron curtain, which had been last rung down a twelve month ago.

"Sidney? You there? Sid? It's Magister. !"

Then they saw it.

"Sid…" whispered Michael, struggling to comprehend the sight.

"Oh, my days!" gasped Phoebe, her hand covering her mouth.

They expected a fellow of a certain age standing on stage diligently exercising his hand-to-eye co-ordination by skilfully keeping six flaming torches aloft. Instead, there lay a crumpled, black, smouldering mass, tinged with glowing red, like a boar left too long on the spit. The shock came in waves as they slowly understood. The closer they dared draw, the more the mass began to take on the awful, recognisable shape. A charred human being. Grey, sweet-smelling smoke gently wafted about the corpse like a gossamer death shroud. Even the wooden stage was scorched in the form of a grisly shadow. The shadow of a man who once was.

"Dear God! Sid…" gulped Michael. "Pheebs, what – what happened here?

Phoebe, with a handkerchief held against her face to mask the stench, was already crouching beside the wood-slat bucket which lay upon its side next to the cooling, black pyre.

She touched the rim of the bucket and rubbed a dab of viscous yellow goo between thumb and forefinger of her ungloved hand.

"The bucket did contain oil, Michael, but it's now empty." Phoebe looked across at the untouched juggling torches. "It looks as if his torches were never soaked in oil this morning. Which rather suggests…"

"…That Sidney was. Pheebs, he was doused in oil and set alight…whispered Michael, looking around and then at the gridiron above. But hard as he looked Michael saw nothing to suggest a terrible accident had occurred. "Someone did this to him. This was deliberate."

"Michael, I do believe it has started," said Phoebe quietly. "I think your friend Connie Dill has just claimed her first victim."

Michael's head was racing. It was a maelstrom of bewilderment and anger and conflict.

Phoebe broke the silence. "We should call for a policeman,"

"No!" Michael was suddenly firm and urgent. "They'll find Sid soon enough. I have to warn the living."

"Connie's remaining victims? But how can we know who she will go for next?"

"She'll start at the bottom of the bill and work up to the top. It's theatrical. And it's what I'd do. Build to the big finish. Wait, that doesn't tick. I was bottom of the bill, I should have been first to die."

"Unless Connie planned for you to perish on the roof of the church?" Phoebe's cold logic endorsed Michael's fanciful theory. "She laid the trap with the hypnotised boy. Yes, we know the trap failed but that's irrelevant. And while you were occupied in Covent Garden, Connie was already making her move here on Sid Picket. No, I believe you're right. She is beginning at the bottom and working her way up."

"After Sid Pickett, next on the bill was Lez?"

"Yes, Lez Warzo," said Phoebe, nodding as she quickly visualised the death list, the Sun Music Hall playbill. "Avian antics."

Michael looked at Phoebe, his eyes were wide, his mouth dry. "Pheebs, I can't ask you to involve yourself in this. Not anymore. It's getting too horrible and it's nothing to do with you. Get yourself a cab and go back."

"And what are you going to do?" said Phoebe, with a glare.

"Whatever I can to warn Lez," said Michael. "He lives across the other side of the river on Roupell Street. Twenty minutes away."

"Then you had better let me drive," said Phoebe, turning and heading for the exit. "I can do it in ten!"

11

Phoebe gunned the Steamo south across Waterloo Bridge and careened her left into Exton Street. Horses reared and pedestrians scattered as the solid, brutal image of the vehicle motored at double the fourteen miles an hour speed limit. The liberalising Locomotives on Highways Act which had made the statute book three years earlier, abolished the legal requirement that self-propelled vehicles be preceded by a man with a Red Flag. Which was fortunate, because Phoebe's flag-bearer would have been flattened in the first ten yards.

"'Lez Warzo – Avian Antics A-plenty'. An ornithological performance I'm thinking," said Phoebe, heaving on the steering wheel and levering more power from the condensers.

"All that stuff," said Michael with his eyes firmly shut and his fists white from holding onto the grip bar while the Steamo slew and swayed. "Trained parrots, red kites, pigeons. Lez cared for them so well and they loved him. Lez Warzo, real name Leslie Warner. Lez taught these birds to talk, perform tricks, swoop high and low over the crowd. One of the great animal acts of the Music Hall. And anyone who jeered was guaranteed an eyeful."

A spit from Waterloo Railway Station stands a side street flanked with small, uniform two-storey 1820s terraced cottages, built of London brick by John Palmer Roupell, specifically for artisan workers. Each of the eighty or so two-up-two-down dwellings comprised a six panel wooden front door set below a glass fanlight, a parlour window beside the front door and two bedroom windows set above. Pitched roofs zigzagged along the length of the street. Everything about Roupell Street – yes, Mister Roupell named it after himself, appears balanced, ordered, beautiful.

"What number Roupell Street?" shouted Phoebe.

"The blue door. Just here. On the right!"

With the Steamo not so much parked, as abandoned, Michael and Phoebe were running across the street when they both blinked in shock as a uniformed Police Constable staggered out of Lez's house, holding his mouth and retching. The bobby slammed the door closed behind him, then bent forward and retched some more. "Hey! What's happening?" demanded Michael. "I know the man who lives here – what's happening?"

The officer shook his hand as he bent forward to suggest his inability to speak. "Pull yourself together, Constable! For goodness sake! What is happening?" insisted Phoebe.

"More as like what's happened," gasped the copper, wiping his clammy face with a ragged handkerchief. "He's dead meat. Dead as likes I've never seen before in me life. It's them birds. In the 'owse. They've all just went for him. All at once. Beaks, claws, pecking and gouging. It's a sight as fit for no man let alone a lady, miss. We got word at the station to stand by the 'owse, but I got here too late to help him. Poor devil . I got here too late! I best go – whistle up for some 'elp. Don't go near the 'owse now, neither of ya, hear me? It's too awful by half!"

And with that the policeman staggered off in the direction of Waterloo Station, fumbling for his whistle with a violently shaking hand. Michael tried the front door but the idiot bobby had latched it shut. He rapped the door knocker frantically shouting Lez's name. Without awaiting a response Michael pushed open the vertical letter box set within the door to peer through. Immediately from within, a flurry of feathers and a vicious beak launched itself at the opening. Michael recoiled letting the brass flap spring back, just as Phoebe peered in through the front window, rubbing the grime from one of the small Georgian panes with a lace handkerchief.

"Pheebs! Don't get near that window," called Michael, fearing what new horror would greet them. His dread was not unfounded. It was a sight grisly beyond belief. Within the front sitting room Lez Warzo, or what was left of him as vaguely recognisable, was sitting by the fireplace in a carved mahogany spoon backed armchair. His blood speckled shirt, waistcoat and trousers hung from his body in shreds. But it was his face. His face was a scarlet death mask of gored flesh, dripping down onto his collarless shirt and waistcoat. And instead of Lez's lovely sparkling blue eyes, you know, there were two hideous black gaping holes.

"Oh, my days. The poor man!" gasped Phoebe. Then SLAM! SLAM! SLAM!

Phoebe jumped back as a blur of bloodied beaks and feathers tried to smash their way through the window panels to attack. "Go for the eyeballs! Go for the eyeballs!" she heard an enraged parrot screech from the other side of the glass. Immediately he was joined by a score or more of his feathered friends, until they became a single, feral flock. Doves, parakeets and love birds with little regard to living up to their reputation, flew with crazed fury headlong at the panes, determined to break through. Some flopped to the window ledge dazed or even dead. Others maintained the attack regardless. The pounding against the window sounded like the lash of rain during a cloud burst. Suddenly a crack splintered up through the centre pane. "Go for the eyeballs! Go for the eyeballs!" jibed the parrot with renewed vigour.

"Pheebs, get back! They're breaking though!" Instinctively protecting the two most precious things in his life, with one hand Michael covered his own face and with the other he pulled Phoebe back from the window. Just as the glass shattered outwards, Phoebe managed to press her parasol, trigger the release and with a smooth 'ZEEOP!' sound the spokes lifted and ballooned the entire grey canopy into shape. Michael and Phoebe backed away behind this improvised metallised shield, struggling to hold the shaft steady as a thundering maelstrom of what seemed to be scores of birds squawked and squeezed their way through the small aperture. Some larger breeds had their breasts slashed open by the jagged edges of broken glass, while others who broke through smashed headlong into the parasol. Those which survived, barely a dozen in fact, took to the wing and flew aloft to freedom. The entire terrifying experience was over as quickly as it had begun. Michael peered from behind the parasol to see the broken window panes edged in dripping red, with beautiful feathers of yellow, blue and green now floating serenely to the floor, as if to try and cover the foul mess of avian carnage that lay quivering on the pavement.

Despite the attending Constable's finest intentions and his distant whistle blowing, his search for reinforcements was proving decidedly fruitless because there was still neither sight nor sound of any other policemen rushing to help. Perhaps it was tea break over at M Division's Southwark Police Station, but whatever the delay, Phoebe was in no mood to become entangled within their official nonsense. Lez Warzo was dead, killed by his birds and no end of form-filling could change the fact. Michael was also keen to avoid any time-wasting explanations. With two of his oldest show business chums slain in the most dramatic, appalling circumstances he was determined to do his darnedest to prevent a third.

With Michael back behind the wheel, the Steamo raced eastwards along Stamford Street, past the Skin Hospital then slewed north across Blackfriars Bridge and continuing on to New Bridge Street, right into Ludgate Hill and only drawing to a halt, at the foot of the grand stairway leading up to the entrance of St. Paul's Cathedral. The effect of such horror on the two magicians was numbing, impossible to fully grasp. Every evening on stage Michael and Phoebe involved themselves with all manner of shocking instruments of torture, but none of that was real. It was controlled and contrived. This most certainly was not.

"Dammit, Pheebs, I still can't believe Connie would do this!" said Michael, banging the steering wheel with the heel of his hand. "It's just not like her!"

"Michael, ten years' incarceration must have a detrimental effect. You have no idea what she's like now. And again, we must consider the facts. Connie warned that you all brought death to yourselves, and so far this morning two of you have."

"I'm dumbfounded, Pheebs. It's like she's using our own acts as a murder weapon."

"Oh my days, Michael," said Phoebe, with a dawning realisation. "You are absolutely right!"

"I know. Just tell me how exactly?"

"That's precisely what she's doing. Sid Pickett or Fek Yu Tu, he juggled blazing torches on stage and died by incineration. Les Warner or Lez Warzo presented a performing bird act and died when his flock turned against him."

"But Sid was hefty," interjected Michael. "He would never have let Connie douse him in oil and set him on fire. And she could never lift that wooden bucket."

"She *could* if she hypnotised him to lift the bucket himself!" yelled Phoebe, inspired, although, her confidence immediately ebbed once she spotted the hole in her theory. "Although it doesn't explain the birds attacking Lez..."

"Tame birds turning wild? Easy. She 'fluenced the birds," Michael was running the idea in his head. It was entirely possible. After all, cobras are charmed by the vibrations made by the charmer's pipe.

"You can hypnotise birds?"

"Pheebs, Connie could hypnotise anything with a pulse. Man, woman, dog. You can't imagine her talent, or her power," said Michael, while the penny dropped for sure. "Remember the parrot screaming 'Go for the eyes'? That's not going to get an audience on your side, and it's not the kind of thing Lez would teach one of his birds."

It became clear that by staging the elaborate Covent Garden up-on-the-church-roof shenanigans, Connie Dill had bought herself more than ample time to cab it across to the Olympic, hypnotise Sid into committing suicide, then skedaddle down to Roupell Street to enrage the birds' and polish off Lez.

"I have to admit there is a macabre symbolic elegance to being murdered by the substance of one's own stage performance," Phoebe nodded.

"Makes Jack the Ripper look like a serial killing nobody."

"Michael, hardly. But according to the playbill the next victim ought to be 'Annie Saunders, The Game Gal with the Golden Gullet'."

"Annie's next?"

Phoebe nodded. "That's if we're now assuming that Connie is working her murderous way up through the billing."

"If Annie's next that's not so good." Michael's face became stern. He yanked on various levers and twisted a stopcock to get the Steamo rolling again. "Pheebs, best you take the wheel again. Get us to Cephas Street as fast as you can – head out east, toward Stepney!"

"But what dreadful demise could Connie inflict on a singer?" said Phoebe sliding along the seat while Michael clambered over her.

"Pheebs, Annie Saunders wasn't a singer."

"Not The Game Gal with the Golden Gullet?"

"No. She was a sword swallower."

12

Sir Cumberland Sinclair had taken the somewhat unusual, not to say audacious, step of summoning Superintendent Melville to a meeting in his very fancy office atop one of the towers of Scotland Yard. Well, no, because it was Sir Cumberland, it was not so much a summoning as an invitation upstairs for a bit of a chat, if Melville possibly had the time. Word had reached the Assistant Commissioner, about the church-top shenanigans in Covent Garden earlier that morning. Obviously, given Melville's involvement, some aspect of national security would appear to be involved and Sir Cumberland wondered if he could provide Special Branch with any assistance? Resources at his disposal? That sort of thing? At all?

Melville saw no profit in evasion and apprised Sir Cumberland of a bare bones résumé, claiming Constance Dill was a dangerous mental patient who escaped with murder in mind. Already one report had landed upon Melville's desk concerning the strange death of a Mister Lez Warzo, Evidently, Sid Picket's inflammable demise had yet to be discovered. Melville explained how, if the death toll were to rise and Constance Dill remained at large, avoiding a firestorm of "Female Ripper At Large! Police Baffled – Again" headlines would be helpful. Melville carefully avoided any reference to Connie's prodigious hypnotic skill.

"Heavens. You're quite correct there, our Melville," said Sir Cumberland. "That must be carefully avoided."

The Superintendent then thanked Sir Cumberland most profusely for his inspired offer of support and yes, with the weight of the entire Metropolitan Police Force behind him, the job of recapturing Constance Dill would certainly be made easier. Sir Cumberland grinned and rubbed his hands together in self-congratulation. Not only had he been the one who suggested Special Branch take on Detective Inspector Skindrick, he had also just made another dashed good suggestion concerning a serial killer and extra manpower.

How wonderful. Melville excused himself and left to deal with more pressing matters.

***

"Duhling, no. Dear old Connie escaping from that asylum doesn't surprise me one iota," said Annie Saunders, The Game Gal With The Golden Gullet, very much alive and pouring good strong tea from a white, bone china rose patterned teapot into two delicate matching cups. Phoebe knew an iota was a quaint word for a very small quantity. Of course, I know it as the ninth letter of the Greek alphabet, but Michael had not the slightest idea of what an iota was, only that it sounded like an exaggerated overuse of vowels.

"But Sidney setting himself ablaze like that, and then poor Lez. I mean, you could understand it if he had been unkind to those birds but he cherished those creatures and they loved him. I always told him, duhling, you've got the perfect Music Hall act. When one of your birds dies, at least it's a hot meal on the table. Nice pigeon pie. Bit of braised parakeet. Help yourselves to a teacake."

"Do you believe Connie Dill could use hypnosis as a weapon?" asked Phoebe.

"Not for one minute, duhling. But then that was our old Connie. Who knows what's she's like now? Not having clapped eyes on her since she was arrested."

Michael and Phoebe were in Annie's front parlour in Cephas Street East London. A relatively new housing development, north of the Mile End Road and the 1757 Anchor Brewery, not a stone's throw away, which gave out a strong whiff of hops when the wind blew in the right direction. You know, it was as much the Ripper's murderous trail, as the construction of London's dockland which had led to a rapid slum clearance and redevelopment of the East End.

Anyway, Annie's house was well situated, slap bang on the corner of Cephas Street and Edwin Street, just along from St. Peter's Church; built in 1838, grey with tall, thin imposing windows and designed by Edward Blore who worked on Buckingham Palace, if anyone's interested.

139

The parlour, bathed in sunlight from the large bay window which looked out onto the street, was dominated by one of those large marble fireplaces with a high mantelpiece. The grate was dressed with a brass companion set of brightly polished coal scuttle, tongs and poker, a focal point for the green velvet chaise and four easy chairs which stood around the square of rich red carpet. The house was more than spic and span, you know, it was the loving work of a home maker. Above the mantelpiece hung an oil portrait of Annie Saunders in her performance days, wearing a theatrically fashioned golden dress, which was low enough at the front to accentuate her figure and short enough to display her shapely legs. She had affected a pose where she was throwing her head dramatically backwards, holding a long sword aloft, mouth open, ready to swallow it down. It was painted, or possibly dashed off, by Walter Sickert, bless him, hardly one of his masterpieces of the Music Hall, but it told the story.

Annie was a beautiful woman then, and remained so now, with dark hair and long face, huge eyes and pouting lips. In fact, the years had done nothing to relieve her of that sensuous allure. Framed theatrical posters advertising productions from a bygone time in which she had performed were framed and hung about the walls, including that fast-becoming-notorious Sun Music Hall show. Yes, this was definitely the home of a show business professional, proud of her past but one who now seemed content to let it go. How so unlike most turns we know who, instead of giving up show business, desperately hang on, until it gives up them. And herein lies the tragedy, because save for the financially astute headliner, of which there were sadly few, the prospects for any old Music Hall performer were decidedly grim, comprising only of bitterness, drink and destitution. And on that cheery note, let me move on.

"After the morning we've had, I can't say what a relief it was to see you alive," said Michael. Only now while sitting in the comfort of Annie Saunders' easy chairs were he and Phoebe finding their heart rates at least slowing to a less alarming level and their complexions returning to something resembling normal pallor.

"And a great comfort to discover that the police had *finally* dispatched a man to stand at your door," added Phoebe.

When Michael and Phoebe had arrived at Annie's home, they were immediately intrigued by a nondescript fellow in a cloth cap, baggy corduroy trousers, a ragged overcoat, smoking a pipe and for all the world looking like he was an indolent worker from St. Katherine's Dock. It was only when they tried to walk up the three stone steps leading to the front of door of number thirty-two did the supposed itinerate became alert and challenged them.

"You two. What's your business here?" the man had said.

"And what makes our business your business, if indeed it is business we're conducting in the first place?" asked Michael.

"This does!" The man produced a fold of cardboard which he held directly in front of Michael face. A Metropolitan Police warrant card. Until recently, you know, a policeman's identification could only be officially confirmed by the decorations on his truncheon. His authority could only be officially confirmed, of course, when he struck you about the head with his decorated length of Lignum vitae.

"It certainly does, detective, keep up the good work!"

"Stop! State your business here," the policeman had insisted, standing between Michael and Phoebe and Annie's front door.

"Us? Pheebs and I, me and Pheebs, we're friends of Annie's," Michael had told the copper. "Well, I'm a friend, Phoebe's never met her before in her life, but Annie and I, we go a-ways back. My name is Michael Magister, by the way, Magister the Magician, currently appearing at the Metropolitan Theatre of Steam, Smoke and Mirrors, Edgware Road. But then, no doubt Mister M has mentioned me." Michael proffered to shake hands, but Melville's man had declined. "You'll find Annie and I have been in the same shows, we toured together. You might even know we figure on the same death list, that's how close we are."

"No visitors allowed at this house. No matter who you might be."

"Whom. It's actually whom you might be," corrected Phoebe. "But it's of no matter – Michael just needs to see Annie, so if you'll very kindly excuse us…"

"I've told you both once. Now you move along as I say, girl, and don't be causing a set to!" said the plain clothes man, not ideally.

"Girl?!" Phoebe had spat the offending word with indignation before turning to Michael. "Did he just call me 'girl'?"

"Michael Magister! My lovely duhling!"

Mercifully, a familiar voice had defused the building tension. A voice belonging to a woman who had opened the front door and was now running down the steps, flinging her arms around Michael's shoulders and kissing him full on the lips with a passion which the policeman and Phoebe both took to be an indicator of some previous intimacy. Annie Saunders, the Game Gal With The Golden Gullet. She was certainly Game, that was for sure. But all that was before the Darjeeling was brewed and the teacakes buttered.

"Duhling, do you know of all the acts that toured in our little show ten years ago, it's only yourself and Tilley who are still in the business," said Annie, looking at Michael. In fact she'd hardly taken her eyes off him since they arrived. "As I said to Anthony only recently, Connie Dill, she was such a lovely duhling, but she was always just that tiny little bit odd. Not that I'm such a one to talk."

"Wait. Annie, you said 'Anthony'?" said Michael. "What's 'Anthony'? A pet?"

Annie reached behind her to the sideboard, picked up the silver oval frame containing a sepia photograph and handed it proudly to Michael. "You might say that. Have a look and see for yourself."

In the picture, Annie was wearing a cream lace wedding gown, her veil thrown back to reveal her beautiful beaming face. She was linking arms with the man at her side, a small, bespectacled fellow with curly black hair, short sideburns, and odd-shaped nose, which was much like an eagle's beak having just flown headlong into a gnarled tree. He affected a slightly diffident look as he stood there in his Sunday best tweed suit with a carnation filling his lapel buttonhole.

"Who's this with you?" asked Michael, "An overcome fan? Can't say I'm keen on his eyes."

"Michael, Annie's dress is the clue," said Phoebe. "The former Miss Annie Saunders is now Missis Anthony. ?"

"Graveolens," said Annie.

Well, Michael nearly choked on his tea. "Wait. Tell me I've got none of that right. You're now actually married in a matrimonial way? And to someone called Graveolens?"

"Duhling, don't start. The time was right for me to settle down and so I wed Anthony. I know, after just six weeks but that's one of those dizzying whirlwind romances for you. He's caring, he's attentive and, do you want to know best of all?"

"I'm not really sure I do…" said Michael, frowning.

"He's nothing to do with the theatre. No interest in the business. He's completely 'legit', he's got a steady job, a proper job! He's a clerical assistant in the department of Births, Deaths and Marriages at Somerset House. He fair turned my head and I'm blissfully happy!" Annie beamed a smile of such genuine love it could only be true.

"That's all that matters. Congratulations, Annie," said Phoebe. "He's quite a catch in this day and age."

"I'm sorry, but two murders and a marriage in one morning is… it's a lot to deal with. And not that I was expecting one, but I'm guessing our wedding invitation was lost in the mail," said Michael.

"Anthony favoured a quiet ceremony at St. Peter's down the road. I know the reverend there. It was lovely, just me, Anthony and a couple of neighbours. And don't you be putting on that face, Michael Magister. I waited long and hard for you. And don't think I'm ungrateful to you and the Professor for where I live. But Anthony, he gives me things, not gifts or possessions, but things I've never had before. Like normality. Security. Everything a theatrical life can never give you, he provides."

Michael scowled at such awful prospects, "And he's living here? In your house?"

143

"Of course he is. But, duhling, just look at us both, now. You and me. Haven't we done well for ourselves? I have Anthony and you have the lovely, gorgeous Phoebe."

"Oh, no. We're not…" said Phoebe, shaking her head and pointing between herself and Michael.

"I understand, my duhling. Your association is purely professional and platonic." chuckled Annie.

"Yes, Annie, it really is," said Michael.

"Duhling, I can't understand why, what's the matter with you both?"

"I'm an idiot and she isn't!" said Michael.

After a long pause Annie nodded wisely. "That makes sense…"

***

Half an hour later found Michael and Phoebe, further refreshed with cups of hot tea and standing by the front door, blinking in the sunshine and bidding Annie a fond farewell. The undercover policeman was nonchalantly leaning in his usual spot, pretending to read *The London Illustrated News*.

"And take no chances, Missis Graveolens or whatever your unpronounceable name is now. Whenever you're here by yourself you open the door on nobody. Least of all any women who can mesmerise. You stay put until the police catch up with Connie," said Michael, kissing Annie on the cheek.

"I still can't believe this of her, ~~Magister,~~ I truly can't," said Annie, shaking her head.

"Who knows?" Michael's sigh implied his agreement. "Take care, Annie."

"Don't be concerning yourself, duhling," said Annie. "Lovely Connie won't do for me, bless her heart. Look out for yourself, Michael Magister. Don't forget, you're on the list as well." She waved, blew a kiss to Phoebe then closed the door.

"Stay sharp eyed, officer," whispered Michael as they passed the policeman. "She's one very special person."

"Right you are, sir," said the policeman, nonchalantly, barely looking up as to not break his cover.

"So what did you think to Annie?" Michael asked Phoebe as he escorted her to the waiting Steamo.

"Rather relieved to find her still alive. It's not what we've been used to this morning. And I was intrigued to discover she is still rather keen on you!" said Phoebe.

Michael smiled and shrugged. "Who can blame her? Ow! That hurt."

It was only when Michael and Phoebe were aboard and firing up the Steamo's condensers that Michael noticed it. That nag in the belly that said something wasn't quite right. Something he'd seen, maybe out of the corner of his eye. Whatever it was, something wasn't ringing true.

"Right there," said Michael pointing. "See, that's the kind of stuff I see and don't understand. Why is it in this part of East London, even the drunks and hobos can wear quality weatherproof footwear!" He was pointing across at a pair of black boots. Boots which were only just visible behind the front area wall of a house on the other side of the street.

"By and large – they don't," said Phoebe. Before Michael could utter another word, she had jumped down from the Steamo and hurried across to examine the boots and their well-heeled owner. Sitting with his head slumped forward and his back against a fence was the hobo. Whom she immediately recognised. Not a hobo at all, but the policeman disguised as an idling docker. The one who challenged them when they first arrived not half an hour ago. Phoebe turned to Michael and screamed "Michael! Annie! She's in danger!"

From the Steamo and from across the street, Michael and Phoebe looked straight at Annie's house just in time to see the man stepping inside and slamming the front door behind him.

13

In the back kitchen, Annie was washing up her tea service in the cream coloured butler sink. The door squeaked open. Annie slowly turned and saw the figure framed in the doorway. Surely it was the policeman from outside.

"Oh, you quite made me jump," she said, placing a hand on her chest for added effect. Then she jumped again, more so, when something long and cruel slid down from the figure's sleeve. The policeman was now holding a sword.

Michael had raced from the Steamo, his fist now hammering on the front door calling Annie's name to no avail. Then he shoulder charged the door but bounced back as it held firm.

"Let me pick the lock..." shouted Phoebe, suddenly at his side, her Picker-Nicker already in hand. A few calming breaths, then a few twiddles and twists with the Picker and the lock was released.

Phoebe pushed open the door with her boot and rushed into the passageway, shouting Annie's name. Michael was right behind her. The front parlour door was wide open, but the room empty. They ran down the hall to the back kitchen. The door was closed. Phoebe booted that door open but then she and Michael stopped dead in their tracks. At first, the sight before them was just too peculiar, too surreal... It looked like a strange gothic statue posed in a manner so extraordinary their minds could hardly process the image quickly enough. Annie was sitting on a pine wood wheel-backed kitchen chair facing them. Except that her head was snapped back as if she were staring at the ceiling. Her wide eyes betrayed that dreadful terror. Her mouth was gaped wide open and her right hand still grasped... what was that? Slowly the image began to make shocking, horrible sense. It must be the hilt of a sword, yes; there was the quillon, the tang, and the grip. Then they saw the tip of the blade. Emerging beneath the seat of the chair and dripping onto a spreading red puddle. Annie Saunders was dead, of the intruder, the murderer, Connie, there was no sign.

Save for the net curtain at the open kitchen window which fluttered in the wind.

~14~

Where was I when this dreadful carnage was occurring? Still at the Met Theatre to be precise, on stage and fiddling with the mechanism which drew the main curtains open and closed. At that time we used a pair of 'traveller curtains', you know those ones which slide horizontally across the stage from either side, to meet in the middle. It was a throwback to the previous theatre management and a little too redolent of those early days of traditional Music Hall for our taste – and far too slow! Wicko was high up a ladder, squeezing into spaces no other man could, giving me a technical assessment of the existing mechanism.

"It's a bit shit," he shouted. Succinct, but much as I anticipated. Despite his surly, work shy demeanour, you know, Wicko was a valued member of our operation. No, really he was.

As for the curtains themselves they were too plush, too velvet trimmed with gold tassels. They looked like the boudoir drapes of a dowager working as a mature, upmarket hooker. And I should know. I quite favoured installing a compressed steam powered piston-braking operation which could drop a metal sheet in an instant. In my mind it worked like this: Michael and Phoebe bade the crowd "Good night' and dropped down to the Dungeon. Then we have the giant green face back projection chat, the image that shatters, then SLAM! The curtain's down before anyone knows what's happened. How dramatic would that be? Of course, it wouldn't come without its intrinsic danger. I know of one magician in New York, at the inappropriately named Comedic Theatre, I believe, who took his bow just as the wire snapped on the Safety Curtain. The Iron dropped and sliced this magician's head clean off. Right there on stage in front of the crowd. They went wild , of course, convinced it was a sensational illusion. I'm told even the promoter clapped his hands and yelled "Wow! Keep that in!" before the grim reality dawned. Well, that's what I heard.

But anyways, the first I learned about Michael and Phoebe's morning from hell was when the red cue light on the wall of the prompt side wing flashed. I took the trap door platform down into the Dungeon, barely hearing Wicko complaining about being left up in the flies. I shuffled to my workbench where the make-up bulbs skirting the edge of the stage mirror also blinked off and on. It was rare for Michael to ever dare use what I call 'The Communicon'. Like all my notions, it was highly advanced and, you know, I preferred to keep these things out of public view until I believed the public was ready to cope with them.

Phoebe and Michael were sitting quietly opposite Mister Garrideb, within the passenger compartment of the Steamotivator. The vehicle was still laid up just along the street from Annie Saunders' house. Uniformed police constables, summoned immediately following the discovery of Annie's body, were now swarming everywhere, in and out of the house, mostly, one suspects, to take a gawp at the grisly sight and to be able to tell their grandchildren they were first on the scene at 'The Infamous Sword Down The Throat Murder'.

With the attention of the Met's finest from J Division at Bethnal Green focussed on the tragedy within, and one hoped on capturing the killer, Michael had pulled a small silver lever hinged onto one of the side panels inside the passenger cabin of the Steamo. With a gentle hiss, a door in the vehicle's deceptively deep roof space had slid open to allow a light brown, dirigible, oh, about the size and shape of a rugby ball, bound with hoops of thin copper to emerge and gently ease itself aloft. The hydrogen filled capsule was tethered to the Steamo by a flex which unwound as it rose, Montgolfier style, to a height of about sixty feet. The metal nose cone of the mini airship swung about, you know, in the way a compass needle is drawn to toward magnetic north, while at the rear, four fins of thin metallised fabric flexed and adjusted to maintain stability in the breeze. The nosecone perked and twitched, finally attracted to the receptor beacon, a device I had installed atop one of the minarets on the roof of The Metropolitan Theatre of Steam, Smoke and Mirrors.

This was pioneering technology constructed and modified to a degree by me; all of it brilliant, most of it stolen, but, as I must reiterate, not for commercial gain, only personal use. I examine other peoples' ideas and simply improve upon them. Like the Communicon. Despite dear Nik Tesla's passionate entreaties to embrace wireless communication in all her wondrous entirety, I ran a flex from the receiver in the minaret straight down through the theatre and into The Dungeon. The line then connected to a block of terminals, coils and switches and then snaked its way along and up into the side of what looked to be a rectangular, wood-framed performer's vanity mirror set on my desk. The mirror with its unforgiving illumination bulbs on either side was supported by two arms on which the mirror pivoted. The entire device was bolted to a box containing an assemblage of valves and capacitors, controlled by brown shellac turn-switches and all ventilated by a hole adorned with a brass scrim. Two aural speakers, the shape of elegant silver horns, stood either side of the screen. I suppose that is all I wish to divulge of the basic mechanics at the moment, but at least you get some idea of the visual beauty of what I called The Communicon.

The lights either side of the mirror flashed quicker still and then remained steadfastly lit. I clicked a switch to the 'On' position and tilted the mirror up to afford myself a better angle. Instead of my own chubby visage staring back at me from the now cream glowing glass, the face I saw was Michael's. The image was sepia and, of course, disrupted by the occasional crisp crackle of misdirected ionised static as you might imagine, but it was very much Michael. His lip movement tended to be half a second or so out of time with the sound of his voice as it emerged from the two speaker horns, but that was a hiccup of 'synchronisation', to use the ancient Greek word. The image also floated and rippled, much as it does when you're looking up at the face of the person who is holding you down and drowning you in the bath tub. All would be addressed in time.

Across London at the other end of the connection, Michael was staring into what looked like the fat lens end of a stubby telescope which emerged on a cantilevered arm from within the seat rest beside Mister Garrideb. Michael got straight to the point, something I appear to have singularly failed to do here. He summarised the dreadful events of the morning thus far: a catalogue of misery, mystery and death. Connie was certainly true to her cryptic threat, resulting in the shocking demise of our dear chums Sid, Lez and Annie.

"In which case," I shouted, "you must both heed Melville's advice and bring yourselves back here, and quickly so, lest Connie Dill adds the corpse of Michael Magister, to her tally..."

A sustained rapping on the glass window of the Steamo cruelly interrupted my words of wisdom mid flow. Apparently, it was Detective Inspector Walter Pym from Melville's Special Branch, and looking none too pleased by all accounts.

"Here, you two – out!" he called.

"We'd be on our way straight back to the theatre now, Prof," Michael shouted, "but I think Pym wants to yell at us."

"Is there anything I might do from this end?" I shouted.

"Yes there is, Artemus," Phoebe's beautiful face leant in to appear on my mirror-screen, "This may have an important bearing. If you have the chance to speak with Father O'Connor, kindly ask him to delve into dealings of a Friar Morten of St. Bernard's Convent. Apparently, this Friar Morten paid frequent visits to Connie at the Hanwell Asylum shortly before she absconded. It all seems rather iffy at best."

I agreed it did and only just managed to assure her that I would approach Connor before her image began to spit, splutter and then fade. While a two-way transmission could comfortably accommodate sound, The Communicon could only operate visually in one direction. I could see them, they couldn't see me, and probably just as well. I pride myself on my brain rather than my looks. Additionally, the stability problems of the dirigible in the variable breeze allowed for only limited communication time.

Once again, it seemed, I would be turning to my holy cohort, Father Connor O'Connor. Bless him. Three times last week Connor had come along to our magic shows to rail and rant about the sins of the flesh, the fires of hell and then write about it in the local rag. It's a rarity in show business to pay someone to denounce your production, but the subsequent boost to our box office proved it to be five pounds and a bottle of malt whisky very well spent. Connor was well known in the parish for his tireless evangelism, spreading The Word of The Lord, and at this time of the morning, I knew exactly where to find such an upstanding, God-fearing paragon of piety. In the pub.

15

"Arrested?" said Michael and Phoebe together.

This was now the second time in fifteen hours they had been paraded before Superintendent William Melville of the Special Branch, only on this occasion they were not standing in his makeshift office in Buckingham Palace . No, this time it was his real office. In Scotland Yard. And a very disappointing affair it was too; a wood panelled cell of a room. You know the kind. Dark, oppressive and smelling of polish, and enlivened only by colourful, detailed maps of Metropolitan police districts and major British ports. Melville sat behind his desk. In front of him lay three open dossiers, one for each of the Connie Dill murders, each containing scenes of crime diagrams and photographs of the victims, presumably filched from their homes. The files had been compiled with impressive speed.

"Indeed," said Melville, quietly. "Arrested."

"On what charge?" demanded Phoebe, with about as much indignation as, well, you might imagine, perhaps even more. Melville, of course, wore his mask of calm, unflappable control.

"On suspicion of murdering or being complicit in the death of Fek Yu Tu, thankfully also known as Sidney Picket, the death of Lez Warzo and the death of Annie Saunders."

"This is an outrage!" fumed Phoebe.

"It so often is…" sighed Melville, patiently.

"Okay. Here's what happened," said Michael. "Yes, we went to the Olympic to see Sid, and then to Lez's house and to Annie's, to tell them about Connie because they deserved to hear it from me. With Sid and Lez we were too late, and with Annie we were that close to saving her. Mister M, these were my friends. Why would I kill them? And if I wanted to, do you think Pheebs would let me? She puts up with a whole heap of stuff, but even she draws the line at my being a murder."

Melville was calm and easy as ever. "I do not think you were in any way involved in the murder of those poor unfortunates."

"You don't?" Michael affected that frankly baffled, frown look he always used when he was, well frankly, baffled.

"In which case," chipped in Phoebe, "this might be an odd question, no, under the circumstances I don't think it is odd! Why are we here?"

"I rely on my experience, knowledge, but also like Mister Magister, I trust my instinct, and to believe that you were responsible for the murders is ludicrous. However, the same opinion is not shared by certain other officers within my department."

"Skindrick," hissed Detective Inspector Pym.

"Detective Inspector Skindrick, is an unbending pragmatist, an officer with little time for the fanciful. The concept of the grey area is entirely unknown to him. All matters are either black or they are white. So, let us now examine the facts in stark black and white as he would view them. Currently with no other suspect in clear purview, and with witnesses describing you and your vehicle at all three murder scenes, what other conclusion might he draw? And I could not defend you."

"Put like that…" was the best Michael could offer. It was tough to fault the man's logic.

"Had Detective Inspector Pym not dragged you here on the pretence of arrest as he did, Skindrick would now have you both under lock and key in Newgate, I dare say, never to be heard of again. And, be assured Mister Magister and Miss Le Breton, I do not allow that to happen to my people. So, if you please, pray enlighten me regarding the events of this morning with clarity and brevity, which means Mister Magister you will please be silent while Miss Le Breton elucidates."

Phoebe tapped each of the three files on Melville's desk. "After we realised Sidney Picket had set fire to himself and discovered that Lez Warzo had been killed by his own birds, Michael suggested the victims were being murdered in the manner of their stage acts, and that Connie was using hypnosis as an instrument of murder. She had 'fluenced Sidney to douse himself with whale oil and strike a match, and Lez's birds were then hypnotised to attack and maim their keeper. It was a theory upon which I still poured considerable scorn. But when we witnessed poor Annie Saunders having just thrust that sword down her own throat, it became clear Michael's idea was borne out by fact. Constance Dill is using hypnotism, mesmerism, mind control, call it whatever you will as a weapon."

"I consider that modus operandi entirely conscionable," stated Melville.

"Good," said Michael. "If only I knew what that meant?"

Phoebe translated for him. "It means the Superintendent agrees. The hypnosis theory, mindful of Connie's ability, does make sense."

"It must be a British thing, this never speaking proper English…"

"That considerable power makes for all the more reason to apprehend Constance Dill with greater expediency," said Melville, looking at Pym.

"Mister M, permission to speak freely?" said Michael.

"I would prefer 'briefly'," said Melville.

"Connie's not the murderer."

Melville raised an eyebrow and repeated slowly: "Hypnosis is the murder weapon but Constance Dill is not the murderer? Explain."

"It's not Connie. It's not her modus whatever. Why after ten years does she suddenly up and decide to break out and start murdering her friends? For revenge? And, if so, revenge for what? We didn't toss her in the booby hatch. We all stood four-square behind her. And more important than anything else and this I believe, Mister M, you will see as the reason Connie's not the murderer. This is the clincher. Connie's too nice."

"Mister Magister," said Melville after a long pause, "I wonder if on this occasion, the acuity of intuition is clouded by your loyalty and affection. Mary Ann Cotton was said to be very nice. It did not prevent her from poisoning three of her husbands to defraud their life insurers…"

But before the head of Special Branch could continue, the telephone on his desk rang loud and shrill. He answered briskly, listened intently, thanked the caller politely, and then looked at Pym. The call had lasted a mere ten seconds but its impact was enormous.

"Thirty minutes ago," Melville said. "Alpheus Armstrong, also known by his stage name of 'Strong Arm' Armstrong, has been found dead at his home in Finchley. An iron bar wrapped around his neck in what appears to be an act of self-inflicted strangulation."

"Oh, no…" said Michael, shaking his head in despair. "Poor Alfie…"

"Again, the murderer overpowered our police guard with guile. Nothing or no one, not even yourselves, could have prevented these deaths," said Melville, considering the situation, stroking his moustache with the back of his hand in contemplation. "My decision stands. The arrest of Constance Dill is our first priority. While she remains at large - nobody is safe."

Michael placed his hands on Melville's desk to take his weight as he leant forward. The loss of four old colleagues in such short order and under such terrible circumstances had truly hit home.

"Detective Inspector Pym, could we possibly have a chair please?" said Phoebe placing her arm around Michael's shoulder.

"No, I'm okay," said Michael, battling with his emotions and straightening up.

Melville unfolded the playbill. "With Fek-Yu-Tu, Lez Warzo, Annie Saunders and now Strong-Arm Armstrong deceased, who remains alive in this company of performers?"

Pym had been doing his homework and flicked open his notebook. "As you said, sir, 'The Great Vance' had already passed away a full decade ago directly after a performance, in the presence of Mister Magister and everyone else on the Constance Dill death list." Pym looked to Michael and received a confirming nod. "And, it's quite true, Miss Vesta Tilley, according to my enquiries, she is mercifully out of the country, on business with her spouse, the impresario Mister Walter de Frece."

"Leaving one remaining performer in harm's way," said Melville, tapping the name, way down at the foot of the playbill.

"Michael," said Phoebe.

Melville stood, signalling the end of the interview. "Her true motive may be uncovered when she is apprehended. Until then, you will now both repair to your theatre and remain there until further notice. And try to avoid Constance Dill."

Once the magicians had expressed their profuse thanks and left, Melville looked at Pym. "They will, of course, do nothing of the sort."

Pym nodded. "And just in case they encounter Constance Dill, I take it, guv'nor , you want me to follow them?"

"If you would be so kind."

16

I had left Wicko busy doing nothing back at the theatre. Now, my face hidden beneath my wide brimmed felt hat and heavy frame shrouded in my long black opera cape, I shuffled across the Edgware Road, and, as anticipated, discovered Father Connor O'Connor in the public bar of 'The Green Man' ale house upon the corner of Bell Street. The patron-landlord of the establishment they all called 'Old Man Griffin'. Griffin because, well, that was his name, and 'Old Man' on account of his thinning strands of shrivelled hair, skin of a dried sheep's bladder and prominent sharp, brown snags for teeth. He was only thirty-two, but local legend said he was born with those features. One must only hope as a baby he was bottle fed.

As for my errant priest, he was to be found slumped against the counter blowing the foam off the top of his third pint of black porter. The appalling, dog-collared poltroon was trying to convince Mairead the barmaid, a long-lapsed Catholic, to re-embrace the ways of the Lord with sayings like, "Come back with me, you heathen hussy, I'll surely ram the fear of God into ye." But the fair Mairead, being a woman of some substance, regarded Father Connor O'Connor with an easy smile which implied that if he tried anything untoward she could throw him to the floor and crush the life right out of him with just one of her ample bosoms, in less than a minute.

"Is that foul excuse for humanity troubling you, fair maiden?" I enquired, as I leant on the bar and watched O'Connor quaff down a mighty gulp of his dark nectar.

"He troubles me not, kind sir," she said. Then leant forward, adding quietly. "Little does the old rascal know my vengeance for his foul talk is to piddle in his glass 'fore I draw his ale. Now, what can it be that I get you?"

"A purely medicinal port and brandy if you please," I said, with my thirst for beer suddenly gone. The expression "This beer tastes like cat's" I'd encountered many a-time before, but I'd never heard "This beer tastes like barmaid's".

The pub was empty for the hour, cool with a hefty aroma of yeast which was most welcome for it mercifully overpowered the odour emanating from the cassock of the Reverend Connor O'Connor. The last time Connor took a bath, John the Baptist was preaching on the banks of the Jordan. He was a true throwback to those days when villagers referred to their local priest as a 'smell smock'. So, anyway, sipping my medicinal, I shuffled alongside the repulsive holy man and slid a pound note along the counter in front of him.

"Thank you for that vocal intervention last night, Connor. Your righteous indignation always adds spice to the show. Same time next Wednesday?" Bribery, you know, oils the engine wheels of commerce like nothing else on earth.

"Professor Artemus More, you filthy spawn of Satan! I shan't be sitting in them bastard stalls at your theatre ever again, Christ alive, them heathen swine near clubbed me senseless, they did," complained the Bible-basher, pointing a gnarled index finger at the areas of grey-purple bruising atop his bald head. "So, re-pocket your blood money and this time we'll call my recompense a go with that wanton Phoebe-woman. Is there not even the remotest of chances? A creature more delicious I have never seen on the whole of God's bastard earth. And if it's religious instruction she craves, sure, I can offer a sermon on the mount. "

"Connor, I'll be level and straight with you now," I lied, "And not just because you're a respected man of the cloth. But dear sweet Phoebe is said to favour the other church."

"Jasus have mercy!" grumbled the presbyter before blessing himself furiously, then snatching up the pound note. "If she's a bastard Methodist then God's having a bastard merry jape and no mistake. So you can get back on your bastard way and leave me be. I'll have no more to do wid ya." He swallowed another mouthful of ale and wiped the foam from his stubble with the back of his veiny hand.

"I would if I could, my old grizzled Papist, but, you know, there's another smallish task I need you to perform on my behalf," I said this with total confidence, because I knew he would comply. "And, hear me out, Connor, because the recompense will not be financial. No. You see, the payment will be the use of a pair – of these."

From inside my cape I produced this cherry wood box, about kind of the size of a good cigar box, and hinged open the lid. Inside, resting upon a purple bed of velvet cloth were what looked to be a pair of brass rimmed goggles, where instead of lenses there were two single inch long adjustable telescopic tubes. That's right, it was Arthur Doyle's 'Goggle-Eyes'.

"Spectacles? By the bloody nails o' the cross, there's nothing wrong with my eyesight as I can't see the way of the Lord," sniffed the unimpressed catechist.

"That might be the case, old friend. But this device affords the wearer a better, clearer, unimpeded method of gazing upon a heavenly body," I said, offering him the frame. "Here. Go ahead. Try them."

Connor rested the Goggle-Eyes on the bony bridge of his broken nose and hooked the heavy shellac arms around his hairy, wax encrusted ears.

"Don't waste precious viewing time on anything other than the fair Mairead. Gaze upon her," I encouraged the devout pervert.

As recommended, Connor turned and pointed the Goggle-Eyes straight at the chest of the barmaid. Then his jaw dropped and his eyes near popped as he saw right through the thick fabrics of pinafore, blouse, vest, brassiere and now found himself gazing upon the unobstructed nakedness of her bosoms.

"Sweet Jasus, Mary and Joseph!" he whispered in awe and blessing himself. Then he tore the Goggles off, rubbed his eyes and quickly put them back on again. It was only after a minute's gawping did the Reverend Connor O'Connor begin snarling.

"This is despicable foulness at work," he claimed. "These be the result of the Godless labours of Beelzebub himself! A disgusting, repulsive affront to humanity is what this is! ... I'll keep them, mind. Just to ensure my pronouncements are well founded!"

It was then I offered the bargain. "For your help in a certain matter, these shocking instruments of the black arts are not only yours for the entire day, but they come with the blood promise of complete ownership of your own personal pair as soon as they are constructed."

As I spoke the pungent priest must have fiddled with the Google-Eyes zoom slider on one of the arms because he recoiled as an apparently now giant bosom reared up in his face. "But, of course I completely understand if you wish to remain steadfast to your holy oath to fight the devil's work."

"Never mind any of that bastard shite," said Connor, now wiping saliva from his stubble. "What do you want me to do?"

***

The inconvenience of Michael and Phoebe's detainment had been ameliorated in the knowledge that Melville appeared more supportive than they had first realised. And that Detective Inspector Skindrick would be an on-going problem. However, they had wasted the best part of an hour, and had been also forced to abandon the Steamotivator, which remained parked and guarded by Mister Garrideb back in Cephas Street. Thus when they emerged from Scotland Yard, Michael hailed a cab with every intention of riding back to Bethnal Green to reclaim the abandoned vehicle . By the way, the word 'cab' in the context of Mister Joseph Hansom's wildly successful passenger transportation vehicle, you know, is a truncation of the word 'cabriolet'. But that's by the by.

Their Hansom had lurched its way up Whitehall, skirted Trafalgar Square and was bypassing the reproduction of Queen Eleanor's original monument outside Charing Cross Railway Station, before Michael said, "Pheebs, while we're picking up the Steamo, I want to speak to this man." From within the gold silk lining of his frock coat he produced a sepia photograph.

Phoebe recognised immediately the loving couple in the image. "Michael, it's Annie Saunders and Anthony

Graveolens. Their wedding picture. You didn't lift this from the file on Melville's desk?"

"Distraction. Sleight of hand. Use it or lose it."

"That is quite appalling and very splendid. I'm rather presuming you wish to speak with Anthony Graveolens to extend your condolences at his tragic loss."

"No, I want to speak with him because he's the killer." Michael flicked a finger at Anthony's image as if his astonishing accusation needed an extra dimension of drama.

That Michael, an unmitigated coward when it came to any form of unnecessary risk, should have filched material from an unsolved murder file and from under the very nose of the head of the Special Branch, left Phoebe in no doubt he absolutely and unequivocally meant it. In fact, Phoebe, found herself so lost for words, all she could manage to say was something along the lines of: "What?!"

"Anthony Graveolens, the man in this photograph is our killer. Sid, Lez, Alfie, and Annie murdered by him. That's our man."

"Michael, you're suggesting Anthony murdered his own wife? And your reason for drawing this conclusion? Your evidence is?"

"Oh, it's a clincher."

After a dramatic pause which Phoebe could tolerate no longer, she snapped: "So, what is it?"

"I don't like his eyes."

"His *eyes*?" Phoebe was bemused. "Michael, that's your evidence? Connie Dill couldn't possibly commit murder because she's too nice, but Anthony Graveolens must be guilty because you don't like his eyes?"

"No, Pheebs, not *just* his eyes. There's something else, just as damning."

"Which is?"

"His name."

"His name?"

"His stupid, ridiculous name. I mean, Pheebs, come on. Anthony Graveolens? Who do you know who calls themselves

'Anthony Graveolens' – apart from Anthony Graveolens. That name just screams out murderer."

"Michael, you know I love you as much as I've ever loved anyone and I do owe you so very much, but can I suggest you wince in pain now, because once again, I'm about to beat you very firmly about the head with my parasol!"

"Pheebs, wait, at least look at his picture. See? Even you'll have to admit they're little beady shifty eyes. Guilty as sin eyes. I tell you, Pheebs, he's our murderer."

"Michael, why don't you just admit that you've taken against Anthony Graveolens because he married Annie! ," Phoebe handed Michael back the photograph, "You don't have to condemn the man as a serial killer because of his eyes in a photograph and he's got a funny name!"

"Which is why we need to meet him face to face. Along here at Somerset House. And look straight into his criminal eyes."

"Michael, I wonder if your usually astute instinct is shifting matters slightly out of kilter?"

"Not enough to know we're being followed," he said, grinning somewhat smugly.

The horse drawn chaos which always reduced east bound traffic along the Strand was, this lunch time, worse than ever, so just past the Tivoli Music Hall (postal address: "65–70 and a half, The Strand" – isn't that wonderful?) Michael tapped the roof of the Hansom and asked the driver to pull over anywhere on the left. While Michael paid the cabbie handsomely and asked him to trot forward and wait outside the Lyceum Theatre, Phoebe alighted, opened her compact mirror to adjust the rakish angle of her bowler hat fascinator while at the same time taking a surreptitious peep at all that was happening behind.

"Is he still with us?" asked Michael.

"My. Yes, he is," said Phoebe. She was looking at the reflection of Pym's cab pulling up and the Detective Inspector stepping out, keeping his back to them to avoid recognition, while at the same time failing miserably.

Following his service with the Royal Artillery, Walter Pym had been a Cannon Row policeman for six years, with an excellent arrest rate, before being singled out to join the Special Branch. "The man gets on with it quietly and efficiently," Melville had assured both the Commissioner of Police of the Metropolis, and the Prime Minister. Pym held back as he snuck a look to see Michael and Phoebe amble along the pavement. Quite the pair of London swells, he thought. Magister was resting his silver tipped walking cane upon his shoulder like it were a Browning rifle, but as for the luscious Phoebe, Pym could happily follow her all day and every day. Look at that sensuous walk.

"And look at that lucky blackguard now!" Pym heard himself say aloud as Phoebe slipped her arm in Michael's.

Then he saw the two magicians stop and have the decency to exchange polite pleasantries with a poor, bedraggled vagabond, most likely a true former rifleman judging by his battered, grimy green topcoat, who was squatting in the doorway of the Royal Adelphi Theatre. Phoebe pressed a couple of coins into the old soldier's hand and received a salute for her trouble. A few doors along Phoebe paused to satisfy some sudden curiosity in the world of postage stamps and gazed into the window of Mister Stanley Gibbons' emporium. Magister appeared not to share her philatelic fascination and strolled on. Phoebe then glanced vaguely behind her, causing Pym to duck inside a shop doorway somewhat smartish. By the time he felt it safe to chance popping his head out for a deft look, Phoebe had apparently also abandoned her interest in ha'penny reds with inverted watermarks, caught up with Michael and was now stepping with him into a bakery shop. From the busy lunch trade, it appeared the savouries, breads and pastries sold therein, proved popular with all sorts.

In fact, the rapid turnover of customers began to cause Detective Inspector Pym no little concern until, following a short interlude, Magister and Phoebe left the bakery, he holding a paper wrapped packet in one hand and his cane over his other shoulder with the other. The couple braved the traffic and crossed to the south side of the Strand. Pym crossed too, dodging between omnibuses and managing to keep his targets in sight. It was only when he finally reached the other side of the street that Pym knew he'd been clocked.

A steady stream of royal blue smoke began billowing from the top of Michael's cane, so much so that it formed a large wispy cloud, which thinned only when Phoebe tossed a handful of white sheets of paper into the air. The sheets looked to Pym, even from this distance, as if they might be five pound notes. It was when Phoebe called "Look! It's free money drifting out of the smoke!" followed by the enthused shouts of avaricious chancers nearby, he knew his suspicions were well founded.

The two magicians then appeared to have taken a swift right turn into the entrance drive of Richard D'Oyly Carte's palatial new Savoy Hotel. By the time Pym had fought and forced himself through the squabbling, money grabbing crowd and turned down into Savoy Place himself, he saw no sign of Michael Magister or Phoebe Le Breton. Nothing except carriages, and toffs and also a solitary vagabond, an old soldier, now in rolled up shirtsleeves, sitting on the kerb, hungrily tucking into a warm mutton and gravy pie. He was also holding a five pound note. And this it turned out *was* genuine.

Pym cursed his stupidity and surmised their method of escape, quite correctly as it happens:

In stopping to speak with the old soldier, Michael and Phoebe had explained their proposition. The veteran then followed them into the busy bakery. Once inside and out of sight, Magister swapped coats and hats with the old chap. Phoebe then escorted the newly attired down and out from the bakery. Viewed from behind, in a busy street, anyone wearing a top hat and frock coat in that style would believe it to be Magister, especially when most of their attention was drawn to Phoebe. Michael, now wearing the threadbare green coat of the Rifleman, remained inside the bakery until Pym had followed the decoy pair right across the street. Michael then quickly slipped up to the Lyceum and his waiting cab. Phoebe invited the real old Rifleman to press the correct button on the walking cane and release the diversionary smoke. Next she tossed a wad of stage prop currency into the air, declaiming, "Look! It's free money drifting out of the smoke!" She then dragged the vagabond into Savoy Place where, in exchange for a proper fiver, she retrieved Michael's hat, cane and coat and quickly disappeared into the lobby of the hotel.

In playing the scenario in his mind, Pym also pondered his future with the Special Branch. Being outwitted by professional exponents in the art of deception was a mitigating circumstance, but would Melville see it that way? After all weren't Special Branch agents supposed to be the masters of deception?

Having first stopped off at Somerset House, Michael learned from the affectedly grandiose clerk at the front desk that indeed Mister Graveolens had been allowed to leave the offices not long earlier, citing grounds of compassion, after receiving some terrible personal news. Michael wasn't in the least surprised that in such a vast establishment of anonymous faces Anthony Graveolens was known. With a ridiculous name like that, how would he not? Michael collared a boy outside gave him a shilling and told him to run down to Savoy Place and return this coat to the old soldier eating the meat pie and resisting attempts to move him on.

"D'you really fink he'll wan' it, mister?" barked the lad, after sniffing the filthy, green garment and pulling a face.

"He'll want it," said Michael, before boarding his Hansom and telling the cabbie, "Cephas Street."

***

Michael paid the driver and tipped well. You may have gathered, among Michael's many failings, a propensity toward over-generosity was one of them. As the delighted driver doffed his cap then clicked and coaxed his horse to trot away and back to the west, Michael walked toward Annie Saunders' house. The police appeared to have vacated the scene of the crime. The Steamotivator, of course, still stood right where Michael and Phoebe had first parked her, along the ways. Mister Garrideb, imperious and intimidating, still sat in the passenger compartment, staring straight ahead, having growled his anti-theft abuse admirably toward several over-interested passers-by.

It was then, as Michael walked towards Annie's house, the magician became increasingly aware of, I don't know, something. It triggered that instinctive warning tingle down the spine, but he couldn't place why. Then he felt as though a pair of eyes, certainly not the Garrideb's, were suddenly burning deeply into the back of his head. Then he heard the words, "Visiting the house of Mister Graveolens are we, sir?"

Michael stopped dead in his tracks. Without turning round to face the owner of the voice, he simply said, "Hello, Connie."

17

"Hello, Magister," said Constance Dill. Michael turned slowly to face his dear long lost friend. She was pale, more slender than he remembered, in fact, upon closer inspection you might think she looked positively wan, but as we wondered earlier, a decade in even a mostly liberal institution like The London County Asylum can have that effect. Connie was dressed as a costermonger, with leather apron, cap, baggy trousers and boots, all of which fitted comfortably. And her smile just beamed wide and bright, lifting her cheeks for a glimpse of her former beauty. Even with a Webley Break Top revolver aimed at his heart, Michael felt an immense wave of joy bathe his entire body.

"Been a fair old while, hasn't it, chicken?" she said. Her voice was given to nasal, with just a trace of the Mancunian about it.

"Far too long for me."

"So? Are you just going to stand there, or what?"

Michael stepped forward and enveloped Connie's slender frame in his arms, she embracing him with equal joy. It was a loving, emotional reunion.

"Connie, what can I tell you? Even after all these years you look... well, okay you look terrible."

"And you've lost none of your winning charm, you saucy bugger," said Connie, smiling. "Alright, I could make you see me as Constance Russell or Marie Lloyd, but I'm not about to waste the bloody energy." Then she pushed him away. "And you're a fine one to talk. I mean, look at you all fancy in your moss stained trousers and shirtsleeves. . And where's your coat? Catch your death you will! All these years and you're still a bloody nightmare!"

"Okay, first my coat is on its way here and second, these fine trousers and this silk shirt, Connie Dill, were all fresh and brand new this morning, but *this,* I think you'll find, is what happens when you're forced to climb onto a Covent Garden church roof and fall off!"

"You fell off that roof?" said Connie, suddenly alarmed.

"Well, not exactly fall – but I might have done, and what were you thinking? Me? On a roof?"

"I knew you wouldn't be too thrilled at that, but I also knew you'd get up there anyway to bring the boy down," said Connie with a shrug.

"Oh, I didn't need to bring the boy down, *he* fell," said Michael, nonchalantly. But when a look of abject horror came over Connie, he added, "Oh, they caught him in a tarpaulin."

"Thank God," breathed Connie. "Mind you, he was a right gobby begger, he was! A nightmare."

After a long pause, Michael said, "Connie, what the hell is happening? Sid, Lez, Alfie and Annie, they're all gone, they all died terrible deaths, So, please tell me, what is going on?"

"What about the police? They know it's me?"

"The Special Branch and every copper in London is saying you're this crazy show business serial killer. But, dammit, Connie, I know you couldn't do those things. You're the kindest person I know. And that's despite the gun you're pointing at me."

Connie sighed. "You were always over-trusting, Magister. I'm nothing but bad trouble, you know that."

Michael felt his ire rising. "Connie, do not say that to me because I will never buy it. I'm not going to ask you to turn yourself in, but at least let me get a doctor to fix you up. They'll never need to know your name."

"I won't be seeing any doctors, Magister!" snapped Connie. "I've had it with them. It was a bloody doctor who did this." She raised the bill of her cap just enough to reveal a silver scar, some years old, running straight across her hair line.

"What's that?"

"They sawed me open to have a bloody rummage round. This Burckhardt, they called him. Gottlieb Burckhardt. Some psycho-surgeon from Switzerland he called himself. In the beginning they were all dead keen to find out how I do what I do. But they still don't bloody know. A decent detective called Melville heard what they were up to with their tests and the like and had me moved, secretly one night, over to Hanwell where those who knew what I can do would never find me. Been there ever since."

"Melville? And who's 'they'?"

"Who knows who anybody is anymore in this world?" she said, with a firm voice.

"Well, at least let me help dig you out of this hole. Tell me what you want me to do."

"What you can do right now is get as far away from me as you can, Magister, for your own sakes. Whatever else happens, I've got to finish what I began." Connie's face had changed. Her attitude hardened and when Michael moved to approach her, Connie raised the revolver two-handed and took aim. "You never bloody change, do you, Magister? Didn't I say in the note you shan't stop me? I warned you not to get involved, but just like you, you take no bloody notice."

Michael froze and not for the first time in twenty-four hours felt his stomach lurch into his mouth as Connie thumbed the hammer back into its firing position with a determined, metal click!

18

The Hansom carrying Phoebe had drawn up behind the Steamo. Phoebe slunk out, somehow managing to juggle Michael's frock coat, top hat and cane plus her trusty parasol in one hand while paying the driver with the other, and all with stylish untroubled elegance. Then she blinked and suddenly, as if from nowhere, another passenger, at first glance a nondescript, possibly well to do woman climbed aboard telling the driver, "Kensington Church Street, when you're ready, cabbie", as she did so.

"Right you are, lady!" chirped the driver, hardly believing his good fortune; first landing a decent fare out to the east and then a paying return journey back up west. 'Handsome in Hansom', the cabbies used to call it. As he rattled the reins to encourage his horse underway, Phoebe blinked again and took a better look at the new passenger sitting in the front of the cab. Far from a well turned out lady, she now appeared to be a pale, drawn figure dressed as a costermonger. All rather peculiar and made not a little more so by the revolver she was holding.

"I've done with him, Phoebe. He's behind the vehicle," said the voice,

"Connie?" whispered Phoebe, before her curious look turned to alarm. "Connie Dill?"

In spite of the fear, no, the utter dread of whatever grim reality was waiting, Phoebe sprinted to the Steamo. She pulled up short. There, on the pavement, sat Michael with his back resting against the vehicle's nearside front wheel. His wide, lifeless eyes were staring straight ahead.

"No! Please, Michael, no!" she flung all she was carrying to the pavement, dropped to her knees and shook him by the shoulders in a panic of urgent desperation. "You cannot be dead! Please, no, you cannot be dead!"

Then Michael blinked, and blinked again. Then swallowed, coughed and looked around, puzzled. "Pheebs?"

"Thank God you're alive!" Phoebe embraced Michael with such genuine relief and affection, that even in his state of woolly-headed stupor he could not help be touched by her display of raw emotion. But then Phoebe let him go and smacked his cheek, shouting "Idiot!" for good measure.

"Ow! Pheebs! What was *that* for?" said Michael.

Truth be told, you know, she couldn't really say for sure. Perhaps it was an expression of relief coupled with the enormous frustration that Michael could be so stupid as to allow himself to blithely wander into such a life-threatening encounter.

"Connie was just here! I saw her! She was brandishing a pistol!" yelled Phoebe.

"Our Connie? The Connie who wants to kill me Connie?" said Michael fighting a dry mouth and an aching head. "I must have missed that, somewhere between me getting here and you hugging and slapping."

"I'm sorry, but you really can be the most infuriating man alive."

"Can you be infuriating and dead?"

"When the time comes I'm rather certain you'll give it a very good try. Can you stand?"

As Phoebe gripped Michael's hand and helped him up onto his feet, she began to question the logic of the situation. Her arrival was far too late to prevent Michael's murder, so why, Phoebe wondered aloud, had Connie not polished him off while she had him so squarely in her gun sights. Why did she not pull the trigger and deal her final card of death?

Michael picked his coat up from the pavement and dusted it off with the back of his hand saying, "Because we both know Connie's not the killer, Pheebs." Michael then pointed at Annie's house. "And the man who is the killer – lives right there."

***

To my astonishment, I found Father Connor O'Connor, rapping furiously upon the locked and bolted glass doors of the front vestibule of The Metropolitan Theatre of Steam

Smoke and Mirrors, Edgware Road, and demanding entry. Following his journey to St. Bernard's Convent, Ealing, Connor was also somewhat unsteady on his feet, which was, you know, either the reaction to whatever fleshly wonders he beheld while gazing through Doyle's Goggle-Eyes, or the result of whatever quantities of the devil's brew he'd quaffed in every ale house along the way.

I typed in the door's lock code, pulled him in and down to the Pit Bar, an airy drinking area with its oval shaped counter which served fortifying refreshments to members of the audience with tickets for the Stalls and the Pit. When officially open an hour before show time, they could all quench their thirsts on a competitively priced array of fine local brews from Devonshire, French wines grown and bottled in the Rhineland, or fine Scottish spirits distilled within a battered copper tank in Doctor Goode's back yard, next to his privy, just round the corner in Church Street. Not that I wholly approved of such deception, you understand, but truthfully, none of the customers had questioned the provenance or questioned the flavour of the beverages, and, well, who was I to correct my experienced, professional bar staff? Besides, the punters were here for the magic!

I poured a full measure of the good Doctor's deep yellow grog and slid the tumbler across to my dishevelled holy associate. Connor knocked it back in one, then screwed up his florid face, hacked up his lungs and spat on the floor. Except it wasn't the floor on which he spat, but Wicko's head.

"Oh, you revolting sack of..." cursed my diminutive associate.

"Jasus, I never saw you down there, Wicko!" gasped Connor, thankfully cutting our manservant off in mid-curse, and rubbing Wicko's head dry with the sleeve of his cassock. "Sneakin' up like a banshee. You'll forgive a distressed man of the cloth, but I'm being served feral cat's pisswater here!" He then slid the tumbler back at me and said, "I'll take another."

A second glass of the offending spirit triggered exactly the same reaction and the entire repeat performance, only this time

Wicko had retreated to a safer, drier distance. "Artemus, y' heathen, I journeyed the omnibus all the ways yonder to the St. Bernard's Convent, God save the holy sisters residing therein by the way, and made certain surreptitious enquires on your behalf concerning your man, Brother Morten. I confess I'd never ever heard of the bastard and I have to tell you in God's name, neither had the Nuns."

"And no mention of Morten at St. Bernard's Church?"

"Neither a hide nor a hair there either. Your man, Artemus, is a will o' the wisp to be sure. A ghost in the mist who doth not exist. An impostor of the worst order besmirching God's holy name," he insisted.

"I suspected as much," I nodded. "Thank you, Connor. You are a credit to your faith."

"Oh, yeah…" huffed Wicko, his arms folded.

"Isn't that the bastard truth! And might I be right in knowing I get to retain ownership of these diabolical spectacles of Satan, as per our agreement?" Connor clutched the mahogany case close to his chest.

"I regret not, you wretched old fiend. But as per our agreement, I shall without fail commission the construction of another pair, just for you."

"You're a stand-up fellow, Artemus, God save and keep you, you evil bastard. Make no mistake, these Goggle-Eyes be among the finest of your tinkerings to date! Take them back now," said Connor, sliding over the case in which they came, "and I'll be on my way."

"Oi. Just a minute, you thieving God-botherer," said Wicko, before instructing me to check inside the case.

Then, as I began to hinge open the lid Connor railed: "Do you dare question the honesty of a preacher of the holy scriptures? Jasus, the leprechauns live about here and you're the bastard king of them, Wicko!"

Unsurprisingly, it was entirely as Wicko expected. The box was empty save for the velvet lining and the imprint of where the Goggle-Eyes were supposed to be. I stared the pious servant of God straight in his bloodshot eyes.

"B' Jasus. They were there whence I began my travels. Have *you* spirited them away?" he protested, then thought better of it, spat again on the floor, patted his filthy black cassock and pulled the Goggle-Eyes from a pocket within. "Wait now. What have we here? Jasus, 'tis but a miracle!"

"Yea, miracle, my arse," said Wicko with contempt.

"A curse on your hobgoblin, Artemus Napoleon More, and all your sciences!" Connor grumbled and cussed some more, too, before adding quietly, "But sweet Heaven, I'll tell you now, that Mother Superior, the Reverend Mother Breena, sure, she has a fine…"

"Thank you, Connor," I told him.

Anthony Graveolens was far less plain in person than his wedding photograph would have you believe. At least that was Phoebe's benevolent first reaction when he invited the magicians indoors. Phoebe put him at no more than twenty-five years of age. And there was little doubt that Anthony Graveolens appeared totally crushed by the enormity of his loss, and by the shocking circumstances which led thereto. Of course, Michael, by contrast, simply saw the cold eyes of a killer, a sharp operator acting out this grieving widower charade, when all the time it was Graveolens who had put his own wife to the sword.

"You can't kid a kidder, pal," Michael thought.

Anthony led them back along the hallway, past the door to the front parlour where elevenses had earlier been taken, and straight along into the kitchen. His waistcoat was still buttoned and his tie and collar smart, although his shirtsleeves were neatly rolled up to the elbows, having made a start on the task of sponging up the blood of his murdered wife. The scene of the crime was much as Michael and Phoebe had left it. All that was missing was the body of Annie Saunders and the wooden kitchen chair upon which she had been skewered. Of course, Anthony Graveolens remained blissfully unaware that Michael and Phoebe had all but witnessed the terrible tragedy, and had they been any swifter they might well have saved Annie.

"You will I hope excuse the appearance," Anthony said. His voice was given to the upper ranges of the octave, somewhat adenoidal, and lent a strange emphasis to most of his verbs. "The police transported my wife to the mortuary at The London Hospital, Whitechapel Road. But that's all they do apparently. Once the police have scribbled down their notes and collected their evidence and clues they very quickly up and leave. You get nought in the way of assistance in the cleaning up process, as you can see for yourselves, not a single bit of it."

"Mister Graveolens, this must be so painful," soothed Phoebe.

"To say it wasn't would be to lie, Miss. And please do call me Anthony. Annie always found my indifference to the rigid formality of names delightfully endearing. I hope you shall not be offended if I continue with my chore while we converse. The sooner it gets done means the sooner it gets done." Anthony twisted another spongeful of red water into a metal pail.

"When I left her this morning for my place of employment, I informed her that I loved her very much. She returned the compliment saying that she looked forward to our spending a convivial evening in one another's company. But then came along that telephone call to my office on the second floor of Somerset House in the Strand, from a policeman who duly informed me of this dreadful circumstance."

Michael and it must be said Phoebe, too, with the best will in the world, couldn't help but wonder how someone as vivacious and vibrant as Annie Saunders could possibly find anything even remotely interesting in a man quite so monumentally dull.

"Detective Inspector Skindrick from Scotland Yard informed me that their major suspect in this murder case is the woman Constance Dill! Of course, I knew of Constance Dill. Annie had spoken frequently and affectionately of all the artistes with whom she appeared on the stages of the various Music Halls. The name Constance Dill often cropped up in the midst of her frequent reminiscences."

"So, Albert..." said Michael, sensing a pause in Anthony's soliloquy.

"Anthony, sir. Actually, it's Anthony," corrected Anthony.

"Quite right," said Michael. "You say Annie talked about the people she worked with. What fine words did she say about me?" Michael smiled and purposefully avoided Phoebe's accusing gaze.

"Truthfully, sir, very little as I might recall. In fact, I hardly remember her mentioning your name at all, as it were," said Anthony apologetically. "That is not to suggest in any way she held you in any lesser esteem." Michael tried hard to suppress a scowl and maintain a generally sympathetic demeanour, but my, it was a struggle as the infuriating little widower continued. "Annie often spoke of how marvellous a hypnotist Constance Dill was. Quite brilliant was how Annie described her. Now, of course, we know quite how brilliant she was, this Constance blooming Dill. If you'll please excuse my common tongue, miss."

Phoebe held up a forgiving hand. "But you believe Connie Dill caused your wife to take her own life?" said Phoebe.

"I must bow to the Detective Inspector's considered view. The woman Dill is on a vengeful murder spree and the Inspector is, after all, the professional in these matters," Anthony's voice began to tremble. "And I myself can foresee no other reason as to why Annie should... do what she did."

"Other than mind-numbing boredom!" thought Michael, before voicing his tuppence-worth. "But I think Skindrick is wrong. You see, I don't believe Connie is responsible for Annie's death, or any of the others."

"And why might you make such a statement, sir, one being at odds and so contrary to the opinion of an investigating officer?"

"Instinct," said Michael. "I have this thing, this instinct about people, Anthony."

"More tangibly," Phoebe pitched in hastily, "Michael appears on the same death list as your late wife. Not fifteen minutes ago outside in the street he was confronted by Constance Dill, who was armed with a pistol. And despite the clear opportunity she declined to shoot him choosing instead to slip away. That *is* rather puzzling."

"Dill was back here? Outside the house? Well, we must surely thank providence for your good fortune, sir. However, her presence in this very street goes a very long way to endorsing the idea that she is, in fact, my wife's murderer. Beyond any reason I can muster," Graveolens mulled over the idea, then sighed. "Oh, my. Now, please do not take me for being a gentlemen of ill-manners but this truly has been the worst day of my life..."

"We understand," suggested Phoebe. "Would you like us to help you clean up here?"

Michael's face became a picture of horror. What was she thinking? Thank God, Anthony declined Phoebe's kind offer and escorted the magicians to the front door. He thanked them most profusely for taking the trouble to come by, express their concerns and pay their respects his dear, departed Annie.

As they walked toward the Steamotivator, Phoebe turned on Michael hissing: "What was the matter with you? Your behaviour toward that grieving man was totally unwarranted."

"But now you've met the man, in person, you'll agree. It's in his eyes. He's our killer. Although technically that should be *my* killer."

"Michael, the only way Anthony Graveolens could murder anybody is by boring them to death."

Michael depowered the Do Not Touch device on the Steamo and as they turned to board the driving compartment he and Phoebe both jumped, as they came face to face with a heart-stopping figure.

"Are you two deliberately trying to lose me my job?" growled Detective Inspector Walter Pym.

19

Detective Inspector Skindrick knelt upon the cold, hard flagstone and blessed himself before the white clothed altar. The flames of half a dozen candles danced and cast their flickering animated shadows upon the chapel's walls. Skindrick's eyes sparkled with that unquestioning, burning zeal which only the truly devout possess.

"*Benedicam tibi, nate,*" incanted The Black Bishop from the shadows. "Bless you, my son. You bring news?'"

"That I do, Blessed Father," said Skindrick, his Celtic brogue always more pronounced in the presence of such a high ranking church official. "The ruthless and cunning angel of death named Constance Dill remains free to walk the streets, but her prospects diminish by the hour. She now finds hersel' branded the most wanted woman in the whole of the metropolis, she does, and it will be but a few short hours before I drag her here by th' hair for ye to do with as ye please."

"You shall not fail me, my son."

"Also, Blessed Father, I am in possession of further information divulged by my man up at yon Asylum. He now reports that prior to her absconding, Constance Dill received at least two visits from a monk by the name of Brother Morten claiming to be from St. Bernard's."

"I am familiar with St. Bernard's," said The Black Bishop, "But I know of no monks cloistered therein; be they of the name Morten, or otherwise."

"Myself, neither, Blessed Father. So, in deep curiosity, I dispatched a keen but loyal constable to St. Bernard's Convent where he met with the Mother Superior, Reverend Mother Breena. She confirmed beyond any doubt there is no Brother Morten thereabouts. But in so doing she informed ma constable of another priest who, earlier in the day, was also at St. Bernard's, making the self-same enquiries about the monkish impostor!"

"And what do we know of this inquisitive priest?"

"They say he is a drunkard an' a disgusting licentious man, Blessed Father. A disgrace to his holy orders," said Skindrick gravely.

"That could be any of them..." sighed The Black Bishop.

"But the Mother Superior identified the individual as one Father Connor O'Connor, of The Church of Our Lady in Lisson Grove, West London," said Skindrick.

The Black Bishop smiled. "Connor O'Connor? Yes, I understand this O'Connor is an over-blown firebrand and was recently known to shriek impassioned denouncement of our friends, the heretic magicians. He is a priest with a voracious thirst, and not for knowledge. Tell me, my son, what is to be made of Connor O'Connor's sudden interest in our mythical Brother paying visits to Constance Dill?"

"I'll have him arrested to find out!"

"No, my son, you shall drag the wretched Father Connor O'Connor to me. Bring him to this chapel tonight where he shall kneel before me and I shall hear his confession. One way or another."

"As ye and our Holy Lord command, Blessed Father," said Skindrick, bowing humbly.

20

Michael, Phoebe and, to my surprise, Detective Inspector Walter Pym, arrived at the Stage Door of The Metropolitan Theatre of Steam, Smoke and Mirrors in fine time for their first performance of the evening, despite the drive from East London taking more than an hour. In Pym's presence I felt it best to play out my role as the subservient "magician's engineer", affecting the role of a shy, almost mute, simpleton. It was quite a stretch, too, as you might imagine, especially as I had decided the use of a cane and a limp, and a dreadful eye twitch probably verged too heavily toward pantomime. Of course, Wicko, our comically malingering manservant, kept out of the way entirely, snuggling into one of the many hiding places he used when avoiding work.

At least Detective Inspector Pym's ill-disguised fawning over Phoebe, and, you know, to her credit, she played along with aplomb, bought me ample time to regale Michael with the fascinating details I gleaned from Father O'Connor's gallivant to St. Bernard's in Ealing.

"So if this Brother Morten doesn't exist, Prof, then whom is he?" pondered Michael.

"The word in this case is 'who', Michael, it's who is he. Whom he might be, is an incidental query. More significantly we must ask ourselves if Brother Morten was instrumental in Connie's dramatic change in behaviour, her escape, her threats and such like. Her demeanour apparently changed following the spurious Friar's first appearance. Was he peddling poison? Because, like you, I truly cannot believe Connie is the killer. But we must lift the cloak of mystery from Father Morten and reveal his true identity if we are to prove Connie's innocence with convincing surety. Come now, we have two shows to perform. Both full houses." As always, I like to think Michael, being American, understood the gist of what I was talking about. I once offered to buy him a dictionary and, do you know his reply?

"That would be terrific. Just don't get me one with too many long words…"

Was Michael always determinedly ignorant or just deceptively flippant? You know, even I could never work that out…

As show time approached I assured Detective Inspector Pym that the security of the theatre's backstage area was akin to that of the Steamotivator. This side of the iron curtain we were impregnable. Nevertheless, he took his guardianship of my magicians seriously and I was grateful for that. Mindful of the manner in which Connie's victims had so far been slain, that is to say killed with items from their stage acts, Pym asked Michael which, if any, of the illusions he performed, might be inclined to endanger life or limb.

"All of them," replied Michael, nodding earnestly. Which Pym found less than reassuring.

***

From his seat in the stalls and with the warm glow of being well fed and watered, Detective Inspector Pym settled down in his stalls seat, pretending to be an enthusiastic member of the audience. If anyone from the crowd approached the stage with murder in mind, he was in a fine place to intercede. Also, Wicko would ring down the iron curtain on my nod. Always assuming he could be bothered.

"Ladies and gentlemen, I give you 'The Steam Cabinets of Suffocation'!" announced Michael from the stage. PHTUM! Either side of him stood two identical shapes, covered in metallised sheeting which were suddenly deluged in light. Both were a good seven feet tall, three feet six wide. Michael made a suitably dramatic gesture, and the two silver shrouds were hoisted simultaneously aloft to reveal a pair of upright, air tight glass chambers, both large enough to comfortably accommodate a person. Each of the four sides comprised three thick panes of bright, clear glass set within heavy metal frames, sea green in colour, and pimpled with rivets.

"Yes, ladies and gentlemen, tonight Phoebe, the Queen of Steam, our Great Goddess of the Aethyr, will once again marshal her immense power, this time to transport me, The Magister, a mere mortal, from inside this locked and bolted chamber – across to this locked and bolted chamber! Now such an uncanny, seemingly impossible feat can only be performed using the volatile mixture of those three essential elements over which, in this world, the Goddess Phoebe alone has total control. I speak, of course, of Aethyr, Steam and Smoke – but no mirrors!"

Now yes, I know that Aethyr, Steam and Smoke are not elements, essential, volatile or otherwise, but trust me, when the crowd is so enthralled and sitting on the edges of their seats, they'll buy any good honest hokum.

Phoebe emerged from behind one of the glass chambers. Dressed in a black tiara, black wasp-waisted corset, trimmed with a short skirt revealing long slim legs clad in black and flesh coloured stripy stockings and black knee-length boots, she sauntered and slunk around Michael, seeming to caress his arms and thighs, while he stood impassive, arms folded. From my vantage point in the prompt side wing I saw Pym in the audience, looking less than pleased about Phoebe lavishing such attention upon Michael twice nightly, seemingly unable to reassure himself this was purely theatre.

"And because the Magister is but the merest of mortals," Phoebe told the audience, "his body might survive the caustic rigors of the elements, but his airways most certainly would not! So for his well-being, he must wear – this!"

Plucked as if from the air, Phoebe revealed a full face gas mask, vulcanised black rubber with brown leather studded straps, two round green-tinged lenses and a circular air filter set to one side. *The rubber was malleable enough to ball up in the palm of her gloved hand. The straps and lenses hidden by her fingers. It was a simple enough production.* You know, it was Thomas Hancock, a Wiltshire fellow, some fifty years ago who patented vulcanised rubber, beating dear old Charlie Goodyear to the rich pickings in this country. Either can claim the credit, we were just grateful, because the reveal would be all the less convincing without vulcanised rubber. But I digress...

Phoebe strapped Michael into the mask, caressing Michael's face to ensure the seal was tight.

"You can breathe comfortably, Magister?" she demanded.

"Urbbleblurrbub!" the audience heard Michael say, his voice muffled by the fearsome black entity smothering his face. Michael wore a frothy fronted white shirt, with the open waistcoat and trousers of a vivid royal blue suit, to contrast starkly with the black rubber horror of the gas mark.

Phoebe enticed Michael with a series of sensuous waves of her arm to follow her from centre stage across to the stage left chamber. She released top and bottom the two metal retaining latches and hinged open the front panel of the chamber, which hissed in protest as the air rushed in. The enchantress then gestured for Michael to enter. Once inside he turned to face the audience.

"The Magister will now be transported from this chamber..." she said, while closing the door and re-latching the locks, trapping Michael within, "... across to its evil twin, that identical chamber some twenty feet away. I now call upon my sycophants, my gaseous exotica; the Aethyr, the steam and the smoke, to do as I command! *Aethyr, vapor et fumus et ingredietur!*"

In full view of the audience, plumes of yellow, white and grey smoke began entering both chambers, swirling and mixing to form a dark fog. The crowd gasped as they witnessed Michael clawing at his mask in a dramatic struggle of death, before being entirely consumed in the dense, caustic cloud.

"*Aethyr, vapore et fumo in deditionem!*" commanded Phoebe, pointing at Michael's tank. All at once, the fog within began to thin, as if drawn back to whence it came. Before the chamber was entirely clear it became increasingly apparent that Michael was no longer there. He had vanished. Phoebe moved swiftly to the second chamber, which still swirled thickly with smoke.

"*Aethyr, vapore et fumo in deditionem!*" she shouted, and just as within the first chamber, the fog began to disperse, revealing Michael slowly dropping to his knees and slumping with his head and shoulders against the side. In his seat, Pym began to shuffle with concern.

"Ladies and gentlemen, having defied death so often, might the Grim Reaper now finally claim his most elusive prey? Only one thing can save him! *Et convertimini, ad Aethyr et vaporem fumi!*"

Upon Phoebe's command, the great cloud of grey murk billowed back into the chamber, again completely enveloping Michael. Once full, Phoebe gave the order, "*Aethyr, vapore et fumo in deditionem*" and again the smoke began to dissipate and reveal a completely empty chamber.

"But what sorcery is this? If Magister is in neither chamber, then his body must be…"

"Here!" came the voice from the back of the theatre. The crowd turned to watch Michael sprint up the aisle and leap up onto the stage and remove his gas mark to reveal himself, alive and well.

The audience cheered and applauded as Michael and Phoebe bowed and gestured at the chambers and one another. Yes, Magister cheats death once more.

Here's how it is done. Michael enters the first chamber and upon Phoebe's cue, from below the stage in the Dungeon, I open the valves on the pipes which pump three colours of smoke into both chambers. It's real smoke, so use of the filtering gas mask is necessary, while additionally serving as a convenient disguise. Once the smoke has filled the first chamber, rendering Michael out of sight to the audience, he descends via a trapdoor riser into the Dungeon and moves to the Drain, the transport device about which you already know. Michael hitches a ride beneath the auditorium to the rear of the theatre where he emerges and waits, watching the action on stage. When the smoke is pumped out of the first tank, Michael is revealed to be gone. Next, once sufficient smoke has filled the second tank, I raise a Garrideb Mechannequin, dressed in the identical costume and gas mask to Michael's, up into the chamber, through the second trap door. On Phoebe's command I reverse the pump and suck the smoke out. The powered cams, pulleys, hinges and compressors within the Garrideb then move his head, his arms and knees in a predetermined sequence, to enact Michael's struggle. On Phoebe orders I pump smoke back into the chamber. When completely refilled, the audience will not see me drop the Garrideb back down to the Dungeon, and pump the smoke out again. Or something like that.

Of course, for dear Detective Inspector Pym, having been charged with keeping Michael from harm, the entire show for him was becoming increasingly difficult: less to enjoy, more to endure. Of course, he was thrilled to see Phoebe in full flow in such exotic costumes, but equally he was racked with uncertainty, wondering if each death defying illusion was playing out as rehearsed, or if the hand of Constance Dill, the serial killer had intervened. Never more was his nerve tested than when Phoebe announced: "Ladies and gentleman, I, Phoebe, the Queen of Steam and Goddess of the Aethyr will tonight commit the perfect murder! My victim shall be – Magister!"

"Yes," chipped in Michael, "I have defied death half a dozen times this evening, saved only by this vision from another dimension. But now it is she who shall render me slain. Naturally, I address only the ladies with that point, because I sense by now the gentlemen in the audience do not care which of us dies on this stage, just so long as it's not Phoebe!"

The men roared their approval, a roar so honest as to dispirit even the most confident magician. You see, that's the thing about magic, it is not just the deception the audience so relishes, but also the thrill of the genuine peril experienced by the magician.

With a dramatic swing Michael produced a straight edged sword from its leather scabbard.

"The Blade of Beelzebub!" he declared. I know, but they love all that. And so do I.

The silver metal sang as it sliced through the air, trailing an arc of white smoke in its wake. The thin sword with its conspicuous handle guard, called a cup-hilt, was light and rigid with very little flex. A fact Michael happily demonstrated by slicing the leather belt, which Phoebe tossed into the air, clean through.

"But first, Phoebe demands a volunteer comes to the stage and test the blade!"

"Who among you has the courage to come forth and assist the Goddess of the Aethyr?" said Phoebe.

Naturally there was no shortage of eager volunteers, all confident of their manly prowess in the face of such beauty. I wonder if, upon reflection, and in the light of Michael's impending doom, it might have been a more sensible option to have summoned Detective Inspector Pym up to the stage to confirm the authenticity of the sword, after all he was sitting right there in the stalls. But, in the moment, it probably seemed but too easy and certainly discourteous. And, you know, it is strange how in each performance, this amorphous creature we call the audience differs so wildly from night to night. But then had this particularly tough, boisterous crowd, discovered Pym was a bona fide Inspector from Scotland Yard, there was every chance he'd have been carted off and strung up from a lamp post high.

While vexed insults, even blows, were traded by the eager fellows in the cheap seats, the volunteer who stole a march on them all was a bearded gent of a certain age. He was a short, round faced sort, bald, save for bushes of grey hair above the ears, dressed as a man of means and most likely letters. I have no idea what caused the alarm bell to sound in Michael's head, but jangle it did. Michael helped the man up to the stage, they shook hands, and the smiling Michael drew the old chap closer whispering, "You even touch her, that sword will cut your balls off." The man looked at Michael, utterly unoffended and heeded the warning with one of those, 'fair enough' nods.

I have no scientific explanation for Michael's uncanny 'instinct' as he described it. I am too much a scientist to admit the existence of 'sixth sense' or 'second sight', but he was certainly spot-on with this old rogue. I was standing in the prompt side wing, listening to Wicko complain as he wafted the distinctive aroma of ether into the air, thanks to a hot shovel upon which ether cubes roasted and smouldered. The scent was supposedly generated by the Goddess whenever she performed her miracles, adding another sensory dimension to the show. Anyway, from my position I had a pretty decent view of the old man from the audience and recognised him immediately as Ashbee. Henry Spencer Ashbee, one of the nation's foremost collectors of erotica and a fellow, you understand, more than well versed in exotic encounters of the flesh. He was into his dotage now, but still potent, having published several volumes of unutterable filth of the most depraved nature, including his notorious *My Secret Life*. Licentious lewdness is detailed upon every page. Not that I've read it, you understand.

Ashbee turned out to be nothing more than politeness incarnate, and after close examination and then the skewering of a wicker basket, he happily confirmed the sharp authenticity of the Blade of Beelzebub. Phoebe then took the sword from the agreeable pervert, and in a cloud of more white steam slipped it safely back into its scabbard. Michael invited a round of applause as Ashbee returned, without incident, to his seat.

"And to prevent any staining of this glorious stage as the scarlet life blood spurts from my neck," announced Michael, smiling, "I shall now be shackled tightly with 'The Garrotting Collar of Death'!" The collar was a wide, black leather choker which Phoebe then strapped about Michael's neck. Immediately he gasped for air, then fell to his knees facing the Stage Right wing so he was now seen in profile by the audience. Phoebe again withdrew the sword from the scabbard and sliced it through the air to produce another arc of steam.

"And so, as the collar chokes the life breath from Magister's body, I, Goddess of the Aethyr shall administer – the coup de grace!"

Phoebe quickly placed the tip of the sword on the back of the collar, and then with a strong thrust, shoved the sword straight into Michael's neck. The silver tip of the sword emerged from beneath his Adam's apple. The crowd screamed and gasped as Phoebe pushed the steaming sword deeper still, the protruding blade extending further out from his neck. Phoebe then slowly withdrew the sword until it was free and she could wave it in the air with a flourish of a victor. Michael gasped, clasped both hands to his throat and slumped forward. The audience was in uproar. Pym was out of his seat and scrambling across legs and laps to reach the end of his row and get to the stage.

"And now, I command the resurrection of Michael Magister! *Revixisset!*" shouted Phoebe, at which point Michael stiffened, gasped, looked shocked, then sprang to his feet and held his arms out, grinning to the crowd, suddenly very much alive. Phoebe unbuckled the collar from Michael's neck and the audience erupted in euphoria.

The original sword blade is steel and sharp enough to pass muster when examined, to slice through a leather belt and to impale the wicker basket. But when Phoebe returns the sword to its scabbard, she clicks a release button on the hilt. This detaches the steel blade. She then attaches the hilt to a new second blade, which lays in the scabbard alongside its more deadly twin. This second blade is forged of vulcanised rubber, painted silver to look like steel. It is quite flexible. The Garrotting Collar of Death is, of course, nothing of the sort. It is a metal collar with a hidden channel, sandwiched between two halves. So when Phoebe appears to push the sword through Michael's neck, the blade slips into the channel which guides it around the neck and forces it to reappear, point first, from Michael's throat.

With Michael apparently restored to life, Pym leant against the auditorium wall. Although I suspect his considerable relief was more concerned with his continued employment rather than his charge's safety.

***

"Are ye not taking yerself across to the theatre for another battering about the head tonight, Father?" asked Mairead, the fulsome barmaid of 'The Green Man' public house, as she pulled on the pump handle to draw yet another glass of black nectar for Connor O'Connor.

"Only when my thirst is quenched!" said the holy man, after draining his tenth pint of the night and banging the empty glass down on the counter. "Why, I might not even bother to go at all if you let me regale you with the story of The Garden of Eden in the back room here. You bring the apple, and I'll show you the Devil's serpent."

"You're a filthy vulgar hog and no mistake," said Mairead, as she slid the fresh pint towards the priest.

"She's warming to me," thought Connor, counting out the ha'pennies and farthings onto the wet bar.

"Ah, good Father," said the Scottish voice. "Will ye not let me buy you that drink?"

Connor O'Connor turned round to gaze at the generous Glaswegian stranger standing there behind him. A thin, sharp featured fellow with a chin perfect for stabbing geese as they say, thought Connor.

"Here's one as not to be trusted," thought Mairead, but when drink-related freemans were on the table Connor's judgement could always be found wanting. He shook the newcomer heartily by the hand and thanked him for his apparent benevolence.

"Would ye mind if I joined ye, Father? For I'm fair interested in the ways of the good Lord and holy writ," said Gersham Skindrick, smiling with assured malevolence.

21

The audiences of both full houses tonight were rewarded with energetic presentations from Michael and Phoebe, and you know, after enduring fourteen exhausting hours of what amounted to endless tragedy and trauma, the idea of performing two magic shows to all but four thousand difficult to please strangers demanded enormous professionalism. Yes, both magicians were young and energetic, but perhaps repeatedly cheating death by all manner of sharp, heavy or suffocating instruments from the fantastical safety of a stage was therapeutic. But now, with the iron curtain rung down, the excitement had drained and Michael and Phoebe found themselves back in the uncompromising reality of real life danger.

Detective Inspector Pym appeared genuinely interested as he wandered backstage with Michael showing him the glorious workmanship and ingenuity of the Steam Cabinets of Suffocation and explaining how adroit a magician must be to understand its mysteries. Not that Michael used the word 'adroit', you understand.

Phoebe was upstairs, in her dressing room discussing ever more costume designs with her artistic school chum, the fair Lady Elsinore Belvoir. Of course, I found neither of these situations ideal. Did we really need to show a policeman our illusions, and did we truly require more costumes? More importantly, it was usual at this time of the evening that I relaxed at the stage manager's desk and sifted through the takings. Our splendid front-of-house staff, orphan brothers who live locally, carry the cash all the way backstage for me in chipped tin boxes. Then I like to smooth the notes flat and pile the coins high to resemble cotton mill smoke stacks. I take comfort (ha, who wouldn't!) in handling the notes, the half crowns, the occasional ten *pfennig* masquerading as a florin, even the copper coinage, right down to the farthings. Time was, you know, when a silver farthing could be quite easily mistaken for a half sovereign. But then the Royal Mint with a drop of darkening acid, sodium thiosulphate, to be precise, at my suggestion, rectified that common ruse.

I find money can bring out the finest in people, but ultimately the worst, and with an officer of the law now present backstage, one who operates in such a dangerous profession and whose remuneration must only be modest, it felt unseemly to be seen handling such fat sums. So I kept the boxes locked shut. Naturally, the fact he may also have direct access to any of Her Majesty's revenue men had nothing to do with it.

Another notable surprise of the evening was the total absence of Father Connor O'Connor. Which was worrisome, because he had agreed to take his place in the stalls once again to hurrumph with holy resentment, loudly denouncing the brazen display of womanliness and blasphemy he was witnessing upon the stage. Why, I'd even stood him a quart of stout at 'The Green Man' to quaff before show time, in order to further fuel his admonishments. Yes, this was worrisome indeed.

The clatter of leather boot heels on the wooden stage, two pairs to be precise, announced the departure of Lady Elsinore. She was a willowy, dark haired beauty, her green eyes served to accentuate her high cheek bones. She wore a brown full length leather skirt, and a white shirt beneath an ox blood leather one piece corset, which swept back over her shoulders in a halter-neck manner. Her throat was dressed with a copper ringed necklace from which hung an oaken cased pocket half Hunter, its clock face looking outward.

Michael and she kissed the air either side of each other's cheeks. He commented upon how lovely Lady Elsinore looked and that wearing a watch about her neck served only to demonstrate how time itself stood still when in her company. It was outrageous flannel of course, which would normally cause any woman to swoon, but Lady Elsinore merely chuckled and pushed him away.

"Well, I can never look at a clock when speaking with you, Michael," purred Lady Elsinore. "For it just reminds me how the time seems to drag."

Her ladyship, no slouch when it came to the cut and thrust of conversation, shared Phoebe's outlook on life: keen to thumb her pert nose at a world where all men were beasts who considered women a burden. So, if it caused bluster, even outrage, to show more than a little ankle in the street, then so much the better.

"Detective Inspector Pym," Phoebe said pointedly. "May I introduce you to Lady Elsinore Belvoir."

"Oh, a great pleasure, your ladyship," flustered Pym. It occurred to me that Pym's shy, awkward manner came not from being in the presence of some lowly aristocrat, heavens he'd spent enough time in the presence of Her Majesty the Queen. No, it was being in the company of such beauty, and if dear old Pym found the lovely Phoebe overwhelming, then the giddying attendance of a second glamorous beauty was enough to bring on a seizure. You see, even in 1899, where Pym came from, anyone who had more white teeth than brown was considered a proper marriageable catch.

"Please, Detective Inspector, the pleasure is mine," whispered Lady Elsinore. "Your courageous work policing the streets is of immeasurable importance. May I express my heartfelt thanks for what you do and if it were within my remit, I would quadruple your salary in a heartbeat."

"Oh, well, s-such an expression of support from one such as yourself is reward enough, your ladyship," said Pym, his mouth dry and the back of his neck wet.

"You, sir, are quite the charmer indeed," Lady Elsinore affected a pose of mock flattery. "Michael Magister might take a lesson in blandishment from you."

"Yes, er, Lady Belvoir, would I be right in thinking your family owns that castle up north somewhere?" asked Pym.

"Heavens, no. Those are distant relatives in Leicestershire," smiled Elsinore. "I'm one of the Eton Belvoirs."

Like me, Phoebe suddenly felt the time was right to push her friend out of the theatre and into her waiting carriage as quickly as possible. "Yes, thank you, Elsinore, we shall all pore over your designs, but your coachman, patient as he is, has waited long enough. Give my best to Lord Gilbert,"

Phoebe and Elsinore offered one another chaste pecks on the cheeks.

"Michael, as ever, you are a dreadful American show off. And Detective Inspector Pym, you are a delight," said Elsinore.

"Elsinore, be careful wearing that watch around your neck. I hate the idea of two hands on your throat," said Michael, as he and she again kissed the air instead of each other. Ever the performer, Michael had claimed the final put-down.

"Permit me to escort you to your carriage," I said, and taking her by the gloved hand, I led, cajoled, even pulled, if you will, Lady Elsinore Belvoir through the Pass Door.

I waved at the Belvoir carriage as it rattled away, then shuffled across the busy Edgware Road to 'The Green Man'. The windows shone bright and yellow, welcoming beacons to the inebriate, much as the lamps of Cornish wreckers luring passing cargo steamers onto the rocks. The heat and the noise from the public bar which smacked you in the face as soon as you pushed open the etched glass front door, was enough to have you reeling back into the street. I managed to squeeze and shoulder my way through the crowd of glassy eyed voluble patrons who always seemed to holler ever more loudly as the evening wore on. Especially when the landlord called for last orders and his request was greeted with a volley of vituperative invective. The fair Mairead brushed by me, collecting whatever jars and tankards she could manage, while fending off groping hands with a smart rebuke or a sharp head butt.

"Where's the unholy Father? I'll never locate him in this melee!" I shouted above the rising torrent of abuse.

"O'Connor? He was away a good hour since," her voice boomed in return. "Went off pie-eyed with a fast fellow. Never seen his face before. A bony sort. Smart suited. Treated the old soak to another quart of stout, so he did!"

The knot of panic gripped me. A man plying the Reverend O'Connor with drink, rendering him incapable, then whisking him away? I thanked Mairead and began forcing myself through the horde towards the exit. But what the barmaid shouted next, all but stopped me in mid stride.

"Oh, and Professor!" she boomed. "Some of the lads said the fellow had the distinct whiff of the mutton shunter about him!"

Mutton shunter? No, it's not slang for what you might be thinking. I had no time to thank Mairead. Here was information I had to impart to Michael, Phoebe and indeed Pym as quickly as possible. Connor had been over-plied with drink and then spirited away by a policeman!

22

"Kneel before the altar, blasphemous dog!" ordered Skindrick, his voice echoing about the damp, empty building.

"Jasus, ya bastard!" complained Connor, as his knees crashed upon the cold flagstone floor. Although he was a priest, Connor was rarely given to the practice of kneeling. He looked unkempt and reeked of drink, but there was nothing unusual about that. Connor's bleary eyes wandered lazily trying to fathom his surroundings. Before him, in the dancing candlelight, there stood a holy altar dressed in a fine white cloth, upon which sat a silver communion jug and chalice. The whiff of polish and dust and candlewax, was unmistakeable. He was certainly in some kind of church, not that that brought much in the way of comfort. Nor did the vast quantities of ale and grog he'd imbibed. O'Connor had never been a fearless intoxicant. He sought tranquillity in booze rather than misguided courage, but he figured the difficulty in which he now found himself may require a good deal of that misguided courage. Especially if he and harm were to remain happily separate.

"If I kneel at this time o' the night, I'm as likely never to get up again. And if it is bastard prayer you'll be wanting, I do more than my share in my own time if you please!"

"Father Connor O'Connor," said a deep, calm voice somewhere in the dark.

"Not necessarily!" replied Father Connor O'Connor.

"The Blessing of the Almighty be upon you," persisted the calm voice.

"And also with you, ya bastard!" said O'Connor. "What's the meaning of any of this? Dragging me away from where I was, to here. Show yourself, whoever you are, with all ya lurking in the shadows like some bastard banshee from the arse end of hell."

"Ye'll show respect to the Blessed Father, ye scum sucker!" barked the appalled Skindrick, as he cracked the recalcitrant supplicant a sharp cuff about the head. He had never known such foul talk to be uttered on consecrated ground.

"I'll consider showing him respect when he shows himself to me and not a bastard minute before," said O'Connor firmly.

Smoothly and silently the tall figure in black stepped into view, a silhouette against the candlelit altar. The hood was drawn over the head, the hands clasped together beneath the voluminous sleeves. The mysterious figure faced the altar, bowed, made the sign of the blessing and turned to look down upon O'Connor. The head, the face, they remained shrouded in darkness, but his vestments proved to be the giveaway.

"Jasus. Shouldn't I have known? There he stands, a son of Loyola, resplendent in his raven cassock. There'll be bastard little in the way of merriment now, lads! A Black Bishop is among us! What do you want from me, Jesuit?" O'Connor almost spat the words. His contempt was a most convincing mask for his now serious concern.

Skindrick again cuffed O'Connor with the back of his hand and our priest toppled to one side, his head throbbing now, more though from the drink than the blow. Seldom, to my certain knowledge, dare such an openly flagrant disregard for the Jesuit Order be displayed. Certainly not to The Black Bishop, who scratched his whiskered chin, intrigued. Connor thought the candlelight caught the lower part of The Black Bishop's face within the hood. Was that a beard?

"Heavens to Holy Mary, you're the fabled Hairy Monk!" said O'Connor.

'The Hairy Monk' was a sobriquet coined by his enemies and one which he detested. And understandably so. However, The Black Bishop elected to ignore the jibes of a drunken sinner and continue with his interrogation.

"So then, Father, I hear you paid a visit today to the Convent of St. Bernard's in Hanwell. That holy place lies some way beyond your diocesan responsibilities. I should like you to tell me why you went there."

"Will your man beat again if I say I've never heard of St. Bernard's?"

"Oh, yes. And much joy it will bring him."

"In which case 'tis with pleasure I'll tell. See, the Mother Superior, that Reverend Mother Breena, she and I have an accord. For mutual benefit, you might call it. She has her womanly needs and I am more than happy to oblige her!" O'Connor then added a knowing look to add further salacity to the nature of their liaison.

"You made enquiries concerning a Father who had paid visits to the London County Asylum, a Father by the name of Morten."

"Not true. You're looking for ought, where there's nought to be found. But then you servants of the Black Pope see intrigue and sedition at every turn, do you not?" O'Connor's voice was sneering, contemptuous.

Again O'Connor felt the sharp burn of Skindrick's slap on his cheek. His head was really beginning to swim now. As if the altar had taken on an animated life of its own, swaying, looming large, then retreating.

"Ye're a disgrace to your holy orders, so ye are!" yelled Skindrick.

"You can look to your man here for plenty of that, so you can!" shouted O'Connor, pointing at The Black Bishop.

"Ye'll tell the Blessed Father as he commands!" shouted Skindrick.

"Why did you enquire about this Father Morten?" insisted The Black Bishop.

"Jasus, all right, I'll tell ya the truth," lied O'Connor, the throbbing in his head was now becoming all but unbearable. "I have a friend who got word of a position becoming available in the London County Asylum. Father Morten, from St. Bernard's, was concluding his ministry at Hanwell, and I felt those inmates interred therein would benefit from my ecumenical visits when he finishes. I was looking for Morten to see if he could offer me anything in the ways of tips and winks as to how I might secure the role for myself. For no one else in London town has more charm and bastard eloquence than me. I'll guide them on the straight and narrow path. Especially if there's additional coin to be earned and the female orderlies seeing fit to express their appreciation of my efforts in womanly ways. See, listen, Jebbie, don't you ever be thinking I took holy orders for the religion! Jasus. Unlike all of you bastard hypocrites, I admit I'm in it for the divine trinity. Respect. Sex. Money. And not necessarily in that order!"

Skindrick staggered backward. He was truly reviled that he was now standing in the presence of someone so utterly sacrilegious. Were his pistol, or indeed a Pulsa to hand, he would have shot O'Connor dead right where he knelt, right there and then. But the response of his Eminence The Black Bishop was more considered - he paused and nodded.

"My son, I believe your bravado betrays the truth of your genuine faith. And you have wandered not so far beyond redemption as you might believe." The Black Bishop turned to his disciple. "The Lord is testing us, Skindrick. He is telling us we have the belief and the power to save a soul even as wretched as this."

"Aye, as ye say, Blessed Father," said Skindrick, hating himself because deep down he truly could not believe it to be possible.

"You can be saved," The Black Bishop told O'Connor. "Come, take the sacrament with me."

O'Connor had realised early in his ministry that one of the many great perks of the priesthood was a few nips of fortified wine at the church's expense at least three times a day. Perhaps, thought O'Connor, a little snifter might settle his complaining digestives. And, frankly, where the bastard else could he be getting a freeman's at this time of night?

"I'm not above taking a drink with any man, even a Jebbie," he said, now beginning to feel that thick churning of the stomach which, by all accounts, tends to accompany the world as it begins to spin.

The Black Bishop faced the altar, prepared the wafer and poured the wine from a silver jug into the chalice. The thick red wine of course was laced with what he called his 'blessed elixir' which hastened the supplicant's passing from this world into the next. Skindrick believed most sincerely that if ever anyone was more destined to rake the hot coals of damnation, rather than bathe in glorious salvation, it was this repugnant being, Father Connor O'Connor. The Black Bishop blessed the silver chalice and offered Connor first the wafer, then the wine. It would be his last drink in this lifetime.

So now, here's the thing. Whether it happened to be the strong porty aroma wafting up from the chalice, coupled with the beatings and the difficult journey pinned to the carriage floor which did it – or – if it was the monstrous quantities of drink he'd quaffed beforehand in the pub, we shall really never know. What we do know is that as soon as Connor put the wine to his lips, he suddenly upped, retched and vomited. He puked once, twice, three times, great spouts of yeasty brown beer all over the cassock of The Black Bishop, who staggered backwards, dropping the chalice and hollering in fury. Before even Skindrick could react, The Black Bishop had toppled backwards against the altar, knocking a candle onto the cloth which immediately ignited. Now shocked into action, Skindrick leapt forward to assist his Blessed Father, but as he did so, Connor heaved up another great quart of bilious alcohol straight in Skindrick's face, causing him to stagger backwards and tumble to the floor, his eyes searing.

I suppose, you know, there's nothing more sobering in life that a mighty up-chuck which smothers not just a bishop, but also a policeman, and more especially if they are both foul and corrupt. So it was that Father Connor O'Connor suddenly found his head to be remarkably clear. The flames, the smell, the chaos all conspired to give him the impetus to pull himself together and take to his heels – but not before he swiped the silver chalice a mighty crack across Skindrick's head as the policeman's hands were up about his face trying to wipe away the stinking slime. With tingling legs, Connor staggered back down the nave for the exit. Mercifully it was a short nave in a small chapel, and following a few unsteady steps he had turned the key, burst through the wooden doors and tumbled into what turned out to be Warwick Street, that side turning off Regent Street. O'Connor quickly lost himself in the night time crowd. With the sludge he called blood now surging back down his calves and into his feet, he told himself to run like merry bastard hell and not look back.

23

With Phoebe safely ensconced aboard her railway carriage, hidden, as you know, in plain sight around the side of the Paddington Goods Yard, Pym now escorted Michael on the short walk to his equally unexpected home, a canal boat.

She was tied up – one of the few nautical terms with which I am familiar – on the Warwick Crescent bank of Little Venice, a broad expanse of water at the confluence of the Regent and Grand Union canals and overlooked on three sides by tall, elegant white stucco villas built in the Italianate style. Michael showed Pym down the stone steps which led to the cobbled pavement on the canal bank.

In the dark, Michael's boat was hard to see, until Michael cranked a lever and the entire vessel was bathed in soft green light. She was forty feet long, fully enclosed, showing a handful of portholes set above the waterline left and right. Onto the side of the raised wheelhouse cabin set towards the back end, the aft I believe they call it for some strange reason, we had screwed a black and white nameplate which read "The Legerdemain". The vessel was to be called "The Prestigitator", but our Sign Writer struggled to squeeze a word containing quite so many Ts into a finite space, so we changed the name to "The Legerdemain", which was not only longer, but also carried within it an abundance of Es. But for some unexplained reason, our temperamental Letterer could cope with that. Artists! In fact, that particular signage was the only 'decoration' to be found on Michael's vessel. While the other dozen or so, mostly residential boats, along the stretch, were a merry kaleidoscope of vivid colours; red, greens and black, with a surfeit of floral illustration, much in that great tradition of the gypsy caravan, Michael's was quite the contrary. Far from showy, it was positively austere, painted entirely in one of the duller shades of battleship grey. Straight rows of rivets followed the lines of the plates and joints, which, while pleasing on the eye of a mathematician, made no real contribution to the spirit of art. She was the ugly duckling of the fleet, and in such splendid, swan-like company it was the boat everyone would most likely walk straight past. Unnoticeable, you might call it, unregistering on the brain, anonymous; and that, of course, was the idea.

Michael stepped aboard, snapped on the cabin light and invited Detective Pym aboard for a warming cup of Mister Twining's finest tea or Mister Taylor's most excellent coffee, or the Cadbury Brothers' best ever cocoa. But the policeman declined, and the two men had wished one another a polite good night. Had it been the gorgeous Phoebe extending the very same invitation, even with a less varied choice of hot beverages on offer, Michael figured Pym would have leapt at the chance. Nevertheless, it was Michael's name on Connie's death list, not Phoebe's, and Pym would be spending the first part of the night watching over a wretched canal boat.

A deft glance around, before closing the cabin hatch behind him and dousing the green flood lamps, told Michael there were at least a couple of uniformed officers making some attempt to melt into the background thereabouts on the canal side and up along Warwick Crescent. No doubt all cursing their lot in the cool night air, but at least they were company for Pym, who took his place up by the black wrought iron gate which stood atop the stone steps. With his hands in his pockets, overcoat collar turned up, bowler brim down over his alert eyes the wait for Constance Dill had begun.

"Unharmed if you please," Melville had told Pym. Nevertheless the Detective Inspector felt the hard, weighty form of the revolver within his trouser pocket. Just in case. Anyway, in three hours he would be relieved. Besides, he was used to more significant protection duty, Tsars, Kings, Presidents and the like. Not bloody magicians. And, actually, would it really affect his career if Dill did manage to shoot Magister? Would it really be any great loss to the nation? But all such thoughts vanished the moment he heard the clopping of a horse's hooves and saw what looked like a Brougham carriage draw up, about twenty yards along from the shadows in which Pym stood.

He squinted and watched as the driver, silhouetted against the lights from the opposite houses, skipped down from the front, swung open the carriage door and helped a shadowy figure step from the front of the cab. It was dressed in a dark full length cape, or cassock, or coat, it was tough to make out, with a hood, very like a monk's cowl, pulled right up over the head. The figure looked up and down the Crescent. Naturally, given the hour, all was still and quiet. With its head down and hands clasped inside the cuffs of its sleeves, the figure moved quickly and smoothly towards Pym and the stone steps down to the towpath. It wasn't the gait of a man, no, it was definitely a woman, surmised Pym. His fingers wrapped around the grip of the revolver. The woman turned to walk down the stone steps. That was Pym's call to arms. If Constance Dill had arrived with murder on her mind, now was the time to dissuade her. Pym drew his gun, levelled the barrel at her head and stepped out from the darkness.

"Officer of the law, madam," he said quietly. "I've a pistol trained upon you. Please do not move."

The figure stood stock still and inclined both her hands upwards. As Pym moved towards her he saw the aft cabin door of The Legerdemain boat swung up and open. The green floods faded up, streaming gentle light upon the canal boat. Magister could clearly be seen.

"Jesus Christ, what's he doing?" thought Pym, before shouting: "Inside! You're a sitting target!"

"It's okay, Detective Inspector, I've got this covered!" insisted Michael as he jumped down from the boat onto the towpath and bounded up the stone steps. Then Pym heard the woman say in a clear, calm voice: "Hello, lover."

The three hidden constables now broke cover with pistols drawn, scampering and scuffing to Pym's side.

"Thank you, Detective Inspector Pym," said Michael. "Thank you, but I promise you, it's fine, I guarantee you this lady is a friend of mine. She's a guest."

"As you say, Mister Magister, but I have every reason to suspect this person is Constance Dill!" Pym was polite but firm. "Kindly show yourself, madam!"

"Detective Inspector, can we at least keep the noise down?" said Michael, his brain whirring, trying to figure out how to contain this fast-becoming-awkward situation. "This isn't Connie Dill."

"Hold on, how do we know? It might be Constance Dill clouding our minds, sir, so please leave this to me. I said kindly show yourself, madam!"

"Okay, Walter, if we continue down this road, it's going to kick the lid off a whole new bucket of worms."

"I think I understand you, Mister Magister, but I say this only once more, madam, kindly show yourself!"

The woman gently raised her hands and threw back her hood as instructed. Even in the green light of the boat her face was beautiful. And, you know, despite the surprise, maybe even the shock, of Pym's gun-toting intervention, her demeanour remained mature, confident, knowing and utterly unflappable.

"Blimey, if Dill's mesmerising me," thought Pym, "it's incredible." He was feeling nothing but blissful wonder as he stared at the woman with her sparkling eyes and dazzling broad smile, one which he felt convinced he had seen before.

"Okay. Leave this to me, Lillie." Michael told the woman before turning to Pym and lowering his voice. "Detective Inspector, this is going to be difficult. Could we at least lose the cavalry? Slip a little out of earshot, but within gunfire range if you prefer. Walter. Please?"

Pym was at first confused, then bemused and later maybe a little amused, simply because he'd never seen this side of Michael Magister before. Gone was the slick-talking devil-may-care attitude. He was now contrite, even, what, pleading? In fact, dear old Pym was so intrigued at this extraordinary development he nodded and the three constables quietly retreated, while keeping their pistols trained upon the woman.

"Detective Inspector, you and Mister M have your secrets, I have mine, and this lovely lady is one of them, and, well, what can I say, other than what you don't know, you don't worry about. So thank you for your concern, but everything here is now fine. I was genuinely expecting a visit from this lady, and for once, well, I don't know how to convince you otherwise,"

Michael turned to his guest with a face of abject apology, screwing up his nose and saying: "As you can see, Detective Inspector Pym of the Special Branch is a terrific policeman, Lillie, and I'm so sorry about this, but, well, when it comes to your honest intentions – he'll need convincing."

"Oh, my dear Inspector," said the woman, "I am quite perfectly happy to prove to you the sincerity of my visit. My credentials."

She unbuttoned her black coat and held it wide open. Save for a pair of black ankle boots, beneath the coat she wore absolutely – nothing. In the green light Pym could clearly see breasts and nipples, a narrow waist, a flat stomach and navel and curvaceous hips and...

"Oh, my word..." said Pym. In fact he wanted to say he had never seen such a thing, but that would not have been entirely true, what with him having courted Ada Bowser from Rotherhithe for a good while. Still, the Detective Inspector tried to take in as much as he could as quickly as he could. Then he coughed and added somewhat hoarsely, "Begging your pardon, ma'am, but I think I know your face."

"That could well be so, Detective Inspector, but may I?" The woman smiled and gestured with her hands that she was still holding open her coat.

"Oh, by all means, please. Thank you," flustered Pym.

The woman re-buttoned her coat and extended her right hand to shake his. "It is a great pleasure to meet you, Detective Inspector Pym of the Special Branch. Lillie Langtry. I'm quite certain Mister Melville still likes to keep my file warm at Scotland Yard."

"Okay. What do you say we all get inside out of the cold!" suggested Michael quickly, still looking about to ensure none of this had been witnessed by nosey neighbours.

Two minutes later found Pym with his revolver firmly back in his pocket, standing aboard Michael's canal boat parlour refusing another offer of that cup of tea, coffee or cocoa. On the other side of the narrow room, with a long leg crossed outside her coat, sat *the* Lillie Langtry, one of the most famous women on either side of the Atlantic Ocean. Her hair was auburn, her eyes bright and violet and her complexion peach perfection, she radiated elegance, beauty and strength of character much of which Phoebe had inherited. A certain age now, but nevertheless it was little wonder that painters, princes and homosexuals alike fought to gain her attention. Michael poured Mrs Langtry a cup of coffee. Black, no milk or sugar.

Despite his enrapture, Pym still managed to take in the details of Michael's boat. The interior was masculine, almost muscular. Pipes, cables, dials, wheels, everything that made the vessel function was on display, surface mounted. Set every couple of yards structural ribs clamped with rivets lined the walls and roof. It was quite beautiful to look at in that industrial kind of manner. If it was forged in copper or brass it was burnished brightly, if it was hewn from wood it was polished to a brilliant sheen. A cunning idea concerning the design of these living quarters involved constructing everything so it could be slid or folded out for use. This applied to chairs, tables, beds, kitchen range, everything that turned the boat into a home. If every piece was slid, collapsed or folded back into its housing set in the walls, floor and roof, "The Legerdemain" would, save for any hardware associated with mechanical function, resemble the empty shell we first purchased.

"Detective Inspector, I am sure you find this wonderful décor brutally chic," said Lillie. "I wish I had converted my own vessel, 'White Ladye', in this glorious fashion. But at least 'The Ladye' sailed, Michael, I did not keep her tied to the dock like 'The Legerdemain'."

"I don't want to get seasick, Lillie," said Michael.

"I doubt the canal network generates much of a swell, lover," quipped Lillie before sipping her coffee.

Pym remembered from the Scotland Yard Lillie Langtry file that 'White Ladye' was a splendid three-masted steam yacht, oh, easily four times the size of 'The Legerdemain'. She was a gift from a spiteful braggart ne'er-do-well named Baird, who dubbed himself Squire Abingdon. Died very early from pneumonia. Much involved in the horse racing world if Pym was right.

"I really ought to thank you, ma'am . Because your chestnut colt Merman, well, he won the Cesarewitch a year or so back, and I had a bit of a flutter on him. You and I both took the bookies to the cleaners that day." Pym told Lillie.

"Oh, that thrills me enormously, Detective Inspector, and you know he only began winning after Lord Beresford suggested we run him without shoes?"

"Part of his appeal, ma'am," said Pym.

"Well, I hope to add to your earnings further still at Goodwood, this year. Now. To business and to rest your mind perfectly at ease, let me explain that Mister Magister has been a very dear friend since my time in the United States. I visit him as often as time and occasion permits."

Lillie's soothing way was so enthralling, how could Pym not believe her? And as you already know, Walter Pym wasn't overly comfortable around stunning looking women. He'd never had the practice or much of an opportunity, so what with the gorgeous Phoebe, and seductive Lady Belvoir, and now this legendary beauty, a famous West End actress and a great racehorse owner, well he was pretty much quite overwhelmed for one day!

Lillie smiled. "I enjoy Michael's company very much because he is charming, infuriating, incredibly clever, very amusing and his *pego* is immense. So, Detective Inspector Pym, thank you, we both feel so much safer in the knowledge we enjoy your confidence. "

Pym nodded, but it was several seconds before he could speak. "Special Branch, ma'am. Discretion is our watchword. Now, I bid you good night, Miss Langtry," he said, before turning to Michael. "Constance Dill remains at liberty, Mister Magister. Never forget that."

"Believe me, Detective Inspector, I don't," said Michael.

Pym stepped from the softly lit warmth of the boat to his vantage point in the cool darkness outside. He would be relieved in an hour. That was hardly enough time to replay the entire encounter in his mind at least a hundred times and reflect on the further insight he'd gained into the mysterious world of Michael Magister. "I mean, come on. Not only has that lucky bastard got it all," he whispered to himself. "He's also got Lillie Langtry."

So you can imagine the Detective Inspector's utter surprise when after only some, what, five minutes, Lillie Langtry re-emerged from Michael's canal boat, strolled by Pym, stopped, turned to face him in the shadows, held out her hand and said, "Detective Inspector, might you kindly help a lady negotiate these steps?" Pym took Lillie's hand and escorted her to the street level. Bloody hell, he thought. He'd only gone and touched Lillie Langtry twice in one night!

"It was such a pleasure to meet you. And please do give my best regards to the Superintendent." Lillie kissed her finger and placed it on Pym's cheek. She then turned and strolled gracefully to her waiting carriage.

24

So what just happened aboard "The Legerdemain" and why did Lillie Langtry depart so quickly? Well, once Pym had left the boat, Lillie had stood, slipped her coat from her shoulders and let it slide to the floor. Michael held up his hand. "Okay, Lillie – stop." He walked around behind her, lifted Lillie's coat up from the floor and wrapped it back around her shoulders.

"Well, something is suddenly the matter," said Lillie calmly.

"There's no simple way of saying this but – from now on we stop seeing one another."

"Because?"

"Something has changed. No, everything has changed."

She took a long pause, then said, "You know about Phoebe?"

"Lillie, what were you thinking? Why didn't you tell me Phoebe was your daughter? If I'd known, I would have stopped all this as soon as she joined the act."

"Oh, lover, that's exactly *why* I didn't tell you. Phoebe didn't know about you and me then, and she does not need to know now. No one has known since I sailed back from America. And does it really matter?" Lillie studied Michael's face, his posture. "My, I see it really does. Michael, don't be naïve. Who suggested Phoebe took on the role of your stage assistant?"

"Arthur Doyle."

"Which was brought about by a whispered word in the good doctor's ear from whom, I wonder?"

"*You? You* gave Doyle the idea? Wait, Doyle? You haven't? Not with Arthur Doyle?"

"That, my lover, is for me to know and for you to agonise over. Besides, Arthur's attentions are drawn to a new friend. You've heard of his Miss Leckie?"

Michael's reaction to that bombshell suggested he had not.

"Meanwhile, Michael Magister, let me allow you one more chance, which is certainly more than I have given any other man. Take this opportunity to pause and reconsider. You may continue with the uncomplicated, exquisite delights we bring one another, and Phoebe need never know. Or end it now, and Phoebe need never know."

"I'm sorry, Lillie," said Michael with an apologetic shrug of the shoulders. "I couldn't live a lie that would hurt Pheebs."

With a gentle sigh Lillie stood, re-buttoned her coat, kissed Michael on the cheek and whispered sincerely in his ear, "Good boy."

Michael helped Lillie up the metal steps to the aft hatch door and out onto the canal boat's deck. "Still our secret?" he said.

Lillie smiled and looked deeply into Michael's eyes. "My dear sweet lover, I keep more secrets than you can ever imagine."

And with that Lillie Langtry stepped off 'The Legerdemain' to continue her truly remarkable life.

25

"For pity's sake, open the bastard door, y'heathen scientist!" yelled the voice.

The Stage Door buzzer was ringing with great urgency down in the Dungeon. I was peering through an angle-poise magnifying glass tightening the final screw on the Aethyr generator, the heart and soul of the reworked Pulsatronic pistol left last night by those incompetent assassins.

"I'm not answering it," said Wicko, sitting on a travelling trunk, dressed in night shirt and cap, sipping cocoa and reading *Country Life* magazine. "Not at this time of night."

I threw a circuit breaker handle which fired up the Spectroscope and looked across at the Visualisation Portal on the table. Once the white flashes of static had cleared, the Visualisation Port revealed the sepia toned image of a vision from hell. It was Father Connor O'Connor, outside the Stage Door and looking frightful even by his wretched standards. He stood, no, more slumped, against the wall, tattered and battered, glaring up at the Spectroscopic Lens, quite the most pathetic sight.

"Connor! Dear Lord, look at the shape of you! I'll be there briskly!" I was shouting into the mouthpiece of the TalkiTube which carried my voice as it snaked along the flexible pipework and emerged, albeit distorted, from the horn-shaped speaker outside by the door.

"All right, I'll let him in," said Wicko, huffing and throwing down his magazine. "But he'd better not spit on me again. Or I'll chew on his knee caps."

The Spectroscope comprised a circular, brass collared lens, front-mounted upon an adjustable leather-made concertina collar which could pull focus and convey the image back along a bundle of copper wires and project in onto the Visualizer Portal. Naturally, the image was far superior to the Scope housed aboard the Steamotivator. I borrowed much of the camera idea from kindly George Eastman, a chum of mine over in Rochester, New York State and another old friend,

Paul Nipkow, with whom I once lodged in Berlin. His spinning Nipkow Disk was an excellent starting point for moving images. But that is by the by.

Upstairs, Wicko tapped in the coded numbers upon the typewriter key board and the Stage Door sprung open with a hiss. Connor tumbled through the door collapsing onto Wicko. Between us, Wicko pushed and I heaved the holy man back onto his feet, and I, as best I could, then supported Connor down to the Pit Bar, where I fortified him with a medicinal port and brandy. Now he sat with his elbows on the counter and his head in his hands, and proceeded to tell me of his nightmare evening, liberally punctuating the narrative with whimpers, foul talk and unholy curses.

"A Jesuit? You're quite certain of that?" I said, after listening to his tale of kidnap, abuse, attempted murder, fire and brimstone, a narrative too richly detailed and too bizarre to in anyway doubt.

"I bastard do. A Jebbie all right!" said Connor, as he tossed back a third 'medicinal', "For a long whiles it's been said there's this high ranking Jebbie Superior, sent across from Rome by the Black Pope himself, to orchestrate any manner of mayhem upon London town. The rank and file clergy, amongst whom I include myself, we all dub him *The Black Bishop*, on account, not only of his black cassock, a trademark of the Loyolan, but also because of his unholy black heart. And he sports a long, black beard. It is for that reason everyone so misfortunate as to encounter his foul presence has dubbed him The Hairy Monk."

"How poetic," I said.

"There he was, all grandstanding there like a bastard in this chapel. In Warwick Street, I'm minded to say it was, but I might be wrong. And posturing there he was, in merry cahoots, with his Jebbie lickspittle. The very scum boil Jebbie who coerced and forced me to take further drink in 'The Green Man', before dragging me away to my certain death at the hand of this Hairy Monk. At least I got to brain one bastard with the communion chalice on the way out."

"That is a very interesting development," I said, my mind spinning back to the attempt on the life of the Prime Minister, yesterday. "The French writer Voltaire was once a pupil at a Jesuit School. He claimed all he learned from them was Latin and nonsense."

"That sounds bastard right, and no mistake," snapped Father Connor O'Connor.

You know, rumours have abounded for centuries concerning the 'Societas Jesu', The Society of Jesus, colloquially known as The Jesuits. The Society was conceived back in the 16th century by a military man, name of Ignatius Loyola, who after surviving a supposedly mortal wound underwent an epiphany, or some such. Loyola then recruited a handful of like-minded students including, interestingly enough, Francis Xavier, and since then his Order has grown, some do say, to become an absolute monarchy within the Church of Rome. The Black Pope to which O'Connor referred could also be known as The Superior General, or Father General, or sometimes Vicar General – gah, don't you wish these people would just for once make up their minds!? To my understanding, the current Father General was the Very Reverend Luis Martín García. The Jesuits are said to be 'the intellectual Catholics', and adopt a lofty superiority. But O'Connor would simply have you believe they are cunning malefactors. Theirs, he said, was the very stuff which spawned "The Massacre of St. Bartholomew's Day", which, if memory serves me correctly, was a 16th century four day orgy of slaughter, which took place all over France. Its intention was to prevent the marriage of Protestant Henry the Third of Navarre to the Catholic French king's sister Margaret of Valois. Thousands, some say tens of thousands of Protestant Calvinist Huguenots were put to the sword by raging mobs. It was a mass murder which caused much rejoicing in Rome despite the direct contravention of at least two of The Ten Commandments.

The Reverend Father Connor O'Connor, when in full Jebbie conspiracy theory flow, would also have you believe the Jesuits were the conniving force behind several attempts on the life of Queen Elizabeth and were linked to the conspirators of The Gunpowder Plot; all intended to steer Britain back on the path to Rome and redemption. Connor also held them responsible for the deaths, by poison, of two American Presidents and the attempted poisoning of a third. But, given his shocking experiences tonight, the crazed ecclesiastic does have an axe to grind...

The next morning, I invited Michael and Phoebe to come by the theatre at their earliest convenience. I had installed Communicon devices in both their residences, you understand. Phoebe arrived on foot as always, but Michael in a Hansom, accompanied by two uniformed minders. Apparently, having relieved Pym and their colleagues, at two in the morning, the policemen had endured such a cold, boring, pitiless night Michael figured they looked like they would never survive the sharp ten minute morning walk along the canal and across Paddington Green. Wicko was cajoled into giving both coppers hot tea and breakfast which cheered them considerably, but not so our dwarfish associate.

Anyway, thus summoned, Michael and Phoebe now sat with me in the Dungeon watching Connor O'Connor, who was also praising the restorative power of Wicko's bacon, liver and coddled egg breakfast, and, for a pleasant change, wiping his mouth with the provided napkin, rather than his sleeve. He repeated his tale of kidnap and the effective use of projectile vomiting as an escape method, in between mouthfuls of egg and lustful glances at Phoebe. She, of course, had added further colour to our potted history of Jesuit conspiracy theories by highlighting the rumour concerning the death of Pope Clement XIV in 1773, poisoned as a punishment for signing a decree abolishing the Order and stating 'that the name of this company shall be forever extinguished and suppressed... and to all eternity be valid, permanent and efficacious'.

"None of which mattered a jot, because fifty years later the Order was reinstated by Pius VII in a Papal Bull," she concluded.

"Bull being the word," said Michael, raising an eyebrow.

To drag the conversation back to religious matters more contemporary, to wit last night's attempted poisoning of Connor O'Connor, I posed two questions. How might The Black Bishop and his thuggish associate come to know of this fictitious Brother Morten visiting Hanwell? Why would it concern them enough to pursue an enquiry? Was it really the exposure of a phoney priest which caused them such angst? Very well, yes, technically that's three questions.

"Angst? Them? Bastard, no. They wouldn't give a bugger," was Connor O'Connor's apostolic assessment. "Even if they got wind of a charlatan working in God's name for his own nefarious ends, it's small beer compared to their grand scale bastard scheming. No. If ever The Black Bishop is involved, the endgame must be big."

"My guess? This Black Bishop, he must have eyes and ears in Hanwell," said Michael. "Connie escapes. So what? That's just another lunatic who's had enough of asylum food. But when the head of Special Branch pitches up and leads the investigation, suddenly that's interesting. And Connie only ups and escapes after meeting with this new Father Morten. Coincidence never happens. The Black Bishop's man on the inside either knows that Connie's a powerful hypnotist, or pokes about and finds out. Powerful hypnotist? Not good on the streets of London. Now, suddenly the Hairy Priest or whatever he is, figures Father Morten could be the key to finding Connie. Why does he want to find Connie? Because an abomination like her, walking the face of the earth with all her powers, makes his God look pretty second rate."

"That's the longest bastard guess I ever heard," said O'Connor.

"Yes!" exclaimed Phoebe, standing up. "Michael's absolutely right. And ever so slightly wrong."

"A statement which at first makes no sense whatsoever, gentlemen," said Michael, "but now Phoebe will stun us with her brilliance."

"Well, hardly brilliance, but anyway, if we assume these mischief-making Jesuits know of Connie Dill's hypnotism, they wouldn't want to eradicate those abilities. I rather wonder if they wouldn't want to harness her powers for their own advantage. Witness the carnage she's caused already. I believe they want to capture her alive and use her as a weapon."

"See? Didn't I just mention her brilliance?" said Michael, proudly.

"A vision from Heaven," said O'Connor, drooling.

We pushed alternative theories back and forth for a while, but none passed muster. No, Michael's explanation of The Black Bishop's involvement and Phoebe's reinterpretation of his motives were quite sound.

"So now we've got three different teams out there looking for Connie," Michael concluded. The Black Bishop and his guy who want her for themselves. Melville's Special Branch who want to get her off the streets and safely back inside."

"That's two teams, y'bastard," said O'Connor. "Who's the third?"

"Us," said Michael.

The Stage Door buzzer buzzed and the Viz Port crackled and fizzed into life for the second time that morning. The face on the screen was familiar. Michael spoke into the TalkiTube.

"Detective Inspector Pym, if you're looking for breakfast, you've come to the right place."

"If only I could, Mister Magister," said Pym. "But you and Miss Le Breton are to accompany us to Scotland Yard immediately. You've been summoned by Assistant Commissioner Sir Cumberland Sinclair."

"Problem?" asked Michael.

"You might say that, sir. Someone's only gone and lodged an official complaint about your behaviour!"

26

Across to the east of London, the morning also found Anthony Graveolens, splendidly attired in a chequered brown three piece suit topped off with a flat cap, bounding down the steps of his Cephas Street villa with a carefree jauntiness that was very much at odds with his expected disposition as a recently bereaved widower. He even tipped his hat to a pair of young ladies who looked at one another in horror at his presumptuousness and then dissolved into a fit of hand to mouth giggles. As he boarded the omnibus and climbed the rear mounted spiral staircase to the open top deck, Anthony appeared unaware of being followed. By the figure which slipped onto the lower deck.

Half an hour of chilly rolling, rattling, stopping and starting later, Anthony alighted at the west end of Fleet Street, just before Temple Bar, clearly with every intention of continuing his journey to Somerset House on foot. In fact, several passengers jumped off at the same time including the mysterious stalker. The street was a hurly burly of early morning 'buses, carriages and carts, each apparently driven by the same kind of urgency and with little regard for anything or anyone who got in the way. Street cleaners hefted great shovelfuls of horse muck into their steaming carts. Yes, my apologies for arising this subject a second time in this missive, but, you know, over one thousand tons of horse manure was cleared from the roads of the capital every day, all to be carried off and dumped against mountainous steaming heaps in the poorer parts of town. I once said to Joe Bazalgette, you know, you've solved the human waste problem, now for goodness sake tackle the equine equivalent. Of course, he did nothing. I expect it will be left to me to come up with some solution.

As Anthony Graveolens pushed and shoved his way through the throng, so the stalker continued to follow him, her narrow, scornful eyes burning brightly. Connie Dill bitterly resented the spring in his step, the phoney hail fellow well met greetings to others, and her fingers tightened their grip on the pistol in her pocket. The shops on Fleet Street were long open for trade. A baker racked up his fresh baked loaves. A pharmacist dusted off his medicaments, brown bottles, liberally laced supplies of cannabis, opium and arsenic, cure-alls aimed at the local newspaper men suffering anything from printer's chest to galloping knob rot. Flower sellers with baskets of freesias battled for custom with pea men selling pots of pods, and frankly the flowers looked a sight more edible. Further along, a butcher's boy dropped a muslin-wrapped ham into the front basket of his bone-shaker bicycle and fanned away the flies.

Connie quickened her pace, and slipped smoothly through the crowd, confident Graveolens knew nothing of her presence. In fact he was slowing down. The butcher's boy threw a leg over his heavy cycle, blinked and pedalled away.

Anthony crossed the Strand to the north side, stopping off at the traffic island on which the Church of Saint Clement Danes stood. Connie remained on the pavement watching him as he went. A clear shot was impossible. She waited for a convenient break in the traffic, drew her pistol, stepped out onto the roadway and raised the weapon. With Anthony Graveolens an easy target, she took aim and BANG!

A tremendous, jagged pain seared through her side. Screams echoed and her world began to spin and the darkness closed in. Eye witnesses later reported that the person in costermonger clothing was crossing the street holding something, and a delivery boy rode his bicycle hard, fast and directly into her side, tossing her into the air. Others agreed it was as if he had deliberately pedalled his cycle straight at the poor costermonger. Connie and the butcher's boy crashed to the floor in a dreadful tangle of limbs, bent bicycle frame and spinning wheels. Carriages swerved and skidded to avoid the melee.

"I never saw! I never saw!" sobbed the butcher's boy, between screams, while he held his dislocated knee, tears stinging his scuffed, raw cheek and his forehead began swelling purple. Connie lay unconscious, a trickle of blood rolling down her cheek and dripping on to the cobbles. Anthony Graveolens elbowed his way through and joined the front ranks of the quickly gathering throng. Fortune was being more than generous this morning because he spotted the butt of the gun protruding from beneath Connie's flank.

Graveolens bent down as if to administer medical assistance, but instead discretely slipped the gun into his hand. He then stood shaking his head, while other onlookers more inclined to good than ghoulish tried to extricate the screaming boy from the mess. Another gent began tapping Connie's cheek shouting, "Boy! Heavens no, she's a woman! Madam! Can you hear me! Have a care! Can you hear me?"

"Don't waste your time, chum," said Anthony, with not the slightest care. "She's a gonna for sure."

The Good Samaritan nodded, but nevertheless felt compelled to place his head on Connie's chest to confirm his pronouncement.

"Halloa! No! I'll wager she might still be breathing!" shouted the gentleman. "Yes! She breathes! Somebody summon an ambulance! And a constable! Be sharp now!"

Anthony Graveolens snarled, turned, shoved his way out of the crowd and walked briskly. That was not the outcome he'd hoped for. Not what he'd hoped for at all.

***

Michael and Phoebe were also finding themselves in circumstances they hadn't hoped for. With the Steamo parked on the Embankment, the magicians were to be found sitting in the Scotland Yard office of a frosty looking Sir Cumberland Sinclair. Well, as frosty a look as the old Etonian bluffer could muster. His office was a grand and well-appointed affair, a large desk, several easy chairs, with portraits of Her Majesty and The Prince of Wales signed by Carl Rudolph Sohn, hanging from the panelled walls. The curved window commanded a fine view of the Thames. Melville sat to one side, having also been summoned to the meeting.

Sir Cumberland eyed Phoebe Le Breton up and down more than once, and with no little incredulity. Heavens, the woman was in a cocoa brown velvet open bust tail coat with a high, stiff collar at the back, and there was a white blouse frilled at the edges and which tested the bounds of decency in regards to the bosomy area. And, by Jove, she wore tan coloured stockings with a leather belt around one thigh like a floozy's garter and brown leather knee length boots secured with half a dozen straps and buckles. I mean, for goodness sake. Then there were those pouting scarlet lips, the bold eye make-up and a look of insouciant defiance. All quite splendid, of course, and lovely on the stage, by crikey, but, really…

And as for Michael Magister, the stage conjuror chap, he was wearing this suit of what looked like velvet. A dark navy blue wide lapelled double breasted tail coat atop trousers of the same material, a white shirt, a black cravat and a brown double breasted waistcoat trimmed with gold braid. Their hats sat on the side table, hers the obligatory bowler with the goggles about the band, and his, the top hat with a time piece strapped to one side. Hardly the attire of a regular chap, d'you think? It all seemed to make Sir Cumberland in his sober black morning tails, wing collar and grey tie feel decidedly under dressed. Mercifully Superintendent Melville brought an even duller complexion to the meeting in his brown Harris Tweed three-piece and brown tie.

"You see, Miss Le Breton and Mister Magister, as the Commissioner and myself were led to believe, you were seconded to Superintendent Melville's department in an advisory role looking into this very unfortunate Hanwell business. What do you think, our Melville, would that be a fair appraisal?" Sir Cumberland looked across for approval.

The Superintendent's nod was barely perceptible. He was never pleased when the Special Branch was referred to as a 'department', it was so much more than that, but he let it go. There would always be more important arguments to win.

"But, do you know, and I'm sorry to have to tell you both, that you quite overstepped the mark when you intruded upon poor Mister Anthony Graveolens's grief. Well, I mean to say, after all is said and done, play fair. The man's wife had just been cruelly slain."

"Graveolens complained?" said Michael, with relief. "Thank you, sir that is a great relief."

"Really, our Magister?" said Sir Cumberland, perplexed. "How can that possibly be a great relief?"

"Well, you see, I and Pheebs…"

"Me and Pheebs. In that usage the correct term is me and Pheebs," corrected Phoebe.

"Okay, me and Pheebs spent the entire day yesterday holding up the investigation, trampling over crime scenes, leaving murder scenes before the police arrived, stealing evidence, and doubtless a dozen other shocking offences Mr M hasn't yet found out about. So to be dressed down purely for intruding on Graveolens's grieving is, frankly, sir, a great relief."

"Oh," said Sir Cumberland. "Yes, I do see your point. "

"Sir Cumberland," said Phoebe, "if Anthony Graveolens felt aggrieved he must have been so overcome with grief he misunderstood us. We went to his house with nothing but good intentions. To offer succour and support."

"Pheebs even offered to help Graveolens mop up the blood," said Michael, still wincing at the thought.

"Yes, I volunteered," said Phoebe with feigned contrition. "And I ask you, gentlemen, does that sound in any way intrusive to you?"

"Fair point you have there, Miss Le Breton. Fair point," nodded the easily pleased Assistant Commissioner. Michael adopted a face of equal contrition. "Once again, it's all my fault, Sir Cumberland, and I can only say sorry. Phoebe suggested proceeding with extreme caution, as she always does, but I insisted we burst right in, and, although it was our enthusiasm and desire to help Superintendent Melville and Detective Inspector Pym as best we could, and by the way, they are tremendous at their jobs, you might want to make a note of that, well, frankly, on refraction…"

"Reflection," corrected Phoebe.

"…on reflection, we were very wrong and, I'll admit erroneous, to intrude on Mister Graveolens's grief. It was a massive mistake and the fault is mine. I apologise."

"Well, our Melville," said Sir Cumberland, not a little relieved, "I suggest that concludes our little get together, don't you think?"

Melville raised an eyebrow and started to stand, no doubt content the get together proved to be quite so little after all. That was until Michael opened his big mouth again, announcing: "The fact that Anthony Graveolens committed all four murders has nothing to do with it."

Melville slumped back down into his chair shaking his head as Sir Cumberland stared open mouthed with shock.

"But… but… but," Sir Cumberland blustered. "You are suggesting that the most appalling series of murders since Jack the Ripper have been perpetrated, not by the escaped lunatic Constance Dill who announced her intention to murder, but by the poor husband of one of her victims?" He looked at Melville, who merely shrugged, while quietly admiring Sinclair's succinct exposition. "But what do you have to support this claim – what evidence?"

"His eyes!" said Michael. "Yes, Sir Cumberland. His eyes. I don't trust his eyes. Have you seen them? The man has evil eyes. Evil. In fact, his people at work all know him as Evil Eye Graveolens!"

"Is he?" asked Sir Cumberland, wrinkling his brow.

"And let's not forget his name," said Michael. "Anthony Graveolens. Isn't that the most ridiculous name you ever heard in your life? Only a serial murderer would have a name like Anthony Graveolens."

"Sir Cumberland," interjected Phoebe, "I too struggle with Michael's instinctive reactions. But he's often uncannily right."

Sir Cumberland suddenly looked at Michael with a peculiar enlightenment which even caught Michael off guard. "My dear Magister. The old second sense is it? A bit of nous-ery thrown in with the old conjuring, eh? Remarkable. What do you think, our Melville? Quite remarkable, what?"

"Indeed, Sir Cumberland," sighed Melville.

"Under the circumstances, our Magister, any line of enquiry is well worth investigating, don't you know. Uncover if this Graveolens fellow is a rum sort," Sir Cumberland really seemed genuinely taken, or 'taken-in' as sceptics of Michael's instinct might prefer to say. Phoebe wondered if those lengthy service postings under the scorching suns of Italy and India had addled the old chap's brain? Especially after he leant forward and said, as if in confidence. "Tell me. Our escapee, This Constance Dill. What are your thoughts on her, old chum? Trusting the old juju, the old instinct, where do you think she might be hiding herself?"

"Impossible to tell, Sir Cumberland. But wherever she is hiding, it's somewhere here," Michael pointed toward the map of London hanging on the wall.

Sir Cumberland nodded and narrowed his eyes. "Very shrewd..." Then he turned to Melville, saying, "Do you know, I think I would appreciate a spot of notice when these fine agents of yours have Constance Dill pinned down, our Melville. I do believe I'd enjoy being in attendance for that escapade, especially if it turns out she's not the murderous type at all and the real culprit is this Graveolens fellow. What do you think, our Melville?"

"Indeed," said Melville.

With that, the Assistant Commissioner, stood up, shook both Michael and Phoebe by the hand, and ushered them to the door, thanking them once again for their excellent work and asking if they wouldn't mind seeing themselves out.

"That man is insane," whispered Michael, as he and Phoebe walked to the stairwell.

"As mad as a mongoose," whispered Phoebe.

"But as a leader of men he could be worse," said Michael.

"No, he couldn't," said Phoebe.

Back in the office, Melville stood to take his leave but Sir Cumberland beckoned him to stay. "Bit of a bad do, all this, our Melville, wouldn't you say?"

"But nothing we cannot handle," said Melville.

"Now then, old chum, I owe you an apology," said Sir Cumberland.

"How so, sir?"

"Detective Inspector Skindrick. What do you think? Bit of a loose cannon? One I feel I foisted upon you."

"That requires no apology, sir."

"The fellow comes from a poor background. Scotsman, see. But made good for himself. Worked hard. Risen through the ranks. Very splendid. I'm inclined to believe he is a spy."

"I know since joining Special Branch he has consistently passed information to you."

"Oh, quite so and for which I apologise, our Melville, but worse than that. I possess a bit of the old Magister nous too, you know. And I'm inclined to believe Detective Inspector Gersham Skindrick also spies for someone else. A force of great evil."

***

As they trotted down Scotland Yard's winding white marble stairwell, Michael and Phoebe turned and collided with Detective Inspector Pym who was on his way up. Breathless and urgent, he carried a sheet of paper.

"Where's the guv'nor ? Still with that idiot?" demanded Pym.

"Walter, whatever is the matter?" asked Phoebe.

Pym waved the scribbled note. "Hot news of Constance Dill! Woman fitting her description was just knocked down by a butcher's bike near Fleet Street. She's unconscious and carted off to hospital. We've got her!"

"To hospital? Badly hurt?" asked Michael, masking his concern.

"Unconscious at least," said Pym.

"Oh. And if you want Mister Melville, I think he went back to his office," lied Michael, ignoring Phoebe's look.

"Right you are. Begging your leave, miss," panted Pym. He and Michael got into one of those annoying, you-go this-way-I-go-that-way muddles on the stairs, before Pym continued up the stairs two at a time.

"Pheebs, what's the nearest hospital to Fleet Street?"

"St. Bartholomew's. Most definitely. And, Michael, why did you lie to Pym?"

"To give us another head start. And let's hope he doesn't miss this…" said Michael, showing Phoebe the Special Branch warrant card he'd just lifted from the Inspector's pocket.

27

It usually took a Hansom twenty minutes on a good run to jiggle its way from Trafalgar Square to St. Bart's Hospital, just there by the Smithfield meat market. But the Steamotivator managed the journey in ten. Admittedly the time was achieved with Phoebe at the wheel adopting that adorable 'point the vehicle in that direction open up the regulator and keep going no matter what' approach to her motoring. In fact she cut such a swathe through the Strand, Fleet Street, left up Farringdon Street, right into Cowcross and over onto Giltspur, that for much of the way it resembled the parting of the Red Sea, with everyone and everything stepping in jig time out of the snorting miracle's path. That's the Steamotivator I'm referring to, by the way, not Phoebe.

The Steamo gasped to a halt by the stone arched entrance of the hospital, the one with the niche above, in which resides the small statue of King Henry the Eighth. It is odd to consider, you know, that for the monarch who imposed such enormous religious and constitutional change upon Merrie England, this is the only statue to be found in London town. Michael leapt from the vehicle, flourished his Special Branch credentials and the Gateman swung open the cast metal full height barrier. Phoebe then eased the Steamo through a second arch and into the quadrangle, an area bounded upon four sides by hospital buildings, and finally parked her by the South Wing, ticking and cooling. The authority of Pym's warrant card enabled Michael to quickly determine where the two casualties of the recent Fleet Street accident had been stretchered.

Time was pressing. Michael figured they only had, what, a ten minute start over Melville. By the time Pym had looked in on Melville's empty office, made enquiries, finally located him, summoned up a police carriage and negotiated the traffic chaos left in the wake of the charging Steamo? Yes, they had a good ten minutes head start. Maybe even fifteen if they struck lucky.

At the top of the stairs on the second floor of the South Wing, Phoebe turned left towards 'Luke', a men's ward, while Michael headed right towards 'Martha', a ward dedicated to women. Michael smiled his best charming smile at the Ward Sister, which brought him little benefit. Sister Concepta Anketel, was a quite splendid, fifty-year-old, no nonsense harridan in a dark blue uniform topped with a crisp white pinafore and starched white headgear resembling a swan about to take flight. A small woman, with little sinuous flesh on the bone, if she was melting to any of Michael's flattery her chiselled, stony face was not inclined to betray it. If he was to gain access to Connie, Michael needed to play his trump card. Sister Anketel carefully examined the credentials which declared him as Detective Inspector Pym.

"You'll see it says 'Special Branch', Sister," Michael pointed out. "I am working undercover, so I know I can rely on your discretion."

"Why Special Branch would take an interest in Miss Dill's accident is naught to do with me. Her condition still has to be fully assessed!" The Sister slapped the card back at Michael's chest and pushed open one of the double doors leading to Martha Ward. "As an authoritarian myself I naturally respect the authority of the police. But be brisk about your business if you please, sir."

"Thank you, Sister," smiled Michael.

"And Detective Inspector Pym. Heed my advice. With that dreadful American accent and that garish mode of dress, a more convincing undercover persona would most certainly be in order."

The air smelled of sharp, fresh carbolic, the spotless glazed green and yellow utility tiles were dazzling, as was the thick linoleum floor. Light poured in through the tall sash windows which must have numbered at least a dozen on the ward. Two rows of beds faced one another with regimental precision, their steel bedheads polished, their linen crisp and cream. It was a stark, bright contrast to the wallowing filth and squalor most of the people endured outside of the hospital. These days, even those clinicians who remained unconvinced of Lister's antiseptic spray had nevertheless all accepted that scrupulous cleanliness and sterilisation were germane in winning the war against infection. Women of varying levels of lucidity, age and disposition, the consumptive, the bandaged, the plastered, the stitched, all lay quietly in wonder at their surroundings and grateful for the care. Mercifully, the emetics, laxatives, leeches and bleeding cups were now banished to the medical annals of yesteryear.

Each bed was haloed by a narrow metal track frame sporting the white linen curtains which could be drawn around for privacy. Sister Anketel had directed Michael to one such bed nearest the door. He drew back the screen and gazed down upon the frail, pathetic figure tucked up in crisp, fresh linen, the bandaged forehead framed against the striped pillow. The last time he'd seen Connie Dill she was pointing a gun at his face. Now she lay unconscious. Michael sat on the side of the bed and warmed her hands together in his.

"You know, most people who want to see me buy a ticket. They don't hold me at gunpoint or get themselves knocked out by, what was that thing, a butcher's bicycle? How did that happen? But, anyway, if you wanted my attention, you've gone the right way about getting it. Oh, and I've looked up and down this ward. The place is full of women. All women. What you need are a few men in here, liven the place up. Both sexes in the same ward, now that *is* an idea. I'll suggest it."

Michael pressed Connie's left hand against his cheek. "The Special Branch and the police still say you murdered Sid, Lez, Annie and Alfie. Okay, you announcing to the world that's what you were actually going to do might have encouraged them into that way of thinking. But, truth be told, Connie, I don't care what they say. I know it's not you. I know its Annie's husband, Anthony Graveolens – can you believe that name? And we'll get him for you. So, anyway, just let me say this. Before you go, which you won't, but – well – thank you. Thank you for tucking me under your great warm kind wing when I first came over to England, a shy, nervous, unknown…"

"Dear God, Magister, when did you start loving the sound of your own voice?" said Connie, in that familiar nasal drone.

Michael's heart leapt. "Connie? Oh, Connie, how are you feeling? Where does it hurt? I thought we were losing you."

"I don't go that easily, you daft beggar," said Connie, slowly opening her eyes.

"So there's obviously nothing wrong this patient. Nurse! This woman is a fraud!"

"Magister, I wish I had bloody shot you now," Connie smiled. "But it's the first time I've woken up to a handsome face in many a long year... I'm sorry, Magister."

Michael kissed the backs of Connie's hands, then her forehead and assured her she had nothing to be sorry about. Well, maybe the gun in his face, but nothing else.

"No, I've caused you and Phoebe such a deal of trouble," she insisted.

"Connie, listen, Pheebs and I, we'll make this turn around. I know the killer is that dullard who married Annie. He is, isn't he? It's Anthony Graveolens. He's the real murderer?"

"I really thought I could stop him on my own, I needed to stop him on my own. I couldn't involve anybody else. You see..." she whispered.

With a sudden clatter, the curtain around the bed was drawn back, Michael blinked with surprise as a portly, bald but bearded gentleman of great presence appeared. Dressed in a black suit with grey bow tie and wing collar, he carried a stethoscope in one hand and in the other a file docket. He glanced at the name on the folder before saying: "Miss Constance Dill?"

"It is, but can it wait a minute?" said Michael, a mite peeved at such an interruption at such a crucial moment.

"Only if we don't want Miss Dill to get better, sir. How do you do. Harrison Cripps, surgeon."

"How do you do. Walter Pym, policeman," said Michael, rising to his feet.

"Quite the nasty bash on the head we've sustained, haven't we?" said Harrison Cripps, scanning the one page in the docket, quickly. Michael wondered why doctors used the word 'we' when they mean 'you'. Is it psychological trickery perhaps? Some attempt at sharing the pain? Cripps then turned to Michael. "Mister... Pym, is it? Yes, I'll ask you to conclude your questioning and afford us some little privacy while I examine Miss Dill."

"Absolutely, sir, the reputation of your medical excellence goes before you," said Michael, despite never having ever heard of the man. "Just make her well again, doc."

"Be assured, she could find herself in no better place, nor in finer hands"

"Michael..." said Connie weakly.

"It's okay, Connie, relax," Michael told her before tenderly kissing Connie's hand once more. "I'll be right outside."

Mister Cripps stood aside leaving barely enough room to allow Michael squeeze from the space beside the bed. Cripps then watched as the overdressed police impostor swung open the door and strode from the ward. Cripps then pulled the curtain again enclosing the bed. But when he turned back to look down upon Connie Dill, she found herself staring up at a sneering face. The face of Anthony Graveolens.

***

Detective Inspector Gersham Skindrick stood in the Scotland Yard office of Assistant Commissioner Sir Cumberland Sinclair, barely able to believe his ears – or his luck!

"Well, our Skindrick, bit of a curious do this," Sir Cumberland was telling him. "The Superintendent is no fool and quickly realised you were keeping me up to date with proceedings regarding the old Special Branch behind his back as it were. Now, I believe our Skindrick, I believe we can dig ourselves out of this mire if you go along and say you're sorry. What do you think, old chum?"

"Apologise? F' spying on Melville?" Skindrick had said with incredulity.

"Apologise is the word, our Skindrick. That should wiggle you back in the fellow's good books, and now's the time to do it. I happen to know the old Superintendent and Inspector Pym are trotting across to the old Bart's hospital for a bit of investigation. Seems this Constance Dill has pitched up in the hospital after an accident…"

Skindrick's face didn't jolt, but his stomach certainly did. Dill at St. Bart's? Here was a chance to grab her for His Eminence.

"…so what say you toddle off to Bart's, make yourself useful to them and then say how sorry you are. What do you think, our Skindrick? I believe the Superintendent will thank you for it."

"I think it's an fine idea, sir. Y'are an inspiring leader of men, sir," said Skindrick. "If y'll excuse me, I'll away t' the hospital forthwith."

"Splendid chap," said Sir Cumberland to himself, as Skindrick closed the office door behind him.

***

Phoebe found Michael leaning back against the yellow tiled wall of the corridor outside Martha Ward. He was rolling a penny through his fingers completely lost in a seemingly troubled world of his own. It was Phoebe repeating, "Michael, how's Connie?" which broke his thoughts. He cast Phoebe one of those squint-eyed, head wobbling 'it's a job to know' looks.

"She was all set to talk when the damned doctor arrived. What did you get from the cycle rider?"

"Henry, he's a butcher's boy. He's in rather a pickle himself: compound fracture of the femur, greenstick fractures of the ulna and radius and multiple abrasions. He's also left with the distinct possibility of internal damage. The abdominal specialist arrived as I left."

"Pheebs, how can you know so much?"

"I've no idea. Blame Arthur Doyle."

"I try to for most things," said Michael. "Pheebs, something's wrong."

"Michael, we are in a hospital, Connie's nearly been killed, and we have a policeman's stolen identity. So yes, I think your assessment is not too far off. Added to which, Henry the butcher's boy said he had no recollection of the accident, none whatsoever. Furthermore, he has no idea why he should be cycling in that direction when his delivery was down to 'The Old King Lud' public house on Ludgate Circus, which is entirely the other way. And he was in rather too much pain to be disingenuous. Otherwise, a street rogue like Henry could have confected a simpler, more convincing lie in a flash. All rather odd, don't you think?"

"Not if he was 'fluenced..." Michael exclaimed, suddenly inspired. "That's it. Dammit, Pheebs, the butcher's boy was 'fluenced. Riding in the wrong direction, no memory of what he was doing and why? Classic hypnosis. Connie hypnotised the boy to pedal straight into her."

"Why would Connie do that?" puzzled Phoebe. "What's to be gained by the accident? Unless – Michael, do you suppose someone else could possess Connie's power of hypnosis?"

28

Anthony Graveolens stared down upon the pathetic figure
laying in the bed. She was grimacing with strain and terror.
The veins on her thin arms stood out like rope-cords as she
gripped the pillow tightly in both hands. The pillow she was so
desperately trying to hold up, away from her face.

"You know you can't fight me, mother," whispered
Graveolens in a gentle, soothing manner. His face was calm,
almost kind.

"Don't you dare call me that," spat Connie. "I gave you life,
but you're no son of mine!"

"We both know that's untrue, and we both know I'm
stronger. And I can take our revenge upon them so much more
sweetly than you ever would. Our revenge. Yours and mine.
On all of them. We cannot forgive for what they did to you.
You've suffered enough, mother. Now you need suffer no
more."

"You're just a murderer." gasped Connie.

"No, no. That's not true. I murdered no one, Connie,"
soothed Graveolens, smiling. "I never touched any of them.
All those uncaring self-regarding scumbags died by their own
hand. All I did was offer the encouragement they needed. But I
did stand by and happily watch them while they did it."

The unseen force bore down even more heavily on the
pillow. Connie fought to keep it at bay, but the weight became
so dreadfully overpowering. Down and down it pushed,
merciless and unrelenting. Her mind was exhausted and her
strength was spent. Connie felt herself pull the pillow down
unto her face. And could do nothing about it.

"That's it. Shhh. Don't fight. It is by far the best way. Soon
it will all be over. They won't be able to hurt you. Or lock you
away. None of them. Ever again."

***

The Black Bishop pressed the earpiece of his candlestick
telephone tightly to his ear, listening intently to Skindrick's

every word. So, the Dill creature was to be found at St. Bartholomew's Hospital. His eyes blazed. It was divine intervention.

"Excellent, my disciple," said The Black Bishop. "You know what to do. At any cost. For it is God's will."

***

"I can think of half a dozen stage hypnotists, but they're all fakers, none of them has Connie's genuine ability," said Michael. "Pheebs, we need to speak with her again. Shame this Doctor Cripps won't hurry up."

"Cripps, yes, he appears terribly impressive," nodded Phoebe. "I just left him across the way examining Henry."

"Cripps? Harrison Cripps? No. Because I just left Doctor Cripps in there with Connie."

"Well, he can't be in two places…"

Then the horror crashed into Michael's head with all the power of a speeding express. "Dammit, she called me 'Michael'! She's never called me Michael! Always Magister. Pheebs – she tried to warn me about…."

Before he finished the sentence Michael burst through the swing doors and into the ward, tumbling and tipping all and sundry out of his way. He wrenched back the curtain surrounding Connie's bed. And there she was for all to see. Lying there, alone. The pillow now resting on her chest. Her eyes wide open. Lifeless.

"Doctor, we need a doctor here – please, anyone!" Michael held Connie's shoulders and shook her in agonised frustration. Phoebe pulled Michael to one side, held Connie's wrist feeling for a pulse, checking her eyes, desperate to find some flicker of life. Phoebe turned to face Michael and slowly shook her head. Michael looked to the heavens, his face a mask of pain which turned to hatred. "Graveolens. Anthony Graveolens did this…"

He then took a breath, and announced to the ward: "Ladies, listen up please. The man who was just here, with this woman. Where did he go? Someone must have seen him!"

Several patients were stunned into open mouth silence by the chaos Michael had caused, bursting in on the ward. A handful remained soundly asleep. It was up to one silver haired, gummy octogenarian who held up a thin, bony finger and pointed to the far end of the ward.

"There," croaked the sweet old girl. "He run down there he did."

But when Michael hurried to her side he saw her eyes were grey and opaque. The woman was as blind as a bat.

"You saw him, ma'am?" wondered Michael.

"A-course I never saw him, young boy," scowled the lady, who then jabbed a finger at her ear. "But I heard him! He ran along to there…"

At the end of the ward a window was wide open. It was certainly large enough to accommodate a small vile man making his cowardly getaway. But Martha Ward was on the second floor. Could he have jumped? Michael slid the sash window higher still and looked left and right along the parapet. Nothing. Directly below him sat the Steamo. In the quadrangle, amid the fountain and the four brand new wooden shelters there were horses, carts, patients, and staff all going about whatever it was they were going about. None of them looked to be in haste and none stood out as a likely candidate for Anthony Graveolens. In fact, the only attention grabbing action was the high speed arrival of a Brougham, emerging in a cloud of kicked up dust from under the arch opposite. Superintendent Melville had arrived.

"Graveolens. He did this! He 'fluenced me, convinced me I was looking at a doctor – but he couldn't fool Connie," Michael told Phoebe. Both had been unceremoniously ejected from the ward, Special Branch or no Special Branch, and were now huddled together in the corridor outside. "And he escaped through the window. Exactly as he did when he killed Annie. He's damned well gone."

***

Graveolens had smothered Connie, then walked quickly to the end of the ward, slipped out of the window onto the cream stone parapet, edged along to the corner of the building and climbed down the black cast iron rainwater pipe to the cobbles below. As he strolled past the Steamo he kicked a well-aimed boot at the left side passenger door. But it only served to jar Graveolens's foot, and rouse Mister Garrideb whose eyes glared green as he hollered metallically, "Clear orf, ya bugger! Gertcha!" But with his work done, the young serial killer strolled satisfied and innocent-looking with his hands deep in his moleskin trouser pockets toward the exit arch. He mooched out into Giltspur Street, looked around, breathed deeply and with a most contented air set off towards Smithfield meat market. Anthony Graveolens couldn't even be troubled to turn up a precautionary collar when he saw the official looking Brougham rattling by at speed.

"Just one more to die," thought Graveolens, as he swaggered along beside the beautiful curlicue wrought iron-work of Smithfield's central Grand Avenue. "That self-important buffoon, Michael Magister."

29

To say that Melville and Pym were disappointed by the news of Connie's murder would be, well, frankly the truth. As they stood in the corridor outside Martha Ward, Magister's report of the events certainly begged far more questions than it answered: he had been hypnotised by Anthony Graveolens, who then murdered Connie behind drawn curtains. But there was no sign of a struggle or injury inflicted upon the corpse, nor did any of the three dozen patients and nurses in the ward see anyone other than Magister himself. Admittedly most of these women were to be found in various states of questionable cognisance, and the only one who was certain she 'saw' this second mystery man was a poor elderly patient who was as blind as Pugh. So, in terms of holding water, Michael's story was much like a bucket with its bottom rusted through.

"But had you not lied to me on the stairs about the Superintendent being in his office, we might have got here a bit sooner and saved Connie Dill," said Pym.

"Detective Inspector Pym, what can I say? I'm deeply ashamed for showing you such a lack of respect, and now Connie…" Michael's voice was almost breaking with contrition. Suddenly he threw his arms around Pym and pulled him close in an elaborate display of contrition.

"Hold up! Hold up! Get off me! Do I look like Bosie?" Pym shoved Michael away and raised a fist of fury ready to duke Michael right on the noble chin.

"Detective Inspector," chided Melville. The tone was enough to unfurrow Pym's brow, lower his fist and regain control. Doubtless his ire, you know, was given more to startled embarrassment than true rage. "If you please, Detective Inspector, I believe your detection skills are required outside. A closer examination of the quadrangle to confirm or deny Mister Magister's report concerning his escaping murderer."

Pym nodded and set about his business, poking around downstairs, cajoling passers-by. He remained unnerved by the incident with Michael. I mean to say, a man who resorts to 'hugging' other men? That sort of thing could land you a two spot in Reading gaol.

Of course, what Walter Pym failed to perceive, during Michael's unwanted embrace, was the magician slipping the Detective Inspector's warrant card back into his inside jacket pocket. A summons for impersonating a police officer was the last thing Michael and Phoebe needed, and when Pym finally, inevitably, discovered his card was gone, suspicions would immediately fall upon Michael. Thus a great show of overly dramatic 'hugging' made for an easy distraction.

Melville looked stern. "The Assistant Commissioner may be sympathetic to your contention that the evil eyes of Anthony Graveolens are evidence enough to condemn the man to the gibbet, but within our real world, a court would struggle to support a conviction."

"Whoever it was, Graveolens or anyone, I was hypnotised into believing he was Doctor Harrison Cripps, before he went on to murder Connie," said Michael firmly.

"Describe the person who hypnotised you," demanded Melville.

"Five feet eight tall, two hundred and twenty four pounds, full brown beard flecked with bits of grey, sad dark eyes, bald, full brows, dark suit and wing collar," said Michael.

"Your talent for observation remains impressive," said Melville.

"Yes, Mister M, my powers are impressive, but it really helps when I'm looking at the man right now."

Behind Melville, the double doors to Martha Ward had swung open, followed by the imposing figure of the real Mister William Harrison Cripps, St. Bartholomew's esteemed surgeon to the Women's Wards and specialist in all matters abdominal. Behind him two sturdy, brown coated porters, one either end of a stretcher, bore the covered body of Connie Dill. Melville held up his warrant card and stopped them.

"Might I?" he asked Cripps.

"You may," came the reply.

It struck Phoebe that these two professionals with the confident bearing of those destined for even loftier plains, both displayed the same courteous efficiency, more importantly the same economy of words; something that would never trouble Michael Magister. Or me.

Melville peeled back the white linen sheet and studied the pale, peaceful face to satisfy himself it was indeed the corpse of Constance Dill. Connie's dead arm slipped down from her side, under the sheet. Michael took her hand, kissed it tenderly, paused, stroked her arm then slipped it back under the white sheet before Melville gave the nod for the porters to carry on.

"My cursory examination would indicate death as a result of the street collision, by reasons yet to be determined," said Cripps.

"Mister Cripps, where are they taking Connie's body now?" asked Michael with a sigh.

"To the mortuary, for a post mortem. Sir, you are a family member or friend?" said Cripps

"Far closer than that," said Michael. "Show business colleague."

"Then you have my sympathy." After twenty years as a cancer treatment pioneer, Harrison Cripps was well versed in the way of compassion, even when it was directed toward the bereaved, who appeared ever so slightly strange.

"Mister Cripps, the scar across Connie's forehead," said Michael. "She told me it came from a brain operation conducted by a Swiss doctor, name of Gottlieb Burckhardt? Does that name ring a bell?"

"My speciality is the abdomen, but my associate Sir Henry Butlin and I have discussed the work of Dr Burckhardt. He maintains a psychiatric clinic in Zurich. A keen proponent of the lobotomy."

"Lobotomy?" said Michael.

"A form of brain surgery, if you will, performed to alter an insane patient's behaviour. But perhaps we should not dwell too much on detail in front of the young lady," Cripps gestured at Phoebe.

"Please, Mister Cripps, which detail of a lobotomy do you suppose will cause me to swoon?" asked Phoebe. "The ice pick itself, or the method where it's hammered into the patient's brain through the eye-socket?"

Cripps bowed to Phoebe, while Michael winced at the thought. "Madam, your point is well made. In answer to your question - no. The scar traversing Miss Dill's forehead was most certainly not a consequence of a lobotomy. I would say less in keeping with cure, and more inclined toward investigation."

"Mister Cripps," said a firm female voice. It was the no-nonsense Sister Anketel. "This is not a public place, kindly move along. Especially you, Detective Inspector Pym, you have caused more than your share of disruption for one day."

Before Melville could begin to even ponder as to how Michael might be mistaken for Pym, his thought was derailed by Harrison Cripps, who was already urging the group toward the stairwell. The eminent surgeon knew the patience of Sister Anketel was not to be tested. Cripps then bade Phoebe, Melville and Michael a good day and set off for the operating theatre to prepare for surgery on the butcher's boy's intestinal bleed.

"I have further enquiries to conduct," said Melville. "So, Mister Magister, Miss Le Breton, with Constance Dill now dead, it appears your obligation to the case is hereby discharged. You may return to continue your theatre."

"But…" Phoebe started to speak, but was cut off by Michael opening his arms and saying: "That's fine by us, Mister M, so how about a farewell hug?" Melville looked impassive and told Michael that he thought not. So, Michael turned to Phoebe who dutifully obliged, but only because she figured Michael was up to some sort of, what he called, monkeyshines. Her suspicions were confirmed when Michael whispered, "We need a reason to stay here."

"Superintendent," said Phoebe, breaking the hug. "Would you mind awfully, before we leave the hospital, if I introduce Michael to the paintings by the stairs of the North Wing."

"The Hogarth Murals?" Melville said brightly. "Indeed. Anyone who leaves this place without viewing them denies himself enormous cultural enrichment."

"Until next time, Mister M," said Michael.

"What next time, Mister Magister? I bid you good day." Melville bowed at Phoebe and headed off to Luke Ward, determined to hear Henry the butcher's boy's side of the story, before Mister Cripps addled his mind with pre-operative laudanum.

30

In the men's ward the whimpering young bicyclist, with head, knees and elbow wrapped in bandages, looking very like an Egyptian pharaoh who frustrates his embalmers by annoyingly clinging to life, pretty much related to Melville everything about the accident he had told Phoebe. It was the boy's loss of memory, the wrong direction of travel and the headache which Melville found particularly interesting.

Then with Sister Anketel's approval, she relented once he suggested there might be evidence of foul play, Melville was back in Martha Ward, methodically examining Connie Dill's hospital bed, above and below. He spoke with nurses, and then with patients, several of whom were vaguely lucid. Everyone saw Magister arrive at Connie's bedside, and several reported they might have seen Mister Cripps join him. Then certainly they all saw Magister leave. But then none recalled seeing Mister Cripps leave, none save for the sightless, gummy octogenarian, who stuck with steadfast rigidity to her statement.

"Heard his footfall, I did. Metal tipped leather boots, they was, which clacked and creaked on the linoleum. Walking slowly along, he was, from there to there." She swung her arm to further illustrate the direction of travel. "And I'll stick a knife in any man who deems me a liar."

Again there was one thing on which many patients and nurses agreed. They had all suffered headaches. Melville strolled to the window at the end of the ward and looked down at the cobbles below and around at the parapet, just as Michael had done. Melville saw that the magician's vehicle had now been moved across the square and was now parked by the entrance arch at the North Wing. The magicians must still be admiring the sweeping Hogarthian masterpieces which dominated the North Wing stairwell.

Melville smoothly slipped out through the window and onto the parapet, where stood for a few seconds. Then, having drawn his conclusion Melville hauled himself back in. He thanked Sister Anketel who said nothing, but pointedly closed the window behind him.

Next, Melville took in the entire panorama of the hospital from below. Four identical wings built of pale Bath Stone enclosed this giant quadrangle, two hundred feet long by one hundred and fifty feet wide. It was an impressive, airy space, designed by that richly skilled Scotsman James Gibbs, almost a hundred and fifty years ago.

Melville stared up at the escape window, his brain methodically working through the events of the last day, the last decade. Mister Magister had confirmed what Melville already knew. Constance Dill's hypnotism required no chicanery, no deception. She possessed the unique ability to cloud the mind and convince people that they were seeing only what she wanted them to see, and make them do exactly what she wanted them to do. All with just a glance, a look in the eye.

Magister had also spoken of Dill's 'innate human decency', a surprisingly flowery phrase. It was a decency which allowed Connie to perform parlour tricks on the Music Hall stage, but prevented her from exploiting her considerable power beyond that. She appeared utterly incorruptible and her distress at causing the death of an innocent had motivated her voluntary incarceration, her withdrawal from society.

At the time, rumours of Dill and her extraordinary power had circulated, but were quickly dismissed as just Freak Show myth, the kind talked up by Barnum. Only a new Irish Special Branch Detective had sought her out and shrouded Constance Dill with a new cloak of anonymity. He knew her power was something the unscrupulous could harness and abuse for their own benefit. So this detective had arranged for Connie to quietly live out the rest of her life, not in prison, but in the reasonably benevolent surroundings of Hanwell. But then suddenly, yesterday, her unexpected escape threatened to overturn that entire carefully constructed status quo. Of course, that young Irish Special Branch Detective was now the Superintendent who ran the entire division. William Melville.

Her innate human decency, yes, that powerful phrase had haunted Melville. Indeed, how could someone who possessed such a virtue suddenly become a merciless, vengeful killer? No. It could not happen. And Michael Magister had been convinced from the beginning that Constance Dill was not responsible for the murders. Might it stretch credibility so much to start believing Magister could be correct about Anthony Graveolens?

"Guv'nor..." Detective Inspector Pym's breathless urgency broke Melville's train of thought. "I found a handful of witnesses who reckon they saw a fella shinning down the rainwater pipe not more than half an hour ago. Most took him to be a building worker, a lead roofer, but down the pipe he came. He then crossed the square and sloped away under the Henry the Eighth archway. There's a severe likelihood Magister was telling the truth. The scuff marks, see, boot marks either side of the drainpipe? They could indicate such an occurrence."

"All in keeping with my own observations. Diligent work, Detective Inspector Pym," nodded Melville. "I see The Magister vehicle remains parked across the square. The work of William Hogarth is clearly fascinating."

31

Michael and Phoebe were all set to board the Steamo when they heard: "The Governors of this hospital were about to commission a Venetian artist to decorate that staircase. When William Hogarth, heard this he became so indignant that he offered his services for gratis. He believed paintings hanging in a Great British hospital should be undertaken by a Great British artist and that it was his patriotic duty to step in." It was Melville. He and Pym had simply appeared from around the back of the Steamo. It was an effective piece of theatre, sneaking up on the blind side.

Melville was referring of course to the two vast, colourful murals which dominate the walls of the broad, airy dark wood stairwell of the North Wing at St. Bartholomew's. And when I say vast, I mean they are enormous. Each canvas depicts a relevant Biblical scene, with a score of figures and wealth of allegory, enclosed within scrolled borders. If you find yourself with the time and opportunity, do wander along to Bart's and see them. They are all but forgotten works of Hogarthian majesty.   One is called 'The Good Samaritan', the other 'Christ at the Pool at Bethesda'. Care and cure is the common theme.

"You know your Hogarth, Superintendent," said Phoebe. "Of the two pictures, 'The Good Samaritan' was painted in 1737, right here in situ with Hogarth balancing rather precariously upon scaffolding."

"But the other picture," said Melville, "'Jesus at the Pool of Bethesda' was painted a year earlier, back at his studio, not far away, and transported here. They join seamlessly at the corner. No one would know they were two separate pictures, composed at different times and in different places. I liken those two paintings to your profession as illusionists, where nothing is really as it appears."

"And I rather think one might say the same of your profession, Superintendent," said Phoebe.

Melville accepted the point against him with good grace, before asking, "I wonder, where is your vehicle's sentinel?"

"Mister Garrideb?" said Phoebe, flashing a look at Michael.

"Slumped on the seat," smiled Michael, apparently tapping the disarm code onto the enamel keyboard before sliding back the passenger compartment door which responded with a hiss. Within the cabin, the mechanical man in his dark overcoat and gas mask lay on one side, as if dozing. His head resting against the seat arm. "Needs recharging. These automata, eh, Mister M? Don't have the stamina of us real people. We'll fire him up back at the theatre. Won't we, old friend?" Michael leant in toward the spent Garrideb, patted him on the lifeless arm, then twisted the wheel, which slid the door shut.

"And Mister Magister. I believe you!" Melville made this sudden announcement for no apparent reason, although, of course, in reality Melville never opened his mouth without some kind of reason.

"That's so good to hear, Mister M, finally!" exclaimed Michael, before wondering. "But exactly what part of anything brilliant we've ever said do you believe?"

"I now believe the presence of a second man in Martha Ward. He was the killer of Constance Dill and he himself is a brilliant hypnotist." Melville was calm, matter of fact and in no way contrite.

"And you suddenly realise this how?" asked Phoebe, her eyes narrowing with suspicion.

"Physical evidence, Miss," reported Pym. "Boot marks on the window ledge, scuff marks on the rainwater pipe. Plus half a dozen good eye witnesses who saw the man descending."

"All the patients in the ward have headaches," added Melville. "Although none of them remember our man was ever there, except, most pointedly, a blind woman."

"And a blind woman couldn't meet his gaze, so therefore couldn't be 'fluenced," said Phoebe.

"Indeed," said Melville. "But if, as you insist, this new suspect really is Anthony Graveolens, an unusual name and a pair of eyes you don't like the look of, do not for credible evidence make."

"Oh, my days, yes they do!" exclaimed Phoebe, as if struck by some glorious inspiration, which, by the way, she had. "On both counts! It is more than enough! Michael has been right all along! All the time he's been boring us rigid, banging the drum about Anthony's eyes, but he's absolutely right, they are the key. Oh, I am such a dunce! But not because Anthony's eyes are evil, which they may well be, but because... they are exactly the same as Connie's!"

"Individuals share the same colour eyes all the time," said Melville. "Grey, green, blue, brown."

"Not with Sectoral Heterochromia," said Phoebe with confidence.

"Exactly!" said Michael with equal confidence, but with no understanding of why.

"It's a condition of the iris. I read about it while working at Arthur's ophthalmic practice at Wimpole Street. Anthony's eyes have blue irises, but with a little brown section. When I looked down at Connie's eyes when she died, I noticed they were exactly the same. Blue irises with a little brown section."

"This condition is uncommon?" asked Pym.

Phoebe nodded: "If memory serves me well, it is present in less than two per cent of the population."

"Don't you just love her?" said Michael, wrapping an arm around Phoebe's shoulder.

Melville paused for thought. "You will, of course, not be offended when I take clarification from an ophthalmic consultant."

"You're in the right place," said Michael gesturing at the buildings which surrounded them.

"But most significantly, Sectoral Heterochromia can be genetic. Which means, gentlemen, there is a strong statistical likelihood that Constance Dill and Anthony Graveolens are related," beamed Phoebe. "And given their ages, quite possibly..."

"Mother and son?" interjected Michael. "Which also means Anthony Graveolens not only murdered four innocent people, he just killed his own mother!"

"Here, hold up a minute, Miss, you said Magister was right on both counts?" said Pym. "That's the eyes. What about the name?"

"It is so obvious I'm rather too embarrassed to admit I didn't realise the connection until now," said Phoebe adopting a coy apologetic face. "It's Latin."

"Of course it is," said Michael nodding and smiling and bluffing.

"Connie Dill. Dill is a herb," Phoebe explained. "And the Latin name for Dill is *'Anethum graveolens'*…"

All three men present said as one: "Anthony Graveolens!"

"Michael, I'm so, so sorry I will never question your instincts ever again," said Phoebe, taking his arm. "You said from the very start that Graveolens was the killer."

While Pym looked impressed and amazed, Melville's face was stern, absorbed in his own world of analysis. He quickly assessed the situation, processed the permutations and made his decision. "If there is even the slightest possibility Graveolens possesses his mother's mesmeric powers, then he certainly warrants the concern of Special Branch. Constance Dill treated her power with respect and responsibility. Graveolens has no such care, as he has demonstrated. He is of greater threat to national security than Constance Dill ever was. He becomes our priority."

"Which is all fine and dandy, Mister M, but aren't we all forgetting something?"

"Michael's quite right," gasped Phoebe. "If Graveolens *is* the murderer he still has one remaining target to kill."

"Me," said Michael.

"Which is precisely what we want him to do," said Melville, with almost a smile

"Excuse me?"

"Let him come for you. Let him make his move. But we shall be ready for him. "

Phoebe grinned broadly. "Well, Michael, this is rather exciting. I do believe the Superintendent wishes to use you as bait."

***

Michael fired up the Steamo, and lurched the metal monster westward towards Fleet Street. Only once they had chugged past the pedestal of Temple Bar, topped with its dragon and decorated, ironically, with statues of Phoebe's father and grandmother, did Michael turn to Mister Garrideb, who was now sitting upright once again beside Phoebe.

"How you doing back here, Connie?" shouted Michael. Phoebe helped Constance Dill remove the gas mask.

"Better all the time, Magister," she whispered. "Better all the time."

32

So. A dead woman, murdered and lying on a mortuary slab ready for a post mortem suddenly appears alive and as well as can be expected, travelling across London in a steam powered vehicle. And all under the very noses of the finest police minds in Scotland Yard? What sorcery was this? Voodoo, perhaps? Some divine resurrection? Certainly not! It was a highly audacious, never to be repeated feat of risen-from-the-dead chicanery, which even dear old Maskelyne would have struggled to fathom.

The plan to extricate Connie did not even exist until her corpse was being hefted from Martha Ward by those two porters, under the watchful eye of Harrison Cripps. You might recall Superintendent Melville asked to confirm Connie's identity and while he peeled back the sheet to examine her face, Connie's arm slumped down off the stretcher. Michael lifted her arm and kissed the back of her hand. It was then that she gently squeezed his hand. Twice. Not a flicker on her face, just two squeezes of the hand. Michael knew then she was still alive and in a state of 'thanatosis'. Not that he would have known that particular word, but he realised she was physically playing possum. After apparently suffocating herself with the pillow, Connie still had the wherewithal to convince everyone else: her murderer, Phoebe, those trained nurses and indeed the eminent Mister Cripps that she was dead.

Michael determined where Connie's body would be taken and conspired with Phoebe. Remember their 'hug'? And the whispered exchange? Michael needed an reason to stay at the hospital and stage Connie's rescue. The excuse to view the Hogarth murals was perfect, because the mortuary was to be found in the same building. The North Wing.

With Melville and Pym setting about their own detective work and with the Steamo now shifted from below the West Wing to the North Wing arch, Michael and Phoebe could make their move. They mauled the Garrideb from the passenger cabin of the vehicle and into the hospital building.

Yes, to begin with he had complained, glowed his eyes bottle green and growled "Clear off, ya bugger! Gorn! I'll 'ave yer!", but the curmudgeonly Mechannequin's throat speaker was quickly silenced by a neat twist of the turn-screw at the back of his neck.

They then supported the Garrideb, one under each arm, as if they were assisting an infirm or more likely drunken relative. Mister Garrideb could manage rudimentary mobility, but you must understand he was still very much a prototype, a primitive form. His gait looked much akin to a sewer-man marching waist-deep through muck. It was only when the Garrideb's gas mask began attracting unwelcome glances, that Michael commandeered an unused bath chair.

Swathed in a scarlet woollen blanket, the Garrideb was pushed apace by Michael, now wearing a stethoscope about his neck, one swiped from the hook on the back of a store room door. Phoebe held the Garrideb's hand and adopted the role of the concerned, comforting next of kin, which seemed to satisfy passers-by until a stern voice demanded: "I say, you there. You two. Where are you taking that patient?"

Michael and Phoebe cursed the interruption, ignored it and simply continued walking. But the stern voice was not easily discouraged. "I asked where you were taking that patient?"

Michael stopped and turned to face the officious voice. It belonged to a heavy fellow, short and wide with a pinky yellow nose in the style of an unripe Victoria plum. His cheeks were dressed in ginger whiskers and his large head covered in wild ginger curls. If the Gorgon had ever dipped her writhing, reptilian hairstyle in a copper full of boiling sulphuric acid, this would have been the result.

"Treves of the London Hospital, if you must know, old man," said Michael, confidently. Phoebe flicked a smile at Michael's attempt at a well-to-do London accent, knowing full well, you know, that the real Frederick Treves, to whom he referred, was Dorset born and bred. "And let me present my associate…"

"Miss Penelope Lister," said Phoebe, bang on cue, extending her hand coyly to be shaken. "How do you do, Doctor...?"

Phoebe's breath-taking beauty almost buckled Doctor Snakehair's knees, as he eagerly shook her gloved hand. He gave his name, but she took no notice. In her mind he was always going to be Doctor Snakehair.

"I present my father, Professor Joseph Lister, whom you probably know as the President of the Royal Society and Surgeon in Ordinary to Her Majesty, and whom you may address as Baron Lister," added Phoebe, firmly and gesturing to the Garrideb.

"I expect you recognise him," said Michael without shame.

"Absolutely! You must forgive my brashness," gushed Doctor Snakehair, lowering his chins onto his chest to hide his embarrassment. "It is the finest of honours indeed to meet such a distinguished practitioner such as yourself, Dr Treves. And, of course your esteemed personage, Baron Lister..."

Phoebe could see the flicker of doubt crossing Doctor Snakehair's face as he gazed upon the Garrideb's gasmask. Quickly she said, "My father recently suffered a well-publicised stroke, this device aids his respiration."

"Doctor," said Michael, adopting a conspiratorial tone, "In his role as President of the Royal Society, His Lordship is keen to continue his practice of inspecting hospitals unannounced, in secret, to assure himself that standards of hygiene and amputation and that sort of medical thing are being kept at an acceptable level. And as you yourself must know, you can never have too much hygiene or amputation."

"We would be most appreciative, in view of his par less condition, if word of my father's visit did not spread," said Phoebe quickly, gazing longingly at Doctor Snakehair.

Totally smitten with Phoebe's loveliness, Dr Snakehair's jowls wobbled with earnest sincerity as he assured her that his oath to the profession and his personal discretion were to be relied upon absolutely.

"Good show, old man, and be assured you will receive his Lordship's highest recommendation. Splendid work and keep up the hypocritical oath," said Michael, pumping Doctor Snakehair's hand once again before demanding directions to the mortuary and then sending him on his way with a further reminder of their confidential pact.

"By the way, Michael," said Phoebe, "its Hippocratic not hypocritical…"

Doctor Snakehair's simpered and precise directions sent them along the corridor into the Otis lift and down to the basement, and along a corridor, at the end of which, above two solid wooden swing doors, the word "MORTUARY" had been elegantly chiselled. Michael and Phoebe shoved open the double doors to discover the mortuary porter standing at his desk and documenting details in a large ledger. Given his gruesome profession in his subterranean surroundings, perhaps it was inevitable he was a pallid and sour-faced fellow. Much like his charges, thought Michael. Mousey-haired, tall, almost gangly, with a long face, sharp cheek bones and lips so thin, an army career as a bugler would never have been an option.

Doctor Snakehair had warned them the porter was an endomorphic type named Staveley Chaddock. Behind Mister Chaddock lay half a dozen corpses, each on its own wooden table and covered in a white sheet. It was Chaddock's role to transport the bodies upon a wheeled bier up from the mortuary to the post mortem room on the second floor, where he was expected to wash and prepare the corpse for the surgeon's cause-of-death investigation. It was a responsible line of work in which Chaddock evidently took enormous pride.

At first sight of Michael and Phoebe, Chaddock looked up from his ledger, turned his mouth down and barked, "No one allowed down here!"

Again Michael and Phoebe explained who they were and why they were in the company of the ailing but indefatigable Lord Lister, sitting here in the bath chair. The confident authority of Michael and Phoebe softened his attitude hardly a jot. Flattery concerning his well-ordered administration of the mortuary, did little to help either, and why would it? They were simply telling the man what he already knew. In which case, thought Michael, he might respond to a contrary point of view. So he told Chaddock that he was happy to disagree with Sister Anketel of Martha Ward. For it was she who had said how ramshackle and disorganised the mortuary was, how it dragged the name of this wonderful hospital down into the mud and how replacing Chaddock, who was frankly a disgrace, would be the most effective solution.

You know, steam had often been seen to emanate from the ears of Mister Garrideb the Mechannequin, but neither Michael nor Phoebe had ever before witnessed such a phenomenon in a human being! The whole of Chaddock's thin face reddened and seemed to swell like a gas bladder, as if it might burst under the pressure of venom and bile. The bait taken, Michael and Phoebe both continued to refute Sister Anketel's opinion in matters concerning not only Chaddock's timekeeping, honesty, literacy, ugliness, temper, but of the cleanliness of the mortuary, and indeed of the cleanliness of Chaddock himself.

Thankfully, the volume of criticism became all too much for the porter who, with much fury, wrestled himself free of his brown apron and flung it down on the desk. With not another word, Chaddock stomped from the mortuary to the waiting lift, determined to challenge that witch Anketel in person!

Before the lift gates were closed Michael was scanning the large airy room and showing every indication of his distaste: narrowed eyes, screwed up nose, those kinds of tell-tale signs. All were without foundation, of course, because the tiled white surfaces were so clean you could fair eat your dinner off them, as many a dear grandmother would say. In fact, any gothic foreboding had been completely whitewashed or sterilised away. Ghoulish sensational seekers sneaking down for a thrill would be bitterly disappointed. The air was sharp with carbolic and a bright light was cast down from half a dozen Edison lamps. Bolted against one wall were two white Butler sinks each boasting bulbous iron taps served by bright copper pipes. White enamel pails of water stood lined up against another wall, all pristine, none bearing a single black bruise of damage.

The torsos of the deceased were entirely covered in crisp white sheets save for their feet which remained exposed; gnarled, calloused or leathery, each pair a revealing character study in their own right. Tied to the left big toe of each corpse was a brown label, detailing the name of the individual, along with the date and time of death. Phoebe explained that each of the bodies required their cause of death to be confirmed as either 'asphyxia', 'syncope' or 'coma'.

Michael shook his head in both wonder and concern, having no desire to get too close to the corpses. "This looks like an audience at The Agricultural Hall, Wolverhampton. Which one do you think is Connie?"

"Magister..." crackled a voice.

"Well, I rather hope Connie is the corpse which has just started to sit up," said Phoebe pointing to a head moving beneath its death shroud in the most unnerving 'Bram Stoker' fashion.

"Connie!" It was as much as Michael could do to supress his yell of joy. He edged quickly between two corpses which had the good grace to remain dead, and to Connie's side. Michael gently folded the sheet back to reveal Connie's face.

"I hoped you'd recognise my sign," she said weakly.

"A dead person gripping my hand? It's the kind of thing you notice," smiled Michael.

"I must say, given your condition following the accident it was quite remarkable you had the strength to convince everyone you were dead," whispered Phoebe, untying Connie's toe tag on Michael's instruction and refastening it to the foot of the female corpse next to her.

Michael pulled back the sheet but quickly flushed and flustered an apology when he realised Connie was totally naked.

"Oh, for God's sake, Magister," wheezed Connie. "You've had worse..."

For the sake of decency, Phoebe helped slip Connie into Mister Garrideb's white shirt, black trousers, tailed coat, gloves and heavy black boots. The gas mask, bowler hat and the red blanket completed the disguise. Michael laid the stripped bare Mechannequin on the corpse table previously occupied by Connie, carefully laying the toe tag conspicuously on the sloped linoleum floor. Mister Garrideb's unclothed body revealed some of the marvellous mechanicals we built which animated the automaton. His head was alarmingly bald and the face featureless; a smooth, taut, yellow rubberised mask of skin, save for two large green glass covered holes from which emanated the lights of his eyes and a circle of silver fine wire mesh which covered the speaker from which Mister Garrideb's limited, abusive vocabulary came forth. His limbs, from shoulder to wrist, and hip to ankle were spare and skeletal; lengths of wood dowel bolted onto brass hinge joints and mobilised by an array of pistons, cams, pulleys and gas tubes. The feet and hands were, of necessity, more realistically moulded, rubber skin covered, to 'flesh out' as it were his gloves and boots. The abdomen and chest cavity were also fully moulded and concealed the motivating power source. It was my variation on Ernst Jungner's nickel cadmium cell, powering a notched speech cylinder the size of a cotton reel. It also supplied the lights of his eyes and heated a steam generating copper cylinder half the size of a tankard, wrapped in an insulating paper and wood fibre fleece. But that's enough mechanical talk for now.

Michael hinged open the chest plate and unhitched the power units within the cavity and yanked the leads down from up inside the neck. Of course, all the moving parts could be pressed into service again elsewhere, but time was critical and only the essential non-combustibles could be salvaged. With his hands full of mechanical giblets, Michael elbowed the chest plate back over to its closed position, then jabbed his elbow upon the now disembowelled Mister Garrideb's shellac navel button. Immediately a hiss of gas emanated from within the Mechannequin's belly. The self-destruction process had begun.

"Who's that poor bugger?" whispered Connie, slumped in the bath chair and still braving the most almighty headache.

"Someone who's happy to help," said Michael, slipping the octopus-jumble of motor, pipes and wires out of sight beneath

Connie's blanket and pushing the bath chair out through the swing doors.

Phoebe paused to take one last look at Mister Garrideb lying on the table, as his arms and legs began to twitch under the white sheet. The twitches soon became convulsions as a black smouldering circle appeared on the sheet and widened over the automaton's stomach.

"Thank you," whispered Phoebe and blew him a kiss before turning to follow Michael and Connie. As the mortuary doors swung shut behind her the smouldering intensified, quickly becoming a ferocious localised blaze. In all my inventions and re-inventions, as I think I may have told you, I install a protective immolation device, in this instance a small bladder of inflammable nectar ignited by the plunger on the Garrideb's navel. In two minutes the Mechannequin would be reduced to carbonised ash.

As for what happened in the corridor outside Martha Ward, you know, I have no idea what the enraged porter Staveley Chaddock yelled at Sister Anketel, but by all accounts her reaction to his verbal onslaught was so explosive the occupants of the entire West Wing felt the aftershock. Chaddock then responded with equal passion claiming that as a woman she should well know her place. This outrage rendered Sister Anketel so frustratingly speechless, her only reaction was to hurl a handy half full bottle of some patient's urine at his head. The missile was off target, but just grazed the scalp above his left ear.

In the comparative calm of the North Wing building, Michael wheeled Connie from the lift along the corridor and out into the fresh air of the square. In less than a few minutes, she was comfortably ensconced within the Steamo and Michael and Phoebe were all set to board when they heard Melville saying: "The Governors of this hospital were about to commission a Venetian artist to decorate that staircase…"

Later that afternoon, a copy of a supressed report finished up on the desk of Superintendent Melville at Scotland Yard. Not that he was there to read it. He was around and about at The Metropolitan Theatre of Steam, Smoke and Mirrors in the

Edgware Road, quietly organising the ambush of the suspected Music Hall serial murderer Anthony Graveolens.

Apparently, the report stated that in the case of the patient Constance Dill, the precise cause of death within Martha Ward, was impossible to determine. Whilst laid out in the mortuary awaiting post mortem examination, her corpse had been decapitated and the head was now missing. However it should be noted that despite being a forty-five-year-old woman Dill somehow had the body of a ninety-year-old. By coincidence, the body of patient Maud Heath, lying next to Dill, had apparently been destroyed by spontaneous human combustion. The hospital's mortuary porter Staveley Chaddock, upon returning to the mortuary had battled to extinguish the raging corpse-blaze with a pail of water, but his only reward for such courage was a pair of singed eyebrows and, inexplicably, a gunshot wound to the shoulder. All that remained of Maud Heath was a pile of unidentifiable black, very soggy ash in the vague shape of a human body. Chaddock was receiving treatment and causing great alarm by claiming that the police were black magic necromancers and the great Lord Lister was an arsonist.

But wait. The report stated that Constance Dill was found headless next to the charred body of someone called Maud Heath and that Staveley Chaddock had sustained a gunshot wound? You may wonder, how so?

33

Galvanised into action by the Assistant Commissioner's news of Connie Dill's location and the Black Bishop's order to kidnap her for his own nefarious reasons, Detective Inspector Gersham Skindrick rode a Hansom to Smithfield with, as yet, no real idea of how to extract the Dill woman from St. Bart's. But he was resourceful and a plan would no doubt evolve once he was there. His mood was sour, his eyes were still sore and he bore a red, scabby gash on his forehead following the encounter with that drunken filth Father O'Connor. So, if success in his mission required extreme prejudice, or even murder, then so be it, he shrugged.

And murder suddenly seemed a highly attractive prospect when he walked through the Henry the Eighth arch and into the quadrangle of Bart's Hospital to see there parked, the absurd horseless steam vehicle driven by that blasphemous magician Magister and his slattern whore assistant. Skindrick left himself in no doubt, if he saw them and circumstances allowed, he would shoot Magister on sight. The harlot he had other plans for.

The Bart's Gateman consulted his lists and directed the wretched policeman to the ward where Constance Dill had been admitted. The presence of Detective Inspector Pym in a corner of the square speaking with a gaggle of nurses was a nuisance, but circumvented with stealth. As he bounded up the central stairs of the West Wing two at a time, Skindrick assessed the difficulty of smuggling a patient out of the hospital. The wing was busy. The magicians and Melville were somewhere about, but with a warrant card and God on his side Skindrick convinced himself he could not fail.

As he turned to climb another flight of stone stairs, the corridor above echoed with what sounded like raised voices. No, it was more than raised voices, more like a full on screaming row. It was an unexpected distraction which might serve him well. Skindrick reached the second floor where the argument was now taking on volcanic proportions, turned to the right following the signage and was immediately doused, full in the face, with half a carafe of warm urine. The vessel which delivered the dreadful soaking then fell to the floor and shattered. As the bewildered Skindrick shook the excess fluid from his eyes, the sight he beheld was quite extraordinary. An angel of mercy in a Ward Sister's uniform, her face contorted with rage, had clearly just attempted to brain a tall, thin man, with a heavy glass weapon containing human waste fluid. The tall, thin man rubbed the side of his head where the jar had barely grazed him, before raising a gangly-fingered hand above his shoulder, as if to strike the woman firmly across the cheek. Skindrick grabbed the man's wrist and advised him forcefully that hitting a lassie, even this hatchet faced harpy, was nae acceptable.

Further oaths and accusations were traded amid much furious finger pointing, and peace was only properly restored in this hallowed palace of healing when the dripping Skindrick produced his warrant card and shouted for silence. Having achieved the quiet he demanded, Skindrick announced he was here to collect Constance Dill, a wanted prisoner, for transfer to a secure unit. But his face fell as fast as his spirits, when the Ward Sister snarled that Dill had died no less than an hour ago. The tall, thin man then pitched in, telling him her corpse currently lay in his mortuary awaiting post mortem, so Skindrick ordered he be immediately taken there, claiming a need to identify the body. Quite a remarkable suggestion, considering Skindrick had never before set eyes upon Connie. But with the object of his mission now deceased, all thoughts turned to retrieving her body. The Black Bishop may wish to slice her open and probe her brain for clues. In fact, hang the body, all Skindrick really needed was the damned head for God's will to be done.

Sister Anketel turned on her heels and stormed back into her Ward to continue her fine work with the sick, while Staveley Chaddock protested his desire to press charges as he led Skindrick, who had turned his collar up just in case he was recognised, back across the quadrangle and down to the basement.

Skindrick wondered, if, with the steam vehicle still in situ, the interfering Magister and his floozy might too be in the mortuary, doing a wee bit of body snatching themselves. They were craven enough. He patted his jacket pocket and felt the reassuring shape of his revolver, as did so many, it seemed, who carried a gun.

Now, it must be said, if poor Staveley Chaddock felt he had endured a fairly torrid time thus far, things were about to get a whole lot worse. He proudly pushed open the swing doors to his mortuary and was immediately repelled by the orange heat of a blaze consuming one of his beloved corpses.

As Chaddock danced around screaming, "Ablaze! Ablaze!" Skindrick forced his way through , stripped the white sheet off a nearby corpse and use it to try and beat out the roaring flames. Chaddock in sheer panic reached for one of his pristine enamel water buckets and flung the contents at the burning body. Unfortunately most of it slopped against Skindrick's back, soaking his jacket thoroughly through. The policeman turned in shock and fury and called Chaddock a blithering idiot, only in far stronger terms, just in time to see the Porter rush from his mortuary still crying 'Ablaze! Ablaze!' presumably to call for all hands to the pumps assistance.

Skindrick stood dripping like a drowned rat, now thoroughly peeved and disinclined to undertake further firefighting heroics. If this burning corpse was Constance Dill, all was lost. But, no! It wasn't! It wasn't Dill's corpse which was crackling and popping and turning to ash. That was Constance Dill's body there, on the table next to the charred ruin! The naked body of an elderly woman clearly displayed a brown label tied to her left big toe. There it was plain as day in clear, neat writing 'Constance Dill'.

"Got ye, y'witch woman!" he sneered.

Speed was now vital. Skindrick looked about. On a shelf, he spotted an elegant mahogany wooden case. He flung open its lid. Yes! Before him lay a pristine array of surgical instruments, the working tools of the pathologist. All of them shiny and silver and above all sharp. Skindrick selected the bone saw, a substantial heavy tool with blade of fine-grade vicious teeth. Aye. Just the job.

For some unimportant reason, Chaddock could not find a single soul prepared to physically help fight his fire, so he rushed back into his precious mortuary only to see the crazed, grinning police detective, wearing a bloody brown overall and holding aloft a dripping head, freshly hewn from the corpse of an old woman. Chaddock screamed in horror, and then screamed again as Skindrick drew his pistol and leisurely shot Chaddock, who was flung backwards and finished up in a crumpled heap on the other side of his desk. Skindrick quickly pocketed his hot barrelled gun and winced as he burned his hip, before dropping the head into the recently emptied water pail. It would make an ideal vessel in which to transport his grisly, but utterly mistaken trophy.

~IN THE END~

"Who loses and who wins; who's in, who's out; And take upon's the mystery of things" — William Shakespeare

I have always pursued a good degree of secrecy concerning our activities here in the theatre. I remain firm in my belief that as little as possible should ever be known by rival illusionists, Her Majesty's Revenue Men and the police.

Thus, this afternoon I found ourselves enduring the unhappy circumstance, thanks to Mister Anthony Graveolens's murderous ways, of The Metropolitan Theatre of Steam, Smoke and Mirrors attracting the undivided attention of at least a dozen plain clothes policeman! All of them smart, sharp and nimble, and all of them deputed by the indomitable Melville to surveil our every entrance.

With the iron Safety Curtain rung down, as you now know, anywhere behind the proscenium arch, that is the stage and backstage area, was entirely self-contained. Our Pass Doors from the auditorium to the backstage area were secured by keyless locks which could only be opened by tapping in the correct passwords upon typewriter-style keyboards. The weak spot we identified when we undertook the lease of the theatre was the Stage Door, which opened out onto the steps down to the yard served by White Lion Passage. But this out of the way artists' entrance was now reinforced with stout wood and metal, inset with a viewing window of inch thick glass, under the ever watchful gaze of the Spectroscopic Camera. Yes, you may recall it was from here that Detective Inspector Walter Pym first abducted Michael and Phoebe as they made their exit. But! Anyone requesting entry through the Stage Door would only be admitted following careful scrutiny.

Not that anyone believed the attempt on Michael's life by the country's most cunning, diabolical serial killer since Henry the Eighth would be made *before* show time. No. The big finale of Mister Anthony Graveolens's death spree would be mounted this evening, during a performance, when Michael stood alone, vivid in the spot light, centre stage before a packed house. This would be Graveolens's glorious moment. The audience would remember this night because of him –

The Legendary Music Hall Killer of Old London Town. Surely?

As the theatre's opening time for the first performance loomed large, I was to be found sitting at the Stage Door desk, nursing a glass of 'medicinal' and tinkering with the cremated Garrideb's salvaged steam power generator. Suddenly, the jangling rasp of the Stage Door buzzer broke my concentration. I looked across at the Spectroscopic Screen and saw the sepia-toned face of Superintendent William Melville, waving his warrant card. His shouts were muffled but I took them to be demands to be let in. Having made much play of satisfying myself as to his identity, I tapped the code letters upon the typewriter keyboard, a charge of compressed steam released the lock and the Stage Door hissed open.

Melville stepped inside quickly and closed the door behind him, saying, "You are the individual they call The Professor?"

"The same," I nodded.

"Mister Magister and Miss Le Breton, if you please. They are to be found where?"

Of course, you must remember that since this gallivant began, Melville had enjoyed little contact with me. He remained gloriously ignorant of my influential role in Michael's and Phoebe's stage careers, a mystique I was happy to perpetuate. To him I was merely the trusted help, 'the *ingenieur*', the eccentric Professor. So as such, I quickly adopted the Shakespearean stance of some lame hunchback, more for my own amusement than anything else.

"On the stage. Through there," I said, offering Melville a kind of head and shoulders gesture towards the Stage Pass Door.

In truth, you know, I was mildly amused at the irony. Here was Superintendent William Melville, the head of the Special Branch, the nation's gatekeeper, the Queen's Cerberus, the knower of all things... not actually knowing about me. I am easily pleased by such little victories. And, calm and courteous as Melville was, I cared little for his succinct, precise manner. As you may have gathered over these long pages, I have no time for brevity.

"Be so kind as to remain vigilant!" he ordered, as he pushed his way through the double doors.

"Mmm," I murmured and turned back to my device tinkerings. In fact, I had become so absorbed in the design minutia of the power source, and he being a masterful exponent of stealth, I failed to hear his return; just felt his warm breath on my cheek, up close and personal as he reiterated quietly in my ear, "I said remain vigilant." In this matter he was, of course, quite correct.

The stage of The Metropolitan Theatre of Steam, Smoke and Mirrors was still and quiet. The only discernible movement came from the dust motes which floated gracefully like lazy midges above a pond on a Sunday afternoon, captured in the yellow shafts of the work lights from above. In such a lighting condition, the illusion of the stage itself was laid bare. Black curtains, black walls, black floor. Focus a score of brilliant lights upon it and click the circuit breakers on and suddenly the dingy stage explodes into a colourful world of glamour and life. But now it stood dormant, stripped of all pretence. In amongst the shadows, the great Throne of Disintegration snoozed, ready to be set. Beyond the Throne stood The Iron Monger's Coffin, our version of The Iron Maiden, with its cruelly spiked door open like a shark's mouth to reveal a deceptively comfortable interior of shiny maroon velvet and brown leather straps.

"Mister Magister?" called Melville, his voice echoed and bounced about the cabinets and boxes. "Mister Magister? It's Melville."

The silence prevailed. A deep, mournful silence. Then the stage creaked. Melville's eyes flashed and his wits sharpened, his tread became soft and the fingers in his overcoat pocket wrapped themselves around the handle of his revolver as they had done on so many occasions in the past. He peered around the vicious door and into the empty Iron Monger's Coffin. He stroked one of the two dozen spikes expecting to feel pliant rubber, but to his surprise found the point hard and sharp enough to draw a bubble of blood from the tip of his thumb. He stepped no nearer. If the door slammed shut now he would certainly be impaled. He moved on to the steam-driven wood chipper, 'The Mincer of Malevolence' we dubbed it. Melville tapped a dormant pressure gauge, tracing the cold copper pipework to the leather conveyor belt which, when fired up, fed a hopper which would hack and chop whatever lay upon it into a thousand chippings. It was originally designed for tree trunks, but we used it for magicians. He looked upstage at the work-in-progress 'Steam Saw of Gore' with its jagged circular blade...

"Dear God," Melville cursed under his breath. Was there nothing on this stage that couldn't inflict the most diabolical demise upon Michael Magister? For methods of fulfilling his murderous legacy Anthony Graveolens was certainly spoiled for choice.

Then he saw it and his blood froze! A grey forbidding - what was it? A Graveyard Tableau, bordered by bent rusty iron railings. The grinning, gap toothed human skull which first caught his eye. The iron cogs to move the jaw. The brass rimmed purple lens screwed into one eye socket. A *mechanical* human skull sitting atop a leaning, cast iron headstone which bore the legend:

"Magister the Magician R.I.P. Rot In Purgatory."

And there, to the right! Beyond the headstone, in the half-light and suspended four feet off the ground; Magister. No, not suspended! Impaled! Skewered through his back by one of the upright iron railings. The sharp spike sticking up a full six inches from his silk brocaded waist coat. Michael Magister's head, arms and legs all lolled, lifeless and down. Blood was trickling from his voiceless mouth.

"Sweet Mother of..." hissed Melville, as he rushed forward to support Magister, lift him off, or, by Christ, try and do something!

"Superintendent Melville?" said the gentle familiar voice. Phoebe appeared, as if from nowhere. Her softly waved titian hair down upon her shoulders, her manner easy and her ruby lips smiling. She wore a royal blue corset trimmed with black lace, matching French style knickers and knee-high black leather boots, but never mind any of that… she was wiping her hands on a cloth.

"Quickly! Help me! The murderous Graveolens did this?" demanded Melville, reaching to lift Michael free from the murderous spike.

"Graveolens? Heavens, no, Superintendent. It was me." said Phoebe, with a chuckle.

As the shock of her indifference struck, Melville was dealt a second thunder bolt as Michael said: "Mister M! Good evening! Welcome to our world!" Michael turned his head to face Melville and grinned. "This is where the magic happens. Allow me to present to you our rehearsal of 'The Graveyard of Death'."

"The title is currently under discussion, Superintendent," added Phoebe. "I would contend that a graveyard is inexorably associated with death, and as a result the title 'The Graveyard of Death' is tautological."

"Then because I have no idea what 'tautological' actually means, I wanted to call it 'The Agony of Impalement'. What do you say? Or is that just too twee?"

With that, Michael removed the rubber spike from his chest and tossed it to Melville, while Phoebe provided a shoulder to help Michael ease himself off the upright ironwork and onto his feet.

"I'd say you're just a little bit keen to know the method of this illusion, Mister, M, "said Michael. "Wondering quite how we do it?".

"Indeed," said Melville, dangling the rubber spike by his fingertips and handing it to Phoebe..

Michael lifted the front of his waistcoat to reveal a heavy metal band around his midriff. He turned and lifted the back to reveal the retaining 'boss' into which the stout upright railing clicked. "An iron corset, a small, collapsible spike concealed in the hand, then simply held against the chest to top off the railing, a swirl of misdirection, a cloud of mist for a little mood, the usual brilliance. You get the idea. Not that you can hold it for too long though." He winced rubbing his back.

"Indeed," nodded Melville, probably very impressed, but too canny to reveal it. "I have plain clothes officers covering every entrance and mingling with the audience. One shall also be seated at the end of every tenth row. There is a 'however'. With an audience of these numbers you must also take responsibility. Be ever on your guard. We undertake a high risk strategy here, and no amount of cavalier badinage can dilute that. Should the resourceful Mister Graveolens appear tonight and we all fail to apprehend him, make no mistake, Mister Magister, he will succeed in killing you. "

"Mister M, we both know courage and I do not sit well together. But with you and Pheebs, I'm in good hands," said Michael. Then he turned to Phoebe. "By the way, should that be 'courage and I' or 'courage and me'?"

2

While many J Division plain clothes men from Paddington Green mingled with the crowd on the Edgware Road, Melville's Special Branch men were allotted covert surveillance positions upon each street corner surrounding the theatre: at Harrow Road, Bell Street, Church Street, White Lion Passage and upon Paddington Green at the rear. All pretended to do whatever was required to appear inconspicuous. As for the head of Special Branch himself, Melville patrolled the pavement across the Edgware Road from 'The Green Man' on Bell Street up to Church Street, pretty much, you know, from where the assassins had taken their pot shots at the Prime Minister not two days ago. His sharp seasoned eyes examined every face with calm, methodical discipline. No one escaped his scrutiny.

Detective Inspector Walter Pym, on the other hand, was feeling distinctly like he'd drawn the stubbiest of short straws when the postings were handed out. He had been lumbered with White Lion Passage, that nasty, narrow, call it 'alleyway' if you will, which flanked the entire south side of the theatre. It was a pedestrian short cut between the Edgware Road and the Harrow Road, which passed the yard leading to the theatre's Stage Door. Why anyone decent should ever want to use White Lion Passage was one of those mysteries of life, because it was cold, dank, smelled like a urinal and after dark became a notorious haunt for activities of the most disreputable nature.

Pym couldn't help but frown at the cushy billet landed by his most hated Special Branch colleague. He imagined this loathsome officer leaning against the counter of the public bar, set in the centre of the frontage to The Metropolitan Theatre of Steam, Smoke and Mirrors, enjoying watching the crowd of drinkers. But that was far from the truth. Detective Inspector Gersham Skindrick was in the bar sneering at the humanity around him feeling nothing but contempt for their weakness. He looked about him at the sea of ale swillers and gin-sluggers and felt nothing but revulsion and disgust. He tried to ignore the raucous babble of a hundred meaningless conversations. Look at them. Men, women an' even some children. Who took bairns to a drinking den?

At Scotland Yard, Melville had briefed his men. Anthony Graveolens, a serial killer with incredible hypnotic powers was their target. Skindrick had arrived late, now washed and brushed up, but caught the salient facts. Having delivered the dead head of Constance Dill to the Warwick Street chapel, he believed God had now rewarded him with the opportunity to capture a living specimen and deliver it to His Eminence The Black Bishop for experimentation.

And what of Michael Magister? Who cared? He and his baffling trickery and his near naked woman… suddenly Skindrick felt the sharp jab of an elbow to the kidney.

"Sweet Jasus, Mary and Joseph, will you not let a holy man near the bar to lock horns with the devil's brew?"

Skindrick looked down at the dishevelled priest with the yellowing dog collar, the stained black suit, the whisky-breath could strip lead paint from a balustrade – and gasped. He could not believe his eyes.

"D'ye no reckon you've had enough there, padre!" said Skindrick.

"And who be you to be telling a purveyor of God's holy word on what should be done? Is yourself bein' the Pope, or the like?" said Father Connor O'Connor.

Skindrick looked around. Everyone in the bar was busy with their drinking or their hollering, they'd not notice a thing. He then grasped Connor's arm and said, "No, y'filth. I am not His Holiness. I am much, much worse."

Connor looked up at the cruel face, the bloodshot eyes, and the scabby wound across the forehead. "Christ on the cross!" he gasped, as he quickly recognised The Hairy Monk's Jebbie cohort from the Warwick Street chapel, the bastard who only last night had snatched him and then tried to separate his body from his soul. Skindrick's grip on his arm was like a crushing vice, and the pain was gnawing into Connor's bones.

"Let me help you home to sleep the booze off, shall I?" snarled Skindrick through gritted teeth. Can you snarl and grit your teeth? Yes, apparently you can.

Connor O'Connor suddenly felt all the blood in his body drain down to his feet. The fear gripped him tighter than the Jebbie ever could. Death was inevitable once he'd been frog-marched from the safety of the saloon. Jasus. There was only one solution he could think of which might aid his escape, so at the top of his voice Connor bellowed.

"Leave me go! Unhand me, you heathen fiend ! This unholy dog manhandles a man of the cloth! He'll smite me down so he shall!"

As might be expected, many a thirsty patron of the saloon knew the holy rogue and took great exception to this stranger's behaviour. Others greatly inflamed with the ale, were spoiling for a fight, and Father O'Connor's pleadings certainly looked like they were calling for such a fervent intervention. All at once, at least a dozen drinkers began jostling and threatening Skindrick.

"Oi! Leave that priest be, arsehole!" was probably the most repeatable of the oaths. Skindrick looked about him. Any one of the throng looked likely to smash a pint pot over his head. Skindrick decided to make a great play of releasing Connor, pushing him away, before reaching inside his coat and producing his warrant card.

"Police! Detective Inspector! Y'll stand back! Back, I say!"

Those of the pickpocketing fraternity, along with others who derived their income from roguery in general, were thoroughly unimpressed by Skindrick's credentials. In fact, they now positively relished the chance to harangue one of Her Majesty's upholders of the law. A melee of jostling, shoving and swearing ensued, followed by punches thrown. Even the few law-abiders present felt distinctly disinclined to assist the detective and back-heeled him in the shins when the opportunity arose. In fact, it was only one poor soul, who was unnerved by the prospect of becoming party to such a fracas, and he slipped quickly out into the street, followed almost immediately at an even brisker, more panicked, pace by Father Connor O'Connor himself.

"Jasus. The Hairy Monk's in league with the bastard bobbies," gasped Connor, to himself as he wiped the sweated grime from his brow with his sleeve. "Even the police cannot be trusted! That I must tell to Artemus More!" And with that intention the cleric headed for White Lion Passage and the Stage Door.

3

For Superintendent Melville it wasn't so much the commotion across the street, or the disreputable holy man emerging from the saloon, which grabbed his attention. It was the fellow who had preceded the bewildered ecclesiastic; the one wearing the brown overcoat and that jaunty cheese-cutter. Could that be Anthony Graveolens? Melville squinted for a clearer view, peering beyond the traffic at the figure which was even now amongst the throng milling about on the pavement waiting for the theatre doors to open. Melville was almost certain it was Graveolens. Almost. Where was he? Yes. There. In person, without question. Anthony Graveolens! Whatever you do, Melville reminded himself, do not meet his gaze. Tipping his bowler down over his forehead, Melville tried weaving his way across the road, but the maelstrom of traffic conspired to make no concession to his urgency, or his rank. Damn, he'd lost him. No wait. There he was. Graveolens. No. Lost him again. Melville was thankful he'd placed the redoubtable Pym in White Lion Passage, at least the Stage Door access to the theatre was guaranteed impregnable. But if Graveolens could melt into a crowd with such ease, there was every chance he could enter the theatre simply by walking in. Melville needed to alert the magicians and scan the audience as they filed in to the auditorium.

The Superintendent slipped through the crowd, swung open the gate and ducked into White Lion Passage. Ahead of him in the dim alleyway, two figures had just become locked in an awkward struggle. Detective Inspector Pym, being stronger and less impaired by the grog, held the holy man face first against the wall. It was nothing he couldn't handle, but the furious volley of language issuing from a man of God was quite an eye opener.

"Yea, all right, Father, that's all fine and dandy, but I am a police officer and this passageway is out of bounds!" shouted Pym. The announcement that he was a police officer appeared only to further enrage the wriggling priest rather than calm him. After receiving a stamp on the boot which made him screw up his eyes and wince, Pym felt the need to adopt a more persuasive method of restraint - just as he became aware of the figure of Superintendent Melville running along the passage toward him.

"I confirm Graveolens is here! Entering with the audience! Go and inform all the others! I'll guard Magister," yelled Melville as he sprinted past, toward the Stage Door.

The first I knew of this fresh development was a rattling, then a hammering on the Stage Door and a rasp of the entry bell. The Spectroscope image spat and fizzed. Bah! This was not the time for the technology to turn temperamental. So I shuffled to the door and peered through the window, cracking my head on the pane as I leant forward. Outside it was Melville, clearly anxious. I clacked out the code on the keyboard keys and the door hissed open.

"Graveolens is entering with the audience. I must warn Magister! Where is he?" demanded the Special Branch man.

"Still on the stage, where you left him. But with the safety curtain down, Graveolens cannot reach Michael from the auditorium." I was keen to display my calmness.

"Keep it thus!" snapped Melville. "And this door locked! Under no circumstance let a soul through. Am I understood?"

I nodded and watched as he walked quickly through the double Pass Doors toward the stage. So, Anthony Graveolens would definitely be in the audience and tonight he would fulfil his promise. Or at least try.

"Magister! Magister!" called Melville, as the doors swung closed behind him. The stage was again in semi light. He looked at the illusions. The cabinets, the blades, the coffin, the headstone – how appropriate. Magister's profession was truly a grim assemblage of deception and lies.

"Mister M! Welcome back! I love repeat business!" Michael emerged from within the open Iron Monger's Coffin. He was now wearing his stage shirt, open necked, beneath his gold brocaded waistcoat. His face was vivid, his eyes enhanced with thin black lines. Make-up on a man was always a little disconcerting to the un-theatrical, but was essential in the full dazzling light of the stage. Michael was riffling his pack of cards, chillingly calm. The relaxed pre-show state of mind he had learned from me and then developed further over the years.

"Your capacity for self-regard is extraordinary," said Melville, who upon seeing Michael adopted a less anxious, more quiescent attitude himself.

"Self-regarding, self-assured, I know, call it what you will. But I figured years back – if *I'm* not cheering for my side, why would I expect anybody else to?"

"Apparently. Magister, you must be alert. Anthony Graveolens has been spotted."

"So, it's show time!"

"He was seen outside amidst the audience, but he will be thwarted." said Melville.

"And that's a shame, Mister M, that's a damned shame."

"A shame?"

"Yes, a shame. You see, I think you should allow him in here, let him come right up on this stage, right here, right now."

"By which you mean?" asked Melville, genuinely puzzled.

"It means I'd welcome the chance to speak with him. Alone. Like this. One to one."

"For what possible purpose?"

"To tell him he knows only half the story," said Michael. "I'd want to tell him that he's murdered innocent people. People dear to me, including his own wife, all for no reason. I'd want to tell him that *everyone* who appeared in that New Year's Eve show ten years ago wanted to testify on Connie's behalf. Me, Sid, Alpheus, Tilley and Annie. Okay, Alfie Vance couldn't because he was already dead, but he would have done. We all wanted to stand up for Connie's side of the story. But the problem was Connie. She wouldn't let us vouch for her. She told the police we were just a bunch of Music Hall vagabonds and liars looking out for one of their own. That's why she pleaded guilty from the start."

"And why would she have done that?"

"She truly felt prison was the only place for her. She was so afraid of her ability, of her power and what it could do, she chose to be locked away. For everyone else's safety. It was her decision and there wasn't a damned thing we could do to stop her. So they just spirited her away. Vanished. And not a day went by without me wondering where she was and how she was. That's why I'd want to speak to Graveolens. To tell him how much we all loved Connie. I'd also want to tell him that compared with his fine and brave, decent mother who was determined to do what she thought was the right thing, he's just a pathetic, insignificant, vengeful nobody. This whole ugly mess has spiralled out of control because he didn't know the full story. Or didn't *want* to know. I would tell Anthony Graveolens that he's an insult to his mother." Michael stared firmly at the figure in front of him. "An insult to the mother he murdered. But then I guess none of that is what you'd want to hear. Is it, Anthony?"

Michael blinked and was looking now, not at Detective Superintendent William Melville of Special Branch. The veil of hypnotism had been lifted. He was staring at Anthony Graveolens, who stood before him sweating, scowling and aiming a revolver at Michael's chest.

4

"Okay, there's no need to be impressed with my instinct, by the way," continued Michael. "I actually figured it was you the moment you came through the door. Sure, I blinked, got the cold chill, the sharp headache, when you do that little thing you do, but here's where you went wrong, pal. The real Superintendent Melville may have a rock bottom opinion of me, but fair play to the man, he always refers to me as *Mister* Magister. You just called me Magister. You slipped up, Anthony. And I see you're sweating up a little there. But then it takes quite some effort to keep that 'fluencing thing going."

"You know Constance was my mother?" said Graveolens. Gone now was the ever so 'umble back of the throat voice he affected. It was replaced instead with a more natural London accent, snide with bitterness.

"Oh, yes, but please, save the applause. Oh, you weren't going to clap? Okay. It was Pheebs who figured out the medical opthal-whatever and made the connection. She has this incredible knowledge, everything sticks in her brain, God, how can you not love that woman? I hold her as dearly as I held your mother."

"You shut your mouth! You say you'd have stood up for my mother in court," Anthony Graveolens had certainly changed from the shy, diffident widower mopping up his wife's blood in Cephas Street. Now he was boiling with that alarming uncontrolled rage you might associate with the murderously unhinged. Michael figured the chances of springing forward and grabbing the gun were slim. Graveolens was maintaining a decent distance between them both. Not that Michael was planning on any such bravery.

Graveolens's eyes narrowed. "You reckon you'd have stood up for my mother. But then what, eh? Nothing. You never once went to see her, you just left her to rot in that hole."

"Graveolens, get a grip, I told you, we none of us knew where she was. If we had known we'd have gone, but no one would tell us."

"But I found her. And I didn't even know I had a mother, till three months ago. Sitting there sifting through my own records at Somerset House I followed this trail of files and found I'd been given away at birth. After that, it wasn't too difficult to find my real mother. And her stage name Lamal, I liked that loose Frenchie translation from D'ill. I'm quite partial to those name games, myself."

"Just as Phoebe realised. You were the priest who visited Connie at the Asylum?"

"Yes. Disguised as one. Those arseholes at the Asylum they never asked. They see a bloke dressed up all religious with a decent story, they're gonna trust him aren't they? I saw Connie three times. It was then I realised I had her powers, too. To make people see what I wanted them to see. I went and looked up everyone who was in that last show with her. You and your lot. But the only one I could find was that Annie Saunders. Stupid cow used her real name on stage, didn't she! So 'stead of killing her right there and then I made her believe I was worth marrying. With a bit of 'fluence. But I only wed her to find out about you lot so's I could take our revenge. Revenge, see. I wanted revenge for Connie and me. 'Cept when I told her I was setting about killing you all, she begged me not to. That's when she escaped and tried to stop me. But she couldn't. And she still can't!" Anthony Graveolens levelled the gun at Michael's head and glared.

"This routine again," sighed Michael as he blinked to see Graveolens become Connie, then Melville, then Phoebe.

"See, now you're just showing off," said Michael.

"Of course I am. But now it's your turn to show off, Mister Big Magician. Let's see the great Magister in action, shall we? Let's see how good you are at catching a bullet in the teeth?"

5

The real Superintendent Melville had finally forced his way across the Edgware Road, twice nearly falling beneath hooves and wheels. He shouldered himself through the crowd on the pavement, into White Lion Passage and straight into Detective Inspector Walter Pym and Father Connor O'Connor.

"Jasus, haven't you bastard bobbies done me enough damage already?" spluttered O'Connor, his lips flecked with foam.

Pym looked across at Melville, once, twice, three times, each with growing incredulity. "Superintendent Melville? Guv'nor? What are you up to?" said Pym, seriously confused. "I thought you just went through…"

"Anthony Graveolens is in the crowd. I am going backstage to warn Mister Magister," said Melville, oblivious to Pym's puzzlement.

"Here, hold up a minute, you've already done that. You've already come by here to warn him not four minutes ago."

"Pym, were you afflicted with a headache?"

"I bastard was," moaned O'Connor.

"How can I really know it's you?" asked Pym, not without good reason. "How do I know you're not Graveolens pulling a fast one on me now?"

"Because, Detective Inspector, I know your police serial number is 3669 and your middle name is Motherby," said Melville. "Does that convince you?"

Pym raised both eyebrows and nodded. Then he and Melville said in unison: "He's in the building!"

"Leave the priest!" snapped Melville, before turning to Connor and adding. "My apologies for your discomfort, Father."

Melville and Pym sprinted for the Stage Door, with the sound of Connor O'Connor's colourful language, none of it graced with forgiveness, echoing behind them. Pym hammered on the door while Melville cranked the bell handle. The cacophony fair made me jump and my stomach turn. The prospect of encountering a serial killer, admittedly on the other side of an impregnable door did not find me bursting with jollification. I examined the image on the Screen, which by some miracle was now working again!. The face looking up at me, urgent and imploring was very clearly that of Inspector Walter Pym. Which seemed unlikely. But who was that at his shoulder? Superintendent Melville as well? Both together? How could that be?

***

"Okay, before you shoot me, let me just say this," said Michael, holding his palms up at Graveolens. "No, wait, I've forgotten what it was. "

Graveolens growled and took aim.

"I remember! Anthony, can I call you Anthony? Anthony, listen, if I tried, I suppose I could pretend to understand why you needed to take your revenge on all of us in the show, because you say we let Connie down. I can see that. But what I can't fathom is how you could murder Connie? How could you smother the life out of your own mother?" Michael stared firmly at the figure standing before him now with barely concealed contempt.

"You saw what they did to her. The operations on her head. What I did to her wasn't murder, it was mercy. Like a dutiful son I gently ended her pain. But I'm not going to end your pain, Magister – yours is about to start."

"Okay, but shooting me? That would be wrong in so many ways and here's why. I've always refused to do that catching bullets in the mouth illusion. That's just crazy. Because my front teeth are part of my winning style, and I promise you this, one day that trick is going to kill someone. Pheebs and The Professor, they want me to rehearse this catching a ball of supercharged Aethyr in the mouth – oh, sure, like that's about to happen any day soon!"

"I don't care how you die, Magister," said Graveolens, now with exasperation. "So long as you die!"

"Okay, I've bought enough time… Pheebs! Get him!" shouted Michael, pointing behind Graveolens.

Graveolens spun around and fired. At no one. He howled at the deception, turned back to fire at Michael but now the magician had vanished. A single playing card span in the air and landed on the stage at Graveolens's feet. It was the King of Hearts. Graveolens fired two wild, frustrated shots at the card.

"I'll find you, you Yankee coward" hollered Graveolens.

"*Yankee* coward?" said Michael from behind something, somewhere. "What are you now, Robert E. Lee?"

Suddenly alone, in the half light, amid the death-dealing cabinets and contraptions, Graveolens felt the entire stage had taken on the atmosphere of an abandoned fairground, with the cast of the old freak show skulking all around him. A chill ran down his back, followed by a bead of sweat. Holding the pistol two-handed, Graveolens slowly, cautiously, rounded the Gravestone with its grinning, mocking skull. Then he listened. Nothing. No creaking. Just the sound of his own breathing. Hissing? That wasn't him! Suddenly a squirt of grey steam hissed from a pressure release valve. It was as if the equipment, the illusions were coming alive and watching him.

What's that? In front of that Iron Maiden cabinet thing! There he is! Magister! Graveolens fired a shot as Michael ducked inside the The Iron Monger's Coffin . The metal door began to close, clanking itself shut, powered by the assemblage of cogs on the lid, turning, clattering. Graveolens fired again. The bullet sparked on the iron work and ricocheted up into the rig, smashing a coloured light. Graveolens ran forward to the metal coffin.

"Big mistake, magician. Now I've got you trapped. Not so cocky now, are you?" Graveolens banged the pistol butt on the door. With his free hand he tried to pull open the door but it remained stuck fast. He examined the cold, black surface closely, the cleverly interlocking cogs, he was so close he could smell the machine oil. Then he spotted the slot by the edge of the door and the inconspicuous lever pointing upward. Graveolens fingered the lever down, The action was surprisingly smooth and easy. The mechanism's cogs turned and clicked and cranked and with a hiss of theatrical smoke, the door popped open. Just a crack. But enough for the macabre green glow from within to outline the rounded shape of the door. Forcing the fingers of his free hand into the gap, Graveolens hauled open the door, which was so surprisingly lightweight he almost pulled himself off balance. Suddenly Graveolens was bathed in the soft, eerie green light which emanated from within the purple velvet lined... and empty Coffin! Gah. Not only had Magister somehow evaded the pointed spikes, he'd also vanished. Again! Bloody, bastard magicians!

6

Both Melville and Pym held their warrant cards against the window pane. From my position within they looked most convincing. And, you know, I not only found it tough to believe Anthony Graveolens could hypnotise a scientist of my great intellect, but also that he could 'fluence me into believing he was two people. Whatever nagging doubt I had about the voracity of these policemen's true identities was swept away when Father Connor O'Connor no less staggered up behind them shaking his fist and furiously demanding I open the bastard door. But you know what immediately swung it for me? The sound of gunshots from the stage. I tapped in the code and the Stage Door swung open.

"Quickly," I urged them. "I heard gunfire from within!"

Melville and Pym drew their revolvers and threw themselves at the Pass Doors to the stage, but shockingly the doors held fast. They had been wilfully secured with something on the other side. The Special Branch men charged the door again with their shoulders, then tried kicking with the soles of their boots, all to no avail. The doors remained stubbornly steadfast.

"There is another way to reach the stage," I told them. "From here…"

***

"Give it up, Graveolens!" called Michael. His voice bounced about the stage. It might have come from anywhere. "You can't win. This is my world. I've got the home turf advantage."

"Michael? Are you all right? I heard gunshots!" Phoebe's clear voice cut through the atmosphere.

She had been lifted onto the stage shrouded in the cloud of blue smoke, which is always triggered when the trap door of the Prompt Side riser opens. Phoebe was armed with the Pulsatronic pistol. As the smoke thinned she saw Anthony Graveolens brandishing his revolver at precisely the same time as he saw her. Only he was ready to shoot.

"Oh, my days!"

Her life-savers, once again, were the thigh-length black leather boots and scarlet corset she was still wearing. The fact the corset was laced loosely at the front didn't hurt with the overall distraction. She was a vision that even old decrepit Pope Leo would have gawped at twice, so it certainly made Anthony Graveolens stop and enjoy the view. His brief hesitation was all Phoebe needed. She dropped to her knees and levelled the Pulsa. With a whirr and a zap, a ball of purple energy burst from the barrel. The tracer sped across the stage wide of her target, shattering a stage light while the unexpected force of the recoil flung Phoebe backwards. She crashed onto her back, and the Pulsa spun across the stage.

"Not terribly elegant," she thought, before rolling and scrambling for cover in the upstage darkness. Graveolens fired twice more in Phoebe's general direction, but his aim was as sorry as hers.

"Pheebs!" shouted Michael "Graveolens is here and it's getting a little boisterous now."

"I rather gathered that!" she called back. "Isn't this exciting!"

"Really?"

Phoebe crouched panther-like behind The Throne of Disintegration, with not the slightest intention of sneaking into the secret under-seat compartment and waiting it out. Not when there was a mind-bending lunatic stalking the stage. Not when this fellow was in full psychopathic flow and wanted one of the most important people in her life dead. No, she was not about to let that happen, thank you very much, Mister Graveolens.

In the shadows across to the left she could hear controlled but heavy breathing; the result of physical exertion and fear. Was it Michael or Graveolens? She eased forward very slowly, very carefully. Ahead of her was the silhouette of a figure. Was it Graveolens? It looked like… suddenly a cool, dry hand wrapped around her face and covered her mouth. Instinctively, Phoebe elbowed her attacker in the side of the stomach, sharp and hard. He released his grip and fell back with a howl of pain.

"Pheebs, what are you doing?" The pain reduced his yell to nothing more than a hoarse whisper.

"Michael? What were *you* doing?" whispered Phoebe, on all fours at his side.

"Stopping you making a noise," complained Michael rubbing his side and pulling himself back up into a crouching position.

"Hmm. I do fear it's rather a little late for that," whispered Phoebe.

"What do you mean?" puzzled Michael furrowing his brow.

Phoebe pointed apologetically to something over Michael's shoulder. "If you'd care to look and see for yourself."

Michael turned. It was Graveolens. Standing above them, grinning with contempt – and taking aim.

7

There was nothing else to be done about it. What the policemen saw, they saw, and hang the consequences. I lifted the lid of that large brown wicker stage trunk which sat by the Stage Door desk. Melville, Pym and O'Connor, too, I suspect, were surprised to see the trunk lined with sheet metal and containing, not the usual flimflam of stage costumes or pretty props, but a flight of metal stairs leading downwards. More's the pity that the urgency of the circumstance did not allow me to enjoy their surprise a little more. Instead, I merely said, "Follow me, gentlemen. Beneath the stage…"

***

In repose, Graveolens's smile was naturally humourless. But now with his revolver pointing directly down upon Michael Magister and Phoebe Le Breton, at all but point blank range, his grin appeared positively demonic. He, the dutiful son, Anthony Graveolens had won. Magister was about to die. The Phoebe woman, huh, a nice little bonus.

"Rather a shame I dropped the Pulsa by the Saw," said Phoebe.

"Pheebs, it's okay. We've all done that at some time," said Michael, his mouth dry and his spine chilled.

"No, it was very silly, unforgiveable and I shall just have to make up for it!" Phoebe then sprang catlike and threw herself up at Graveolens. Before he could react the two of them were tumbling and scrapping across the stage. In the melee, Graveolens lost his pistol. Phoebe tried to pin him to the floor. Graveolens pushed her off with ease and scrambled to reach the gun, his panic rising. Phoebe grabbed at his leg to heave him back, but he kicked her away, then scrambled some more, grasping and feeling about the floor for the weapon. Again Phoebe came at him pouncing on his back and wrestling him furiously onto his side. Elbows, knees, it was a desperate fight to the death. Graveolens hefted her away, struggled to his feet, saw the sword rack and snatched at a rapier, but pulled only the grip and hilt. It was a sword with no blade.

"That's magic for you!" smiled Phoebe. Graveolens flung the hilt at Phoebe which she dodged with ease. Then they both saw the pistol. Lying by the Gravestone. They both made a dive. One hand grabbed it. The struggle of strength brought them both to their feet, then

THUNG! THUNG! THUNG!

The entire stage was engulfed in full, dazzling light.

"Stop!" shouted a voice.

Phoebe and Graveolens briefly blinded, squinted and peered into the yellow brilliance. Slowly the image came into focus, as first a silhouette, but from the stance and the frame, Phoebe knew it was most definitely Michael. There he stood, by the Saw, fifteen feet away aiming the Pulsa directly at them. Michael had found it precisely where Phoebe had said. He had thrown the hefty circuit breaker which powered the show lights above. A hand over his eyes shielded much of the glare and a few rapid blinks adjusted his eyes more quickly to the burning light. Before him stood Phoebe. She was holding the revolver, training it on her assailant...

...Phoebe.

Michael blinked again. What? That had to be impossible. Yes, it was definitely impossible! Nevertheless there was no doubt about it. Michael was staring at two Phoebes. Two identically dressed Phoebes, both blinking at the light, with one pointing the pistol at the other. Anthony Graveolens had to be one of them - but which one?

"It's all right, Michael, it's over! I have him, look! I have him!" said the Phoebe holding the gun.

"Michael! Shoot him before he shoots me!" implored the other Phoebe.

Michael stared and swung the Pulsa left and right, back and forth between the two figures, totally flummoxed.

"Pheebs, I'm seeing two of you! He's 'fluencing me! Graveolens is 'fluencing me! Which is the real you?"

"Michael, it's me!" said the Phoebe holding the gun.

"Don't listen to him, Michael, I'm the real Phoebe!" said the other.

"Nobody move. Pheebs, and Pheebs, listen to me. Okay, the only way to settle this – Pheebs, if that really is you, you'll put the gun down."

"No, Michael. I've got him. If I put it down he'll grab it!" urged the Phoebe holding the gun.

"Michael, he's going to shoot me!" implored the Phoebe who wasn't.

"Don't listen to him, Michael! He's the real Graveolens!"

"Michael, you know I'm the real Phoebe!"

"I'm the real one!"

"Michael... just go with your instinct!"

Exactly! Michael looked at one then the other and fired the Pulsa. The ball of purple energy spat from the end of the barrel, screamed across the stage – and missed! He actually bloody well missed! The sphere of Aethyr smashed into The Mincer of Malevolence shattering the wooden framework. The next thing they heard was the crack of a pistol. In that instant, the Phoebe holding the revolver was jerked around, blood spurting from her shoulder.

"Pheebs!" shouted Michael. But by the time Phoebe slumped to the floor she was Anthony Graveolens. The real Phoebe rushed forward for Michael to embrace her.

"Wasn't *that* rather thrilling," laughed Phoebe.

"Stand aside, Mister Magister!" ordered Inspector Pym, holding his revolver before him as he rushed forward to secure Graveolens's weapon. Not that it posed a threat, Graveolens was too busy wailing and cursing to the heavens.

"Shoulder wound, guv'nor," reported Pym. "Nice and painful, but not life threatening!"

"Walter?" said Michael, with a tone of incredulity. "How did you know which Phoebe to shoot?"

"I didn't," said Pym above Graveolens's cries. "But the Superintendent did." As he hauled the serial killer to his feet as roughly as possible, Pym nodded to the group behind the magicians. Phoebe and Michael turned to see me, Father Connor O'Connor and Superintendent William Melville, smoking gun in hand and wearing a pair of Arthur Doyle's Goggle-Eyes. He looked much like a myopic fish, but that's as maybe.

"I had the advantage, Mister Magister," said Melville, "With your man's optical device, how could I be mistaken?"

I pointed out to one and all that even a hypnotist of prodigious ability could not confound a scientific device which sees directly through clothing.

Phoebe stood, hands on hips looking at Melville. "Superintendent? Do you mind?"

Flustered, Melville quickly removed the Goggle-Eyes. "Madam, my apologies."

"Here, guv'nor , can I have a quick go?" wondered Pym, easily restraining Graveolens, whose screams of pain and criticism of the Holy Trinity went largely ignored. Except by Father Connor O'Connor, who swiftly booted the serial killer in the belly.

"Do not take the Lord's bastard name in vain, you disbelieving heathen!" ordered the furious, but idiosyncratic cleric.

"What happens now?" asked Michael.

"We have a murderer to process," said Melville. "You two have a show to perform." With that Melville nodded and followed Pym and his whimpering prisoner to the Stage Door.

"Melville," I said, firmly, holding my hand out. "My Goggle-Eyes if you please!"

The Superintendent stopped, said, "Indeed," and handed the device back to me. I was not about to let him walk off with anything which was rightfully mine. Especially after being referred to as Michael's 'man'!.

"The Pulsa works a treat, Prof," said Michael, waving the elegant weapon.

"Michael Magister, may you never cast doubt over my marksmanship again. Whoever you were aiming at, me or Graveolens – you missed us both!" said Phoebe.

"Pheebs, I promise you I was aiming at him," he then turned to me adding, "You might want to look at the Pulsa again, Prof – it pulls a bit to the right."

"Oi, you lot," said Wicko, rubbing his eyes and stretching as he emerged from beneath the false seat of The Throne of Disintegration. "What was all that noise and fuss about?"

***

"Weapons discharging pulses of energy," mused Superintendent William Melville, as he sat in the quiet, comforting austerity of his Scotland Yard office. "Steam driven motor carriages, optical devices enabling the wearer to peer through almost anything. Mister Magister and Miss Le Breton will prove themselves to be enigmatic assets indeed...and a very significant problem."

Elsewhere, The Black Bishop simply glared with hatred... and began to plot his merciless vengeance.

8

It was during the week that followed that Superintendent Melville made his remarkable offer; that Michael and Phoebe be retained as consultants, advising upon the more complex, outlandish and arcane incidents which the Special Branch increasingly found itself facing. Like mind-bending psycho hypnotists, for example. We told him we would consider it.

Pym let slip that thanks to Father Connor O'Connor's identification, both drunk and sober, along with confirmation from mortuary porter Staveley Chaddock, ex-Detective Inspector Gersham Skindrick had been arrested and charged with murder, kidnap and treason. Skindrick proudly admitted the offence, but steadfastly refused to speak about The Holy Black Bishop, whose identity and whereabouts remained a mystery. The chapel in Warwick Street was raided, but no evidence of murderous ceremonies was discovered. It was a beautiful little building, kept under lock and key.

It was Saturday morning when Michael stepped aboard Phoebe's railway carriage and as if from nowhere, *from the hidden pouch in his waistcoat,* produced an envelope and handed it across.

"Tidings of comfort and joy, Pheebs. Have a look at this."

Phoebe examined the envelope. It was addressed to "Magister, The Metropolitan Theatre of Steam Smoke and Mirrors, 267 Edgware Road, Paddington, W." The orange halfpenny postage stamp bearing Victoria's head was franked with an Uxbridge postmark. Inside, Phoebe found a slip of paper bearing no message. Just an address. Written in the self-same hand: "Cottage Number 2, Barrack Yard, Chalfont Saint Peter, Buckinghamshire"

"But there appears to be no message," she said.

"No, Pheebs. That *is* the message. Can I just see the envelope again?"

Michael held the envelope up close to Phoebe's face, glancing between her and the Henry Corbould profile of

Queen Victoria on the postage stamp. "You know there *is* a resemblance..." he said.

Phoebe's reaction was terse and involved reaching for a blunt instrument.

***

Ninety minutes later and twenty miles westward, Michael was splashing the Steamo through the ford of the River Misbourne, scattering water fowl and drawing unpleasant looks from village locals. But a cheery wave coupled with: 'Apologies, he's rather an idiot driver!' from the beautiful Phoebe Le Breton, sitting alongside the idiot driver, did much to placate their ire.

"Passed the turning, just need to swing her about," said Michael as he turned the Steamo left into the imposing coach entrance of the redbrick 'Greyhound Inn', built by Judge Jeffreys, The Hanging Judge, which had served travellers with a greater sense of direction than Michael for more than three centuries.

The village of Chalfont Saint Peter is set in the heart of the rolling Buckinghamshire countryside midway between Aylesbury and London. The ancient village comprised of rows of terraced cottages, a few shops and a thousand public houses, or so it seemed. The name 'Chalfont' comes from 'Caedles Funta', the fount of Caedle apparently, which leaves me none the wiser, and somewhat less inspired to find out more.

"B'chryser! Imz gon back'ards nah!" yelled one Chalfontian, in his broadest Bucks accent, which, I believe, roughly translated meant something like, "By the son of God! That fellow is now intent on reversing his vehicle!"

Michael swung the Steamo round, out of The Greyhound Inn and splashed back through the ford, this time in the other direction. The 18th century Gothic tower of St. Peter's church soared up to their right, and on the left after 'The George Inn' and 'The Carpenter's Arms', but before 'The Baker's Arms', Michael steered a sharp left through a coaching entrance into Barrack Yard. More a square than a yard, it was a cobbled area bounded on three sides by dwellings. On two sides stood a quirky hotchpotch of old half-timbered and whitewashed cottages, which somehow continued to stand and defiantly thumb their noses at time and gravity. At least on the third side was a uniform terrace of five wood and brick built cottages with tiled roofs.

Number 2 Barrack Yard was the end of terrace cottage. A ground floor with one window to the side, an upstairs window and a gable window set into the roof. The idyll was completed with a profusion of colour from wallflowers and sweet peas which flourished in the small front garden beneath the window.

The wooden front door shuddered, catching the flagstone floor, as it opened. A woman stood framed in the doorway.

"Hello, Phoebe. Hello, Magister." The voice was unmistakeably nasal, tinged with a northern accent.

"Hello, Connie," said Michael.

9

Michael and Phoebe sat in easy chairs as Connie handed out steaming cups of tea all served in her new best floral pattern bone china.

"No one's going to come looking for you again. To the Special Branch, to Hanwell, to the world you're dead. And looking at the villagers round here, you're in the right place," said Michael.

Connie ignored his jibe and smiled at Phoebe's indignant reaction to it. "My own cottage in this lovely little village, fresh water pumps and wells, a butcher, two bakers, seven pubs all within a stone's throw and a workhouse along the way if push ever comes to shove. And there's a new six-bed cottage hospital just been built, up at the top of Gold Hill Lane. What else am I going to need? And all that's thanks to the pair of you."

They were sitting in the small living room, the front door opened directly out onto the Yard. The beamed ceiling was low slung and the walls were plastered and whitewashed contrasting artistically with the small brick built fireplace. In one corner a flight of narrow, uneven stairs curved upwards and round. The room was just big enough for three easy chairs and a low table. A red and gold coloured mat covered most of the flagstone floor. Through an open door leading out to the back, Michael saw another room with a wooden table and two chairs, a larder cupboard and a small, black cooking range. Everything was clean and just so. Exactly what you would expect of Constance Dill.

"It really is so charming here. And The Professor is arranging a monthly stipend," said Phoebe, looking around.

"That glorious, generous rogue, what would we all do without him?" said Connie, warmly. I know I am twisting the truth of her comment a little there, but then I am telling the story and that was really the essence of her eulogy to me.

"It's us that owes you, Connie. Me more than anyone," said Michael holding Connie's hand.

"We," correct Phoebe. "It's we who owe you."

Connie looked at Phoebe. "Hasn't he told you?"

"From the tone of your voice, I'm rather supposing he hasn't…" smiled Phoebe.

"You're right. No more secrets, Pheebs. Confession time, cards on table, whatever you want to call it, none of those President George W. Bush shenanigans. Here's what happened. Here's why I'd do anything for Constance Dill.

"When I first came over to England, with The Professor, I couldn't perform for the English audience. Couldn't do it. The Americans in New York, they were so much easier, because I was one of them and they were as rough as me. But for the English, I couldn't do it. I dropped cards, mangled my words. You're still teaching me to speak correctly. It wrecked my confidence, and I became this shy, embarrassed little conjurer far from home with no plans to get back on stage anytime soon."

"I don't believe it for one moment," said Phoebe.

"No, Phoebe, it's all true, he was a wreck. God, it was a nightmare! " Connie assured her with a smile. "Carry on…"

"Pathetic? Anyways, my nerve was gone. So The Professor heard about Connie and she hypnotised me. Made me confident, assured, debonair, and most probably quite unbearable – it's all down to Connie. But this fly, cocksure, vain, wise cracking, buffoon? It's not the real me. The real me was dull and shy. Connie created the monster which is Michael Magister, Pheebs, and if Connie wanted to she could have me revert straight back to a retiring little puppy with just a blink of her eye and click of her fingers. It's why I owe her so much. It's why we went through everything we went through. I've been under Connie's spell for ten years. The Michael Magister you see is just an illusion."

Phoebe sat with her mouth open. "I don't know what to say. I am astonished. I rather knew there was some degree of play acting, but I never for once thought your entire persona was pure artifice. I'm… and there was I, terribly concerned you'd be upset when I didn't tell you I was Queen Victoria's granddaughter!?" Then she quickly turned to Connie adding, "Which, by the way, you didn't hear."

"Pheebs, we all keep secrets. My secret is I'm a real, genuine phoney," said Michael

"Well, now we're being entirely honest and all that, what you've said just then Magister isn't strictly true," said Connie. "The part about my hypnotising you, Magister, yes, that's quite right. Yes, I 'fluenced you to help restore your stage confidence, even boosted it, if you will. But after two performances and without you even noticing I blinked, clicked my fingers, as you put it. You were only hypnotised for a day, you idiot. I just didn't bother telling you. Whatever you are now, that is the real Michael Magister. God help us...you're a nightmare" Connie then reached for a small bowl. "Sugar anyone?"

***

Following that glorious morning of honesty and reminiscence with Constance Dill, Michael and Phoebe boarded the Steamo and chugged east, towards London, the great epicentre of the British Empire; the grand metropolis of horses, carts, industry, architecture, design, invention and Victorian era majesty. The new century was looming large and who knew what glories that would bring. Certainly Connie had convinced Michael and Phoebe that working with William Melville's Special Branch, and making sense of the most bizarre mysteries of the age, would be a rewarding and exciting experience. Michael warmed to the idea of the reward and Phoebe was particularly attracted to the prospect of further excitement; the strange, the mysterious, the bizarre, solving the unfathomable, explaining the inexplicable. Yes, that would make a fascinating addendum to their careers on the stage of the Music Hall. As if it wasn't enough being Michael Magister, the Industrial Age Illusionist and Phoebe, The Queen of Steam and Goddess of the Aethyr.

And, regarding this new diversion, there one very puzzling peculiarity which Phoebe felt the need to address right there and then. She turned to the handsome, stylish, glib, brilliant, protective and utterly infuriating magician sitting next to her, and asked:

"Michael. Who is President George W. Bush?"